PRAISE FOR *SILENT SEA* . . .

"A thriller that matches—and often surpasses—other epics about the silent service. A first-rate piece of fiction rooted in reality."
—Herman Kogan, "Critic's Choice," WFMT Chicago

"A spine-tingling narrative of submarine men and their WW II experiences. Factual episodes are set forth with such realism that each one is a classic."
—Maurice 'Mike' Shea, RADM, USN (Ret.)

"Harry Homewood has surfaced again with an undersea drama as fascinating as *Final Harbor*."
—Bill Mauldin

. . . AND *FINAL HARBOR*

"A remarkable, gripping submarine tale . . . I couldn't put it down."
—Clay Blair, Jr., author of *Silent Victory*

"One of the best books I've read about World War II—and the *best* I've read about life and death under the sea."
—Bill Mauldin

Bantam Books by HARRY HOMEWOOD

FINAL HARBOR

SILENT SEA

SILENT SEA

Harry Homewood

BANTAM BOOKS
TORONTO · NEW YORK · LONDON · SYDNEY · AUCKLAND

Silent Sea and the characters portrayed therein are wholly fictional. Any similarity between the characters and actual people, living or dead, is unintentional.

*This low-priced Bantam Book
has been completely reset in a type face
designed for easy reading, and was printed
from new plates. It contains the complete
text of the original hard-cover edition.*
NOT ONE WORD HAS BEEN OMITTED.

SILENT SEA
*A Bantam Book / published by arrangement with
McGraw-Hill Inc.*

PRINTING HISTORY
McGraw-Hill edition published June 1981
Bantam edition / June 1983

This book is dedicated with profound respect to the 3,508 officers and men of the United States Submarine Service who sleep peacefully beneath the sea in unmarked graves.

In particular, this book is dedicated to Vice Admiral Glynn R. Donaho, USN (Ret), who distinguished himself as an aggressive and courageous submarine commander—and who was, as well, an inspiration to those fortunate enough to have served with him.

"I wish to have no Connection with
any Ship that does not sail fast,
for I intend to go in harm's way."
JOHN PAUL JONES, USN

PROLOGUE

On December 7, 1941, the Japanese bombed Pearl Harbor. When the attack was over the major surface ships of the U.S. Pacific Fleet were burned and sunken hulks. Fortunately, the submarines were untouched by the holocaust of that Sunday morning. They took up the burden of carrying the war to Japan and became known, with justification, as the "Silent Service."

Plagued by unreliable torpedo exploders for almost two years, slowed by erratic diesel-engine performance, ripped internally by the internecine political warfare of Admirals clinging to outmoded concepts, the American submariners fought two bitter wars: one against the Japanese, the other with their own high command. But as new submarines were built and commanded by younger and far more aggressive men, the submariners won their intramural war, almost eliminated the entire Japanese Merchant Fleet, and badly crippled the Japanese Navy.

By April 1945, the U.S. submarine force in the Pacific had so tightened the noose of naval blockade around Japan's throat that the enemy was finished as an industrial nation, unable to fight a war effectively.

Proof of this is found in the fact that on April 5, 1945, the Japanese High Command decided to send a battle fleet headed by Japan's mightiest battleship, the *Yamato*, to crush the U.S. invasion fleet at Okinawa. Yet there were only 2,500 barrels of oil available to fuel the Japanese ships, not enough for the 1,000-mile round trip from Japan to Okinawa. The *Yamato* and her escort sailed without sufficient fuel and with no air cover—there was little or no aviation fuel to be had—and the Japanese battle fleet was smashed, the *Yamato* sunk, by U.S. carrier planes. It was the last major naval sortie Japan was able to mount.

The American submarines paid dearly for their victory over Japan. One of every five men who went to sea in submarines in the Pacific died in combat, the highest percentage of casualties of any branch of the U.S. Armed Forces.

CHAPTER 1

The twin-engined Mitsubishi Zero-1 medium bomber, called a "Betty" by American forces, cruised on a westerly course across the southern end of the Gulf of Leyte. To the bomber's left the northern peaks of Dinegat Island were wreathed in a soft haze. To the plane's right the waters of Leyte Gulf sparkled in the late afternoon sunshine, the slanting rays of the sun making the water almost opaque.

The bomber's crew, bored with their daily routine, searched the sea looking for the telltale dark, cigar shape of a submarine beneath the surface. The plane's commander looked out his windshield at the southern end of Leyte Island, squinting against the sun and then at his wrist watch. With a grunt of relief he banked the bomber to the right and headed for the airport outside of Tacloban, fifty miles north.

"Another day's work done," the copilot said. "I don't think we'll ever see anything out here."

"There's nothing to see," the pilot said. He made a minute adjustment to the trim tab controls as he steadied the plane on its course. "The Americans are not complete fools. They wouldn't risk putting their submarines so close to our airfields." He wriggled in his seat, trying to ease the cramp of sitting in one position for hours.

1

"No, not complete fools," the copilot murmured. "May I make the landing, sir?"

"No," the plane commander said.

Far back of the cruising bomber the U.S.S. *Eelfish*, Fleet Submarine, U.S. Navy, cruised slowly at a depth of 125 feet, safe from the searching eyes above. The submarine, 312 feet long and only 16 feet wide amidships, its widest point, was a new ship, commissioned at New London, Connecticut, in late 1942. Its main weapons were standard for a U.S. submarine of that time: 6 torpedo tubes and 16 torpedoes in the Forward Torpedo Room, 4 torpedo tubes and 8 torpedoes in the After Torpedo Room. Unlike submarines built before World War II, its topside armament was massive. Two 5.25-inch wet-type guns built of stainless steel and monel metal dominated the main deck fore and aft. A 1.1 rapid-fire quad pom-pom gun was mounted in the center of the cigaret deck just behind the ship's bridge. Forward of the bridge and below it on a platform there was a twin .20-millimeter machine gun.

Designed originally for long-range reconnaissance, the *Eelfish* was powered by four 1,600-HP diesel engines and carried 112,000 gallons of fuel oil, enough for a cruising range of more than 12,000 miles. Like all U.S. submarines on war patrol, the *Eelfish* carried a stock of essential spare parts; its crew knew that if the ship were to be disabled, and they could not repair it themselves, they would get no help from their own forces.

There was sufficient frozen and canned food aboard to feed the crew of 72 officers and men for 90 days. The Kleinschmidt evaporators in the Forward Engine Room could make up to 1,900 gallons of fresh water a day from sea water to offset the more than 4,000 gallons of fresh water used each week for cooking, cooling the diesel engines, and replenishing the water in the 252 huge storage-battery cells that provided power for the submarine when it was submerged.

Although living conditions were by most civilian standards cramped, there were some creature comforts. Each man in the crew had his own bunk with a good mattress. Each bunk had a reading light and an individual air-conditioning vent. An ice-cream-making machine dominated the Crew's Mess, and two washing machines stood in the crew's small shower space.

The crew of the *Eelfish* was an odd mix that had become common in submarines by mid-1943. They were all volunteers; submarine service was purely voluntary, but unlike the submarine crews prior to 1941, the men of the *Eelfish* were almost evenly divided between Reservists who had enlisted for the duration of the war plus six months and Regulars, career Navy men.

The mix of Regulars and Reserves was born of necessity. When the Navy's prewar submarine building program went into high gear just before the bombing of Pearl Harbor the Navy found it did not have sufficient qualified submarine men to man the new ships. The Navy's solution to the problem was to pick men who had experience—and after the war broke out men who had made one or two or three war patrols—to form a cadre aboard the new submarines, fleshing out the rest of the crew with Reservists who had volunteered for the rigorous training at the Navy's Submarine School in New London. By mid-1943 half of the men aboard new submarines were Reservists whose first experience at sea was aboard their submarine.

The senior enlisted man aboard the *Eelfish* was Chief Torpedoman Joseph J. Flanagan, called "Monk" by his friends because of his perpetual scowl, his thick thatch of black hair, and his long, powerful arms, which hung from a set of wide, sloping shoulders.

Flanagan held a position found only in submarines. He was the "Chief of the Boat," a classification that put him above the rest of the enlisted men and just below the officers of the Wardroom. As an enlisted man he was required to give rank its due honor. In actual practice the Chief of the Boat reported directly to the Captain and the Executive Officer.

The leading petty officers were almost all Regulars. Steve Petreshock, TM 1/c, a stocky, usually soft-spoken career man, ran the Forward Torpedo Room with quiet efficiency and a dedication to detail. In the After Torpedo Room Fred Nelson, TM 1/c, hawk-nosed, a big man who stood well over six feet, ran his torpedo room with the same efficiency. But where Petreshock was quietly insistent, Nelson was more often noisily firm.

Chief Ed Morris, a dour, pipe-smoking Chief Electrician's Mate, drove his crew of electricians with a heavy hand to keep the electrical end of the *Eelfish*'s diesel-electric propulsion system in perfect operating condition. In the galley Elmo "Scotty" Rudolph, like Chief Morris a veteran of more than a dozen years of submarine duty, turned out three meals a day and a midnight snack for the crew of 72 men on only four large hot plates and two small ovens.

When Lieutenant Commander Mike Brannon, USN, had reported to New London to take command of the *Eelfish* he was a veteran of three war patrols aboard the U.S.S. *Mako*. Two days after he had reported for duty he sat with his wife Gloria in the sparsely furnished quarters the Navy had provided, holding his small daughter in his lap.

"I can't believe it," he said, easing his heavy, six-foot frame in a creaking wicker chair that was the only seat in the small living room other than a threadbare sofa. "I've got one Academy man in the Wardroom, John Olsen, the Executive Officer. I'm lucky, he's a hell of a good man. He was on the S-Thirty-Seven when the war broke out. They fought their way out of Manila and down to Australia. But he's never been on a big Fleet submarine. John's got his hands full learning the ship and making sure the Regulars in the crew teach the Reservists port from starboard.

"The rest of my Wardroom are Reserves. My Gunnery and Torpedo Officer is Bob Lee, Robert E. Lee if you please, a Lieutenant, Junior Grade. He's a lawyer. My Engineering Officer is another J.G., Jerry Gold and he's a dentist, for God's sake! That is, he graduated from dental school but he didn't get a chance to take his exams or whatever they have to take to go into his own practice."

"Why isn't he in the Medical Corps if he's a dentist?" his wife asked.

"Don't ask me, Gloria," Brannon said. "The Navy apparently found out that Jerry has a lot of mechanical aptitude so they made him a line officer and sent him to Sub School. His number one man, the Assistant Engineering Officer, is an architect named Perry Arbuckle." He shook his head.

"They're good men?" Gloria Brannon asked.

"Oh, heck, they're wonderful. Bright as hell. But not one of them has ever been to sea. Lee is so smart that he scares me. He's not very big, sort of skinny, but he's all brain. Jerry Gold is a big man, I think a pretty tough dude if you crossed him, but he's very willing and he's damned bright to boot. Arbuckle is a cagey sort. He's bright as hell but he gives me the impression that he'd never blow his stack in a crisis. We'll have to have them over pretty soon. I know, this place isn't big enough for the three of us let alone entertaining anyone. We'll do it at the O-Club. Maybe early next week."

"What about your other officers?" his wife asked.

"What others? That's all I've got! I get one more man, not the two or three I could use, but not till we get to Australia. That means that Olsen and I will have to stand four on and four off on the bridge at sea until the other officers are qualified to stand a sea watch." He eased his small daughter off his lap and got out of the creaking chair with care and began to pace the living room, his heavy shoulders hunched.

"The trouble is we need submarines so damned badly in the war zone. We don't have any surface fleet to speak of, outside of a few carriers. And we're building submarines almost faster than we can find crews for them. Half of my crew are Reservists who have never been to sea."

"You had some Reserves aboard the *Mako*," his wife said.

"Sure," he answered. "But we had time to train them. I don't have the time now, honey. In four weeks they're going to hold sea trials and the Navy will accept the ship from the builders. Then we'll have a week, one week, to shake down the ship and the crew.

"Then we leave." His big Irish face softened. "I thought when I lucked out and got new construction we'd have about a year together, the three of us. It comes down to five, maybe six weeks or so."

She nodded, her eyes bright with unspilled tears. "It doesn't seem fair," she said. "It isn't fair, damn it!" She blinked and smiled, but a tear ran down her cheek.

Lying in his bunk in his tiny stateroom in the Forward Battery Compartment of the *Eelfish* Mike Brannon woke as he sensed the slight shift upward of the ship's bow. He heard the whine of the motors raising the periscope and the voice of the Chief of the Watch in the Control Room advising Lieutenant Lee in the Conning Tower that the ship was at periscope depth. He rolled over and closed his eyes, listening to the soft murmur of water against the submarine's submerged hull and drifted back to sleep.

"Periscope observation at sixteen hundred hours," Lieutenant Lee said. "No shipping in sight. No aircraft in sight. Sea is calm. Down periscope. Control, go back to one hundred and twenty-five feet."

Bill Brosmer, Quartermaster l/c, entered Lee's observations in the ship's log in his neat, crabbed handwriting. He reached into the hip pocket of his khaki shorts for a comb and pulled it carefully through his thick, curly red beard.

"Same damned report we've been making every hour for the last week," he growled. "Ain't seen one damned ship. This patrol area is dead, Mr. Lee."

"The people in Fremantle seemed to think we'd see some good targets here," Lee said. He shrugged his thin shoulders. "It should be a good area. There are a lot of troops up around Tacloban and there's two big airfields up there. With lots of troops and airfields there should be supply ships coming and going."

"But there isn't," Brosmer said.

"Have to be patient, Bill," Lee said. He lounged against the edge of a shelf that held the sonar gear.

"We can't complain, you know. This is our first war patrol and we got those two big Jap destroyers when they were sinking *Mako*. A lot of submarines have never had a chance to fire torpedoes at even one destroyer. The Old Man is a good shot."

"How's he taking the loss of the *Mako*?" Brosmer's eyes were half shut, his face noncommittal, his voice carefully casual.

"Pretty hard," Lee said. "He put the *Mako* in commission just before the war broke out. He made three war patrols on her as the Exec under Captain Hinman. From what John Olsen has told me Hinman was the closest friend our Old Man had." He turned his head and looked at the gyro repeater to see if the helmsman was on course.

"If we hadn't been twenty miles away when the *Mako* told us they were going after a convoy and invited us to come over and help them, maybe the Old Man could have sunk those two Jap destroyers before they blasted *Mako*. He talks about that quite a bit, the Old Man does. About getting there sooner." He looked at Brosmer, his brown eyes guileless.

"Does the crew talk much about the *Mako*?"

Brosmer looked at his comb and pulled a long, curly red hair out of the teeth. "Damn," he muttered, "must be gettin' bald in the chin." He turned toward Lee.

"Yeah, they talk about it." His voice was flat. "It's like, well, it's like we got sunk, you know what I mean? *Mako* was the same class ship we are, damned near our spittin' image except we got a new SJ radar.

"But the crew, well, they think about how it was when the *Mako* was sinking out of control into six fucking thousand fathoms of water where she went down. I do it myself. I wonder what the Quartermaster who had my job on the *Mako* was doing when she was sinking so fucking slow. Was he standin' in the Conning Tower like I'm doing now, talking to an officer? Did the Conning Tower just squash in on him and kill him quick? Or did he drown? Gives me the creeps so I don't think about it any more. Rest of the people, the crew, most of them think about the same thing."

"Did you lose any friends on the *Mako*?" Lee's voice was soft.

"No, I didn't know anyone aboard her," Brosmer said. "Some of the guys knew some of the *Mako* crew, the Regulars, I mean. I think Petreshock in the Forward Room knew some of the crew. I'd guess that the Chief of the Boat knew a few. From what I hear she was a good ship. Two things die when what happens to the *Mako* happens. The ship dies and the crew dies." He took a long, deep, slow breath.

"I know one thing, sir, and you can maybe tell this to the other Reserve officers in the Wardroom. I think maybe the Old Man and the Exec, they might know it already. The crew of this ship was just another crew before the *Mako* went down. Now it's different. We're *Eelfish*. It's like it was before the war when I was in the Thirty-Seven Boat with Mr. Olsen.

"You could get in a fight in a bar in Manila or up in China and if you hollered 'Thirty-Seven Boat!' anybody from the ship who heard you would come runnin', ready to fight even if the odds was twenty to one." He pulled the comb through his beard and stared at the hairs in its teeth. "That's the way this crew is now, sir. All for one and one for all. Used to take years before a crew felt that way about each other. This crew got that way in one night, listening to the *Mako* go down."

Lee looked away from Brosmer's intent eyes. "Does the crew feel that way about the officers? I mean, four of the six of us are Reserves."

Brosmer grinned suddenly, his teeth flashing white in the dense red beard. "Get yourself in a fight next time we're in Perth, Mr. Lee. Holler '*Eelfish*' real loud and find out."

"Would you come running?"

"I'd do my damndest to beat the Old Man and Mr. Olsen. I figure either of them would fight any time."

Mike Brannon rolled over in his bunk and looked at his wrist watch. Almost sixteen thirty hours. He'd had almost seven hours of sleep, the longest stretch he'd enjoyed in a week. He got out of his bunk and hitched up his wrinkled khaki shorts. On a submarine on war patrol all hands usually slept in the khaki shorts that were the unofficial uniform of the day; there was no time to get dressed if the General Quarters alarm went off. Pete

Mahaffey, Officers' Cook l/c, stuck his head through the two green curtains that served as a door to the stateroom.

"Evenin', Captain." Mahaffey's hand and muscular black forearm came through the curtain with a cup of hot coffee that had been liberally laced with canned evaporated milk and sugar.

"Thank you, Pete. Come in. What's new?"

"Same as yesterday, same as the days before that, sir. Nothing in sight topside. Mr. Olsen's waiting on you in the Wardroom with his charts, sir."

"Tell him I'll be in as soon as I shower and shave," Brannon said. He sipped at the hot coffee.

"Sunday sir. No showers today. Showers go on the line tomorrow, sir." Brannon nodded. Submarines on war patrol observed water rationing. Making fresh water out of sea water by electrically heating the sea water to the boiling point and then collecting and cooling the steam was a hot, miserable chore that was thoroughly detested by the Engine Room people. Brannon let down the stainless steel washbowl from its clips and ran a few inches of hot water into it. As he washed his face his mind flickered back, as it so often had this past week, to the night when he and John Olsen had stood on the bridge after the torpedoes he had fired had blasted the two Japanese Fubuki destroyers that had been depth charging the *Mako*.

The flotsam of the second destroyer was floating off the port beam of *Eelfish* as Brannon and Olsen listened to Paul Blake, the young sonarman of the *Eelfish*, talk to the *Mako* by sonar, repeating each word the *Mako*'s sonarman sent so that Brannon could hear and the yeoman could take down the words in his notebook.

The report by *Mako*'s sonarman had been succinct: *Mako* had made a night surface attack on a small convoy. Two big Japanese destroyers had apparently been lying in wait behind the convoy. Heavy gunfire killed Captain Hinman, the Executive Officer, the Quartermaster, and the lookouts on the bridge. The *Mako* dove and came under heavy depth charging. The After Torpedo Room was ripped open and flooded with water and *Mako* had struggled to the surface just as the *Eelfish* arrived on the scene and sank one of the destroyers. The remaining destroyer had opened fire on the *Mako* with deck guns and hulled the submarine in the Forward Torpedo Room. The sonarman signaled to the *Eelfish* that the *Mako* was sinking, slowly, inexorably, out of control.

Brannon stared at his face in the stainless steel mirror over the washbowl as he rubbed lather into his beard, reliving again the scene on the bridge of the *Eelfish*.

"Mako is at four hundred feet and sinking," Paul Blake said from the Conning Tower.

"Oh, God!" Brannon said. "What in the hell can we do?"

"Not much," John Olsen said slowly. "Not much except pray, sir."

Mike Brannon wiped his eyes with the back of his hand.

"Tell them," his voice broke, "tell them we are praying for them. Tell them that." He turned away, sobbing.

He waited, the tears streaming down his cheeks, listening to the measured sound pulses of the Mako's response. Paul Blake in the Conning Tower called out each word to the yeoman, and on the bridge Captain Brannon and John Olsen heard Blake's voice.

"The Lord is my shepherd . . . I shall not want . . . He maketh me to lie down in green pastures . . . He leadeth me beside the still waters . . ."

There was silence.

"Sir." The sonarman's voice was small, hardly audible. "Sir, transmission stopped and I heard a big crunching noise."

Brannon looked at his Executive Officer, his eyes streaming. *"My God, John, the water is six miles deep here!"*

John Olsen nodded and in a soft voice finished the words of the Twenty-third Psalm.

He reached for his razor and shaved, forcing himself to stop thinking about that night. There was no joy in knowing that he had sunk *Mako*'s killers. Finished, he combed his hair and went into the Wardroom, smiling his thanks at Mahaffey, who had put a fresh cup of coffee and a sweet roll in front of his place at the table.

"What's on your mind, John?" Brannon asked. He bit into the roll, savoring the sweetness of the prune filling.

"This damned gulf is too wide to patrol submerged," Olsen growled. "Fifty miles is too wide. Takes us all day, submerged, to cover half of the distance. Takes us all night on the surface to go from one side to the other. Too much can slip past us. I'd like to go up the gulf a little way, about twenty, twenty-five miles, half way up to Tacloban." He pointed at the chart. "We'll be here when we surface tonight. By the time we've finished charging the batteries we'll be off the east of Leyte Island. We could turn north and run at ten knots up the coast for a while. Stay close enough to the coast so the mountains hide us from radar in case they got a night-flyer out there or a patrol boat. If we don't see anything in a couple of hours we could come right and angle back to our area and be there before we have to dive for the day.''

"Sounds reasonable," Brannon said. He reached for Olsen's pack of cigarets and took one. "Work out the courses and speeds." He waited as Olsen busied himself at the chart. He looked at the result and nodded assent.

"Enter the courses and speeds in the Night Order Book," Brannon said. "Might break the monotony." Olsen slid out from behind the Wardroom table and unfolded his long, lean length. "Hope we run into something," he said. "The crew's getting itchy."

In the ship's galley Scotty Rudolph stared balefully at a big dishpan full of boned steaks. He turned to a messcook.

"Get one of them jugs of papaya juice I bought in Fremantle and mix a cup of the juice and a cup of Wooster sauce together and paint each side of each steak with the gunk. Put a thin coat each side. Use that brush hangin' from that ventilation duct.''

"What's that for?'' the messcook asked.

"Aussie beef is tough. They feed their cows on grass. Papaya juice is a tenderizer, but you got to be careful, you can't use it full strength. That stuff will turn the toughest steak you ever saw into gray mud you put it on full strength and leave it on. Hour or so should be about right. Make them steaks nice and tender.''

The *Eelfish* surfaced an hour after the sun had dropped behind the mountain ranges of Leyte Island. The submarine's four big diesels belched a small cloud of black smoke and then settled down to a steady pounding, three of the engines charging the two giant storage batteries, the other engine moving the *Eelfish* at a sedate six knots. Mike Brannon climbed through the bridge hatch and took a deep breath of the fresh night air.

"Nice night, Jerry," he said to Lieutenant Jerry Gold, the ship's Engineering Officer, who had the Bridge Watch. "Going to be a quarter moon in a couple of hours." He went aft to his night station, the cigaret deck area back of the periscope shears. He leaned against the 1.1 quad pom-pom gun mount that stood in the center of the cigaret deck and raised his night binoculars to his eyes to search the horizon. Above him, in the lookout stands in the periscope shears, the three lookouts adjusted their night binoculars and searched the sky, the horizon, and the sea.

A few minutes before midnight Mike Brannon heard Lieutenant Gold reciting the litany that all Officers of the Deck on a submarine must go through when they are relieved of the Deck Watch. He listened as Gold told Lieutenant Bob Lee that the battery charge had been secured at twenty-three hundred hours, that number one main engine was on the line and making turns for six knots, the lookouts had been relieved, the below-decks watch had been relieved, the fresh-water tanks had been topped off and the evaporators were being shut down, depth set on all torpedoes was four feet, all torpedo tube outer doors closed. Course was 285 degrees, true.

"You're relieved sir," Lee said to Jerry Gold.

"Thank you," Gold said. "The Captain's on the cigaret deck and he hasn't had a cup of coffee for two hours."

"Why don't you send up some coffee for the Captain when you go below?" Lee said with a grin. Gold nodded his head and dropped through the hatch to the Conning Tower.

John Olsen brought Brannon's coffee to the cigaret deck, balancing the two coffee mugs one on top of the other.

"Thanks, John," Brannon said. He sipped at the hot, sweet liquid. "Anything on your mind tonight?"

"I'd like to make a radar sweep at zero zero thirty, sir," Olsen said. "One sweep to get a fix on the mountain peaks on Mindanao and Leyte for navigational purposes."

"Very well," Brannon said. He walked forward to the small bridge. "The Exec will make a radar sweep at zero zero thirty hours, Bob. He'll tell you when he lights off the radar."

"Aye, aye, sir," Lee said. "Radar sweep at zero zero thirty, ten minutes from now." He moved to one side as Olsen went down the hatch.

Brannon heard the SJ radar antenna begin to turn, and from below decks he could hear the voice of Elmer Rafferty, the radioman who doubled as a radar operator, calling off the bearings and ranges to the mountain peaks on Leyte and Mindanao islands. There was a short pause and then Rafferty's voice went up a notch in tone.

"Contact! Several small pips bearing zero eight five, sir. Range is . . . range is one five zero zero zero yards, fifteen thousand yards, sir!"

"Secure the radar," Olsen's voice was sharp. "Bridge! Tell the Captain that radar has a contact bearing zero eight five.

Range is one five zero zero zero, fifteen thousand yards. Radar is secured, pending Captain's orders."

Lee turned and saw Brannon standing behind him. "I have the word, Bob," Brannon said. He lowered his head to the Bridge transmitter.

"Control. Let's get another radar bearing on those contacts. Make it short but get a good bearing and range." He looked upward as the radar antenna steadied on the bearing, and then he heard Rafferty's voice.

"Positive contact bearing zero eight four, sir. The range is closing slightly, closing a little bit. Contact is coming this way, sir."

"Secure the radar," Brannon ordered. "Come right to course three one five. All ahead full. Mr. Olsen to the bridge."

"Steady on course three one five, all ahead full is answered, Bridge." The helmsman's voice from the Conning Tower was flat, unemotional. Brannon heard the coughing roar of the other three diesel engines starting and then the quickening of *Eelfish* under his feet as the ship picked up speed.

"Very well," Lee answered the helmsman. He turned and repeated the information to Brannon as Olsen climbed out of the hatch and went back to the cigaret deck.

"That radar contact look solid to you?" Brannon asked.

"Jim Michaels was in the Control Room when we lit off the radar," Olsen said. "He's damned good on that thing. They told us in Fremantle when we took him aboard that he was the best they ever saw. I tend to believe him when he looks at those little spots of light and tells us he's got a solid contact."

"Several pips might be a convoy," Brannon said. "Go below, John, and start the plot. I want to stay on this course until we know more about the contact, until we know its speed and course. Once we've got that I want to be put on a parallel course, an opposite course to that of the contact. I want to run past the contact at no more than four thousand yards. Clear?" Olsen nodded and went forward to the bridge and down the hatch. Two minutes later his voice came over the bridge speaker.

"Bridge. Tell the Captain that we want to make two radar sweeps, one now, one in five minutes. Recommend slowing to ten knots until we have course and speed of the contact."

"Very well," Brannon said. He turned to Lee. "Keep the lookouts sharp. We should be seeing whatever is out there in a little while." He raised his night binoculars as he felt the *Eelfish* slow down.

The minutes crept by. Olsen's voice came out of the bridge speaker.

"We're going to make the second radar sweep, Bridge."

"Very well," Brannon said. He walked forward to the bridge and stood beside Lee. Above them the radar antenna was making short, jerky sweeps.

"Targets bear zero five seven, Bridge," Olsen's voice said from below. "Range to the targets is now nine five zero zero yards. Repeat, ninety-five hundred yards. Target course is one eight zero, dead south. Target speed is one zero, repeat, ten knots. Distance to the target track is now four one zero zero yards, repeat, forty-one hundred yards.

"We've got several targets out there, Bridge. Suggest we come right to course zero zero zero. Request permission for another radar sweep to determine disposition of the ships in the convoy, sir."

"Very well," Brannon said. "Execute course change. Let's make this next radar sweep a solid one, Control. Is Mr. Michaels at the radar?"

"Yes, sir," Olsen answered. "Mr. Michaels and Rafferty are manning the radar. Plot is running, sir."

"Very well," Brannon said. Olsen was showing no signs of excitement, Brannon reflected. He was doing his job calmly, plotting the problem, figuring the courses and speeds to bring *Eelfish* into contact with the enemy as Brannon wanted that contact to be made. He braced himself as the *Eelfish* heeled as it came to the new course.

"We have a good idea of what's out there, Bridge," Olsen said through the bridge speaker. "We make it a convoy led by one small ship, probably a small escort vessel.

"Back of that escort there are two larger pips. They are running abreast of each other one thousand yards back of the escort in the van. These two ships are eight hundred yards apart. Then we have two more ships. These pips are even larger. These two are aft of the first two ships at a distance of one thousand yards. They are following in the wakes of the ships in front of them. There is one more ship, a smaller pip, dead astern of the second line of ships. We assume that ship is an escort. It is one thousand yards astern of the second line of ships. We have also picked up one small pip abeam of both sides of the convoy at a distance of five hundred yards from each side of the convoy. Assume them to be small escort vessels, sir. The entire convoy is spread out along course one eight zero over three thousand yards of ocean, sir.''

"Very well," Brannon said. He stood at one side of the bridge, his mind sorting out the information given to him, figuring out the plan of attack he would make.

The classic, the approved manner of attack on a convoy would be to reverse his course and run out ahead of the convoy. He had enough speed to be able to do that. Then he could submerge *Eelfish* and wait for the convoy to come to him. Once they did so he would open fire.

The classic approach was a good one, Brannon thought. What it didn't allow for was that the water was too shallow, only 180 feet deep. That wasn't deep enough to give him the room to maneuver away from a determined depth-charge attack. Once he started shooting from ahead of the convoy it was certain that the escort in the van and the two on each beam would rush to the attack. The escort astern would likely herd his sheep off to safety while the other escorts pinned down the submarine. Brannon turned the problem over in his mind, his face somber in the starlight.

"I have ships!" the starboard lookout called out. "I got several ships bearing zero four zero, Bridge.''

"Very well," Lee said. He looked at his Captain.

"Very well," Brannon said. He bent his head to the bridge transmitter.

"Plot, give me a range to the target's course line.''

"Range to the target track is four zero zero zero, repeat four thousand yards, sir.''

"Very well," Brannon answered. "Plot, here's what I want: We'll run on this course at this distance from the enemy track until the last ship in the convoy is to our beam to starboard. Then I want to come right and run to the enemy's course and come right again so that we'll be dead astern of the convoy. We'll attack on the surface."

He waited a moment so the plotting party down below could make notes. Then, his voice calm, Brannon said: "Set all torpedoes for two feet depth. Repeat two feet. Gun crews to the Control Room in red night goggles. Sound General Quarters.''

He heard the muted clanging of the General Quarters alarm and the rush of feet down below as the crew raced to their battle stations.

He listened as the reports poured in from each compartment of the ship. All battle stations were manned. Depth set all torpedoes two feet. All torpedo tube outer doors were closed. Course is zero zero zero. Speed is ten knots. Plotting party standing by. Brannon nodded to Lee and steadied his elbows on the teak bridge rail and raised his binoculars to his eyes. He could see the targets plainly, one small ship out ahead of the others and then two lines of ships. He bent to the transmitter.

"Radar. Are you sure there's a small ship abeam to starboard in the convoy? I can't see him at all. Take a look through the periscope to verify."

Brannon heard the search periscope sliding upward above him and then the voice of Lieutenant Perry Arbuckle, the Assistant Engineering Officer who manned the Torpedo Data Computer in the Conning Tower, said, "Bridge, confirm a small ship close aboard the second ship in the line. He's very close to that ship, sir."

"Very well," Brannon said. "Plot, give me a time at this speed when we will be abeam of that last ship in the convoy."

"Twelve minutes, sir. One two minutes."

"Plot a course to the enemy track, John," Brannon said, "then turn the plot over to Mr. Lee and come up here. I need you up here for this action."

Olsen climbed out of the hatch, his lean face beaming. "We've got a lot of ships out there, Skipper. All of them waltzing down the garden path just as nice as can be. How are we going to hit them?"

"I'm going to fall in behind the convoy," Brannon said. "I'll give Plot time to give me a shooting setup on that Tail End Charlie back there, the last ship in the convoy. He might be an escort, and I want to get rid of him before anything else. Then I'll set up to take the ship that will be on our port side as we go in, the second line of ships."

"Gun crews are standing by, sir," Olsen said.

"Good. If the convoy breaks up and scatters, as I think it will, we can add to their confusion by opening fire with the deck guns. They might discourage the escorts from getting nasty while we're working in the middle of the convoy. Pass the word below to break out extra ammunition for the deck guns and have the ammunition party standing by to pass it topside if we call for it. This thing could get a little hairy, John, just a little bit hairy before we get through."

"Could get a little hairy?" Olsen said to himself as he went *forward to the hatch to pass the word about the ammunition party. "By my late Swedish father's ass it could get hairy!"*

"Last ship in the convoy will be abeam to starboard in ten minutes, Bridge," Lee said from down below. "Suggest we come right to course zero nine five and make turns for flank speed, sir, twenty knots. When we reach a point astern of the convoy, sir, that will be in five minutes and twenty seconds, we can come right to course one eight zero. At that time the last ship in the convoy will be two two zero zero, repeat twenty-two hundred yards dead ahead of our position."

"Execute the course and speed changes at the proper time," Brannon said. He waited, feeling the vibration in the deck under his feet as the *Eelfish* picked up speed and began to turn to starboard, heeling sharply. A bow wave curled over the starboard side of the bow and splashed the gun sponson. Brannon felt a sudden alarm. If a Japanese lookout on one of the ships out there saw the bow wave there would be hell to pay. He gritted his teeth, watching for a searchlight signal, a star shell from the convoy, a sign that *Eelfish* had been seen. The convoy plodded southward without a change of course or speed, and Brannon let his breath go out in a long sigh. He bent to the bridge transmitter.

"Mr. Lee!" Brannon's voice was sharp. "You will execute speed changes after a change of course. Repeat, execute speed changes after a change of course. We made a big bow wave and there's some moon and starshine up here. You were given the order to change course and speed. You will do it in the future in that manner."

"Aye, aye, sir," Lee's voice was subdued. *Eelfish* rushed through the night toward the convoy's wake. Down below in the ship the telephone talkers relayed the conversation to the people at battle stations.

"Old Man's getting cranky," a reload man in the After Torpedo Room said with a grin. "Chewin' that feather merchant's ass out in public."

"He's got a right to do that," Fred Nelson said. He glared at the torpedomen and the reload crew under his charge, his fierce eyes staring from either side of a big, hooked nose.

"Old Man's fighting this ship. You do what he says you do. You do it right, first time. Without being told to do it right. That's what bein' a submarine man is all about. You do things right the first time without being told how to do it." He turned as the telephone talker raised a hand.

"Lee is asking for permission to execute a right turn and to open the outer doors in the Forward Room before he goes to flank speed,'' the talker said.

"Fucker's gettin' smart,'' Nelson grunted. "He's the Gunnery Officer. He should know you can't open them outer doors on the tubes in the Forward Room you goin' faster'n ten knots. Not without gettin' a hernia.''

"Old Man gave him an 'execute.' Here we go: Open doors on tubes in the After Room!''

"What doors, fuckhead?'' Nelson snarled. He grabbed a Y-wrench and fitted it in place on the stud that opened the torpedo tube outer doors.

"Outer doors,'' the telephone talker said.

"Do your fuckin' job right, first time,'' Nelson snapped.

"All torpedo tube outer doors open, Bridge,'' Lee reported. "Steady on course one eight zero, making turns for flank speed.''

"Very well,'' Brannon answered. "Give me a shooting setup on this Tail End Charlie at the after end of the convoy. He sure as hell isn't an escort, he's a small island freighter.

"I want to take him as we go by him at eight hundred yards if that's okay without any big course changes.

"Keep that problem running and then give me a shooting set-up on the bigger ship that will be to our port as we come up on the second line of ships in the convoy. I'll take Tail End Charlie as we go into the convoy, and then I'll take the bigger ship on our port hand and after that it will be Beulah bar the door!'' He drew a deep breath.

"Now hear this,'' he said into the bridge transmitter. "This is the Captain. We've maneuvered into position astern of a convoy of five ships and at least three escorts. We're going to run the *Eelfish* right up under their skirts from the rear and give them a goosing like they never had before!'' He straightened up and looked at John Olsen.

"John, I want you on the TBT on the cigaret deck. You use the fish in the After Room. Shoot if you see a good target. Keep me informed. Save at least two fish in case those escorts try to run up our backsides.'' Olsen nodded and ran back to the Target Bearing Transmitter, a pair of night binoculars mounted on a pelorus that transmitted the relative bearings of a target to the Conning Tower.

In the Forward Torpedo Room Steve Petreshock slapped his hand against the warhead of a reload torpedo, his face exultant.

"Hear that?'' he said to the torpedomen and the reload crew.

"Hear that? The Old Man's gonna go right up their ass on the surface. He's got the gun crews standing by in the Control Room. He's gonna raise hell!"

"I heard what he said," one of the reload crew said. "I heard him say there's at least three escorts up there. Three of them Jap destroyers can make us mighty sick. Ship's cook told me there's only a hundred and eighty feet of water in this fuckin' place. That ain't enough water."

"Knock off the shit," Petreshock snapped. "You engine room snipes ain't good for anything but cleaning the bilges and being in the reload crew because all you've got goin' for you is a strong back. This Old Man knows what he's doin'. He's a fightin' son of a bitch!"

In the Control Room Bob Lee looked down at the neat plot John Olsen had drawn of the maneuvering of the *Eelfish* and his own additions to the plot. It all looked so, well, schoolbookish, he thought. Like a problem out of a book about how to solve the problem of firing torpedoes at an enemy. All neat and easy. Elementary. He looked at the Chief of the Boat, Chief Torpedoman Joseph "Monk" Flanagan, who was lounging against the ladder to the Conning Tower, his eyes hidden behind the dark-red night-vision adaptation goggles. Flanagan's jaws moved constantly as he chewed on a large wad of gum. Lee bent over the plotting board as Rafferty and Jim Michaels began to feed Arbuckle and Lee a stream of data. He heard Arbuckle's voice in the Conning Tower.

"Bridge, you've got a solution on the first target. Range to the target is eight five zero yards, repeat eight hundred and fifty yards."

"Stand by forward," Brannon said. "Stand by...don't get me off course, damn it! Stand by..."

"Fire one!" Brannon yelled. He felt the jolt in his feet and legs as the 3,000-pound torpedo hurtled out of the torpedo tube, driven by a giant fist of compressed air and water, its steam turbines screaming into life as the torpedo passed down the tube. He counted down from six to one.

"Fire two!"

"Give me more speed, damn it! Give me a solution on that second target." He heard Olsen's voice from the cigaret deck before he heard the crumping boom of a torpedo exploding against a ship.

"Hit!" Olsen yelled. "You got a hit on the first target! Second fish missed ahead."

"Give me a setup on the second target, damn it!" Brannon yelled.

"You can shoot, Bridge." Arbuckle's voice was high with excitement. "You can shoot!"

"Fire three!" Brannon yelled. He counted down to one.

"Fire four!" He spun and looked to starboard. "Target to starboard in the second row is turning away to starboard," Brannon yelled into the bridge transmitter. "Give me a setup on that target!"

"Escort coming in from starboard, bearing one one zero!" The starboard lookout's voice was a high scream.

"Hit!" Brannon yelled. "Hit on the second target!" He stared for a few seconds at the orange blossom of flame at the second target's starboard bow.

"Battle stations surface!" Brannon yelled. He jumped to one side as Chief Flanagan literally seemed to bounce upward out of the hatch, and then he disappeared over the side of the bridge rail. He heard the Chief of the Boat's voice cursing as he wrestled open the ammunition lockers in the Conning Tower fairing as the gun crews poured upward out of the hatch and went over the rail.

"Deck guns standing by and ready," Flanagan's voice was a bull-like roar from the deck.

"Collision!" the starboard lookout screamed. Brannon jumped in panic.

"Collision between that big ship on this side and the escort that was comin' in," the lookout yelled. Brannon whirled and saw the two ships locked together, the larger ship's bow buried deeply in the small escort vessel.

"Olsen!" Brannon shouted. "Shoot at those two ships!"

"Escort comin' in from the port side, bearing zero two zero, Bridge!" the port lookout was yelling loudly. "Son of a bitch is shootin', Bridge!"

"Forward gun!" Brannon shouted over the bridge rail. "Take that escort under fire! Adjust fire by shell splashes!"

The deck gun boomed, and Brannon saw a column of water rise on the port side of the onrushing escort vessel. The gun roared again and a second column of water soared upward in the moonlight, close to the escort's bow. The escort began to turn to its starboard and Brannon heard John LaMark, the Gunner's Mate on the 1.1 quad pom-pom, yelling from the cigaret deck.

"I can hit that bastard, Bridge!"

"Commence firing, pom-pom!" Brannon yelled. He watched

as the deadly "Chicago Piano" began to spit its stream of high explosive shells toward the escort vessel. As he turned away to look around he heard LaMark's high-pitched yell: "Gotcha, you bastard!"

"*Hit!*" Olsen was yelling from the cigaret deck above the steady roar of the pom-pom. "Hit, dead center!"

"Plot," Brannon yelled into the bridge transmitter, "give me a setup on the ships up ahead, damn it!"

"We've lost contact, Bridge," Jim Michaels called out. "Last-time we had a contact with them they were going in all directions, sir!"

Brannon heard Flanagan's yell from the forward deck and turned and saw the escort vessel, its bridge a burning wreck, reeling under the combined assault of the 5.25-inch deck gun and the pom-pom. He saw a sudden explosion in the escort's hull and the ship began to roll over.

"Cease firing!" Brannon shouted. "Radar, give me a picture of what we've got. Olsen, what in the hell is going on back aft?"

"The target that collided with the escort is sinking, sir." Olsen's voice was cracking with excitement. "The escort he hit broke up and went down. The first target you shot at, back aft, has rolled over, bottom side up. Second target is down by the bow but still underway."

"Plot," Brannon snapped into the transmitter. "Give me a course and bring me in to six hundred yards on that second target. We'll take him with gunfire."

"Come right to zero zero five, Bridge," Lee answered.

"Execute course change," Brannon ordered. He waited as the *Eelfish* heeled around in a sharp turn and steadied, running toward the second target.

"Radar range to the second target is six zero zero, repeat six hundred yards, Bridge," Lee said.

"Both deck guns, set range six hundred yards," Brannon called out. "*Commence firing!*"

He flinched as the two 5.25-inch deck guns roared in unison and then settled down to a steady barrage of fire. He saw the flashes of the hits in the ship's bridge and superstructure and then a steady series of explosions as the gunners lowered their sights and began to pound at the ship's hull. A great gush of steam and fire exploded out of the target's midships section, and the ship seemed to rear slightly, like a wounded animal. Then it broke in two and the bow and stern began to drift apart.

"Cease fire! *Cease fire!*" Brannon yelled. "Plot, give me some information, damn it!"

"Ships up ahead have all disappeared from the radar scope, Bridge. We can come left to course one eight five, Bridge. That will take us toward where the rest of the convoy was when we started the action."

"Close torpedo tube outer doors," Brannon said. "Secure the Battle Surface party. Make the course change and give me turns for flank speed as soon as the torpedo tube doors are closed." He went to the port side of the bridge as the deck gun crews poured into the bridge and went below. When the last of the gunners had gone below Brannon bent to the bridge transmitter.

"We'll stay on this course until we see the other targets or we're sure they got away," he said. "Give me a constant radar sweep until further orders." He straightened up and looked at the luminous dial of his wrist watch, blinked his eyes and looked again. He had opened fire on the Tail End Charlie at 0130. The minute hand on his watch was creeping toward four minutes after two. Thirty-four minutes? He shook his head. It had seemed more like thirty-four hours. He felt a hand touch his arm and turned and saw Olsen.

"I got a hit, Skipper! First torpedo I ever fired at an enemy ship and I hit him right in the midships section. That ship that was all tangled up with the escort!" His face suddenly sobered. "I missed with the second fish but I hit him good with the first one, blew him apart!"

"You had a sitting duck," Brannon scoffed. Then he reached out and found Olsen's right hand and pumped it with his own.

"I'm kidding, John! You did a damned fine job. You covered our stern and kept me informed." He paused. "I wonder where in the hell those other ships went? There were two of them in that front line of ships and one escort."

"We plotted them at ten knots," Olsen said slowly. "I guess they could make fifteen, anyway. They were a good what, twenty-five hundred yards ahead of Tail End Charlie when you started shooting. How long were we engaged?"

"Thirty-four minutes," Brannon answered. Olsen nodded and did the mathematics in his head.

"They could have gotten about fourteen, fifteen thousand yards out ahead of us plus the distance we lost when we turned and went back to take that one freighter with the deck guns. Jim Michaels said that we picked them up at fifteen thousand yards because there were several of them together. If they scattered and were that far out in front we might not be able to make a radar contact."

Brannon nodded and turned to stare at the dim horizon aft of the *Eelfish*. "I've got a hunch that we'll have company, John. The Japanese have aircraft at Tacloban, and there's enough moon and starshine to help them if they come out to search for us. Go below and get our position nailed down and put me on a course back to the patrol area. Pass the word to stand easy on Battle Stations. Galley can serve coffee. Smoking lamp is lighted. I'll keep the deck watch until we secure from General Quarters. Send the regular lookouts up as soon as they're adapted to night vision." Olsen dropped down the hatch. The regular lookouts came up to the bridge a half hour later and as the Battle Stations Surface lookouts went below Brannon patted each man on the back and murmured a "well done."

"Contact! Aircraft bearing one six zero, Bridge!"

"Clear the bridge!" Brannon yelled. He waited until the last lookout had dropped down the hatch and then he punched the diving alarm with the heel of his hand and punched it once more. He went down the hatch, pulling the hatch cover closed behind him, and the *Eelfish* slid quietly under the sea.

CHAPTER 2

Edward "Doc" Wharton, the ship's Chief Pharmacist's Mate and the only medical man aboard the *Eelfish*, was loading a syringe in the Crew's Mess. His patient, the second loader on the forward deck gun, was seated at a mess table. One man on each side of the second loader held him as he fought for breath in tortured gasps. Wharton slid the needle gently into the flesh of the man's muscular shoulder and pressed the plunger home as Chief Flanagan walked into the compartment.

"What's wrong with him?" Flanagan asked.

"He's hyperventilating, Chief," Wharton said. "He's breathing so fast his lungs can't get any oxygen, and that makes him black out. Excitement, that's all. I've given him a weak shot of morphine, enough to knock him out for a little while so his breathing will slow down. He'll be okay. We have to watch him until he comes back to normal, but he's okay."

Flanagan looked around the compartment. The crews of the deck guns were babbling excitedly, ignoring the Pharmacist's Mate and his patient. The high they had been riding in the deck gun action was still with them.

"All right, you people," Flanagan growled. "Let's knock off this bullshit. You people sound like a zoo."

John Wilkes Booth, the ship's yeoman who had manned the .20-millimeter machine guns, grinned at Flanagan.

"Hell, Chief, it was just like a turkey shoot back home in Alabama. We just purely shot those bastards right outa water, didn't we?"

Flanagan stared at the black-haired yeoman. "Next time we get into one of those flails I wish you'd keep your big mouth shut. It's bad enough when those twin twenties of yours are hammering right over our heads on that forward deck gun, we don't need you screaming like someone had shoved a big corn cob up your ass and sat you down hard!"

"I wasn't screaming, that was my Rebel yell. You got to yell if you're fighting, Chief. All us good ol' Suth'n boys give out with the Rebel yell when we get in a fight. Scares the damn Yankees outa their skulls!"

"You'd better Rebel yell your ass up to that cubbyhole you call an office," Flanagan growled. "The Exec is writing up the contact report, and he'll be looking for you to do a little fightin' on that typewriter."

Booth slid out from behind the mess table and looked at the second loader, whose head was resting on his arm on the table.

"Old Doc does pretty good with that needle for a Reservist who used to sing in front of some damned band, doesn't he?"

"I didn't sing in front of any band," Wharton snapped. He ran his hand over his carefully combed wavy blond hair. "I was a featured ballroom dancer with a full orchestra. Not a band, an orchestra. There's a hell of a difference. Shit, singers are a dime a dozen in show business. Dancers, good dancers, are hard to find." He rolled his eyes upward. "Man, I had me a partner, a tall redhead, she was built like a brick shithouse! If you ever saw her, Booth, your gonads would shoot right up to your stomach. That is, if yeomen have gonads."

Booth grinned at the Chief Pharmacist's Mate. "All that good civilian background sure helps to make a submarine sailor, doesn't it? Damned submarine navy is just like the Army. The

Army takes a civilian who's a first-rate restaurant cook and makes him into a truck driver.'' He rinsed his coffee cup in the sink and put it back in the cup rack. "I guess that being a professional ballroom dancer is the right background for a bedpan cleaner.'' He went forward and through the hatch as a gust of laughter swept the Crew's Mess. Chief Wharton grinned and took the sleeping loader's wrist in his hand and began to take his pulse.

"LaMark," Flanagan said to the ship's Gunner's Mate. "The Exec wants a reading on how much ammunition we shot off and how much we got left. Like right now."

"Got it right here, Chief," LaMark said. He took a piece of paper out of his pocket.

"That isn't going to do the Exec any good in your pocket," Flanagan said.

"I'll take it to the Wardroom right away. Man, that quad pom-pom is sure a fire hose, ain't it? I could have cut that damned escort vessel right off at the water line if you people on the deck gun hadn't got lucky and blew it up. I pure blew that ship's bridge into firewood."

Flanagan faced the people still sitting at the mess tables, his powerful sloping shoulders hunched belligerently.

"I want you people on the gun crews to know that for a bunch of sorry peckerheads you did a pretty damned good job." He looked at Steve Petreshock, who was sitting with Fred Nelson, the torpedoman in charge of the After Torpedo Room.

"The torpedoes ran good. Like they are supposed to run. Old Man told me he was happy about that so you two people can feel happy. Just make sure the rest of the fish we still got run good. As soon as the Exec gives me the word I'll be able to tell you when to start the reload." Petreshock and Nelson grinned their appreciation.

"All the rest of you people"—Flanagan's voice was a low rumble—"get your asses outa here. The baker's got to have some room to mix his bread dough." He drew a cup of steaming coffee from the urn as the men left the mess room. Scotty Rudolph came out of the galley with a smoking hot, freshly baked cheese Danish.

"Just out of the oven, Chief. They taste pretty good when the cheese is still hot, but don't burn your damned tongue." Flanagan nodded his thanks and sat down at a mess table. The ship's cook sat down across from him.

"You people did an awful lot of yellin' and a hell of a lot of shootin' up there tonight. I like to broke my damn back shoving those shells up through the ammo chute. Those things are heavy."

"Ninety-two pounds each," Flanagan said.

"What in the hell was goin' on?" the cook said.

"Well, I don't rightly know what went on before the Old Man hollered for Battle Surface. But when I went over the bridge rail there were ships all around us and the Old Man is yellin' at the Exec, he was aft on the cigaret deck, to shoot some damned target."

"I wear the battle phones back here," Rudolph said. "I know the Old Man hit two ships with fish from the Forward Room and the Exec knocked off one ship with a couple of fish from the After Room. But you don't get any dope over the phones when there's a Battle Surface going on."

"Well," Flanagan said. He sipped at his coffee and chewed a bite of the pastry. "We were manning both deck guns and doin' nothing and all of a sudden the Old Man yells for the forward gun to take out an escort that was chargin' at us from up forward on the port bow. We couldn't get any radar ranges, radar was busy with gettin' ship ranges for torpedo targets. Old Man yells for us to adjust range by shell splashes. That ain't the easy way to do it, you know, because the gun keeps shooting longer for the first five, six rounds as the barrel heats up.

"But that number two baker of yours, that Willie Stevens we made pointer on the forward gun? He did a hell of a job. Got a hit with the third round and held the point of aim right in there and the escort is tryin' to get away and we're movin' all the time.

"Once we tore that bastard all up the Old Man comes about and reverses course and both guns went to work on a freighter he'd hit with a torpedo. I guess we hit him with maybe fifteen, twenty rounds. We musta hit his engine room, the boilers, because he blew into two pieces. I tell you, Scotty, this Old Man is a heller. Not like the skipper I had on my first three patrols out of Brisbane. That bastard wouldn't surface if there was an escort vessel within ten miles." He pushed himself to his feet.

"I got to see the Exec and get the word on reloading the tubes. Like you said, they taste better when they're hot. I like the way you put raisins in the cheese part."

Captain Mike Brannon sat in his accustomed place at the head of the Wardroom table. He finished a plate of scrambled eggs and bacon that Mahaffey had put in front of him.

"I don't see how you can eat those powdered eggs and that

canned bacon and look as if you were enjoying it," Olsen said. "I can't get that stuff down."

"I thought it tasted pretty good," Brannon said. "I must have been hungry. Let's get down to business. I want to get some sleep after they finish reloading the tubes."

Olsen looked down at his notes and put a clean piece of paper in front of him. "Let's get the tonnages of the ships we sank down on paper. I didn't get too good a look at that first ship you hit. Not until it was aft of us, and when I saw it then it was bottom up. How big was it?"

"Not too big," Brannon said. "She looked to me like one of those inter-island freighters. Pretty decrepit, from what I could see. I saw a lot of lines and other gear hanging loose from her booms. I'd guess about a thousand tons. No more than that."

"I'll put her down for one thousand tons," Olsen said. "The other two targets we hit with torpedoes; I got a real good look at the one I fired at. Pretty good size, I'd say. Maybe three thousand, thirty-five hundred tons. That one and the one you hit looked like they could have come off the same shipyard ways. Thirty-five hundred tons, that seem right?"

"Let's not be greedy," Brannon said slowly. "You feel awfully silly when you get back to port and they read your patrol report to you, and when they come to the part where you say you sank a five-thousand-ton ship they read you an intelligence report that says the Japanese reported losing a two-thousand-ton ship. They ask you nasty questions about your judgment and infer that if you can't judge the size of a ship you can't work out a torpedo problem. No. Make both those ships three thousand tons."

"Yes, sir," Olsen said. "The two escort vessels. I think they were pretty small. About five hundred tons each. Do you agree?" Brannon nodded his assent and Olsen made some notes.

"That one escort, the one that got rammed out to our starboard," Olsen continued. "Can we take credit for that one? The bigger ship rammed it when it started to make a run on us. Damned near cut it in two. It went down when I hit the bigger ship with a fish."

"I don't see why not," Brannon said. "If we hadn't gone in on the surface and started shooting, that freighter would never have rammed the escort. Hell yes, we'll claim it. What does that give us as a total?"

"Let's see," Olsen said. "The Tail End Charlie is one thousand tons. Three thousand each for the two freighters and two escorts at five hundred each. That makes seven thousand tons of merchant shipping and a thousand tons of escort vessels. Add the two big Fubuki destroyers we sank when the *Mako* went down and we've got one hell of a bag!''

"Wait until they start the nitpicking in Fremantle and Brisbane," Brannon said dryly. He fished a cigaret out of Olsen's pack on the table and lit it. Mahaffey, in the tiny Wardroom galley, saw him light the cigaret and came out with fresh cups of coffee.

"Those people on the Staff in Fremantle and Brisbane," Brannon said, "all they do is go over our contact and patrol reports with a fine-toothed comb to try and find anything they can to gig you on. They always do that. I think they believe this is how you fight a war." He leaned back in his chair and yawned. "What's the status of our torpedoes and ammunition?"

"We fired six fish from the Forward Room last week at the two Fubukis," Olsen said. "You fired four more out of that room tonight, so we've got six fish left up there. Six in the tubes, no reloads. I fired two fish out of the After Room tonight, so we've got four in the tubes and reloads for Nine and Ten tubes back aft. The deck gun forward fired twenty-two rounds and the gun aft fired twelve rounds. No problem there. We've got plenty of ammo for the deck guns. That one point one pom-pom is another matter. That thing goes through ammo like my ex-wife used to go through my paycheck. We're down to just under fifty percent of that gun's ammo supply. We're better off in the twenty millimeter stuff. We have about seventy percent of our supply left for that gun, and we didn't use any fifty-caliber stuff at all."

"The twin twenties?" Brannon said. "I don't remember telling the twenties to fire. I can't even remember them firing, and God knows I should be able to remember that. They built that pregnant lump out in front of the bridge for a gun platform for the twenties when they decided to give us the pom-pom and put it on the cigaret deck."

Olsen grinned at Brannon. "Well, sir, you know our demon yeoman John Wilkes Booth. You can't get that good old Southern boy near a fight and not expect him to join in.

"That escort vessel that was rammed to our starboard? The escort had a gunner on it who was all guts. His ship was cut nearly in two. He was sinking, and he opened fire on us with a machine gun. Booth took care of him. He poured that twin twenty into him until he silenced him. I didn't see what he did on that escort you took under fire on the port bow, but Flanagan told me that Booth was really going to it with the twin twenties and screaming his head off. Flanagan told me that he bounced

Booth about the screaming, and Booth said he was just giving his Rebel yell. Flanagan said it scared half the gun crew to hear him yelling.''

"I don't remember hearing him yell, either," Brannon said.

"I wouldn't worry too much about that," Olsen said with a grin. "You were a fairly busy fellow during that action tonight. Bob Lee said he was nearly a wreck when you finally secured the Plot. He did pretty well, didn't he?''

"Not nearly as well as he should have," Brannon said slowly. "Lee is bright enough, God knows. Sometimes he scares me, he's so damned bright. But he hasn't as yet gotten the knack of anticipation in a battle situation. Arbuckle has to depend on him for information, and even when I was yelling and hollering on the bridge I could hear Arbuckle shouting at Lee for more information. I can't have that, John.

"I want you to take the complete plot of tonight's action and sit down with Lee and Arbuckle and go over it step by step. Show them what you would have done and when you would have done it and why. Show Lee and Arbuckle where they have to be thinking with me, thinking as I think. I shouldn't have to ask for information that they should be giving me automatically, and I won't have any more of it in the future. Another thing," Brannon paused. "I think that Lee is losing weight. He wasn't any fat man when he came aboard, but it seems to me that he's getting a lot thinner. Maybe he's worrying about his job, about things like that. I'd like you to find out.''

"Captain," Olsen said. "I'm not a doctor.''

"You're the Executive Officer, John," Brannon said. "A good Executive Officer should be able to do anything, any damned thing his Captain asks him to do." He grinned at Olsen. "Art Hinman used to lecture me on that when I was his Exec. I got to the point where I could almost read his mind.''

"I'll try, sir," Olsen said. "Anything else?''

"Yes. Tell Jerry Gold that he did one hell of a job of compensating this ship. We were in almost perfect trim when we dove, and that was after we'd fired six fish and used up one hell of a lot of heavy ammunition. He's a damned good diving officer, and I want him to know that you appreciate that and that I appreciate it." He looked at Olsen.

"The radar," he said softly.

"What about the radar?" Olsen said. "It worked just perfectly. I thought Jim Michaels was full of crap when he came aboard in Fremantle and told me what that SJ radar could do. He wasn't full of it at all. The way he can read that thing, the way he's taught Rafferty, they told us exactly what we had out there and they even gave us damned accurate readings on the relative size of the targets."

"That's it," Brannon said slowly. "*Mako* didn't have this new SJ radar. If we hadn't left *Mako* when we did—we were running out ahead of *Mako* you remember—we'd have picked up that convoy and Michaels would have been able to tell us there were two big destroyers hiding back of those ships. We could have ambushed those damned destroyers that killed the *Mako*. But we left her and the *Mako* never knew what she was walking into."

"My God, Skipper," Olsen's voice was low, intense. "You just can't think about what happened in that way. We left because we had to leave. Our patrol orders told us where we had to go and when. For God's sake don't live with the idea that we did anything wrong, because we didn't!"

"I don't think we did anything wrong," Brannon said slowly, his voice soft. "I just keep wondering about how it would have been if we had decided to stay with *Mako* just an hour or two longer. I know it's sort of foolish, but I do." He stopped and looked down at the table top.

"I thought about Art Hinman when we were coming up on that convoy tonight." Brannon looked up, and Olsen saw that his eyes were fixed on something far distant.

"The first night surface attack we made in the *Mako* Art Hinman told me to take the TBT on the cigaret deck, to protect his stern and to keep him informed. Just as I told you to do tonight. Like you did tonight I fired two fish out of the After Room. Like you I got one hit. Like you those were the first torpedoes I ever fired at an enemy." He turned his head and focused his eyes on Olsen.

"I had a funny feeling tonight, John. A very odd feeling. I felt as if Art Hinman was on the bridge with me and that he was joking with me and telling me to go right up the convoy's rear end. I thought I heard him say that when we started shooting torpedoes the convoy would scatter and then I could use the deck guns. I don't know, John, it seemed natural to me that Art Hinman seemed to be there."

"I don't think it was unnatural, sir," Olsen said. His lean face was somber. "My mother believed that when a person died his or her soul went back to God. But if that soul knew that someone the soul had loved on Earth was in trouble or needed help, the soul could go back and give that help." In the small Wardroom galley Pete Mahaffey cocked his head as he listened, and then he began to shake his head in disapproval.

"I thought it was only the Irish who are fey," Brannon said.

"No," Olsen replied, "the Swedes have a long history of that sort of thing." He slid his long, lean frame from behind the Wardroom table.

"I think I'll take a walk through the boat," he said. "I'll have the contact report all typed up for you when you get up."

"Tell everyone who's awake that they did a hell of a good job," Brannon said. "Especially the people in the torpedo rooms. The fish ran good and the exploders on the ones we got hits with worked." He rose and followed Olsen out of the Wardroom and went to his stateroom.

He turned on the small light over the mirror and washbowl and blinked in surprise. His face was grimy with the smoke and soot of the gunfire. He ran hot water into the bowl, washed, kicked off his sandals, put his socks and shirt in a small laundry bag, and stretched out on his bunk. He heard Pete Mahaffey's loud whisper through the watertight door opening to the Control Room that the Captain was in his bunk and the low order from the Chief of the Watch to get-a-one-degree-up-bubble-and-hold-it-there-damn-it.

He closed his eyes. If only Art Hinman had had the new SJ radar on *Mako*. If only *Eelfish* had stayed with the *Mako* a little longer. If. If. If.

He waited for sleep to come.

CHAPTER 3

The Control Room Auxiliaryman, who also served as the watch messenger, knocked softly on the bulkhead of the Captain's stateroom three times during the eight to twelve morning watch to report that a periscope observation had picked up enemy aircraft. Each sighting was of planes far out on the horizon. Brannon acknowledged each report and drifted back to sleep. He had expected the Japanese would send out aircraft from their field at Tacloban to search for the submarine that smashed up their small convoy. He had expected, too, that the airmen would overshoot the search area; most fliers tended to think about distance in terms of scores of miles per hour, not in terms of a submarine's slow progress of two or three knots under water.

He awoke when he heard the torpedomen from the Forward Torpedo Room scuffling past his stateroom on their way aft to the Crew's Mess for the noon meal. He rose and went to the Officers' Shower in the Forward Room and put on clean clothes. Pete Mahaffey came in to collect his dirty laundry.

"Cook's got roast beef and mashed potatoes today, sir. I finally taught that man that a little garlic is better than a lot. Gravy is mighty tasty. I can serve when you're ready, Captain."

"I'll eat when the other officers are ready, Pete," Brannon said. "I don't like eating alone."

After Mahaffey had cleared the table Brannon began reading the contact report that Olsen had written. After he had read it and approved it the report would be encoded and sent to the Submarine Commands at Fremantle and Pearl Harbor. He read slowly, weighing each word, each phrase. More than one submarine commander, as he well knew, had come to grief because of a carelessly worded contact report and had been undone by a caustic footnote appended to the report by the Admirals in Fremantle and Brisbane.

Brannon wrote his approval on the side of the contact report and then carefully worded a last paragraph. He noted that targets were extremely scarce in Surigao Strait, and *Eelfish*, with all due respect, requested a more productive patrol area. Olsen came into the Wardroom, and Brannon showed him the paragraph he had added.

"I know that the squeaky wheel gets the grease," he said. "But the mosquito that buzzes also gets slapped."

The answer to the contact report came from Fremantle two nights later. There was a short sentence of congratulation on the sinking of three freighters and two small escort vessels. In response to the request made by the Commanding Officer of the *Eelfish* for a more productive area, *Eelfish* was needed in her assigned patrol area and would stay there until all torpedoes were expended or until early September, whichever came first. Future discussions of patrol areas could be done after *Eelfish* had returned to Fremantle.

"I told you they'd find fault down there in Fremantle," Brannon said after he had read the decoded message that Olsen brought to the cigaret deck. "Those fellows sit around in that fancy headquarters of theirs down there. They sit around drinking coffee and trying to figure out ways to make the people at sea feel like a thin dime.''

"You mean that place they call 'The Bend in the Road'?'' Olsen asked with a grin. "I had to take a message over there when we were in Fremantle. You can't have a messenger boy going to that place unless he wears at least two gold stripes. That place is really something, Captain. I mean that is some sort of luxury!''

"I know," Brannon growled. "That place is full of people who are making a career out of kissing the asses of Admirals. Doesn't make any difference which Admiral, just so the ass is gold-plated. They're a bunch of yes men.

"Admiral Christie is a hell of a good man. At least I think so. But he's surrounded with ass kissers. Every one of those people knows there's something wrong with Christie's pet project, that Mark Six exploder, but not one of those people have got the guts to say anything to Christie. They keep agreeing with him that we're missing the targets when that damned exploder doesn't work. Listen to this sentence." He tilted the message flimsy so he could catch the light of the moon.

"Quote and unquote: It is the opinion of this command that shooting more than one torpedo at a target is an unnecessary waste of torpedoes, which are in very short supply.

"Hell, I know torpedoes are in short supply. But if their damned magnetic exploder worked the way it's supposed to work, sure we could fire one fish at each target. And if the torpedo went off underneath the target, the way the exploder is supposed to work, that's all you'd need, one torpedo to one target. Pearl Harbor has, finally, recognized that fact, and if you're operating out of Pearl you get exploders that have been modified to work only on a contact hit. But not in Australia. You'd think we were in a different Navy out here. I was told in Fremantle by a four-stripe Captain I worked for when I was a youngster in submarines that Admiral Christie has openly defied orders to modify the exploder, orders that came right from Admiral Nimitz!

"What's worse, that General MacArthur, he's playing off one Admiral against another to get his own way. He's got submarines running all over the damned ocean doing things he thinks are important, that he wants done. You should hear what some of the other submarine captains have to say about some of the missions they've had to carry out for Dugout Doug. The job of a submarine is to get out and sink enemy ships, not go chasing around landing commando troops and giving food to people in the islands. They can do that stuff with aircraft and do it better.''

"You must have a hell of a gripe session when all you skippers meet in Fremantle,'' Olsen said. Brannon looked at his Executive Officer and saw the friendly grin.

"Oh, we do,'' he answered. "We really let down our hair. Not that it does a damned bit of good. It just lets off a little steam. And I'm pretty sure that what some of the skippers say gets back to the Admirals the next day.'' He turned away and stared at the dark bulk of Dinegat Island. A lone sea bird floated by overhead, its mewling cry a lost and lonesome sound. He turned back and faced Olsen.

"Ordering us to stay here on station is punishment for using up six fish on three small targets, for saying, as I did in the contact report, that we fired a spread of two fish at each target. I said that deliberately, and they know when you say that you fired a spread, no matter if it's two fish or six fish, they know that you're firing to get contact hits, not using their damned magnetic exploder.''

Olsen raised his head and sniffed appreciatively at the fresh night wind. "I wouldn't read all of that into this message, sir.'' His voice went down a notch and became gentle.

"You may be right, but the thing is—you've got those people by the short hair and you've got a downhill pull. You sank ships. They can't ignore that. Two big destroyers ten days or so ago. Three small freighters and two escorts the other night. That's seven ships down with twelve torpedoes and some ammunition. They can't say that's wasting torpedoes or ammo. Hell, if you'd used all twelve torpedoes to sink the two big destroyers I bet Admiral Nimitz would turn hand springs!''

Brannon grinned and shrugged his shoulders. "Okay, John. You're a good listener, a good friend. I won't sound off again.''

Eelfish sent its departure-from-station report to Fremantle and Pearl Harbor after receiving orders to return to port and turned toward Australia with twelve torpedoes in her tubes and reload racks. Her course took her southward through the Sea of Mindanao, the Sulu Sea, and the Celebes Sea, down the length of Makassar Strait past the big island of Borneo, across the Java Sea and through the justly feared strait between the islands of Bali and Lombok.

Lombok Strait was narrow, with a strong tidal current. When the Japanese discovered that American submarines were using the Strait as a shortcut, to avoid going to the east and through the

Arafuru Sea, they fortified the strait with heavy guns and patrolled it with aircraft.

Running the Strait submerged was considered dangerous because of the strong currents and uncharted rocks. Most submarine captains preferred to time their arrival at the Strait in the dark of night and make the twelve-mile dash at full speed, risking the danger of shellfire and aircraft.

Once *Eelfish* had cleared Lombok Strait and was well into the Indian Ocean the men in both torpedo rooms began the laborious work of pulling the heavy torpedoes out of the torpedo tubes, rolling them over and removing the exploder mechanisms to restore the exploders to the condition they had been when delivered to the ship.

The principle of the controversial Mark VI exploder mechanism was brilliant. Prior to the development of the Mark VI, or the "magnetic exploder," as it was called, all torpedoes were fired to hit the target ship's hull and explode on contact. The mechanism that exploded the warhead on the torpedo upon contact was simple and reliable.

The unalterable laws of physics decree that since water cannot be compressed to a measurable degree, the major part of the explosive power of a torpedo warhead would vent upward along the side of the ship that was hit. Only a small part of the warhead's explosive force would be directed against the target's hull.

If a method could be found to explode a torpedo warhead *under* a ship's hull the laws of physics would ensure that most of the warhead's explosive power would go upward into the air-filled ship's hull, thus breaking the ship's keel, its backbone, and destroying it.

The United States, Germany, and Britain all developed an exploder that would do this. Much of the work of development was done in the 1920s and early 1930s. The principle used in all three exploders was similar. A metal ship's hull passing through saltwater creates an electromagnetic field (EMF) around the hull. A simple antenna built into the torpedo warhead could detect that EMF field. A small propeller mounted in the warhead that was used to arm the contact exploder could also be adapted to run a tiny generator that would charge a capacitor tube with electrical energy.

When the torpedo fitted with the magnetic exploder was fired it was set to run five to ten feet beneath the target's hull. When the torpedo entered the target's EMF field the antenna in the warhead would detect the field and relay the impulse to the capacitor tube, which, after a slight delay to allow the torpedo to get beneath the target, would release its electrical energy and fire the torpedo warhead. The target would be destroyed.

The British and the Germans both used their own version of the magnetic exploder in the early months of World War II. Both sides found that the magnetic exploder was unreliable. Both sides abandoned the magnetic exploder by 1941 and went back to the more dependable contact exploder.

Despite this evidence, the U.S. Navy continued to use the magnetic Mark VI exploder, its defenders arguing that the exploder was perfect, the people using it imperfect in that they consistently missed their targets. This attitude, bitterly criticized by submarine captains who were certain they were not missing every target, did not change until late in 1943, until the evidence that the Mark VI was unreliable was so overwhelming it could not be ignored. However, the orders from Pearl Harbor that the torpedo exploders be modified to work only on contact were ignored by the Admirals in the Submarine Command in Australia.

Submarine captains leaving Australia on war patrol routinely ordered their torpedomen to modify the magnetic exploders to work on contact only. Routinely, those same officers lied in their patrol and contact reports so that the Admirals in Australia wouldn't know about it. Returning to Australia with torpedoes aboard meant that the exploder mechanisms had to be removed from the torpedo warheads and put in the condition they had been when received. John Olsen called it a miserable charade. Mike Brannon agreed with him.

Chief Monk Flanagan, his shirt dripping with sweat from his labors in changing the exploders in the After Torpedo Room, stopped at the coffee urn in the Crew's Mess where Lieutenant Commander John Olsen was drawing a cup of coffee.

"The Chief of the Boat working?" Olsen chided Flanagan. "I thought when you attained that exalted position you didn't have to work anymore, just tell others what to do."

"Those people in the Torpedo Shop in Fremantle check those exploders with an eagle eye," Flanagan grunted. "They'd love to have a solid case where they could prove that we modified the exploders so they could drag someone up in front of a court-martial. So I'm working." He sat down beside Olsen on a mess bench.

"This is all a bunch of damned foolishness, you know."

Flanagan kept his voice low so the cook on duty in the galley wouldn't hear him. "Hell, we wouldn't have to do this crap if we were working out of Pearl Harbor."

"I know," Olsen said cheerfully. "Count your blessings. We're lucky we're going to go into Fremantle and to a hotel in Perth for the R and R period. If that Admiral Carpender over in Brisbane had his way we'd be going to our rest and recreation up in Exmouth Gulf. You could have two weeks of playing soft ball in the sand and cool off with two beers a day."

"I heard about that deal," Flanagan said. "Chief Yeoman in the relief crew, guy I knew a long time, told me they even had a name for that deal. They called it Operation Potshot. You know why it didn't go through?" Olsen shook his head.

"A couple of real hard-assed submarine officers, guys who'd made patrol runs and were too senior to go back to sea on a submarine, they got together and decided that the Admiral was cruising with too much right rudder. They started a big study project on the whole thing. This Chief Yeoman said they've been making studies for months and they're going to keep making studies until the Admiral forgets about it or else he gets transferred." Olsen grinned.

"What gets me," Flanagan continued, "is this whole business of treating a submarine sailor as if he was some sort of a dangerous animal. What in the hell is wrong with letting us have some R and R in a city where they've got decent restaurants and bars? What's wrong with a submarine sailor rolling in the sack with some woman—if she's willing?"

"I don't see anything wrong with it at all," Olsen said. "All I know is that the whole command down here is FUBAR. Fucked Up Beyond All Recognition. You come into port after a patrol run and if you tell Admiral Christie that the Mark VI exploder he developed doesn't work you'll find yourself so deep in hack that you might wind up reading weather instruments on some mountain up in Alaska. Last time we were in port I heard that Admiral Christie doesn't ever allow himself to get into a conversation with the big boss in Brisbane, Admiral Carpender, because if he does he's afraid he'll get into a shouting match and he'll wind up in hack. I haven't figured out yet how you put an Admiral in hack, but I guess other Admirals know how to do that."

"Hell of a way to fight a war, isn't it?" Flanagan asked. "I'll bet none of those Admirals ever made a war patrol. They should have been with old Stoneface Mealey when he had the *Mako* that one run and went into Truk and hammered about eight, nine fish into that battleship and then got the immortal shit kicked out of the *Mako* by about a dozen tin cans. Maybe they'd realize when a man comes in from a tough war patrol he rates something better than a softball game, sand fleas, and two cans of beer a day."

"I'm pretty sure Admiral Christie recognizes those things," Olsen said slowly. He stood up, and Flanagan rose. "I guess both of us had to blow off a little steam, Chief. Let's keep it between ourselves, okay?" Flanagan nodded and went forward, ducking his head and raising his foot to go through the watertight door opening to the Control Room. Scotty Rudolph came out of the galley.

"Got some fresh prune Danish," he said. "Like one?"

"No, thank you," Olsen said. He looked at the W.T. door where Flanagan had disappeared going forward. "That Chief Flanagan, he's a remarkable sort of man."

"Yeah," Rudolph said. "He's one of those old-timey Chief of the Boats. I seen a few of that kind in the fourteen years I been in the boats. Flanagan's hard but he's fair. Do what he tells you and do it right and you're okay. Fuck up and he'll have your ass in little pieces. I like that kind of a Chief of the Boat. You always know where you stand. I figure we're lucky to have him."

Olsen nodded and rinsed his cup and put it in the cup rack. *We're lucky to have Flanagan, he thought to himself as he went forward to the Wardroom. Lucky to have Flanagan and damned lucky to have Mike Brannon. With those two and a little luck maybe I'll live through this damned screwed-up war.* He pushed through the curtains at the door of the Wardroom and saw Mike Brannon sitting at the head of the table.

"Torpedo exploders are all returned to their original condition," he said. "What's got you looking like death warmed over, Captain?"

Brannon pushed a message flimsy across the table. "I've got to see the Staff as soon as we get in. They want three extra copies of our contact and patrol reports. That only means one thing to me, that I'm going to get reamed out for something. Damned if I know what for."

"Keep one thing in mind, sir," Olsen said. "Don't let them forget it, either. You sank ships. Not one of those people has done that."

CHAPTER 4

The U.S.S. *Eelfish* moved along the west coast of Australia, an hour away from the seaport of Fremantle, only hours away from two weeks of rest and relaxation for the crew in the city of Perth, twelve miles up the Swan River from Fremantle. Overhead a clumsy PBY-4 dipped its wings in a salute to the submarine and the *Eelfish* bridge watch waved back happily.

Jim Rice, a tall, heavily bearded torpedoman, was sitting in the bight of a double bowline knot on the end of a line that had been rigged over the starboard side of the Conning Tower. He braced his bare feet against the side of the Conning Tower and with great care began to touch up the small battle flags that he had painted on the side of the Conning Tower. Two small cans of paint, one red, one white, hung from a cord around his neck. His tongue stuck out of one corner of his mouth, a red tip in a thicket of black beard, as he delicately added a little white paint to the array of flags; four Rising Sun flags that stood for two Fubuki destroyers and two escort vessels sunk by the *Eelfish*, three white flags with a red ball in each flag's center for the three small merchant ships *Eelfish* had sent to the bottom in Leyte Gulf. Captain Mike Brannon leaned over the side of the bridge and grinned at Rice.

"Going to make a career of art when the war is over, Jim? You've got a nice touch with a brush."

"No, sir," Rice answered. His white teeth gleamed in the center of the black beard. "Once this war is really over I'm gonna find me a nice rich widow and spend the rest of my life sleepin' between silk sheets and eatin' good. No more of those twelve to four watches at night for me."

"I always heard that most rich widows are old and fat," Brannon said.

"Don't matter, Captain. You can always find a nice young filly on the side for hard ridin'."

"Two women?" Brannon's eyebrows rose. "You're asking for trouble with two women. Double trouble."

"No trouble for a good submarine torpedoman," Rice said airily. He looked up as the PBY-4 dipped low over the submarine, its engines thundering.

"Get lost, you bastard! You're making me nervous and I don't want to smear these nice little flags."

Down on the main deck John Olsen was talking to Chief Monk Flanagan.

"Captain's a little worried, Chief. You sure the Base exploder shop won't be able to tell if we modified the exploders?"

"They won't be able to tell, sir." Flanagan looked at the plane overhead. "Those bastards in the exploder shop are getting cute. Chief in the Afterbody Shop, the torpedo shop on the tender, he tipped me off that the exploder shop on the Base was putting a little drop of clear shellac on some, not all, of the exploder studs that fasten the exploder to the warhead. Not much shellac, not enough to notice it when you backed out the studs but enough to see it if you're looking for it.

"They keep a little notebook, mark down which studs they shellacked on which exploder. That way, if you noticed a little flake or two of shellac when you backed out the stud and if you made a mistake, put some shellac around every stud or if you didn't see it at all, they'd have you.

"What I did was to get a can of the same kind of shellac. And a notebook. When we remodified the exploders we went by our own book so each exploder would be exactly the same as it was when we got it. I'd bet some good money they won't know we fucked with their damned exploders, sir."

A lean destroyer closed on the *Eelfish* from the starboard side, a signal light on its bridge blinking furiously.

"They're saying they'll lead us in, sir," Bill Brosmer said to Bob Lee, who had the OOD watch. He raised a signal gun he had brought to the bridge as the *Eelfish* neared port.

"You want to receipt affirmative and say thank you, sir?"

"Make an affirmative reply and say thank you," Lee said. He turned to Captain Brannon. "Sir, the destroyer will lead us in to the harbor."

"Very well," Brannon said. "Tell the destroyer we'll take up position five hundred yards astern." The destroyer's signal lamp blinked in reply and Brannon watched as the graceful ship swung ahead of the *Eelfish* and took up position, slowing its speed to accommodate to the *Eelfish*. Deep in the harbor another signal lamp began blinking.

"The *Pelius* is making a signal to us, Mr. Lee," Brosmer said.

"Tell him to go ahead," Lee said. Brosmer raised his signal gun and cradled its rifle butt in his shoulder. His index finger clicked the trigger signal on the lamp. The signalman on the submarine tender answered in a blur of light flashes.

"He's telling us to moor alongside the outboard submarine, starboard side to, sir," Brosmer said.

"Acknowledge," Lee said. Ahead of them the destroyer signal lamp began to repeat the message.

"What the hell," Brosmer growled. "Doesn't that bastard think we can read code?"

"They don't know we've got you on the bridge, Bill," Mike Brannon said genially. "Acknowledge and tell them thank you. This is no day to be getting picky." He turned to Bob Lee.

"Let's set the maneuvering watch. All hands not on watch or working will muster topside in clean dungarees, shined shoes, and clean white hats. Tell Chief Flanagan to get his line handlers organized."

Chief Flanagan lined up two ranks of off-duty crewmen on the afterdeck and put Chief Pharmacist's Mate Wharton in charge. He took the line-handling party to the foredeck.

"I want two men for each line," he said. "For those of you who haven't done this before remember one thing. Don't try to catch the monkey fist on the end of the heaving line they'll throw you from the other submarine. That monkey fist is loaded with lead and you'll break your hands. Let the monkey fist fall and grab the heaving line, and haul in the mooring-line eye and put it over the cleats. That's all you got to do. Then you gather up the heaving lines and coil them up nice and neat. Now stand by your line-handling stations." He turned to the bridge.

"Off-duty crew in formation on the after deck, Bridge. Standing at ease. Line-handling party is stationed."

"Very well," Lee said.

Flanagan turned to look at the bulk of the U.S.S. *Pelius*. There were four submarines alongside the tender, and on the outboard submarine Flanagan could see groups of men standing beside coils of mooring line. A submarine on war patrol carries no mooring lines, no anchor, and no anchor chain. The possibility that depth charges might tear open the mooring line lockers and that the line might foul the submarine's propellers, the danger that depth charges might knock the anchor loose and that it would roar out with its G30-foot length of chain and thus immobilize the submarine under water were too great to risk. Nor did submarines on war patrol keep their bronze-wire lifelines, which were usually strung on posts along the edges of the deck. Those might rattle under water and give away the submarine's position. Only the heavy stanchions that had a special fixture on their tops to accommodate the spud of a 50-caliber machine gun were left in place, and those stanchions were braced and welded to make sure they couldn't rattle.

The *Eelfish* eased in toward the outboard submarine in the nest next to the *Pelius,* Captain Mike Brannon watching carefully as Lieutenant Robert E. Lee, his voice crisp as he issued orders to the helm and the maneuvering room for changes of speed, maneuvered the submarine toward its berth. As the bow of the *Eelfish* passed the forward deck gun of the submarine it was to moor alongside, Lee raised his voice.

"Rudder amidships. All back one-third. Pass mooring lines aboard." The heavy lead-loaded monkey fists on the ends of the heaving lines whipped across the *Eelfish* deck, and the line handlers hauled in the mooring-line eyes and slipped them over the cleats.

"All stop! Double up all mooring lines." Lee turned to Captain Brannon. "Ship is moored, sir."

"Nice landing, Bob," Brannon said. "You've got a really good feel for the ship." Lee grinned like a little boy. "Bridge! Permission to take the gangway aboard?" Flanagan's voice came from the afterdeck.

"Permission granted," Brannon said. He walked back to the cigaret deck and dropped down to the deck as a short, heavyset officer, his Captain's eagles gleaming on his shirt-collar tabs, put one foot on the gangway.

"Permission to come aboard, Captain?"

"Welcome aboard, sir," Brannon responded. He waited as the Captain and his staff crossed the gangway, saluting the American flag, which hung from its staff at the ship's stern, and John Olsen, who was standing at the gangway.

"I'm Sam Rivers," the Captain said to Brannon. "Operations Officer for Admiral Christie. The Admiral is coming aboard in a few minutes. Let me extend my congratulations for a fine patrol, sir."

"Thank you, sir," Brannon said. He turned as Admiral

Christie came bounding down the gangway, his hand extended to Mike Brannon.

"'Damned fine patrol, Mike!'' the Admiral cried. "Damned fine, two Fubukis, wow! Good shooting!''

"Thank you, sir,'' Brannon said. "I just wish we could have got them before they got the *Mako*.''

The Admiral's smiling face became grave. He put his arm around Brannon's heavy shoulders and walked him up the deck away from the group of Staff officers.

"You did everything you could, Mike. It wasn't your fault, not in any way. You followed your orders, your patrol orders, the way every officer in this Navy has to follow his orders. You made all possible speed to come to the *Mako* when they told you they had a convoy and invited you to share in the action. We all know that.'' He stopped and removed his arm and turned to face Brannon.

"I want you to know this, Mike. I cried when I read your contact report, the part about the *Mako* transmitting the Twenty-third Psalm as the ship was sinking into the Philippine Trench, out of control. My God, what brave men! And how terrible it must have been for you, to have to stand and hear that message and not be able to do anything. I cried, Mike. I did.''

"I've got to write to Art Hinman's bride,'' Brannon said. "They were only married, together, a few weeks, you know. I don't know what to say, I've never met her.''

"I wrote to her,'' Admiral Christie said. "I told her that based on what you had told us, what the *Mako* told you, that Captain Hinman died instantly when the *Mako*'s bridge was swept by very heavy gunfire. I think it makes it a lot easier for someone who has lost a loved one if they believe that the loved one died instantly, with no pain or suffering.'' His face sobered. "I've had to write too many of those letters, Mike. Too many. But you write to her. You should.''

"That's good of you, sir,'' Brannon said. "One other thing. I'd appreciate it if someone in your office could give me a roster of *Mako*'s crew. I knew most of them and I'll spend my rest period writing to their survivors.''

"I'll take care of that,'' Admiral Christie said. "Now, if you don't mind, let's talk about other things. The exploders worked all right?''

"Yes, sir.'' Brannon's voice was suddenly flat, without emotion. "I missed with some fish. John Olsen missed with one he fired, but those we were accurate with, they worked.''

"The only real criticism I have, Mike," the Admiral said, "is that you shot too many torpedoes at those small freighters. One torpedo for each would have been enough. By the way, we can't give you a kill on that patrol craft that was rammed by the freighter. You didn't have anything to do with its going down, but we'll give you a damage on that one."

"The patrol vessel wouldn't have sunk if we didn't go into the convoy, sir." Brannon's voice was suddenly edged with an anger he tried to conceal. "It was our direct action that caused him to get rammed. My contact report noted that the patrol ship fired at us and we had to silence him with our machine guns."

"I'm sorry, Mike," the Admiral said. He slapped Brannon on the shoulder. "All the same a damned fine patrol. I'd like to see you at my office for a debriefing in, oh, about three hours. I'll have one of my aides come down and pick you up. The buses to take your crew to the hotel in Perth will be here in two hours, a little less." The two men turned and walked up the deck. Admiral Christie stopped and turned to face Brannon.

"I'll tell you this, before the briefing, and you'll hear it again from my intelligence people. It should make you feel a little better about the *Mako*.

"When you blasted those two Fubukis you killed the man we call the 'Professor.' His name was Captain Akihito Hideki. He was the best antisubmarine man they had in their whole Navy. Our code breakers in Pearl Harbor said the traffic about his going down in your attack was very heavy. You've probably saved a lot of our own submariners by sinking him. Try to keep that part in mind." He stopped at the gangway, saluted, and bounced across the swaying gangway to the next submarine. Mike Brannon watched his bounding progress across the other submarines and into the vast hull of the submarine tender, wondering where he got his energy, how he retained it under the enormous weight of his responsibilities. He turned as John Olsen walked up to him.

"We've got to paint over one of those Rising Sun flags on the Conning Tower, John. They're giving us a damaged on that patrol boat that was rammed."

"I know," Olsen grumbled. "I damned near swung on that ass of a Lieutenant who works for the Staff when he told me. You'd think he'd just hit a home run or something. Son of a bitch has never made a patrol run and he's drawing submarine and sea pay for working here on land

"I gave the tender permission to bring fresh fruit and mail aboard, sir, while you were talking with the Admiral." He looked at Brannon.

"Did he say anything about the exploders, sir?"

"He asked if they worked," Brannon said. "I told him the simple truth, that the ones we got hits with worked fine. He didn't ask anything more than that, I didn't offer anything more than that." He looked down the deck at his crew, many of them sitting on the deck reading their mail while they ate the cold-storage apples and oranges that were a standing feature of a return to port.

"The buses will be here in a couple of hours, John. You'd better tell the Chief of the Boat to get the crew ready to go to the hotel. I want you to take over for me. I've got to go to the Admiral's office this afternoon." Olsen nodded and went in search of Chief Flanagan. He found him sitting on the after capstan eating an orange.

"Read all your mail already?" Olsen asked.

"Didn't get any," Flanagan said. "I was brought up in an orphanage. Stayed there until I was seventeen. Then I enlisted in the Navy. Makes it kind of convenient. I don't get any mail so I don't have to write any letters." He nodded toward Paul Blake, the sonar operator who was standing by the side of the ship staring at the water.

"Blake got one of those Dear John letters. His girl back home dumped him for some Four-F civilian. He's taking it pretty hard."

"Is there anything we can do?" Olsen said.

"I don't know," Flanagan said. "I've got to think about it some. He's too good a kid, too damned good on that sonar for us to lose, to go sour over some silly-assed broad. I might get him pissy-assed drunk or something. I don't know."

"Captain wants all hands to be ready to get on the buses in two hours, Chief. You'd better take care of that now."

"Aye, aye, sir," Flanagan said. He wadded the orange peel in a big hand, walked forward to where a big trash can had been placed, and dropped the peel into the can. The yeoman, John Wilkes Booth, came over the gangway holding a piece of paper in his hand.

"Some dude out in the country from Perth has written a letter to the Staff, Chief," Booth said. "He says that next Monday he'll throw a big barbecue for up to twenty of the crew on his ranch. They call the countryside the 'outback' in this part of the world. He says he's got horses to ride and that if we bring our own rifles and ammunition the guys can hunt kangaroos and emus. Staff has already okayed drawing rifles and ammunition for anyone wants to go." He handed the paper to Flanagan.

"I'll announce it at quarters," Flanagan said. Booth turned and looked down the deck.

"Hey, Geronimo," he yelled at a swarthy Machinist's Mate. "Some rancher out in the country wants to take us huntin' on horseback for kangaroos. I'll put your name down for the hunting party and we'll find out if you can really ride a horse."

"You do that," the Machinist's Mate said. "I'll show you how to ride bareback, like I used to do back home."

"Shit," John LaMark said. "You Indians didn't have enough money to own horses. You walked around dressed in an old crummy blanket until you came in the Navy and they gave you a sea bag full of new clothes." He ducked as the Indian threw an apple core at him.

"You know my name," the Indian said. "My name is Charles Two Blankets. And they were good blankets. I didn't have to go to Small Stores to get a pair of shoes if I wanted shoes. I just shot me a deer, skinned it, and tanned the hide and made me a pair of moccasins. You white people would starve to death if you lived in my part of the desert and the mountains. You know something else, wise ass? I don't have to stay on this ship with clowns like you if I don't want to. Friend of mine on the tender come down here a little while ago. He told me they're looking for Indians who can speak the Indian languages. It's better than code for sending messages. We begin to talk in Apache and that old Jap won't know what the fuck to do."

"How you gonna make smoke signals big enough to be seen in Pearl from out here?" LaMark inquired innocently. "You gonna burn both your blankets?"

"Ah, shit," the Apache said. "You just make sure you sign up for this huntin' trip and I'll get you on a horse and ride you until your soft ass comes apart at the seams."

"I'll personally take both your asses apart at the seams," Flanagan said. "Get squared away for the trip to the hotel." The sailors who had bunched up to listen to the exchange between Charlie Two Blankets and LaMark broke up and went below to get themselves ready for two weeks at the hotel.

In the ship's Wardroom the Lieutenant in charge of the Relief Crew, which would repair whatever had to be repaired on the

Eelfish and paint ship, pushed his coffee cup to one side and smiled at Mike Brannon and Bob Lee.

"I'm obliged for your hospitality, gentlemen, and I appreciate how little needs to be done and how clean your ship is. We'll move you tomorrow and take off torpedoes." He paused and lit a cigaret.

"You'd have to do duty here to realize how dirty some ships are when they come in, how much gear has broken down. When we get an *Eelfish* it's a big break." He rose and left the Wardroom. Brannon turned as Olsen came through the green curtains and sat down.

"The crew will be ready when the buses get here, sir," Olsen said. "The Squadron Office sent word that when you're ready to go ashore they'll provide a car. You and I are being quartered in a house the Navy's rented for the duration. If it's all right with you, I'll go over with you when you're ready."

"Might be a while, John. I've got to write a letter to Captain Hinman's widow." He paused and drew a long, shaky breath.

"I don't know what to say. I never met her. I knew his first wife—she was killed when they bombed Pearl Harbor. We were at sea on our way to Pearl. When we got to Pearl they told Captain Hinman that his wife was dead.

"You can imagine how he, how all of us felt. Then, near the end of last year, after we'd got into some trouble for modifying the torpedo exploders, they sent me to take over the *Eelfish* in New London and they sent him on a bond-selling tour, war bonds." He funbled in his shirt pocket for a cigaret and nodded his thanks to Olsen as Olsen extended his cigarets.

"The Navy assigned a Wave Public Affairs Officer to go with him on the bond-selling tour. He wrote me a lot of letters about that tour. Only thing that made it bearable was the Wave officer. Art said she was a hell of a bright woman and very pretty. Well, it happened, they fell in love and got married. The bond tour ended and he got the *Mako* back and went to sea. They'd only been together a few weeks." He looked down at the table.

"It's not only a duty, I feel I owe it to him, to her, to write to her. I'm no damn good at this sort of thing, John." Olsen saw a wetness in Brannon's eyes.

"Maybe," Olsen said in a low voice, "maybe I could sort of draft the letter for you, sir. I didn't know either of them, but I think I could do it, if it's okay?"

Brannon rose, turning his face away from Olsen.

"I'd be very grateful to you if you did, John. Her name is

Joan, Joan Hinman.'' He pushed through the green curtains and
went aft.

CHAPTER 5

In a basement room located behind a supply office in a building
on the Naval Base at Pearl Harbor, a man in a worn smoking
jacket and scuffed bedroom slippers shuffled across the floor to a
desk piled high with charts and papers.

"How's it going?'' he asked the man behind the desk. The
man looked up at him, rubbed his eyes, and yawned, lines of
utter weariness etched in his face.

"It doesn't go,'' he said.

"You'll get it,'' the man in the smoking jacket said. He
shuffled over to a table standing against one wall of the room,
and rummaged in a cardboard box and found a sandwich. He
unwrapped the food and ate it, staring reflectively at the men
who were working at desks in the crowded room.

The men he commanded were an odd group. Some were
officers who the Navy had decided were good enough to be kept
on but not good enough, for various and obscure professional
reasons, to be promoted to higher rank.

Others were enlisted men, among them the ship's band of the
U.S.S. *California*. When that battleship had been holed by
Japanese aerial torpedoes and had settled to the bottom in the
harbor on December 7, 1941, the ship's band had, fortunately,
escaped injury. But their instruments went down with the ship.
Literally unemployable, in the eyes of the Navy, the ship's band
members had been assigned to the basement room to work in
what was called the "Combat Intelligence Unit,'' a cover name
for a top-secret communications group of intelligence experts
who were desperately trying to crack the complicated Japanese
military codes.

The members of the *California*'s band had shrugged and gone
to work, guided and instructed by the half-dozen professional
code breakers in the basement room. The musicians proved to be
adept at cryptanalysis, and some experts were led to believe that

there was a subtle connection between the mysteries of cryptology and music.

The immensity of the task of breaking the Japanese military code was almost beyond human comprehension. The five-digit code was not extraordinarily difficult in itself, it was the refinements the Japanese had introduced that drove cryptanalysts almost to tears.

Once a message had been encoded in five-digit code groups, that numerical code was then further enciphered. To do this the Japanese had prepared a list of 100,000 five-digit number groups. The Japanese encoder took the encoded message to that list of 100,000 five-digit code groups and picked a place at random on the list. Starting at that place the five-digit numbers in the encoded message were subtracted, group by group, from the numbers on the master list.

To decode the message the recipient had to know where in the 100,000 group list the encoder had started his subtraction and then perform the reverse mathematics. Without knowledge of the actual list of five-digit number groups in the 100,000-group list a cryptanalyst was faced with a task that might take years to solve—if it could be solved at all.

However, the use of such a massive list of master code groups raised the possibility of garbles and mistakes. The Japanese recognized this and decided to use only number groups from the master code list that were divisible by three. This reduced mistakes, but it soon gave the American cryptanalysts in the small basement room a surprise tool—which they used to good effect.

A further complication for the cryptanalysts arose immediately. Japanese is written, mainly, in Chinese characters called *kanji*, but Japanese can also be written in a phonetic form called *kana*. One form of *kana* used Roman letters, but another form had its own code to represent the more than fifty symbols of the phonetic system.

The cadre of men in the secret basement room had started their work prior to the attack on Pearl Harbor. They were hampered in that work by a distaste for all forms of intelligence operations that was shared by most ranking U.S. military leaders.

That attitude had a precedent: In 1929 the then-Secretary of State, Henry L. Stimson, had refused to fund the State Department's code-breaking intelligence operation with the remark, "Gentlemen don't read each other's mail."

The work that had been done by the State Department's

"Black Chamber" was divided between the Army and the Navy. By 1941 the two military services, in a rare display of cooperation, had joined their code-breaking resources and had become efficient enough to be able to intercept and decode Japanese diplomatic messages and deliver them to the State Department and the White House before the Japanese diplomats in Washington received those same decoded messages. Too often the remarkable successes in breaking Japanese diplomatic codes were ignored, too often such messages were delayed in reaching people who had authority to initiate action. Morale among the code breakers went down.

Most of the men in the basement room in the Pearl Harbor Naval Base worked a minimum 84-hour week. Some, notably the handful of professional cryptanalysts who formed the backbone of the Combat Intelligence Unit, worked even longer hours. The boundaries of rank and rate were ignored once the men were in the room. The weary man in the red smoking jacket and bedroom slippers commanded the group not only by virtue of his commission as a full Commander of the United States Navy but also because of his intelligence, his knowledge of the Japanese language, and his vast knowledge of Japanese ship movements. Everyone in the group shared one consuming interest: to crack the Japanese military codes, to get one part of the codes broken so that they could go on to reading more and more of the codes. They literally lived in the basement room, eating sandwiches and soup brought in from the Navy galley on the base. More often than not they slept on cots in the basement room, unwilling to leave the room, unable to physically leave the nagging probabilities of this group of numbers or that group.

As time went on some success in reading portions of the Japanese military code was achieved. But with this success came a danger: If information about Japanese ship movements gleaned from the code breaking were to be widely disseminated it was certain the Japanese would realize their codes had been broken and would change them. That possibility brought a paralysis of fear to the code breakers.

They moved cautiously to prevent the Japanese from learning that their codes had been broken. Information of vital interest to the planners of the Pacific war was given out guardedly, in many cases, "sanitized" so its origin could never be revealed. The burden of these decisions weighed heavily on the cryptanalysts. In the end it was the endless work of this group, their utter devotion to their jobs, that was the linchpin on which the success of the Pacific war turned.

In Fremantle Mike Brannon sat in a wicker chair facing Admiral Christie and his staff. The chair creaked under his solid weight as he shifted position. The Admiral looked up from a folder on the table in front of him.

"Mike," he said slowly, "it's time we took you and the other submarine Captains into confidence, the deepest, the most secret confidence we can emphasize.

"From time to time we have been getting reports from our intelligence people in Pearl Harbor about Japanese ship movements. These reports have turned out to be amazingly accurate. These intelligence reports are called Ultra Codes, and they are so damned secret that not very many people have even seen them.

"You and other submarine Captains will be getting Ultra intelligence when you're on war patrol. But we've got to be awfully careful that we don't give away what our people in Pearl have accomplished. So Washington intelligence people have suggested a system, a code within a code.

"For example: You might get a message telling you to leave one end of your patrol area and go to the other end and cruise on such and such a course on such and such a day. That part of the message will contain a separate code within a code, and when you decipher it—you'll be given the code books before you go to sea—you'll learn that you will proceed to a different part of the area on a different day and patrol on a different course. The information about what targets you can expect will be in yet another code, which we're sure the Japs haven't begun to crack. But if they crack the standard code we use to direct submarines and learn that you're supposed to go to, let's say, the east end of your patrol area—when you're really going to the west end as per the code within a code—then if you sink the targets the Ultra people sent you the Japs will think that their ships got nailed by some submarine that just happened to be passing through that area.

"In short, we can't take a chance of letting the Jap know we can read his codes. We have to assume that the Jap can read some of our codes, but we're awfully damned sure he can't read our top-secret codes. Is that clear?"

"Yes, sir," Brannon said. "It's an operation of, well, misdirection as far as the Japanese are concerned, sir."

"Exactly," the Admiral said. "And that leads me to point

number two. In order for this thing to work your navigator has to know where your ship is every hour of the day and night. I'm not saying this applies to you, Mike, but there's too much slack, too much sloppiness out there on war patrol. Sun sights aren't taken by periscope every day at noon. Star sights are taken every three or four nights, not every night. That sort of thing has to stop. You have to know where you are every moment, we have to know. If a valuable target is coming we have to know which submarine is in the best position to intercept. When Captain Mealey was sent to intercept the battleship en route to Truk—that was an Ultra operation by the way—we knew exactly where the *Mako* was because Captain Mealey runs a damned taut ship.'' The Admiral stood up.

"I don't want to keep you from your R and R, Mike. My aides will be in touch with you when you go back to your ship. Our intelligence people will brief you fully on the new codes we'll be using.''

Brannon left the Bend of the Road compound in the car the Admiral's aide had provided for him. He grinned to himself as he settled back in the car seat. If the code breakers in Pearl could send him targets he'd be happy. Maybe with this new system there would be less aimless cruising in the hope that an enemy ship would come by.

The bus loaded with *Eelfish* volunteers for a day's hunting and barbecue pulled up at a rambling group of buildings in the flat desert country that Australians call the Outback, ninety miles east of Perth. A burly Australian rancher held a gate open, and the bus rolled through and stopped. Chief Flanagan got out of the bus and walked up to the rancher, who was closing the gate.

"I'm Chief Flanagan of the *Eelfish*, sir,'' he said.

"Jim Briggs, here,'' the Aussie said. He stuck out a work-hardened hand. "Welcome to you and your people.''

"I'll line up my people,'' Flanagan said. "Then you can talk to all of them at once, Mr. Biggs.'' He turned and growled out orders and the twenty men who had volunteered for the day's outing shuffled into two ragged lines.

"This is our host, Mr. Biggs,'' Flanagan said. He turned to the Aussie. "All yours, sir.''

"Too right,'' the Australian said. "Well now, chaps. Not to stand on ceremony or things like that. But a few words of warning.

"This is what we call the Outback. Mainly desert. Very little water, very damned little. Most places there's no water at all. Nearest water from here is about eighteen miles. So you don't leave the ranch without two water bottles hanging from the saddle.

"You'll hunt in parties of five men, two parties out at one time. Each party will be under one of my trackers." He turned and indicated two small, very black men who were standing to one side.

"Joe and Pete are abos," Biggs said. "Abo is our way of saying aborigine for short. Some people call them Stone Age men, and I guess the tribes that live far out in the Outback are Stone Age people.

"Joe and Pete are men of great dignity. Great ability. They can see farther with their naked eye than you can with a pair of bloody binoculars. They can smell water two feet under the sand where you can see nothing but dry sand. They can live all their lives on raw lizards, ants and bugs, and grubs that would turn your bloody stomachs. And mine.

"The point I make, chaps, is that these are good men. Far better men than I am in their own way. If either of them is mistreated or made fun of you'll have to answer to me and, I'd guess, your cobber here, the Chief. Now, one other thing, you'll be on horseback. Any of you ever rode before?"

Chief Pharmacist's Mate Wharton stepped out of the line. "Some of us have ridden before, Mr. Biggs. But we have a real Apache Indian with us and he said he'd show us how it's done." Wharton smiled.

"An American Indian?" Biggs said. "Never seen one of those gentlemen. Will you step out, sir, and introduce yourself?"

"Charlie Two Blankets," the Apache said, stepping out of the line. "I think some of our tribal trackers could go up against your people. Any time."

"In your country, yes," Biggs said. "Out here, no. It's different, y'see, like our cricket and your baseball."

"Charlie Two Blankets is the greatest bronco-busting rider in the Navy, Mr. Biggs," Chief Wharton said. He was smiling at the Australian. "If you've got any horses that need breaking ol' Charlie is the man to break them for you. At least that's what he tells us."

The Australian looked at him, the sun lines around his eyes crinkling as he smiled.

"Well, yes, chaps. I do have a horse that none of my Abo people can handle. Bucks like a mad thing if you get near the beast. Maybe Mr. Two Blankets would have a go at breaking him." He turned to Flanagan. "If you'd allow it, sir?"

"It's up to Charlie, I guess," Flanagan said.

"Go on, Indian," Wharton jeered. "Let's see you do your stuff on the man's wild horse." Charlie Two Blankets shrugged.

"Show me the animal," he said.

Biggs led the way toward a large corral. Walking beside Flanagan he dropped his voice to just above a whisper.

"Served my time in our Army, First World War," he said. "I know what that handsome chap's up to, egging on the Indian man. Hope the Indian can ride. Do you know?"

Flanagan shook his head.

The horse in the corral looked wild. It threw its head back and snorted loudly, its eyes rolling, as the group of men neared the corral. Charlie Two Blankets eyed the animal for a moment and then stooped down and undid the laces of his shoes and kicked them off. He took off his socks and placed a sock carefully in each shoe. Then he stripped off his dungaree shirt and trousers and walked up to the corral bars in his shorts. He vaulted over the top rail, dropped down in the dust of the corral, and walked toward the horse.

"Be careful, cobber!" the Australian called out. "That beast is dangerous!"

The Apache trotted toward the horse, making a sound deep in his throat. The horse laid back its ears and charged across the corral at the man. The Apache feinted to his left, and as the horse veered the Indian pivoted and took two running steps, and his hands shot out and grabbed the horse's mane. In one smooth, sinuous movement, aided by the horse's quick burst of speed, the Apache was on the horse's back. He raised his voice in a high, wailing cry, and the horse bucked violently, rearing high on its hind legs, shaking itself from side to side to dislodge the man on its back. The horse neighed in a high scream, and the Apache answered with his own scream. The horse bucked, gyrating wildly, coming down with all four hooves hitting the ground, twisting and bucking across the corral in high jumps. The Apache clung to the horse's back, his hands clenched in the mane, his powerful legs locked against the horse's barrel.

"God, he's a burr, that one!" Biggs said. The horse went upward, twisting. When the horse came down the Apache reached forward with his right hand, bending low over the horse's neck, and grabbed the horse's right ear. He pulled the head back savagely, and then with his bare heel he kicked the

horse again and again in the side of its head. Then he leaned
forward and bit the horse's ear. The horse screamed, ran a few
steps forward, and then stood, its sides heaving. The Indian sat
very still on the animal, and then he leaned forward and began
crooning in a low hum into the horse's ear. He rapped the sides
of the horse with his bare heels, and the animal trotted a few
steps and then stopped. The Apache leaned forward over the
horse's neck and crooned again, softly. He tapped the sides of
the horse gently with his feet and the animal raised its head and
then trotted docilely around the perimeter of the corral. Charlie
Two Blankets slid off the animal's back and walked around to its
head and stroked the long smooth muzzle, crooning gently as he
did so.

The Apache led the horse over to the side of the corral, his
right hand entwined in the mane.

"Here's your horse, Mr. Biggs," the Indian said. "He knows
a man can hurt him and he knows a man can be gentle with him.
Treat him kindly and you've got a good animal. Now I got to get
dressed before this sun gives me a bad burn." He vaulted over
the top rail of the corral and pulled his shirt over his bronzed
shoulders. Flanagan walked over to him as he finished dressing.

"I'm damned glad you didn't get yourself killed, Charlie. I'm
damned glad you hadn't bullshitted people about the way you
can ride."

"Indians don't speak with forked tongue, Chief. Only white
man has a forked tongue. Didn't you ever see any cowboy and
Indian movies when you were a kid? Now I want to see some of
these wiseass submarine sailors ride."

The Australian walked over to Charlie. "I've been talking
with my two chaps, sir. They want to know what kind of a tribe
you come from. Can't very well tell them about America, the
Outback is all the world they know. They think they may be
related to you by tribe, and I'll thank you not to laugh, sir. To be
related to an Abo is the highest honor they can think of. They'd
like to touch you so their medicine and yours can mix."

"I understand," Charlie Two Blankets said. He faced the two
aborigines and drew himself to his full six feet of height. He
bowed his head slightly toward the two smaller men and stretched
his arms out, his palms facing the sky. His voice rolled out in a
sonorous chant, the liquid vowels and clipped consonants of the
Apache language hanging in the still Australian air. The two
aborigines stood quietly, watching him. When he had finished
they stepped forward, their arms outstretched, palms upward.

Gravely, they turned their hands and touched the Apache's hands, palm to palm. The older of the two aborigines turned his head and spoke briefly in his own tongue to Biggs.

"He says he doesn't understand your language, breaker of horses, but he would like to know what you said. He is sure you made a prayer to the Rain God. That's the most powerful god these people have because water is so scarce."

"I made a prayer to the gods," the Apache said. "I asked my gods to protect them and give them many children."

Biggs turned and spoke to the two aborigines, his deep voice chopping at the guttural speech. The two men smiled.

"Right thing to say, cobber," Biggs said. "Children and water are the only resources these poor devils have when they're on their own. Tonight they will pray to their gods and ask that their strength enter you while you sleep."

On the bus that evening Chief Wharton walked down the aisle and perched on the arm of the seat where Charlie Two Blankets was sitting.

"I take back everything I ever said when I kidded you on the ship. You are just one hell of a horse rider. And some kind of rifle shot, too. You must have hit that one kangaroo at about two hundred yards and that damned thing was running and jumping."

"I don't like to kill a pretty animal like that," the Indian said. "You should never kill animals unless you can eat them and that Australian fella said the only part of a kangaroo you can eat is the tail. He said they were pests, that they eat his crops. I don't think I'd want to eat that thing's tail."

"Might be better than roast sheep," Wharton said. "I'll be tasting that mutton for a week."

The next morning Flanagan went looking for Paul Blake. He found him in the hotel dining room eating his breakfast.

"Mind if I sit down?" Flanagan asked.

"No, I mean, yes, sit down, Chief."

"What have you been doing with yourself?" Flanagan asked. "I thought you'd sign up to go out on that thing we went on yesterday. Hell of a good time. You hear about the Indian?"

"Yes, sir," Blake said. "Everyone who didn't go has heard about that. Must have been something to see. The reason I didn't go . . ." He blushed suddenly, and Flanagan felt awkward.

"Reason I didn't go, Chief, I met a girl. I mean, it's not, I'm not living at her house or anything like that. She took me home to meet her parents, she lives with them. They're real nice folks,

just like my own folks. Her father is in charge of the Port
Customs or something like that.''

"How'd you meet her?''

"Day before yesterday some Red Cross people came to the
hotel to see if they could do anything for us, for the crew, like
sew on buttons or even write letters home. Most of the fellows
were out somewhere. I was the only one here. I was sitting in the
lobby and I was trying to write a letter to Ginny, that was my girl
back home until she decided I was too far away.'' Flanagan saw
the younger man's eyes blink a little bit.

"Well, anyway, I had tried and tried to write a letter to Ginny
and I couldn't say what I wanted to say and there were some
crumpled up pages on the deck around my feet and she asked me
if I'd like her to write the letter. So I gave her the letter from
Ginny.''

"The Dear John letter?'' Flanagan asked softly. Blake nodded.

"And she wrote Ginny a real nice letter. She just seemed to
know what to say. So I asked her if I could buy her lunch and she
said yes and then we went to the zoo and walked around and she
took me home to meet her father and her mother. Real nice
people, Chief. Her father walked me back to the streetcar, they
call them trams here, and invited me to go back there for supper
tonight. You could go with me if you want.''

"Thanks, but no,'' Flanagan said. "You go ahead, but don't
foul things up by making a run on the girl or something like
that.''

Blake's face flushed. "I wouldn't do anything like that! She's
a nice girl. Her mother and father treated me like I was their son.
They're going to take my picture today and send it to my folks.''

Flanagan stood up. "Okay, son. Take things easy.'' He walked
away, glad that the boy's disappointment over the Dear John
letter had evaporated quickly. He saw Lieutenant Lee coming
across the hotel lobby, motioning at him. He stopped and waited
until the officer came up to him.

"You mind if I ask you to come out to the ship, Chief?'' Lee
said. "They've got some sort of a problem with some torpedoes.
I don't know what it's all about, but I've got to go out there, and
I'd like you to come along if you don't mind. It shouldn't take
long.''

"I don't mind,'' Flanagan said. Lee led the way outside to a
jeep, where a sailor sat behind the wheel.

The *Eelfish* was now moored inboard, next to the bulk of the
submarine tender. Flanagan walked down the steep gangway and

saw that some relief crew sailors were closing the torpedo-loading hatch to the After Torpedo Room. Up forward Steve Petreshock was supervising a relief-crew gang as a torpedo was being lowered to rest in the loading skid.

"What the hell are you doing here?" Flanagan said to Petreshock. "You're supposed to be in the hotel and what in the hell is going on, taking fish aboard? We're not supposed to get new fish until after we get back from the hotel." He turned to Lee.

"We're not going to have our usual week to ten days in port after the R and R," Lee said. "They want us back at sea as quickly as we can get there. So they load the fish today."

"And you?" Flanagan said to Petreshock.

"Well, we got the word yesterday morning that they were going to load fish, so me and Nelson decided to come down today and make sure they did it right," Petreshock said. "Nelson's in the After Room, and he's got some kind of problem. Don't know what it is. I been busy up here."

Flanagan nodded and went to the Crew's Mess hatch and went down the ladder, followed by Bob Lee. Fred Nelson was in the After Room with a crew of torpedomen from the submarine tender.

"What's the problem, Fred?" Flanagan asked.

"These people are giving us destroyer fish, Mark Fifteens, for the tubes back here," Nelson said. "Mark Fourteens for the reloads."

"What difference does that make?" Lee asked.

"Mark Fifteen fish are longer than our regular Mark Fourteen torpedoes," Flanagan said. "I've heard you could use Fifteens in the After Room because the tubes back here are a lot longer than those up front so's the fish will clear the screws and the stern planes. But I never heard of any boat firing Fifteens."

"It's a real fuck-up!" Fred Nelson said. He stared at the tender torpedomen balefully, glaring at them from his six feet four of brawn, his eyes hot.

"Way it is with these damned fish," Nelson said. "Way it is is that the fish are just that much too long so when the fish is lined up with the tube you can't open the inner door because the warhead sticks out too far.

"That makes it that when you want to load a fish you got to open the inner door first and then jockey the damned fish back and forth until you get it lined up. That ain't too bad sittin' in port. But when we have to pull these bastards to routine them at sea it means we do the routining with the inner door open and the Old Man wants them inner doors closed when a fish is outa the tube.

"And that ain't the only thing. They had to put a modified

guide stud on these here Fifteens because the regular guide stud don't line up with the stop bolt in the tube. Means that when you load you got to bleed down the impulse air and dry-fire the tube and hold down the firing key. Then you got to ease the fish in the tube inch by inch until you can feel the stop bolt touch the guide stud and then you ease it in a little bit more until you can feel the stop bolt drop down into the slot on the guide stud.''

Flanagan stood quietly, his mind sifting through the problem. He looked at Nelson.

"That would mean that when you want to pull the fish to routine it you have to bleed down the impulse air and dry-fire the tube and hold the firing key down while you pull out the fish. Hell, you can't do that unless you bypass all the safety interlocks!''

"You got the picture," Nelson said sourly. "With them safety interlocks disconnected any clown goes between the tubes and touches a firing key and we've got a fish fired in the tube with the outer door closed.''

"There's another thing." One of the relief crew torpedomen spoke up. "When you pull a fish for routining you got to be awful sure you dry-fire the tube and hold that firing key down because if you try to pull the fish without doing that the modified guide stud will bend up and the only way you'll get that fish out of the tube is to go topside, open the After Trim tank manhole, go down in the tank and take off the stop bolt housing, and then remove the guide stud. That ain't anything I'd want to do out in a patrol area.''

"How come you give us these fish?" Flanagan asked.

"We're short of torpedoes," the relief crew man said. "We're putting four fish, Mark Fifteens, in the after tubes of every submarine until further orders.''

"Big pain in the ass," Nelson said.

Riding back to the hotel in the jeep Lieutenant Lee turned to Flanagan.

"What do you think, Chief?''

"I guess it will work out," Flanagan said slowly. "I don't like the idea, but if they're short of fish they're short of fish. Nothing we can do about it. Thing that bothers me is that we've got to change routines back there in the After Room. With the safety interlocks on the tubes disconnected, having to dry-fire the tube to pull a fish for routining, you have a chance of a casualty. We're going to have to work out some new routines, do a lot of drilling back there." He sat back on the uncomfortable seat.

"What's important, sir, is that we've got some damned good people in charge of those two torpedo rooms. Nelson and

Petreshock gave up one of their rest days to come back to the ship to supervise loading the torpedoes. That's a hell of a thing to do, you know."

"I know," Lee said.

CHAPTER 6

Admiral Christie was in a testy mood. Mike Brannon got word through the grapevine before he went to a conference about his new patrol area. The gossip had it that General MacArthur's politicking had undercut Christie in some manner. Brannon was warned to be on his best behavior, to say as little as possible.

"Those tankers that come out of Balikpapan." Admiral Christie walked over to a chart standing on an easel near the conference table. He pointed at the port city of Balikpapan on the east coast of Borneo. "Those tankers are supplying Admiral Koga's fleet based at Truk. Those tankers have got to be stopped. That's our first priority."

Mike Brannon shifted in his chair and stared at the chart. It had been just north of Balikpapan that *Mako* had gone roaring in on three loaded tankers and four destroyers in a night surface attack earlier in the war. Brannon remembered the awful moment of fear he had felt as he watched the bubbling trail of the second torpedo he fired from *Mako*'s stern tubes at a destroyer that was coming full tilt at the *Mako*'s stern. Those brief seconds that had seemed like hours after the wake of the torpedo led into the side of the destroyer's bow and then the tremendous explosion as the torpedo sheared off the entire bow of the attacking destroyer.

"Are you paying attention, Brannon?" Christie's voice was sharp, petulant.

"Yes, sir," Brannon said. "I was Exec under Captain Hinman in *Mako's* third patrol off Balikpapan."

"I know that," the Admiral said. He pointed at the chart again. "The oil coming out of those fields there is said to be so pure that they don't have to refine it before using it. They just run it through a filter. The Australians have ship watchers in the hills along the coast of Borneo, the east coast. Those ship watchers report that the tankers leave Balikpapan, go north of Celebes and then toward the Pacific. We have other intelligence reports that the tankers are going to Truk, to supply Koga's fleet." He paused and looked at his assembled staff and Mike Brannon.

"If Koga ever decides to move that fleet out of Truk, we haven't got anything in the area strong enough to stop him. The only thing we can figure that's held him in port so far is that he's short of oil for his fleet. But if he gets enough oil, if he moves out to sea, he can cut us to ribbons. And once he's done that, well, there wouldn't be any General MacArthur returning to the Philippines.

"It boils down to stopping the tankers. That's our first priority. They'll be escorted, but ignore the escorts. Get the tankers."

"Tankers are hard to sink, as you know." Sam Rivers, the Operations Officer, a squat, heavyset four-stripe Captain spoke up. "We've had reports from submarine Captains who tell us of hitting a tanker with as many as six torpedoes, hitting them in the sides of the hull. Those tankers are so compartmented that they can suck up a half-dozen torpedo hits at or below their waterlines.

"What you have to do—" the Operations Officer paused a moment, looking hard at Brannon. "What you have to do is to believe in the Mark Six exploder. If you fire one, no more than two torpedoes set to run beneath the tanker, if you make your approach properly, then you'll have a kill. No tanker, no matter how well compartmented, can live with its keel, its back broken."

"The tankers burn," Brannon said. "The two we hit off Balikpapan in *Mako* burned like blast furnaces. Maybe that unrefined oil has something in it that makes it burn easily."

"That's been thought of," Rivers said. "We've been trying to find a Dutch engineer who worked at the oil fields in Borneo who might know the chemical makeup of that oil, but we haven't found him yet. Your safest bet is to rely on the Mark Six exploder. I worked with Admiral Christie developing that exploder and we know it works." Brannon nodded, his face carefully expressionless.

"We're putting *Eelfish* just north of Celebes," the Admiral said. "You should have good targets, good hunting. You can expect the tankers to be well guarded. Ignore the escorts, go after the tankers." He rose from the chair where he had been sitting while his Operations Officer was talking.

"I know that once you've hit and sunk destroyers you get a sort of fever, you want to keep going after them. Take an aspirin, do something, don't let that fever overcome your priority, the tankers. Just bear in mind that if Koga gets enough oil at Truk he's going to go out to sea, and if he does General MacArthur's invasion route to the Philippines will be vulnerable.''

Mike Brannon leaned against the pom-pom gun mount on the cigaret deck, aft of the bridge, looking at the long, straight fluorescent wake the *Eelfish* trailed behind her as the ship walked the long sea miles up through the Indian Ocean on a course for Lombok Strait. In another ten or eleven days *Eelfish* would be on station, north of the northernmost tip of the oddly shaped island called Celebes. As he so often did when it was quiet on the bridge he let his thoughts run back to the night when the *Mako* had gone down, hearing again in the innermost parts of his mind the slow, steady pulsing of the *Mako*'s sonar beam spelling out the words of the Twenty-third Psalm.

The more he thought about it, the more he was convinced that John Olsen's shrewd conjecture that *Mako* had been ambushed was correct. *Mako,* without surface radar, had probably bored in to attack what the lookouts had been able to see, a line of small freighters proceeding cautiously down the east coast of the island of Samar. What the lookouts had not seen, what a surface radar would have picked up, was the presence of two enemy destroyers lurking closer to the coast, their silhouettes lost against the island's bulk. Once committed to the surface attack, *Mako* had been trapped by the destroyers, riddled with gunfire, and then fatally damaged before the ship could dive deeply enough to evade the destroyer attacks.

It was strange, Brannon thought, how the odds of success veered so sharply in the problems of attacking with a submarine or being attacked while in a submarine. An attacking submarine, if it could make its approach undetected, carried the odds in its favor. If the Captain made all his observations correctly, if the torpedoes ran hot, straight, and normal, if the exploders worked properly, then the target could be hit and destroyed.

The chance of escape from the retaliatory attacks by the enemy's destroyers were not good. If the destroyer Captains were experienced; if they were dogged and patient; if the water in which the attack was made was not deep enough to give the submarine ample room to maneuver, to go very deep; if there were no layers of heavier saltwater under which the submarine could hide the odds were with the destroyers. . . . He turned as he heard Lieutenant Bob Lee going through the ritual of taking over the OOD watch at midnight. The Quartermaster going off watch came back to the cigaret deck.

"Mr. Lee brought you a cup of coffee," he said.

"Thank you," Brannon said. "Nice night."

"Yes, sir," the Quartermaster said. "Hope it's raining when we get to Lombok Strait. That place scares me."

"Me, too," Brannon said. "Pray for rain or at least an overcast."

Eelfish, running at full speed, traversed the dangerous strait between the islands of Bali and Lombok and raced out into the Java Sea, heading for Makassar Strait. Six days later *Eelfish* submerged an hour before dawn off the northernmost tip of Celebes Island.

Lieutenant Michaels, who wore several hats as the ship's Commissary, Radio, Radar, and Sonar Officer, came into the Wardroom an hour after *Eelfish* dove. He handed Mike Brannon a sheet of paper covered with groups of numbers.

"This message came in before we dove," he said. "I broke it down, but all I get is another code, sir."

"Okay, Jim," Brannon said. He nodded at John Olsen, who was sitting at the table with his charts in front of him. "Let's go into my stateroom, John, and see what we've got."

An hour later Brannon looked at the words he had decoded from the message Michaels had given him. He handed the paper to Olsen, who whistled in surprise. Brannon reached for the chart Olsen had brought in with him. He laid the chart on his bunk, and with a pair of parallel rulers he covered the compass rose on the chart, then moved the rulers to *Eelfish's* position and drew a light pencil line on the chart.

"They're coming right down our street," he said to his Executive Officer. "Where are the dividers?" He took the dividers, pricked off the distance along the course line, and leaned back.

"I make it they'll be here about midnight tonight, maybe a little after midnight."

"If the people in Pearl Harbor who got this information know what they're doing," Olsen said slowly. "Seems too good to be true, three tankers and only three destroyers? Big tankers?"

"They know their business in Pearl," Mike Brannon said. "I didn't tell you this before, but Admiral Christie told me that those people in Pearl who work with the Japanese codes have gotten so good that last April they broke a coded message that said Fleet Admiral Yamamoto and his staff were going to fly out of Rabaul to visit bases in the Solomons on an inspection tour. The code breakers had his itinerary, the numbers and types of planes in his party, down pat.

"A big bunch of long-range P-38s flew out of Guadalcanal and ambushed Yamamoto's planes and shot every damned one of them down. The Japanese lost the best Admiral they had and his Chief of Staff and a lot of other high-ranking officers."

"I never heard about that," Olsen said.

"Damned few people have," Brannon said. "From what the Admiral told me they had a hell of an argument in Pearl about using the information they had gotten from the codes. The people who broke the codes were afraid that if they went after Yamamoto the Japanese would know that their codes were broken and the code breakers would have to start all over if the Japanese changed their codes. But Admiral Nimitz and Admiral King in Washington figured that Yamamoto was so valuable to the Japanese war effort that they gave the order to go ahead with the ambush."

"Japs didn't realize their codes had been broken?"

"Two things argued against it," Brannon said. "Or that's what I've been told. First of all, there were some heavy storms, real bad ones, along Yamamoto's route. One of the planes sent a message about the storms. Apparently none of Yamamoto's planes reported an attack by the P-38s. And we have never claimed any credit for shooting down the Admiral and his group. But keep that to yourself, all of it. I don't think the other Wardroom people need to know about it."

Eelfish surfaced a half-hour after full dark, the water streaming from her superstructure, the four big diesel engines coughing into life and then settling down to a muted roar as three of the engines went on the battery charge.

In the Forward Torpedo Room Steve Petreshock checked and rechecked the torpedo tubes, his anxious eyes searching for evidence of any small fault that would hamper a successful firing. Jim Rice watched him.

"What I'd like to know," Rice said, "is how those people in Fremantle know we're supposed to see a convoy of three big oil tankers and some destroyers out here? Hell, we ran all the way up here and never saw one damned ship, not even a fishing boat."

"I don't know how they know," Petreshock said. "Get some oil and take care of that gyro spindle on number two tube, will you? Son of a bitch feels a little sticky to me, and I don't want a fucking spindle hanging up.''

"Does seem funny, though," Rice said as he went between the tubes with an oilcan. "If those tankers do come along it will be the first damned thing that's happened the way it was supposed to happen since I been in this fuckin' submarine navy.'' He squirted some oil on the gyro spindle shaft and worked the spindle back and forth gently.

"So far, seems to me, the Jap is outfumbling us. If he was half as smart as the Japs is supposed to be, he'd have won this damned war by now." Paul Blake leaned out of his bunk above the reload torpedoes on the port side of the room.

"If the Japs had good sense they would have invaded Pearl Harbor. If they had they'd have won the war right then.''

Lieutenant Arbuckle came out of the Officers' Head, buckling his belt.

"If the Japanese ever bombed the Panama Canal, they've got submarines that can carry small planes, or if they used saboteurs to blow up the Canal locks we'd be in a nasty pickle. I share the wisdom of the bearded savant, Mr. James Rice, Esquire: The Jap is just outfumbling us." He ducked his head and lifted his leg to go through the watertight door opening to the Wardroom, to Officers' Country.

Brannon heard the sharp word "Contact!" come up the bridge hatch, and he turned and went forward to the bridge space.

"Contact, Bridge." The voice of the Chief of the Watch was tinny over the bridge speaker. "Radar contact bearing zero zero five, repeat zero zero five. Range is one four zero zero zero repeat fourteen thousand yards. Several pips on the radar, Bridge."

"Sound General Quarters!" Brannon snapped. The muted clanging of the alarm floated up through the bridge hatch and Brannon could hear the steady thud of feet down below as the crew raced to Battle Stations. He listened to the reports coming over the bridge speaker.

"All Battle Stations manned, Bridge. All torpedo tube outer doors closed. Repeat closed. Depth set on all torpedoes is four feet. Repeat four feet. Plotting party standing by in the Control Room."

"Very well," Brannon said into the bridge transmitter. He turned to Lieutenant Lee.

"Go below, Bob and start the plot. I'll take the bridge. I want intermittent use of the radar. I don't want them to pick up the radar if I can help it. Tell John Olsen I want him up here for a minute.''

Olsen climbed the ladder to the bridge and stood beside Brannon.

"They're a good quarter-hour behind schedule, Captain.''

"We'll have to speak to them about that,'' Brannon said. "How far north of Celebes are we?''

"Fifteen miles north of Celebes, sir. We're about dead center between Celebes and that little island of Biaro. We should have a three-quarter moon in about an hour.'' Both men looked upward as the radar antenna moved in a small arc.

"Targets bear zero zero two, Bridge. Range is closing. Range is now one three zero zero zero. Repeat thirteen thousand yards. We'd like to double-check range with another radar observation in three minutes.''

"Target speed?'' Brannon asked.

"We make that fifteen knots, Bridge, but we'd like to double-check that, too.''

"Very well,'' Brannon said. He stood, chewing his lower lip as he worked out the problem in his head. At 13,000 yards the targets were almost seven and a half miles away. At fifteen knots the targets would cover a mile in just under two minutes. That meant the targets would be abreast of *Eelfish* in about fifteen minutes. He turned to Olsen.

"I'm going to attack submerged. We have to assume they have radar. We're too far away from Celebes to use the island as a background. Right now we're too small a target to be picked up, but they'll sure as hell find us if we stay on the surface. Go below and take over the plot. Tell Mr. Gold that when I dive I want to run at forty feet so I can use the radar as long as I can.'' Olsen nodded and dropped down the hatch. His voice came over the bridge speaker a few minutes later.

"Recommend we stay on this course, Captain, at least until we have a better picture of the targets. Mr. Gold has the word on depth. Plot is running.''

"Very well,'' Brannon answered. He looked upward at the lookouts.

"Clear the bridge!'' he shouted and stood to one side as the three lookouts thudded down into the small bridge space and then dropped through the hatch. Brannon punched the diving alarm twice with his fist and slid down the ladder, pulling the hatch cover closed behind him. Brosmer spun the hatch wheel closed, dogging the hatch down tight.

"Forty feet,'' Brannon called down to the Control Room.

"Forty feet, aye," Jerry Gold answered. He watched as the bow and stern planesmen eased the *Eelfish* down to forty feet and leveled the ship off.

"Forty feet, zero bubble, sir," Gold called up the hatch, his voice betraying his pride. His last-minute shifting of water from the variable ballast tanks to compensate for the fuel consumed during the four and a half hours *Eelfish* had been on the surface and for the flour the baker and the messcooks had lugged from the Forward Torpedo Room to the Crew's Mess had resulted in a perfect diving trim.

"Very well," Brannon said. "Mr. Michaels, please come to the Conning Tower ladder."

Michaels climbed a few rungs and leaned his back against the rim of the open hatch. Brannon looked down at him.

"I'm going to depend on your radar for as long as I dare stay at this depth," he said. "I want quick readings, on and off. I'll give you bearings from the periscope so you don't have to waste time searching for the targets." Michaels acknowledged the order and went back down the ladder. Brannon turned to Paul Blake on the sonar.

"Let me know if you hear anything at all out there."

"I'm just beginning to get some faint propeller noises, sir," Blake said. "Too faint to tell anything."

Brannon nodded and relaxed, leaning against the chart desk. Lieutenant Perry Arbuckle, wearing one of his telephone ear muffs cocked on his temple, grinned at Brannon.

"Life in the Navy is just one long waiting in line," he said. "You wait in line to eat, you wait in line to get paid, you wait in line to go ashore, and now we wait to shoot."

Brannon grinned at the irreverent Reserve Officer. "I'm glad we're not in that line of ships coming toward us," he said. "Might get noisy." He turned as Blake spoke.

"I've got steady propeller noises bearing zero zero two, sir. Solid heavy propeller beat."

"Radar," Brannon called down the hatch. "Sound has a bearing at zero zero two. Give me a picture." He waited, hearing the muffled conversation between Michaels and Rafferty down below.

"We have six targets on the radar scope, sir," Michaels called out. "Range to the first target, a big pip, sir, is one one zero zero zero. Repeat eleven thousand yards. We have three big pips, one behind the other. We have one smaller pip out to port and ahead of the three big pips. We have two more small pips well back, well astern on the starboard side of the three big pips, sir.''

"Very well," Brannon said. "Secure the radar. Plot, how does it look from here?"

"We can stay on course for another four minutes, sir," Olsen said. "That will bring the targets to within fifty-five hundred yards, sir. At that point we can come right to course zero zero two and let them come right across our bow."

"Very well," Brannon said. He stood quietly in the Conning Tower, glancing at his wrist watch from time to time as he sorted out the factors of the problem in his head, plotting the intricate approach to the moment of the final truth that faces every submarine commanding officer in war; when to give the orders that would send torpedoes shooting out toward the enemy, what the guarding escort vessels might do in retaliation.

"I have several sets of propeller noises, sir," Blake said. "Slow and fast screws. Pretty broad spread of sound, sir, but I'd say the first heavy screws bear zero one zero, sir."

"Very well," Brannon said. He looked at his watch.

"Radar bearing," he said.

"Targets bear zero one three, sir. Range is five three zero zero. Repeat fifty-three hundred yards. We have the same formation, sir. Three big pips in a line, one ship out ahead to the port side of the convoy. Two ships well aft to the starboard side of the convoy. Target course is zero eight eight. Target speed is one five, fifteen knots, sir." Olsen's voice followed hard on the heels of Michaels's report.

"Recommend we come right now to course zero zero two, Captain."

"Execute the course change," Brannon said. He looked at Arbuckle, who had cranked the data Michaels had given into the TDC.

"Give me the torpedo track distance to the targets," Brannon said.

There was a short silence from below, and then Olsen said, "First target will be in position in six minutes, sir. Torpedo track will be two thousand yards."

"Too far!" Brannon snapped. "Give me a speed that will shorten that down to a thousand yards. Give me one more radar bearing."

"First target in line bears three four three, sir. Target course is zero eight eight. Target speed is one five knots. Repeat, fifteen knots. Range is six zero zero zero yards. Repeat six thousand yards.

"Recommend we come right to course zero two zero, sir," Olsen called out. "Recommend we make turns for five knots, sir."

"Secure the radar. Execute speed and course change. Sixty feet." Brannon snapped out the orders, bracing himself as the deck slanted down sharply.

"Sixty feet, sir," Gold called out. Brannon nodded at Brosmer to raise the periscope. He put his eye to the big rubber eyepiece that shielded the periscope lens. He saw the ships ahead of him and to his port side, three big oil tankers, one behind the other. Out ahead of them a destroyer was moving away from *Eelfish*. He swiveled the periscope to the left. One destroyer, far back along the starboard side of the convoy was moving toward him. He turned the periscope, searching for the other destroyer.

"Damn it," he said. "I've got two destroyers up here. Can't see the third one."

"He might have gone around the stern of the convoy, sir," Michaels said. "He did that once before and then came back, sir."

Brannon stared through the periscope. The ships were lit clearly by the moon, moving in a line like ponderous elephants. Below him he could hear the small sounds of the Control Room, the muttered commands of Jerry Gold to the men on the diving planes, the shuffle of paper as the Plotting Party penciled in the last bearings of the targets.

"Let's start the dance," Brannon said. "Open all torpedo tube outer doors. Stand by for shooting bearings." Brosmer, the Quartermaster, moved over and stood on the far side of the periscope, his head turned upward, ready to give the bearings to Arbuckle on the TDC. Brannon centered the cross hairs in the periscope lens on the first tanker.

"Bearing on the first tanker in line . . . Mark!"

"Three four two," Brosmer said.

"Range . . ." Brannon cranked the range knob with his right hand. "Range is two thousand yards." He swung the periscope around to his right. "The lead destroyer is way over on the other side." He focused the periscope on the lead tanker. "Come on, you big, fat cow! Come on, baby!" He swung the periscope to the left. "Destroyer on the convoy's starboard beam is well back. Range to that destroyer is . . . three five zero zero yards. Thirty-five hundred . . . Plot. What's the time factor to close to one thousand yards?"

"One minute, sir."

"We've got a constant shooting solution, sir." Arbuckle's voice was steady, calm.

Brannon watched the lead oil tanker loom larger and larger in the attack periscope's lens. Farther back—he estimated about 750 yards—the second tanker was following in the first tanker's wake.

"Twenty seconds, sir," Arbuckle said. "Shooting problem is go, sir."

"I'm going to shoot two at the first tanker and then we'll set up and try for two more at the second and two at the third . . . stand by . . ."

"Fire one!" Brannon felt the jolt in his legs and feet as the first torpedo hurtled out of its tube. He counted down from six to one.

"Fire two!" Brannon swung the periscope to his left.

"Number one and two torpedoes running hot, straight and normal, sir," Blake reported from his sonar station.

"Mark!" Brannon snapped.

"Three four six," Brosmer said.

"Range to the second target is eleven hundred yards." Brannon's voice was quiet.

"We've got a solution to shoot," Arbuckle said. A muffled boom shook the *Eelfish.*

"That was a hit!" Olsen said from the Control Room. "It timed out for a hit, sir."

"Fire three!" Brannon barked. He counted down.

"Fire four!"

"Both torpedoes running hot, straight and normal, sir," Blake reported, his young voice loud in the Conning Tower. Brannon swung the periscope to the right and saw the first tanker listing to starboard but still underway. He swung the periscope back to the left and saw a sudden gout of spray shoot up near the bow of the second tanker. Then he saw a huge orange flame back near the tanker's stern that swelled and burst into a tremendous explosion.

"Hit!" he yelled. "Hit on the second target!"

"I've got fast screws bearing two six zero, sir!" Blake said suddenly. Brannon swiveled the periscope around and saw the destroyer that had been farther back on the convoy's starboard beam racing toward him. He swung the periscope to the right. The first target, still listing, was underway but with no sign of smoke or fire. Brannon saw the white bow wave of a destroyer cutting across the listing tanker's bow.

"Right full rudder," he snapped. He swung the periscope back and forth, looking first at one destroyer and then the other.

"Down periscope!" he snapped. "Take me down! Four hundred feet! Fast, damn it, fast!" He grabbed at the bridge ladder for support as the deck tilted sharply beneath his feet as *Eelfish* burrowed deeper into the sea.

"Fast screws bearing two six one. More fast screws bearing three five four," Blake reported. He was shifting on his stool, gathering his legs beneath him, his face dripping perspiration as he tried to sort out the welter of sounds in his mufflike earphones.

"Passing two hundred fifty feet, down angle fifteen degrees," Jerry Gold said.

"Very well," Brannon replied. "Rig for silent running. Rig for depth charge."

The destroyer screws could be heard now, drumming through the submarine's hull in a high, thin sound that seemed to set everything in the submarine vibrating. The sound got louder and then one ship passed almost directly overhead, the *Eelfish* shaking in the volume of sound.

"Rudder amidships," Brannon ordered. He looked up as a high, sharp, cracking sound penetrated the *Eelfish*, the sound of a depth-charge exploder mechanism going off, and then the depth-charge explosion shook *Eelfish* savagely. Another sharp crack and then two more pierced through the tremendous noise of the first depth charge, and the world of the *Eelfish* crew became a nightmare of explosions that twisted and racked the submarine's thin hull, twisted the ship in the vortex of underwater explosions, knocking loose everything that wasn't screwed or bolted down. Cork insulation rained from the overhead and light bulbs and gauge glasses shattered. Shards of glass were scattered over everything.

"More fast screws, sir, I can't tell you a bearing, too much noise!" Blake's face, powdered with flecks of pale green paint from the cork insulation, was agonized as he tried to get a bearing on the destroyer above. He winced as the sharp crack of a depth-charge exploder mechanism sounded in his earphones, and then the *Eelfish* was caught again in a roaring, smashing, series of depth-charge explosions.

"Left full rudder, five hundred feet," Brannon said. He looked upward as the drumming sound of a destroyer's propellers filled the interior of the Conning Tower with sound. *Eelfish* staggered through the explosions of the sinking depth charges that twisted the long, slim length of the ship, straining the rivets and welds that bonded the thin skin of the ship to its frames, throwing men off their feet.

"Damage reports," Brannon ordered. Olsen spoke quietly into the sound-powered telephone set that hung around his neck. He turned his face upward to the Conning Tower hatch.

"Some small leaks, sir. Nothing serious. Most of the lights are broken, using battle lanterns in all compartments. Some bruises, one bloody nose. No broken bones, sir."

"Very well," Brannon said. He dropped through the hatch to the Control Room and looked at the plot.

"Didn't get a chance to shoot at the third tanker," he said calmly. "Didn't dare take long enough to shoot at the two destroyers. They were coming at us from two different angles." He looked up as Blake's voice came down the hatch.

"Two sets of twin screws aft, sir, one bearing one seven five, one bearing one six zero, sir. Both coming this way." In the Control Room Brannon could hear the sound of the screws building to a thunder. He looked at his wrist watch.

"Right full rudder, all ahead two thirds," he said.

The destroyers attacked as a team, depth charges rolling from their squat sterns, their Y-guns hurling the clumsy charges far out to each side. The *Eelfish* staggered under the attack.

"They might not stick around too long," Olsen said in a low voice. "You blasted that second tanker. You hit the first one, I timed that one for a hit. The tankers are more important than we are to them. They might leave in a while."

Brannon nodded and reached for a towel that Pete Mahaffey had hung from the fathometer. He mopped his dripping face and looked at the thermometer hanging near him. It read just over 105 degrees. The humidity reading on the dial just below it stood at 98 percent. He handed the towel to Olsen, who rubbed it over his face and neck.

"Here they come again!" Blake called down. "First ship bears three four five. Second ship bears three five eight, sir. Both coming fast!"

Once again the thunder of the destroyers' screws filled the *Eelfish* hull. Brannon looked briefly at the plot. "Right full rudder," he said. The helmsman strained at the big brass wheel, pulling it around by brute force.

"He's dropped!" Blake's voice had a sudden maturity. Brannon braced himself at the gyro table, his knees bent to take the shock of the explosions. He heard the helmsman muttering to the brass wheel.

"Take it easy, old girl," the helmsman said. "This ain't nothing to what you can take." He grabbed at the wheel as the *Eelfish* reeled to port and then to starboard as the depth charges exploded. John Olsen pressed the talk button on his phone and spoke softly. He listened and then turned to Brannon.

"No serious damage, sir."

"Very well," Brannon said. "Let's hope you're right, John. Maybe they'll put more weight on protecting the tankers we didn't get than keeping on us. They aren't too good. They haven't used a sonar on us once. They've been attacking using passive listening and by guesswork."

"Damned good guesswork," Olsen said. The two men looked upward as Paul Blake reported.

"One set of screws, dead slow, bearing one six zero, sir. Other set of screws has speeded up and is going away from us bearing one nine five. That set of screws is going away, sir!"

Brannon reached for the towel and mopped his streaming face. "You're guessing pretty good, John. One of the dogs has gone back to his sheep. All we have to do is be cute and let the other one get discouraged and maybe he'll leave. Pass the word, dead silence about the decks. I don't want to hear anyone even cough. Make turns for dead slow."

An hour crept by with whispered reports from Blake that the enemy destroyer was still above but far out to one side. *Eelfish* crept away from the destroyer, running as silently as possible. Olsen looked at the clock on the bulkhead above the helm. The glass face of the clock had been shattered, but its black hands continued to move.

"Another hour should take us in the clear," he whispered to Brannon. "He's got to get discouraged and go back to his other ships."

The eerie silence in the *Eelfish* was suddenly shattered by a whining scream from the after end of the ship. Brannon whirled around.

"Belay that damned noise!"

The high, whining sound kept rising in pitch. Blake's voice came down the hatch.

"Destroyer is picking up speed, sir. He bears two seven five! He's speeding up."

"Damn it, shut down that noise!" Brannon snapped. Olsen looked up from his telephone, his face stricken.

"After Torpedo Room reports that the torpedo in Number

Seven tube was fired accidentally with the outer door closed! The torpedo is running hot inside the tube!''

"Here he comes!'' Blake wailed from the Conning Tower.

CHAPTER 7

The moaning scream of the runaway torpedo vibrated throughout the length of the *Eelfish*. Mike Brannon turned, his face grim.

"Flanagan, what in the hell can be done about this?''

"Only one thing to do, Captain. Get back there and open the inner door of the tube and snake that son of a bitch out of the tube somehow and shut the engines down.''

"You ever see it done?'' Brannon asked.

"No, sir, but I sure as hell am going to find out how to do it.''

"Get back there. Lee, go with the Chief. Keep me informed.'' Flanagan headed aft, opening each watertight door as he came to it. Lee, following him, closed the doors behind them.

The thunder of the destroyer's screws drowned out the noise of the runaway torpedo as Flanagan and Lee hurried through the engine rooms. The first depth charge of the renewed attack went off with a shattering roar, throwing Flanagan against the guard rail of an engine in the After Engine Room. Lee heard him curse quietly as he regained his balance.

The scene in the After Torpedo Room was one of frantic activity. Fred Nelson had put in place the heavy bars that joined the skid supports on either side of the torpedo room and had moved the reload torpedo for Number Seven tube on to the crossbars. His reload crew, working with sheer muscle, had moved the 900-pound spare torpedo skid from the port side of the room over the tops of the reload torpedo in front of Number Eight tube and the torpedo that was now in the center of the room and put it in position in line with Number Seven tube. Flanagan and Lee ducked under the torpedo that was sitting on the skid cross bars and duck-walked their way up to the after end of the room to the clear space in front of the tubes.

"Cussed that damned extra skid every day since we left Fremantle,'' Nelson said. "Now I could kiss the son of a bitch.

At least we got something to put that bastard on that's running away in the tube. If we ever get it out.''

"You got any bright ideas on how we're gonna do that?" Flanagan grunted.

"Petreshock called from the Forward Room while you were comin' aft,'' Nelson said. "He figured the exhaust comin' out of that tail cone would be hot enough to fry a man so gettin' a line or a cable around the tail assembly to haul the bastard out would be a bitch unless we had asbestos hoods and gloves and we ain't got any of them. He thought maybe we could shove a slewing bar down the tube, if we can reach the fish, and jam it in the screws.''

Flanagan shook his head. "Burn your damned hands off trying to put a slewing bar in the tube. You got some steel cable back here?'' Nelson nodded.

"Get some steel cable. Make a coil, three or four turns about two feet across. Lash it together so it makes like a butterfly or a figure eight with a belt or something. We can feed a cable down one side of the tube so we don't get burned off at the elbows and maybe whip it around until it catches in the screws. Might even catch good enough so we could use the cable to pull the fish out.'' Nelson went scrambling forward on his hands and knees underneath the torpedo in the middle of the room. Flanagan turned to Lieutenant Lee, who had put on the Battle Station talker's telephone set.

"Tell the Old Man what we are going to try to do, sir. Tell him we'll do it as quick as we can.'' Lee nodded and spoke into the telephone. He listened and then made a thumbs-up sign to Flanagan, who turned and looked at the cable that Nelson had prepared. He nodded his approval and picked up the heavy wrench that was used to revolve the bayonet ring that held the solid bronze inner torpedo tube door closed.

"All hands, out of the way. When this son of a bitch of a door comes open there's gonna be noise and heat and gas like you never saw.'' He put the wrench on the stud and spun it viciously. The door flew open and a high-pitched scream filled the room as boiling hot exhaust gases belched out of the tube. Flanagan crouched below the level of the tube and to one side. Nelson gave him the looped end of the cable and Flanagan gingerly fed the loop into the tube. Nelson fed him cable as he pushed the loop down the tube. He felt it hit something solid.

"It's at the fish,'' he grunted. "Hold on to me, Fred, so's I don't slip and get in front of that damned exhaust.'' Both men staggered as four heavy depth charge explosions shook the stern of the *Eelfish*. Flanagan took the cable in both hands and began to whip it up and down and to one side. Suddenly the cable jerked through his hands, and there was a grinding noise of gears shearing themselves to bits and the sound of the propellers stopped. The hot exhaust continued to pour out of the torpedo tube. Flanagan turned and saw that Nelson was laying out a block and tackle and fastening the cable to one block. The reload crew, coughing in the increasingly foul atmosphere of the torpedo room, were crouched on their knees in a line, ready to begin hauling on the block and tackle to pull the torpedo out of the tube. Flanagan turned to Lee.

"She ain't frozen in the tube, sir. See that little bit of water leaking past the fish?" He pointed at a thin stream of water running out of the torpedo tube.

On the surface up above the *Eelfish* the sonar operator on the Chidori destroyer looked at his Sonar Officer.

"Whatever it was making that funny noise has stopped, sir. Shall I begin a sonar search?" The officer nodded and the sonar man punched a button. A sonar beam began pulsing out into the ocean, searching in a circle. Suddenly the beam bounced back, ringing loudly in the Sonar Room of the destroyer.

"Target bears zero two zero, sir," he said calmly. "Range to the target is five hundred yards." The Sonar Officer murmured into the telephone he wore, and the Chidori's bow reared high and then settled down as its engines went to full speed.

The first depth charge exploded above the Forward Torpedo Room of the *Eelfish*, driving Petreshock to his knees in front of the torpedo tubes, lifting the upper bunks upward and out of their chain hooks to fall with a crash against reload torpedoes. In the Control Room the bow planesman saw the bubble in his inclinometer move sharply, and he began to strain against the big brass wheel to tilt the bow planes upward to compensate for the downward push of the depth charge.

The sudden slant down by the bow that was caused by the crushing force of the depth-charge explosion brought the torpedo sliding out of the tube as Flanagan yelled a warning. The torpedo, its tail cone belching a stream of burning hot exhaust gas, its turbines howling inside the afterbody, slid down the reload skid and crashed into the thin metal side of the Engineering Log cubicle and jammed there. A 24-inch thick stream of sea water driven by the 500-foot depth *Eelfish* was cruising at, burst into the torpedo room out of the tube, slamming against the warhead of the runaway torpedo. Flanagan ducked under the stream of water, grabbed the bottom edge of the tube's inner door, and tried to close it. It moved easily and then it stopped, kept from closing by the warhead of the torpedo. He ducked back under the warhead and the rock-hard stream of water and realized that Nelson had shut down the torpedo's engines.

"Clear the room!" Flanagan bellowed, his voice loud in the suddenly silent torpedo room. "All hands get out except Nelson. Close the watertight door. Maneuvering Room, open the salvage air valves, get a pressure in here soon's these people get out and close the door!"

The electrician on watch with Chief Morris in the Maneuvering Room pulled the watertight door closed and dogged it tight as Chief Morris, standing on the padded bench seat, reached up and opened the salvage air valves. Air under a pressure of 225 pounds to the square inch roared into the sealed-off torpedo room. Lee pressed the talk button on his phones.

"Sorry about the noise, Captain," he said calmly. "The torpedo is out of the tube. It's jammed into the Log Room bulkhead. We can't close the inner door on the tube because the warhead is in the way. The tube will be secured as soon as possible. Salvage air is being bled into the room to try and keep the water level down. Water is now knee deep and still coming."

"Very well," Brannon said into the phone Olsen had handed him. He gave the phone back and turned to the auxiliaryman at the high-pressure air manifold.

"As soon as that son of a bitch upstairs makes another run, as soon as you can hear his screws, blow Number Six Main Ballast tanks. All of them." The auxiliaryman repeated the order and moved his wrench to the blow valve.

"That bastard up there isn't going to have any trouble finding us," Olsen said.

"He hasn't had much trouble since that fish was fired in the tube," Brannon said. He looked at the bubbles in the inclinometers in front of the bow and stern planesmen. The *Eelfish* was assuming a downward slant by the stern.

In the flooding After Torpedo Room Nelson had retrieved the block and tackle the reload crew had dropped into the water as they scrambled out of the room. He methodically untangled the wet lines and hooked one block over the horizontal surface of the torpedo's tail fin. He carried the other block aft and hooked it into the skid. Flanagan joined him and took hold of the line.

"Take it easy on the haulin'," Flanagan grunted. "We got a

down angle by the stern. I don't want this son of a bitch to hit the inner door and jam that fucker up." The two men pulled carefully, and the torpedo slid out of the thin metal of the Log Room. Flanagan took the block off the tail and carried it to the nose of the torpedo. He pushed his hand and arm into the stream of water roaring out of the tube, wincing with pain as the water slammed into his flesh, and found the nose ring on the warhead. He got the hook in place and turned to Nelson.

"Get outboard of this fucker and when you're set try to shove the ass end of the skid over far enough so the tail will clear the Log Room. Then we can pull the bastard back in the skid so's we can get the inner door closed." Nelson nodded and scrambled under the torpedo and braced his back against the hull. He put one big foot against the skid and pushed.

"Harder, Fred, harder!" Nelson heaved again and the skid moved another few inches. He scrambled toward the tail of the torpedo and explored the position of the skid and the edge of the Log Room bulkhead.

"She's gonna clear," he said, and ducked under the torpedo and took hold of the line on the block and tackle with Flanagan. The two men heaved mightily and then heaved again, fighting the downward angle *Eelfish* had assumed because of the increasing weight of the water pouring into the torpedo room. Lieutenant Lee heard Flanagan sob with effort and scrambled upward on the skid in the middle of the room, peering intently at the inner torpedo tube door and the warhead nose. The torpedo inched away from the inner door.

"That's it!" Lee yelled. Flanagan came splashing forward and saw Lee's white face in the eerie glow of the battle lanterns.

"This is what they give you that extra submarine pay for, Mr. Lee," the Chief of the Boat said. He ducked under the stream of water and worked his body between the torpedo-tube inner door and the hull. Using his arms and legs he began to push his back against the inner door, narrowing the two-foot stream of water pouring out of the tube. He heard Nelson grunting as he scrambled under the warhead and eased his tall frame up beside Flanagan, who was straining, holding the door partially closed against the more than 200 pounds of pressure the stream of water was exerting.

"Lemme get a shoulder in next to you," Nelson muttered. The two men pushed and the door gave a few inches. Nelson got his foot against the side of the ship's hull, and with a loud grunt he heaved backward with all his strength. Lieutenant Lee,

standing by with the door wrench, slipped it over the stud and
threw every ounce of his 150 pounds downward. The bayonet
ring caught and Nelson spun away from the warhead and grabbed
the wrench from Lee and finished closing the bayonet ring. Lee
thumbed the button on his phone set.

"Inner door on Number Seven tube is secured, Control.
We've got about four feet of water in the room. Torpedo is now
being strapped into the skid."

Mike Brannon looked at the inclinometer bubble. The *Eelfish*
was sagging dangerously downward by the stern. He turned to
Jerry Gold, the Battle Stations Diving Officer.

"Next time that guy up there speeds up to make a drop on us,
as soon as he's committed, start pumping the After Room
through the drain lines."

"Aye, aye, sir," Gold said. He spoke briefly into his telephone
set, and in the After Room Lieutenant Lee relayed the message
to Flanagan and Nelson. Nelson shrugged.

"Fucking sump stop valve to the drain line is under four foot
of water. I'm so wet now it don't make any real difference." He
ducked down under the water and emerged a half-minute later,
water dripping from his hooked nose.

"Bilge sump stop valve to the drain line is open, sir," he said
to Lee. "Now all we got to do is wait until that old Slant-Eye up
there drops some more of his shit-cans and maybe that stupid
fuckhead on the trim manifold can pump some of this damned
water outa my room."

"You won't have to wait long," Lee said, "He's on his way."

The attack was sharp and heavy. *Eelfish*, her bow at 450 feet
and her stern sagging below 500 feet, staggered through the
attack. As the continual roar of the exploding depth charges went
on, the man at the trim manifold ran the drain pump at high
speed. In the After Torpedo Room the water began to recede and
the down angle by the stern began to ease.

"If he comes back again we'll do it once more," Brannon
said. "I can't afford to pump the After Room dry. Number Six
main ballast is empty and I can't flood it because the damned air
bubble from the vents would give us away too damned much.
Even at night that son of a bitch up there could see that air
bubble.

"We've got a seven-degree down bubble by the stern, sir,"
Jerry Gold said. "We can hold pretty good if we can get that
down to about four degrees, sir."

"Very well," Brannon said. "Get ready to pump, I can hear that bastard coming!"

After three more runs, dawn streaked the sky, and the destroyer gave up the hunt. Paul Blake, listening with all his being, heard the sound of the destroyer's screws fade and then disappear. In the Control Room Mike Brannon nodded his acknowledgment of the information. He turned to Jerry Gold.

"Switch to hydraulic power on the bow and stern planes and the helm. Bring me up to sixty-five feet." He climbed the ladder to the Conning Tower, wondering at the weariness of his legs and then realizing that for hours he had been braced against the depth-charge explosions. He swung the periscope in two complete revolutions and saw nothing. He ordered Gold to bring the ship up to forty feet and took a radar sweep. No evidence of any ships. He walked to the hatch.

"Jerry, tell the engine and maneuvering rooms to stand by. I'm going to surface after one more radar sweep, and I'm going to stay up there as long as I can. I want a battery charge started as soon as the main induction is open. Start pumping that After Room now and keep at it until it's dry." He waited for the radar report and then punched the surface alarm three times. *Eelfish* rose, sluggishly, her stern sagging. The bow broke water first, rearing toward the sky, and then the Conning Tower burst through the surface. Brannon opened the hatch and scrambled back to the cigaret deck. The afterdeck of the *Eelfish* was under water from the gun mount aft. He heard the drain pump straining down below, and as he watched he could see the stern beginning to rise slowly. He turned as Jerry Gold, who had the OOD watch, spoke to him.

"Charging batteries on three main engines, Captain. Chief Electrician says if you can give him an hour he'll have enough juice crammed back in to go down until after dark tonight if we behave ourselves and don't go chasing anything."

"Very well," Brannon said. "Jerry, I'm going below. I want to take a look at that torpedo room. Keep the lookouts on their toes. If you see anything larger than a sea gull dive the ship."

He stopped in the Maneuvering Room where Chief Ed Morris was overseeing the battery charge.

"Give me an hour or so, Captain," Morris said. "After that we can dive and make out easy for a good twelve, fourteen hours."

"I'll try to give you more than that," Brannon said. He

stepped through the watertight door opening into the After Torpedo Room.

"Afraid you'll have to duck down and crawl, sir," Lee called from the torpedo tubes. Brannon ducked under the torpedo that was blocking the room and scrambled along until he reached the clear area in front of the tubes. He stood up gasping for air.

"Whew," he said. "Air back here is foul."

"You should have smelled it when we had the watertight door closed and that torpedo was belching exhaust gas in here," Lee said. "I don't know how the Chief and Nelson could work in that air."

Brannon looked at the two men. "You did one hell of a job," he said slowly. "I won't forget it."

"Mr. Lee just didn't stand around, sir," Flanagan said. "He stayed back here after I ordered the room cleared. He was one hell of a lot of help, sir." Brannon nodded.

"You have any idea of the condition of the outer door, Chief, Nelson?"

"It's either knocked off or it's hanging by its hinges," Flanagan said. "Nelson tried to close it but when he put the Y-wrench on the stud it just turned. Easy. So we lost the connecting linkage between the stud and the door for sure. But I don't know if it's still there or not. That's not what's worrying me, sir."

"What is?" Brannon said.

"The warhead is leaking, sir. Must have split when it hit the outer door. When you mix sea water with the Torpex in the warhead you get stuff called exudate. Exudate is explosive. But we can handle that."

"What else?" Brannon asked, looking at Flanagan's hard face.

"I think we got an armed warhead, sir. The stream of water coming out of the tube was hitting the front of the warhead square. The little propeller that arms the warhead was right in the path of that stream of water."

Brannon looked at the dull coppery sheen of the warhead and then at Flanagan.

"Anything hits that warhead with a force of four pounds of impact," Flanagan said slowly, "anything hits that warhead, it's gonna explode!"

CHAPTER 8

There was a dead silence in the After Torpedo Room. Mike Brannon licked his lips and looked at the Chief of the Boat.

"You're sure the warhead is armed?"

"I got to figure it that way," Flanagan said. "That little propeller on the underside of the exploder, we call it an impeller, it spins when the torpedo goes through the water. It arms the exploder at about four hundred and fifty yards.

"That stream of water coming out of the tube was hitting the warhead full on the nose. I figure the stream of water would turn the impeller enough times to bring the fulminate of mercury cartridge up out of its safety chamber in the exploder. Once that happens, all you've got to do is to hit the warhead with a force of four pounds and she explodes."

"Be fatal," Fred Nelson chimed in, his eyes staring belligerently from either side of the big hawk nose that dominated his face. "If this baby goes off the warheads on the other fish in the room go off with a sympathetic explosion, they call it, Captain."

"Don't scare me," Brannon said slowly. He looked at Flanagan. "I guess the only answer is to get the exploder out of the warhead?"

"That's the only thing I can think of, sir," Flanagan said. "But it ain't gonna be easy to do, sir."

"Why not?" Brannon said. "You've had enough experience taking exploders out of warheads to modify them and then to put them back the way they were if we didn't fire them."

"First place," Flanagan said, "we'll be working from the underside of the fish. Normally, we roll the fish over in the skid so the exploder is on the top side and we can work on it. When you roll a fish over it doesn't come easy. You got to put a steel cable sling around it and use a slewing bar and sort of jolt the damned thing until it finally rolls over.

"Then we take out the studs and screw two lifting tools into the exploder base plate, there's tapped holes for the lifting tools. And then, and this is the way it is every exploder we've taken out, damned near, it won't come out of the warhead. You pull on the lifting tools and you hit the edge of the exploder with a rawhide maul and you work it out gradually.

"We can't take a chance rolling this fish over because we might jolt it too hard. That means we got to take the exploder out from underneath and it means we can't hit it with the maul and if the bastard sticks and won't come out, I think I'll put in for a transfer."

Brannon chewed his lower lip, thinking. He shrugged his heavy shoulders.

"What's got to be done has got to be done," he said slowly. "I'm going to stay on the surface for a while. We've got to get some charge back in the battery. Once we've done that we'll submerge, go down to about three hundred feet so we'll have a nice steady platform to work with and we'll get the exploder out." He stooped and looked at the underside of the warhead. A steady stream of viscous drops was falling from a split in the nose of the warhead, the drops falling soundlessly into a pile of soft rags Nelson had put on the deck.

"We'll have to do something about that warhead," Brannon said. "If exudate is dangerous we can't have it leaking into the room."

"Once we get the exploder out we can roll the fish over," Flanagan said. "Then we can seal it with something."

"Okay," Brannon said. "Don't let anyone get near this torpedo, Nelson." He turned to Bob Lee. "Let's go up to the Wardroom, Bob. I want you to dictate everything you saw and know that happened back here to the yeoman. When he gets that typed up we can have Chief Flanagan and Nelson read it for accuracy and for additions." He looked at Nelson and Flanagan.

"You're damned good men," he said slowly. He started to duck under the torpedo to go forward and then straightened up. "Chief, later I want you and Nelson to sit down with me and talk about how this happened. I don't want to crucify anyone, I don't think we have to do that, but I want to know everything so we can make sure it doesn't happen again. We've still got those Mark Fifteens in the other three tubes." He ducked under the torpedo and went forward, followed by Bob Lee. Nelson turned to Flanagan.

"Got me a helluva mess back here, Chief. Ain't hardly gonna be any room to live back here, let alone do our work. What do you want me to do about Dumont? He's the dumb fuck who fired the damned fish in the tube. Said he saw a leak in a grease fitting above the gyro repeater and was going to look at it and a depth charge threw him off balance and he hit the firing key for Number Seven."

"Don't do anything," Flanagan said. "I'll handle it, I'll do something if something has to be done. I want to talk to the Old Man about it first, and to John Olsen. Dumont's a pretty good man."

"Yeah, he's a good man," Nelson said.

"Leave it there," Flanagan said. He scrambled under the torpedo and went into the Maneuvering Room. Chief Morris looked at him from the padded bench seat where he was sitting, his foot propped negligently against the edge of the control panel.

"How's your ears after all that pressure, Monk?"

"Didn't notice any pressure," Flanagan said. "I was worried about getting my ass wet. That damned water sure came in fast through that open tube. Thought I might have drowned before we got that inner door closed."

"Nah," Morris said. "The air pressure in the room would have stopped the water a good three feet from the overhead. You could have breathed in that bubble."

"You're a cheerful fuck," Flanagan grunted. He went forward to change clothes.

Standing on the ship's bridge, Mike Brannon filled John Olsen and Jerry Gold in on the condition of the exploder. Olsen's eyes widened.

"My God, if we get depth charged again the jolts from the depth charges might set it off!"

"I don't think so," Brannon said. "We took some hard knocks when that fish was out of the tube, and it seemed to take it. The real danger is in someone getting careless and hitting the warhead itself." He turned to Gold.

"How's the battery charge coming?"

"Chief Morris says he'll have a full can in another hour, sir. We can secure any time, but when we do he'd like twenty minutes, if we can give it to him, to ventilate the battery compartments. He's been charging at a high amperage rate, and there's hydrogen in the battery ventilation system."

"Something in the water, bearing zero four five, Bridge," the starboard lookout yelled.

Brannon and Olsen raised their binoculars. In the distance the water surface had a peculiar iridescent purple sheen broken by several white objects.

"Let's get over there, Jerry," Brannon said. Jerry Gold nodded and spoke quietly into the bridge transmitter, and the *Eelfish* turned to starboard and began to close on the odd purple sheen in the water.

"That looks like oil all over the water, Bridge," the starboard lookout reported. "I can see some two, three life rings, and there's a guy hanging on to some sort of wooden crate or something that's floating and he's waving at us."

"Control," Brannon said into the bridge transmitter. "Give me a radar sweep, air and horizon."

"Radar reports all clear, Bridge."

"Very well," Brannon said. "Chief of the Boat to the bridge with a boathook, a life line, and two seamen. Gunner's Mate to the bridge with a submachine gun."

"We've got an oil slick up ahead, Chief," Brannon said. "There's some life rings in the slick. I want to get one of them, two if you can. There's a man hanging on to a crate or something a little to starboard of the life rings. I want to get him, too, but these people often would rather die than be captured. So ignore the man. Maybe if he thinks we won't pick him up he'll come aboard." He turned to John LaMark.

"Gunner, if we pick this swimmer up I want you to watch him like a hawk. If he shows a knife or a gun, shoot him." He turned back to Flanagan.

"If you have to go down on the pressure hull remember it's got some oil on it. We're running through some oil now. Use a safety line."

Down on deck Flanagan tied a double bowline in the end of a coil of 21-thread manila line one of the seamen was holding. He put his legs through the two loops of the knot and pulled the line up his legs to his crotch. He took the bitter end of the line, put it around his waist, and tied it to the standing part of the line. The seaman gathered up the slack.

"Don't worry, Chief. I won't lose you."

"I'm not worried," Flanagan growled. "But you'd better worry if you do." He sat down on the deck and eased his way down on to the pressure hull, holding the boathook ready. As the ship slowed and eased by a life ring stained with oil, Flanagan reached out and snared the ring and lifted it up on deck. The man holding on to the crate was a scant ten yards distant.

"Left ten degrees rudder," Brannon yelled out in a loud voice that carried over the water. "That's good, Chief. We've got what we want."

The bow of the submarine began to swing slowly away and the man holding the crate thrashed his legs in a violent dog paddle.

"Don't leave me!" the swimmer's voice was high-pitched with fear. "Please don't leave me!"

"Son of a bitch speaks English," Flanagan said. He looked at the submarine's bridge.

"You want me to get this sucker, sir?"

"Might as well," Brannon said, his voice loud. "Gunner, stand by to shoot that swimmer if he makes one wrong move." He turned to Olsen and said in a low voice, "He spoke English, so he must understand it."

"He doesn't have to understand," Olsen said. "Look at LaMark!"

Brannon looked at the deck where LaMark was elaborately going through the process of pulling the cocking knob on the .45 caliber submachine gun back and letting it snap forward. He raised the machine gun to his shoulder and aimed it at the swimmer, his finger on the trigger.

In response to Jerry Gold's delicate maneuvering the *Eelfish* slid through the oily water, closing on the swimmer. As the submarine eased toward the swimmer Flanagan held out the boathook and the man abandoned his wooden crate and swam desperately toward the boathook and grabbed it with both hands. Flanagan, his feet braced against the pressure hull, pulled the man to the side of the ship.

"You savvy English?"

"Yes, sir," the swimmer's teeth were chattering with fear.

"Okay," Flanagan said. "I'm going to give the end of this boathook to that sailor and he'll pull you aboard. You make one wrong move and that man with the machine gun is going to cut you into two pieces. You understand?"

"Yes, sir," the swimmer said. He reached out with one hand, his fingers scraping the pressure hull. Flanagan passed the boathook to a seaman on deck and the swimmer, hanging desperately to the end of the boathook, scrambled up on the pressure hull and then to the deck, where he huddled on his knees, his hands clasped in prayer.

"On your feet," Flanagan ordered as he climbed up on deck and took off his safety line. "I'm going to search you. Gunner, blast this man if he makes a move." Flanagan ran his hands around the pair of white shorts the man was wearing.

"No weapons on him, sir," Flanagan called to the bridge.

"Bring the prisoner to the cigaret deck," Brannon ordered.

"Secure the deck party." The two seamen herded the prisoner down the deck and up to the cigaret deck, where he raised his hands.

"Take the prisoner below," Brannon said. "Gunner, you guard him. Get Doc to look him over and give him some food and water. I'll be down later."

"Jerry," Brannon said. "Tell Maneuvering I want to secure the battery charge. As soon as the battery is ventilated we'll go back down. I want a radar sweep every five minutes. Some of the friends of that prisoner might come back to look for him."

Thirty minutes later the *Eelfish* slid very gently beneath the sea, sinking almost vertically to 300 feet. Mike Brannon went to the Forward Torpedo Room where LaMark was guarding the prisoner. Doc Wharton was closing up his first-aid kit as Brannon came through the watertight door opening.

"He's pretty good, sir," Wharton said. "He's got some small burns from the fuel oil but nothing to bother with. This oil must not burn as much as the oil did at Pearl. I was in the hospital there, at Aiea, and I saw guys who had been in oil in the harbor who were burned a hell of a lot worse than this guy."

Brannon nodded his head. He looked at the prisoner, who was standing with his back against a bunk, watching John LaMark, who was fondling his submachine gun.

"You spoke English when you were in the water," Brannon said to the prisoner. "Will you tell us your name?"

"Yes, sir," the prisoner said. "My name is John Yamati. I graduated with a master's degree in engineering from Stanford in nineteen thirty-seven, sir."

"And went right home to Japan," Brannon said.

"No, sir. I went home in nineteen forty-one, early in forty-one, sir. My mother had died, and I stayed there to help my father. He's quite old. I was there when the war broke out. I was put in the Merchant Marine. I was the chief engineer of the ship you sank, sir."

"What ship was that?" Brannon asked.

"You have a life ring so there is no point in refusing to answer your questions, sir. I was serving on the oil tanker *Takasaki,* ten thousand tons. You hit our ship with two torpedoes. One did not explode. The other hit us aft, in the boiler rooms. The ship exploded and sank."

"Where were you?" Brannon asked.

"I was on the bridge, getting some air," the prisoner said. "I am grateful, very grateful to you for saving me." He bowed from the waist.

"Well," Brannon said. "We'll extend the courtesies of the Geneva Convention to you and probably a lot more. Which is more than your people do for ours."

"I can give you my word as an officer, sir, that I will obey your orders." The prisoner bowed again.

"Uh huh," Brannon said mildly. "I'll figure out how we're going to handle you later. Petreshock, we'll keep the prisoner up here. The Gunner's Mate has some handcuffs. If the prisoner wants to sleep, let him, but cuff one of his hands to a bunk rail. If he wants to sit up, same thing. I don't want him made uncomfortable, just safe. Is that clear?"

"Yes, sir," Petreshock said. Brannon nodded and went aft, followed by Olsen and Bob Lee. Brannon stopped in the Control Room where Flanagan was standing.

"Let's get this thing over with, Chief."

Fred Nelson had the tools needed to remove the exploder from the torpedo's warhead laid out on a clean towel on deck in front of the torpedo tubes.

"Been thinkin' on this, Chief," Nelson said to Flanagan. "Important thing is to not shear off any of them studs that hold the exploder in the warhead. We'll have to make damn sure the wrench is square on the stud and solid and take a slow strain to get the stud started out.

"If we can do that we can take out all the studs except those on two corners, diagonal corners. After that we'll sweat gettin' the exploder outa the warhead."

Flanagan nodded his approval. "I'll take the first half of the studs. You get down under the warhead with me and make sure the wrench is solid on the stud, hold it there while I take a strain." He turned to Brannon.

"We'll go ahead now, Captain. Cross your fingers, sir." He crouched under the warhead. Nelson got down on his knees beside him and carefully fitted the socket head of the wrench into a recessed stud hole in the exploder base plate. Flanagan began to exert a little pressure and then a bit more pressure, and with a sudden, sharp noise, the stud turned.

"Next one," Flanagan grunted. The two men worked in almost total silence, stopping only when Nelson stopped to mop his sweating face. Nelson fitted the wrench on to one stud after the other, Flanagan's powerful forearms bulging with the strain of exerting maximum power with a delicate touch. At the halfway point Flanagan paused.

"You want to take the rest of them, Fred?"

"Keep on goin'," Nelson muttered. "You've got the touch now. I might shear off a stud." Flanagan nodded, wiped his hands on a towel, and began on another stud. After almost forty minutes of concentrated effort he crawled out from under the warhead.

"Only two studs left, Captain. One on each corner, diagonally. Both of them are a little bit loose. We're ready to try and drop the exploder, sir, soon's I get my breath."

"Take all the time you want," Brannon said. "When you take those last two studs out, how are you going to handle the exploder?"

"One of us will have to get under the warhead and push up against the exploder while the last studs are coming out. Then I'll screw in the two lifting tools and try to wiggle it free."

"If you don't object," Brannon said, "I'll get under the warhead and hold the exploder."

"That thing is heavy, Captain," Flanagan said. "Must weigh forty, fifty pounds. Maybe more."

"I know," Brannon said. He wiped his hands on his shorts.

"Okay, sir," Flanagan said. "You get down here, on your knees. Put both your hands up against the exploder. Fred, you guide the wrench for me."

Brannon got onto his knees under the warhead, his head craned upward, his two hands on the exploder.

"No," Nelson said. "No, sir. Let me place your hands for you. I want you to spread them out so if this thing happens to come free it won't drop cockeyed and jam. We can't let it sag at either end." He positioned Mike Brannon's hands. Flanagan began to back out one of the two remaining brass studs. He finished and Nelson moved the wrench to the last stud. Brannon heard Flanagan mutter.

"Dear God, make this son of a bitchin' thing come out nice and easy."

The wrench turned slowly and then more slowly and Brannon felt the sudden weight of the exploder on his hands.

"Stud's free," Flanagan said. "Hold everything just so until I put the lifting tools in."

"Never mind," Brannon gasped. "It's coming out!" His neck swelled with effort as he slowly lowered his arms and the exploder slid out of the warhead. Nelson, on his knees beside

Brannon, leaned over and gently put his hands under the edges of the exploder and took its weight. He swiveled sideways and let the exploder down onto his thighs and drew a deep breath.

"Son of a bitch, that's the first time I ever seen one of those bastards come out like that!" He rested the weight of the exploder on his legs and then slid it downward and lifted it gently to the deck. He peered into the exploder.

"The son of a bitch is armed, all the way!" he said in an awed voice.

"Hold it steady," Flanagan said. Very cautiously he put his hand into the interior of the exploder and began to turn the gear that extended the fulminate of mercury cartridge out of its safety chamber. Working slowly and patiently he turned the worm gear backward until the dangerous explosive charge was safely housed in its safety chamber. He sat back on his heels and took a deep breath as Nelson quickly unscrewed the safety chamber from its base and took it out of the exploder. He gave the small, heavy safety chamber to Lieutenant Lee.

"I think this would be safer in the magazine, sir," he said. "Safe enough the way it is but we've got no stowage for it back here."

Brannon looked at Flanagan and smiled. "We make a hell of a good team, the three of us, Chief."

"We had one thing going for us, Captain, the luck of the Irish. Like Fred said, that's the first exploder I ever saw that came out easy." He reached upward and grabbed the handle on the inner door of a torpedo tube and hauled himself to his feet. He turned to Nelson.

"You'd better unstrap that fish and roll it over so the exudate will stop dripping. Might try sealing the split with some Tacki-wax. If that stuff will seal exhaust valves in the fish against sea pressure it should seal a crack in the warhead. Then get this damned room in some sort of shape."

In the Wardroom Mike Brannon relaxed over a cup of coffee. He looked at John Olsen.

"Hairy experience, John."

"Wasn't any fun watching you," Olsen said. "I kept telling myself that I might as well be back there as up forward. If that thing blew, the whole ship was going to blow."

"Yup," Brannon said. "Now let's figure out what we're going to do with this prisoner, how we're going to handle him."

"He seems like a fairly decent sort of guy," Olsen said. "Doc said his English is very good."

"It'd have to be good if he got a masters in engineering from Stanford," Brannon said. He paused and chewed at his lower lip. "I know that the Geneva Convention says we aren't supposed to ask him any questions, other than his name and that sort of thing. But if he'd volunteer some information, that might be a help to Fremantle." He motioned to Mahaffey in the galley.

"Please go forward and tell Petreshock that I'd like to see the prisoner."

Petreshock brought the prisoner into the Wardroom. Brannon noted with approval that someone had given the man a pair of dungaree trousers and a shirt and that his feet were shod in submarine sandals. The prisoner stepped inside the Wardroom and bowed deeply from the waist.

"Sit down, Mr. Yamati," Brannon said. Pete Mahaffey slid a cup of coffee in front of the Japanese, who looked upward and then started to get out of his chair. Petreshock pushed him back down.

"This is for me?" the Japanese asked. "I thank you for your kindness."

"Until we get back to port you'll eat the same food we all eat," Brannon said. "On a submarine in our Navy the officers and men eat the same food. You may have all you want. You may have coffee whenever you want it if there is someone to bring it to you. You can take a shower twice a week, as we all do. You will not be physically mistreated. You will be handcuffed, one hand, to a bunk rail when you sleep or to a torpedo skid when you are sitting. I don't think that is unreasonable."

"It is most generous of you." The prisoner took a long drink of the coffee. "The coffee is excellent, sir."

"Do you smoke?" Olsen asked.

"Yes, sir."

Olsen slid a packet of cigarets across the Wardroom table. The prisoner took a cigaret and lit it from a box of small wooden matches given to him by Petreshock.

"I'd like to talk to you a bit, Mr. Yamati," Brannon said. "Your ship, as the life ring showed, was the *Takasaki*, an oil tanker. You said she displaced ten thousand tons."

"Yes, sir."

"You were bound where?"

"Tokyo, sir."

"Going a little bit out of your way, weren't you?" Olsen said. He slid the cigarets back to the Japanese. "Keep them, I have more. You could have saved a lot of sea miles going up the west coast of the Philippines.''

"Your submarines, sir,'' the prisoner said. ''The west coast of the Philippines is not too dangerous for us, but farther north it is very dangerous.''

"Are you married?'' Brannon said. ''I'm not prying into your personal business, sir. But if you're married we can ask the Red Cross or the Swiss to notify your wife that you are a prisoner of war and safe.''

''I am married, sir,'' the Japanese said. He bowed his head and then raised it. ''My wife lives in San Francisco. She is an American girl I met in college. I have a son, sir. I have never seen him. If it is possible to inform her I would do anything I can for you.''

Olsen slid a piece of paper and a pencil across the table. ''Write her full name and address,'' he said. ''She'll know you're well and safe within seventy-two hours.'' The Japanese unashamedly wiped moisture from his eyes.

''She has not heard from me since the war began,'' he said. ''I had one letter telling me of the birth of our son. Nothing else. I do not know how to thank you, sir.''

''Just behave yourself until we get back to Australia,'' Olsen said. The prisoner rose and bowed to Mike Brannon and to John Olsen. Petreshock took him back to the Forward Torpedo Room and sat him in a canvas chair. The prisoner extended his left arm along a torpedo skid and Petreshock handcuffed him to the skid. He reached upward and opened a small locker and took out several packs of cigarets.

''I'm trying to quit smoking,'' the torpedoman said. ''You can have these. More if you need them. Can't give you any matches, but the man on watch will give you a light.'' The prisoner got to his feet and bowed and sat down.

Brannon's contact report was transmitted that night. It included the conversation with the prisoner. When the report reached Admiral Christie he called a staff meeting.

''I just don't believe what that Jap prisoner said.'' Sam Rivers, the Operations Officer, thumped the table with his thick index finger. ''We know those tankers are heading for Truk. The ship watchers on Borneo and on Celebes have told us so!''

''That's what we think we know,'' Christie said slowly. ''We should know about those tankers. There's two of them still going in that convoy with three destroyers. We should know about them in a few days. We know from Brannon's report the base course they were on approaching the eastern end of Celebes. We know what course they'd take to Truk. And we have seven submarines between the Islands and Truk, waiting for them. One of those submarines should pick them up in a couple of days."

"I still don't know why this guy would volunteer that sort of information," Captain Rivers said. "Damn it, he's a college graduate. Masters degree. Smart. He knows he doesn't have to say anything like that. I think he's trying to help his own side, not us."

"You make a good point," Admiral Christie said. "The only thing we can do is wait. Meanwhile you'd better get a message off to *Eelfish*. Tell them to come home. Route them so they'll run into as little as possible. I don't want that damned ship to tangle with any Jap destroyers with an outer door gone from a tube, and Mike Brannon is the type to tangle with anything and everything he sees."

Two days later, as the Staff sat around the big table in the conference room at the Bend of the Road, a Marine sentry rapped on the door. He handed Admiral Christie an envelope marked "Urgent." The Admiral waited until the sentry had closed the door behind him and slit the envelope open with a pocket knife. He read the message and looked down the table.

"This just came in from Cy Austin in the *Redfin*," he said. "A tanker convoy, two tankers escorted by three destroyers came right down Cy's track off the east coast of Samar. The convoy was moving north at twelve knots. Cy went in on the surface at night and got three hits in a tanker that was listing to starboard. The other tanker and the three destroyers went over the hill. North over the hill. Cy tried to chase but he was driven down by planes. He thinks the planes came out of Tacloban." Admiral Christie looked around the table.

"That prisoner Brannon's got was telling the truth. Brannon reported getting a hit in one tanker that got away, listing to starboard. His report said the hit he got in that tanker was a low-order explosion. This is without any doubt the same damned convoy and it sure as hell isn't headed for Truk!" He pushed his chair back and stood up.

"If we've been wrong about where those tankers out of Balikpapan are going we've got seven submarines out there on the route to Truk and the only thing they're going to be doing is to send weather reports." He stopped, his face grim.

"We'll do some talking about this after dinner. Meet me here at nineteen hundred. Sam, get Austin's contact report off to Pearl with an urgent on it for the Ultra people. Something is awfully screwy in Denmark.''

''Or in Borneo,'' Sam Rivers muttered.

CHAPTER 9

The orders from Fremantle routed the *Eelfish* down the eastern side of Celebes Island through the Molucca and Banda Seas and then westward along the north side of the archipelago called the Lesser Sunda Islands to Lombok Strait. Mike Brannon walked into the Wardroom and sat down. He yawned hugely, and John Olsen moved his charts to one side so Mahaffey could put a cup of coffee in front of Brannon.

''How's the route home look?'' Brannon said.

''They've given us three different days, three times when we can enter Lombok Strait,'' Olsen said. ''I figure if we can run on the surface for a couple of days, and we should be able to do that, we can make the first ETA for Lombok.'' He indicated the thin pencil line he had drawn on the chart.

Brannon pulled the chart around in front of him. ''We should be able to run some of the way on the surface. At least down to the point where we turn west. I don't think there's much, if any, shipping on the east side of Celebes. No reason to be.

''That brings up the danger of sunburn. The lookouts, none of us, have seen much daylight this trip. You'd better issue an order for shirts and hats to be worn while topside. I don't suppose that Doc Wharton has got any suntan lotion in that magic box of his.''

''I mentioned that to him before you woke up, sir. He says he's got cocoa butter for burns and he's got iodine and that he can make a good suntan lotion out of that stuff. I never heard of that but he says it works.''

Brannon grinned. ''I guess they'd think we were crazy if we tried to draw suntan lotion as part of our supplies. Who ever heard of needing suntan lotion on a submarine?'' He looked around as a very gentle rap sounded on the bulkhead beside the green curtain that served as a door.

"Permission to speak to the Captain?" Steve Petreshock's face appeared through the curtain.

"Of course, Steve," Brannon said. "Come in. Sit down."

Petreshock leaned over the Wardroom table. "I'd like to keep it low, sir. Don't want my voice to carry up forward. It's about the prisoner, Captain."

"What about him?"

"Well, sir, he's getting awfully friendly. He sits with me on watch, on the four to eights, sir. I okayed that because I thought he was kind of lonely, maybe a little scared about what's going to happen to him.

"So I encouraged him to talk a little, to tell me about going to school in the States, his wife, that sort of thing. It sort of led from one thing to another and he's told me about how it was in Japan after he went back for his mother's funeral, all about his old man. He really thinks a lot of his old man. About how they drafted him into the Merchant Marine and how it is there, the living and the working on the oil tankers he's served on.

"After I'd get off watch and go back aft I'd write down everything I could remember he said." He reached in his shirt pocket and took out a thick packet of paper and put it on the table.

"Lot of stuff in there about Balikpapan and the oil they get from there, Captain. I thought some of it might be useful to you."

"I think it might be," Brannon said. "Thank you. Keep listening to him. Write down whatever he says, no matter even if it's about girls or food or anything."

"There's something else, Captain. He's sort of opening up real good now with me and with the guys who live in my room. I figured if maybe we could let him eat in the Crew's Mess, I'd be with him all the time as a sort of guard, I figured with all the guys around him he might open up even more. I didn't push him, but this morning he started to tell me about how many times he'd been in convoys that were attacked by submarines and what their orders were when they got attacked. I figured that if all hands were tipped off to treat him good that he might really open up."

Brannon looked at Olsen, who nodded approvingly.

"Sounds all right to me," Brannon said. "But what sort of reason are you going to give him for changing the way he eats, for letting him go back to regular chow?"

"I thought a little about that," Petreshock said. "He's a sailor and he's an officer. He's pretty bright. I'll just tell him that he's the first prisoner we ever had and that we didn't realize that he was no danger in the mess hall at chow time and that it would be easier on us, on my people, if one of them didn't have to carry his chow tray to him. He washes his dishes in the sink in the room, sir. Says that one of us shouldn't have to clean up after him. I think he'll think everything's okay.''

"Keep coaxing him to talk a little but don't push it," Brannon said. "John, you'd better get hold of the Chiefs and tell them what's going on and have them coach their people to treat the prisoner nice and to talk with him but not try to interrogate him or anything like that.''

The crew, as Petreshock had anticipated, welcomed the prisoner at the mess table. His fluent command of English, his obvious pleasure at being out of the war, and his keen engineering interest in the *Eelfish* led him to recount funny stories about his undergraduate days at Stanford. He began to tell stories about his shipmates in Japan's Merchant Marine, how one day a lookout on a tanker he was serving on threw an entire convoy into panic when he sighted a periscope. Later, after heavy depth charging, a dead whale came to the surface. The lookout had seen the whale spouting and had mistaken the gust of spray from the whale's blowhole for a periscope. Scotty Rudolph got into the act, asking the prisoner for Japanese recipes and very carefully writing down what the prisoner told him. After each meal Petreshock took the prisoner back to the Forward Torpedo Room and shackled him to a torpedo skid and then went back to the Crew's Mess to write down everything the prisoner had said, aided by Scotty Rudolph, whose ear for gossip—a faculty shared by most ship's cooks— and whose memory spurred Petreshock's own memory of what had been said.

Eelfish ran on the surface for two days and nights through seas empty of Japanese shipping. As the submarine approached the Lesser Sunda Islands Brannon gave the order to submerge during the daylight hours so enemy air patrols wouldn't spot them. It was an hour past noon on the second all-day dive when Perry Arbuckle motioned to the Quartermaster of the Watch to raise the search periscope for the hourly check on sea and sky. He swung the periscope around and gasped.

"Captain! Captain to the Conning Tower!''

Brannon scrambled out of the Wardroom and ran into the Control Room and up the ladder to the Conning Tower.

"What have you got?''

"Snakes, sir! Millions of snakes, long brown snakes with yellow bellies all over the ocean! They're swimming with us!"

Brannon looked through the periscope and saw that the surface of the sea was covered by a mass of sea snakes, all swimming steadily westward. He shuddered and recoiled as the periscope lens brought a snake's head into close view.

"My God!" he muttered. "Imagine swimming in the middle of those things. I'll bet they're poisonous, too." He turned and went to the ladder, and started to descend. "Next time, Perry, try to pick up something we can shoot at. I'm going to get a few hours' sleep." He grinned at the Reserve Officer and went down the ladder.

An hour later Arbuckle walked to the periscope and waited for the Quartermaster to raise the long steel tube. He put his eye to the lens and froze.

"Captain to the Conning Tower!" Arbuckle's voice was hardly more than an agonized croak. Mike Brannon, roused from a deep sleep, stumbled through the Control Room and climbed to the Conning Tower.

"Not more damned snakes!" he grumbled. He put his face to the big rubber eyepiece on the periscope and the Quartermaster saw his shoulder muscles bunch up.

There, almost dead ahead of the *Eelfish,* a submarine was lying, fully surfaced. He twisted the periscope handle to bring the submarine focus and saw the insignia on the side of the Conning Tower: U-135.

"Down periscope!" Brannon snapped. "Sound General Quarters. Rig for silent running. Set all torpedo depths two feet. Open the torpedo-tube outer doors." He waited, fidgeting, listening to the small noises of the crew hastening to their battle stations. John Olsen, a battle telephone set hung around his neck, climbed three steps of the ladder into the Conning Tower.

"All battle stations manned, sir. Torpedo depth set two feet. Torpedo tube doors open. Sonar is manned. The Plotting Party is standing by."

"Sonar reports no contact," Paul Blake said from the after end of the Conning Tower.

"Up battle 'scope," Brannon said to Brosmer. The Quartermaster punched the button that controlled the battle periscope and the oily tube slid upward. Brannon went to his knees and caught the two handles of the periscope as they rose above the deck, snapped them outward, and rode the scope upward, his eye at the lens.

"Mark!" Brosmer looked upward.

"Bearing is three five zero." Brannon heard the gears in the TDC clicking as Arbuckle cranked in the bearing.

"Range is one zero zero zero, one thousand yards. Angle on the bow is zero eight zero port. There's a lot of people on the deck and the bridge of that damned sub! They're staring into the water."

"You've got a solution," Arbuckle said from the TDC.

"Stand by Forward . . . My Irish oath! A damned U-boat in this ocean . . . stand by."

"Fire one!" He counted down from six to one.

"Fire two!"

"Both torpedoes running hot, straight, and normal." Blake's voice was loud in the Conning Tower. Brannon hung on the periscope handles staring at the enemy submarine. He saw a man on the bridge of the submarine suddenly wave his arms and point at the surface of the sea. There was a flurry of activity among the men on the deck of the submarine and then the first torpedo from the *Eelfish* hit the U-boat and exploded with a great gout of water and fire. Seconds later the second torpedo slammed home into the heeling submarine and blew it apart.

"Two hits!" Brannon yelled. He pulled the periscope around in a 360-degree search for other ships.

"Come to forty feet," he called down the hatch. "I want a radar search." He waited as the *Eelfish* planed upward. Rafferty, manning the radar, reported no contacts other than two small ones bearing three five eight.

"Those are the target," Brannon said. "Stand by to surface. Chief of the Boat to the Conning Tower with a boathook and a safety line. Two seamen to the Conning Tower for deck rescue party. Maybe we can get another prisoner."

The *Eelfish* surged upward, and Brannon climbed the ladder to the bridge hatch, hanging on with one hand, turning the wheel that undogged the hatch with the other. He heard Jerry Gold say "Twenty feet, sir," and he pushed the hatch open, gasping as the residual water in the bridge flooded down the hatch.

Ahead of the *Eelfish* the German U-boat had broken into two pieces, its stern rising out of the water before it began to slide down to the sea bottom. Flanagan climbed over the bridge rail followed by two seamen.

"Chief," Brannon yelled over the bridge rail, "if we can get a prisoner I want one. For God's sake don't fall over the side, don't even get down on the pressure hull." Flanagan looked at the water and drew back. The surface of the sea was alive with long, sinuous, swimming snakes.

The submarine's bullnose eased slowly through the snake-covered water as Brannon conned the *Eelfish* toward a mass of debris on the surface. He raised his binoculars and searched the debris. He saw shattered bodies, pieces of what looked like mattresses, and other debris. Flanagan and the two seamen, trotting up and down the deck looking at the water, searched for a survivor but saw none.

"You see anyone alive, Chief?" Brannon called down to the deck. Flanagan shook his head.

"Deck party below," Brannon ordered. He waited until Flanagan dropped down the hatch and then moved to the port side of the bridge to get out of the way.

"Clear the bridge," he ordered and as the Quartermaster followed the lookouts down the ladder he punched the diving klaxon button twice and dropped through the hatch opening, pulling the hatch closed.

"Sixty-five feet," he ordered. He turned to Perry Arbuckle. "Make a continuous periscope observation for the next ten minutes. Then go to one hundred feet and resume regular submerged patrol. Periscope observations on the hour. I want the sonar manned for the next hour. Stand easy on Battle Stations. Smoking lamp is lighted. Close torpedo tube outer doors." He went down the ladder to the Control Room where John Olsen was standing at the gyro table with the plotting party. Brannon picked up a telephone and thumbed the button that connected him with all compartments.

"This is the Captain," he said. "An hour or so ago Mr. Arbuckle saw an ocean full of swimming snakes. A few minutes ago he saw a German U-boat, lying to on the surface with a lot of people on deck. I assume those people on the German submarine were looking at the snakes. We scored two hits on the U-135, and it broke in two and went down. We searched for survivors and found none." He put the phone down and turned to Olsen.

"Damned submarine was just sitting there, John. She was lying to. Half of the crew must have been on the deck. Looked like a Sunday afternoon at New London."

"We don't have much of a plot, sir," Olsen said. "Just the firing data and the one set of bearings and range."

"Didn't need much," Brannon grinned. "I saw one guy on the bridge begin to wave his arms. I think he must have seen the wake of the first torpedo because the people on deck began to mill around just before the fish hit. I didn't see anyone jump over the side, though, so I don't know what he was waving at."

"Hell of a choice," Olsen said. "Jump over the side into a mess of big snakes or stand still and get hit with a torpedo."

Admiral Christie read the *Eelfish* contact report the next morning at a breakfast meeting of his staff.

"That's the second U-boat that's gone north into the Java Sea out of the Indian Ocean," the Operations Officer said. "And it's the second one we've sunk." He grinned at the Admiral.

"I thought Mike Brannon had run out of Irish luck after he lost that outer door. So we order him to come home and he bags a German U-boat!"

"That part in the *Eelfish* contact report about the sea being covered with snakes, big snakes," the Operations Officer said, squirming in his chair. "I hate snakes!" His assistant, a chubby Commander, looked up from his plate of ham and eggs.

"You're in the right part of the world for snakes, sir. Australia is the only continent where there are more venomous snakes than harmless ones."

"Belay the small talk," Christie said. "We've got a lot of work to do." He looked at his Staff Engineer.

"What about repairs to the *Eelfish*? How long?"

"Can't say, Admiral. Can't tell until she gets here. We don't know if she's lost the outer door. We don't know if there's any damage to the tube itself. Have to wait until she's here and we can send a man over the side to look. If she needs a new door, if the tube is okay, we'll have to order a door from New London and have it flown out. That's one thing we don't stock in spare parts, a new outer door for a torpedo tube."

"Have you ordered a new door?"

"No, sir."

"Well, damn it, order one! *Eelfish* won't be in here for another nine, ten days. By that time maybe we can have a new door here."

The Staff Engineer shook his head slowly. "Sir, I'll bet you a new set of khakis that when we get all the paperwork done and air mail it there the people on the other end will tell us that we have a Class Z priority and that they can't ship the damned door until there's a full moon or some other damn fool thing."

"Never mind exercising your boundless optimism," the Admiral said. "Get the order in by radio, not air mail."

"Yes, sir," the Staff Engineer said. Admiral Christie looked around the table.

"I can't fault Mike Brannon for that casualty on the outer door. With Mark Fifteen torpedoes in the after tubes it can happen. It did. But he had a damned good patrol all the same. One tanker down, a good big one, a prisoner who speaks good English and who's talking a blue streak, and a German submarine. He deserves a medal for this one."

"He deserves a kick in his big Irish ass," Captain Sam Rivers, the Admiral's Operations Officer grumbled. "Three nice fat tankers coming along in a row. The nearest escort way back on the flank and he gets only one of the tankers. He should have got at least two."

Admiral Christie grinned at Captain Rivers. "Sam, I do believe we'll send you out on a war patrol. When you bag a great big Jap cruiser we'll hold an ass-kicking ceremony on the dock because you didn't get a battleship! You are the hardest damned man to please I ever saw!"

The *Eelfish* eased carefully into a berth alongside the submarine farthest outboard of the submarine tender in Fremantle, and Admiral Christie bounded over the gangway.

"Damned fine patrol, Mike," the Admiral boomed. "Shame you had that casualty, but you did a damned fine job." The Admiral pumped Brannon's hand and the two men walked forward on the deck.

"We've got the prisoner below, sir," Brannon said. "He talked a blue streak, especially after we sank the U-boat. I've had all that typed up and it's with my patrol report. I hate to say this about the enemy but I have to, sir. He's a very nice guy. Very nice. I wouldn't want to see him thrown into some crummy jail cell or strung up by the thumbs. What will they do with him?"

"Our intelligence people here want to have some long talks with him," Admiral Christie said. "We notified his wife, you know. I wrote her a letter. Once our people here are through with him he'll be sent back to the States and put in a federal prison. Probably near 'Frisco I'd think. That way his wife could visit him."

A Chief Warrant Torpedoman followed by two Chief Torpedomen came down the gangway and picked their way throug the *Eelfish* crew, who were sitting on deck, eating fruit and reading their mail. The Chief Warrant spotted Flanagan and the trio came up to him.

"Monk," the Chief Warrant said, "Good to see you. What the hell happened in the After Room?" He turned to the two Chiefs with him.

"This is Chief Torpedoman Monk Flanagan, Chief of the Boat. Monk, Randy Nuthall and Bob Wilson. They're my tube experts. Can we go down to the After Room?"

"Glad to meet you," Flanagan said to the two Chiefs. "Have to use the Engine Room hatch, Mr. Glover. We've got the reload fish for Number Seven in the middle of the room. Can't get down the hatch."

He led the way, and when the other three men finished scrambling under the reload torpedo and stood up at the after end of the room, Chief Warrant Pines said, "Why don't you start at the beginning, Monk?"

Flanagan nodded and told how the tube had been fired, the noise the runaway torpedo had made in the tube, and how he and Fred Nelson had decided to get the fish out of the tube.

"How in the hell did you get a line around the tail of that damned fish?" Wilson said. "My God, the screws turning up maximum rpms, the hot exhaust gases?"

"You take a look at the screws back there on that fish," Flanagan said. "That steel cable all wrapped up in the screws, that's how we did it. We didn't have to pull the damned thing out of the tube. The Jap dropped a charge right above our bow. You can see the damage up there when you go topside. The boat took a down angle by the bow and this fish came sliding out. Jammed its busted-up screws in the bulkhead to the Engineering Log Room. Then we had to jockey the damned fish out of the bulkhead and then move the after end of the skid over and pull the fish away from the tube so's we could get the inner door closed. It wasn't what I'd call a picnic."

"Water coming in all the time?" Wilson asked. Flanagan nodded. "Got to be waist deep before we got the inner door shut. Helluva mess."

"How many of you back here?" Chief Nuthall asked.

"The Gunnery Officer, he's a Reserve named Lee, Fred Nelson, the guy who has the After Room and me. They bled high-pressure air into the room to keep the water down, but it didn't do much good. The Old Man had to wait until the tin can up above would drop charges, and then he'd put the drain pump on the line and get some water out."

"What about the outer door?" Warrant Glover asked. "Is it still there?"

"I don't think so," Flanagan said. "Nelson didn't hear it banging or anything on the way home. I'd bet it's gone."

"The Squadron Office told me something about the warhead being armed," Glover said

"The stream of water coming out of the tube spun the impeller and armed the exploder," Flanagan said. "We dropped it out and disarmed it."

"You've had a lot of experience taking exploders out of warheads," Mr. Glover said with a crooked grin.

"Mr. Glover." Flanagan's face was set, expressionless, as he looked at the shorter man. "Between you and me and these other two Chiefs we all know damned well that the Mark Six exploder doesn't work the way it's supposed to work. You got to know that every boat that goes to sea out of Australia is modifying the exploder to work on contact. And you know something else. It's all a bunch of fucking nonsense. Pearl Harbor modifies the torpedo exploders for contact before they give them to the boats. But out here, shit!" He laid a hand on the warhead of a reload torpedo. "The way this room is, full of fish, partly flooded, we couldn't change the exploders back to the way we got them."

The Chief Warrant Torpedoman looked at Flanagan, the crooked grin still in place. "You figure you're looking at a court-martial? Stop worrying. The big boss over in Brisbane, Admiral Carpender, he's been relieved. Admiral Kinkaid took over. He's an old buddy of Admiral Nimitz. Admiral Kinkaid has put out the word, and when he puts out the word you obey. The exploders will be modified in the shop before you get them.

"Admiral Christie's no dummy. He's whipped and he knows it. As of now you don't have to go through that crap of modifying the exploders and then changing them back on the way home.

"Now what the hell else is wrong with this fish? At least you got the bastard shut down, and it looks like the air flask and the after body might be okay. No discoloration in the metal that I can see."

"The tail cone has got to be all messed up inside," Flanagan said. "When I got that wire into the screws I know it chewed up the idler and the bevel gears. The gyro is okay. We took it out and checked it and stowed it away. I'd guess the depth and steering engines might be okay. I don't know about the main engine.

"The warhead split when it hit the outer door. It's been leaking exudate. We sealed the split with Tacki-wax, but I guess you'll have to deep-six the warhead." He paused.

"Okay for me to tell the Old Man about the exploders? He's kinda worried."

"I don't see why not," Warrant Glover said. "I knew Mike Brannon when he was a cub, down in Panama. He's good people. Just tell him to act surprised when he gets the official word."

"We'll go over the side tomorrow morning," Chief Wilson said. "Take a look at the door area of the tube. If nothing's busted up we can hang a new door for you as soon as we get it. When we got a copy of your Skipper's message I told 'em we didn't have a spare door. But they fucked around for three days. Then the paperwork took another three days. You know what the Navy is like.

"If we're lucky we should have a door in another three, maybe four weeks. Then we got to requisition dry-dock space for you. No telling how that will come out. We might get you in dock the next day, might take a week or two. That shouldn't make you too hot under the collar. The beer is awful good here, and the ladies are something out of this world."

"If you want to drop by for lunch at the CPO quarters on the tender tomorrow," Chief Nuthall said, "We could give you a report on what that tube looks like. If you're interested."

"I'm interested," Flanagan said. He led the way up to the deck. John Olsen saw him climb out of the Engine Room hatch and beckoned to him.

"You'd better get the prisoner ready for transfer, Chief. They're taking him to our intelligence people at the Bend of the Road. But this is an Australian port and we have to observe protocol; they're sending a squad of Aussie soldiers to take him over there. Make sure he's in clean clothes and tell him to be on his best behavior."

Flanagan stood to one side as the prisoner climbed out of the Forward Torpedo Room hatch, blinking in the bright sunshine. He walked slowly down the deck, speaking to crew members, shaking hands. At the gangway a small, wiry Australian Army sergeant had drawn his squad up in formation. He extended a sheaf of papers to Flanagan.

"Just sign this top one, cobber," the sergeant said to Flanagan. "I keep that one to show you turned this bastard over to me. The others are for your office wallahs to file away. Thank you, cobber, and now we'll take this slant-eyed bastard to your people.'' He grinned evilly at the prisoner, and Flanagan felt a shiver of premonition.

"You will go with these people to our headquarters,'' he said to the Japanese. "I wish you luck.'' The prisoner bowed from the waist.

"You have treated me humanely and with much kindness,'' he said. "I offer you my hope you survive the war and live in peace and happiness.'' He bowed again and turned to the squad and smiled.

"Good morning, gentlemen. A nice day for a walk.''

"I'll good morning you, you yellow son of a bitch!'' A soldier in the squad reversed his rifle, raising it, aiming the steel-shod rifle butt at the prisoner's head. He drew back his arms to smash the prisoner's head as Flanagan started toward him.

"Hold it soldier!'' Mike Brannon's voice was a whip. The soldier turned, his rifle still upraised, and looked at Brannon, who was standing on the cigaret deck.

"Ground that rifle and come to attention, soldier!'' Brannon roared. He climbed down from the cigaret deck and walked, stiff-legged, his eyes flaming, to the Australian sergeant.

"Identify yourself, Sergeant. Name. Rank. Unit. Name of your commanding officer.'' Brannon took a piece of paper and a pen from his breast pocket and wrote, as the sergeant, standing stiffly at attention, carefully gave the identification Brannon had demanded.

"This is an American prisoner,'' Brannon said slowly. "American. Not Australian. He will be treated by you in full accordance with the Geneva Convention Articles of War. You will escort him to our headquarters as instructed. You will do so without harming him in any way. I am going to telephone as soon as you leave and a doctor will be on hand to examine him. If there is one mark on him, one mark, Sergeant, I'll have you court-martialed and shot! Is that clear?''

The Australian looked into Brannon's blazing eyes.

"Perfectly clear, sir.'' He saluted, his hand quivering at his hat brim in the approved Australian manner.

"Beggin' your pardon, sir,'' he said. "These chaps of mine, me, we fought in New Guinea, sir. We know what the Jap did to our nurses when they captured them. I can't blame any of my chaps for wanting to brain this bast— . . . this prisoner, sir.''

Brannon returned the Australian's defiant stare. "I think I know how you feel. Bear in mind that this prisoner was not at New Guinea. He is not a Japanese soldier. He is an officer in their Merchant Marine. Based on his conduct aboard my ship I am confident that he will make no effort to hinder you in your work or to escape. Which means that if you report that you had to shoot him dead because he tried to escape I will still have you court-martialed. Carry out your orders, Sergeant." He returned the sergeant's salute and watched the squad form around the prisoner, each man carefully keeping his distance, and march up the gangway and into the submarine tender. He turned to John Olsen, who had come to the gangway.

"We brought that fellow so damned far and got so much out of him and they'd have killed him on my own quarterdeck!"

Olsen nodded. "I don't think the Aussies will ever forget the atrocities the Japs committed against their nurses. I don't think they should forget. It was a beastly, evil thing to do."

"Let's get the Chief of the Boat started on getting the crew ready to go ashore," Brannon said. "We, you and I and Bob Lee, have got to sit down with Admiral Christie and his staff this afternoon." He turned to go down the deck, and John LaMark, who had the gangway watch, spoke in a low voice.

"If that Aussie had moved that rifle butt one inch toward the prisoner's head I'd've shot the son of a bitch in the kneecap!"

"Gunner," Brannon said, "the forty-five pistol the deck watch carries is supposed to be unloaded."

"Yes, sir," LaMark said. "I musta forgot that order, sir." He pulled the gun from its holster and pointed the muzzle skyward and released the clip. He put the clip in his pocket, worked the slide, and caught the live cartridge as it was ejected from the gun.

"Full clip and one up the spout," Olsen said in a dry tone of voice. "Gunner, you're a bad man, you know that?"

CHAPTER 10

Flanagan rapped at the bulkhead outside Brannon's stateroom and went through the green curtain in response to Brannon's reply. Brannon turned from the washbasin and the small locker above it where he was packing his shaving gear.

"Chief Warrant Glover came aboard with a couple of his Chiefs, tube experts, a while ago, Captain. They'll look at the tube tomorrow morning. I guess the two Chiefs will go over the side with shallow-water diving gear. I'm coming back to the tender for the noon meal and they'll give me a report then."

"I'd appreciate it if you get in touch with me," Brannon said, and Flanagan nodded.

"There's something else, sir. You're not supposed to know it so when you get told, Mr. Glover would be happy if you look surprised.

"Admiral Carpender over in Brisbane has been relieved and a new Admiral, Kincaid, has taken over. He's issued orders to modify the Mark Six exploders, just like they do in Pearl. Mr. Glover, I knew him a long time ago when I was Second Class and he was a Chief Torpedoman, he says not to worry about our exploders back aft not being put back the way they were."

Brannon smiled. "Ah, that's a load off my mind, Chief. What about the tube door, have they got one?"

"No, sir. They've ordered one from New London. What will happen, I guess, is that they'll scavenge a door from a boat they're just starting to build. One of the Chiefs said it might be three, four weeks getting here, and when it gets here, not before he said, then they'll requisition time for us in the dry dock so they can hang it. Provided the tube itself hasn't been damaged."

Brannon cleaned out the small locker over the washbowl and packed the shaving gear in his bag. "Looks like we're going to be here awhile. I don't like it but there's nothing we can do about that.

"I've told Mr. Gold to muster the crew when the buses get here. That will be just before noon. Mr. Olsen and Mr. Lee and I have to go to a debriefing at headquarters. One of the Staff officers told me that the paymaster will be in the hotel lobby right after the noon meal at the hotel. Keep the crew together until everyone's been paid. And please get in touch with me after you talk to the two Chiefs tomorrow."

"Will do, sir," Flanagan said.

The Operations Officer, his lined face grim above the silver eagles on his collar tabs, turned to face Mike Brannon.

"The point is, Captain Brannon, you damn well know that you disobeyed orders and modified those torpedo exploders. Your patrol report conveniently leaves out the depth setting for the torpedoes. You people must think we're idiots! You know your orders; you are to set torpedoes to run at a depth of from five to ten feet below the estimated draft of the target so the magnetic exploder will detonate the warhead beneath the target and break its keel. You fired two torpedoes at the first tanker and missed. You fired two at the second tanker and got one hit. That's damned bad shooting, Mister!''

"We got a hit on the first tanker, sir," Brannon said. His normally pleasant face was set and grim. "I observed a low-magnitude explosion against the starboard bow of the first target. I so reported in my contact report and my patrol run report. I observed a hit and exploder failure against the hull of the second tanker. The second torpedo fired at that target worked and the target blew up. Three hits out of four torpedoes is not, I submit, bad shooting.''

John Olsen, sitting beside Brannon at the table in the conference room of the headquarters building, could feel the chill in the air. Bob Lee, sitting beside Olsen, stirred restlessly. Olsen turned his head as Brannon took a deep breath.

"With all due respect, Captain Rivers, I am not going to argue about the Mark Six exploders. Too many submarine commanding officers have already done that. I can add nothing to that argument. You must know, again with all due respect to Admiral Christie, to you and the Staff, sir, you must know that most submarine Captains have very little faith in the Mark Six exploder.''

"You are coming dangerously close to insubordination, sir!'' Captain Rivers's harsh face was set, his eyes blazing.

"With all due respect, sir, I am a ship's captain—''

"At our pleasure," Captain Rivers snapped.

"Yes, sir," Brannon said. "I submit that I intended no insubordination. If I gave that impression then I apologize for stating my thoughts in a clumsy manner.'' Brannon stared past the close-cropped head of the Operations Officer, his eyes looking out the window at the lush greenery of the grounds.

"Sam, let me say a few words," Admiral Christie said from his place at the head of the table.

"Mike, I helped develop the Mark Six exploder, as you know. I helped develop the Mark Fourteen torpedo. I know that the exploder, the torpedo, work. If the approach to the target is made correctly, if the observations by the Commanding Officer are accurate, if the torpedoes are fired to run at the correct depth, if those torpedoes have been properly cared for—remember that part, Mike, because I am going to come back to that—if all those things are done I know that we have a torpedo and an exploder that are far superior to those of any other submarine navy in the world!

"Now let me say this, and what I am going to say does not apply to you or to the *Eelfish*.

"I have submarines come into this port and into Brisbane with their torpedoes so poorly maintained that those torpedoes would not have run if fired. I have seen some torpedoes with alcohol and water tanks half full. They wouldn't have run five hundred yards if they were fired.

"I have seen relief crews rig block and tackle and have to use the tender's crane, sir, to get torpedoes out of the tubes! The tube rollers were so poorly cared for that the torpedoes were literally frozen in the tubes. If they had been fired they wouldn't have even gone out of the torpedo tubes!"

"Sir," Bob Lee blurted out, "sir, every torpedo on the *Eelfish* is pulled out of the tubes and routined on a regular maintenance schedule. Every torpedo we have will leave the tube and run properly when it is fired!" His eyes widened and then squeezed shut as he suddenly realized what he had done. He, a Reserve Lieutenant, Junior Grade, had interrupted an Admiral, had spoken without being asked, had dared to contradict an Admiral.

Admiral Christie, his square jaw set, stared at Lee. Then the Admiral's glare softened.

"Well said, youngster. I am delighted to hear that." He turned to look at Mike Brannon.

"You see my point. I am faced with constant criticism of the Mark Six exploder and the Mark Fourteen torpedo by submarine Captains.

"I am faced, also, with the disturbing fact that some of those who criticize the loudest come into port with torpedoes that I know will not run if fired, not run properly." He lowered his head and stared at the table top for a long minute. Then he raised his head.

"Perhaps there is justification for criticism on both sides. Whatever there is, it is ended as of today. The Mark Six exploders will be modified in the shop before you get them. And I will relieve at once any Commanding Officer who does not command as he should, who is not sufficiently aggressive against the enemy.

"Now that we have passed that barrier, I want to commend you, Mike, Olsen, for the cleanliness of the *Eelfish*." He nodded his head toward Bob Lee. "And you, sir, for the excellence of the torpedoes you brought back and your conduct during that casualty in the After Room. That's what we want to hear about next; will you tell us, in full detail, Mike, what went on back there?''

Brannon wet his lips and nodded. He carefully went through each step of the casualty, from the accidental firing of the torpedo in Number Seven tube to the disarming of the exploder and the removal of the fulminate of mercury cartridge.

''You must have had a helluva time keeping a decent trim with the After Room flooding and under depth-charge attack,'' Captain Rivers said.

''Mr. Olsen and Lieutenant Jerry Gold, who is my Battle Stations Diving Officer, performed flawlessly. As did Lieutenant Lee, who stayed in the After Room when it was flooding.''

''I've looked over your recommendations for medals, Mike,'' Admiral Christie said. ''I'm awarding Silver Stars to Olsen, Lee, and Gold and to Chief Torpedoman Flanagan and First Class Torpedoman Nelson.'' He looked up from the papers in front of him and grinned.

''Now tell me, Mike, what in the hell did you think you were accomplishing by getting under that warhead and catching the exploder?''

''I don't really know, sir,'' Brannon answered. ''I guess I thought it was my duty, something I should do to share in the risk of the operation.''

''Oh, hell!'' Captain Rivers snorted. ''If the damned warhead had blown, every warhead in the torpedo room would have exploded in a sympathetic explosion and the whole ship would have been blown to bits!''

''But it didn't happen,'' Christie said with a grin. ''I've awarded you the Navy Cross, Mike. The medal ceremonies will be held after the R and R period. My yeoman will be in touch with you. Now let's hear about this U-boat sighting. I looked over your contact and patrol reports, and you didn't even have a preliminary plot. Hold it until we get a fresh pot of coffee.'' He nodded at a junior staff officer, who rose from the table and went to the door. After a mess cook had delivered the coffee and left the room the Admiral nodded at Brannon.

Brannon went through the incident slowly and carefully. Admiral Christie shook his head when Brannon told him of being called to the Conning Tower because the surface of the ocean was covered with swimming snakes.

''Must have been a terrible sight,'' Christie said.

''Yes, sir,'' Brannon said. ''Eerie is the word that came to mind at the time." When he had finished describing the sinking of the U-boat, the Operations Officer spoke.

"The Germans have a few U-boats in the Indian Ocean. They never bother us. Once in a great while we get a report of one of them as far east as Bali. The one you sighted and sank was only the second one to ever go through Lombok and into the Java Sea that we know about."

"The other one was sunk by a Dutch submarine skipper," Christie said. "Captain Goosens got the U-168 coming out of Surabaya and sank it and took survivors aboard. Two for two is about as good a batting average as you can get. Hard on the U-boats though." He stood up, and his staff stood up with him.

"Thank you for coming by, Captain Brannon, gentlemen. Enjoy your R and R." He looked at Bob Lee, a small smile showing on his lips. "And you, sir, always defend your Captain when you're right." He stretched, the strain of the burdens he carried showing in his face.

Seated in the car that took them away from the Bend of the Road, Olsen reached over and shook Brannon's hand.

"Congratulations, Mike! A Navy Cross! By God, you deserve it. And thanks for putting me in for a Silver Star."

"I put in for a Navy Cross for you, John, and for Bob and Flanagan and Nelson; you for your work as the Executive and Plotting Officer and Bob, Flanagan, and Fred for what they did in the After Room. They told me when I met with Captain Rivers before we all went in there that you would get a Silver Star, that your time was coming. Bob got knocked down to a Silver Star because he's not Regular Navy, he's a Reserve. Flanagan and Nelson got reduced to a Silver Star because they're enlisted men and they didn't die. Captain Rivers doesn't believe in giving medals to enlisted men if he can avoid it. I'm sorry my recommendations didn't carry much weight."

"I'm grateful, Captain," Lee said. "Silver Star or Navy Cross, neither one is going to count when I hang out my shingle as an attorney after the war."

"That's right, you're a lawyer, aren't you?" Olsen asked.

"Yes, sir," Lee said. "I passed my bar exam for California, and then the Navy reached out and said the proper place for a young lawyer was on a submarine. I'm sort of glad they did. I like the *Eelfish,* I like you people."

"It must have cost Admiral Christie an awful lot to admit his pet exploder isn't working the way he thought it would work,"

Brannon said slowly. "I admire that man. It took an awful lot of backbone to face up to that. I don't think I could have done it."

"He's a pretty good dude, for an Admiral," Olsen said. "He could have jumped all over rambunctious Bob when he spoke up in defense of our torpedoes."

"I could have bitten my tongue off," Lee said.

"You got away with it because Christie is a decent man," Mike Brannon said. "You've used up all your luck in that department. One other thing, John, and you can tell the Chief Petty Officers when you see them: We're going to have to do our own refit this time. The relief crews are overworked at this particular time, several boats are in or are coming in, and because we're going to have to wait for that outer door they decided our people would do their own overhaul."

"Going to be some unhappy sailors," Olsen said. "Not that we've got much to do, other than painting the ship inside and out. That's a big job."

"It won't hurt them," Brannon said.

Flanagan found Chiefs Nuthall and Wilson in the CPO Quarters on the tender. Both men were dressing in front of their lockers.

"We just went over the side and looked at your tube," Wilson said. "The water in this harbor is filthy, you know that?"

"Was the door gone?" Flanagan asked. "How did the tube look?"

"Door's gone clean as a whistle," Nuthall said. "We couldn't have taken it off any cleaner if we had tools. We scraped the paint off all around the hinges and looked for hairline cracks with a light, but we couldn't see anything wrong. We'll do a better job of that once we get you in dry dock."

"Supposing you find a few cracks?" Flanagan said with a grin. "That mean we have to go back to the States?"

"'Fraid not," Wilson said. "What we'd do then is to throw some welds on every crack we could find, hang the door, tack weld it shut, and you'd go to sea with one less torpedo tube. You ready for chow?"

"What are you going to do with the guy who fired that fish in the tube?" Nuthall said as the three men sat down at a table covered with snowy linen and laid with china that was decorated with the name of the submarine tender.

"You gonna transfer him and give him to us, in the relief crew?"

"I don't think so," Flanagan said. "He's a good man. Young,

but he's good. Fred Nelson, the guy who has the After Room, wants to keep him. The Old Man is just letting him stew in his own juice for a while. I don't think he'll do anything unless the Staff gets stiff-necked about it." He unfolded a white napkin and laid it in his lap.

"You people live pretty good," he said as he eyed the menu the messcook brought.

"They have to treat us good," Wilson said, a grin splitting his cherubic features. "We're the folk who are winning the war, didn't you know that?"

"I'm glad someone's winning the damned thing," Flanagan said. He looked up at the messcook, who was standing, order pad in hand.

"I'll have a steak, rare, and two fried eggs with the yolks runny, if that isn't too much trouble."

Wilson and Nuthall placed the same order. The messcook left and came back with three salads and a tray of dressings.

"You don't live too bad on the boats," Nuthall said. "From the stores I see going aboard before a patrol run you don't lack for much."

"Food's good," Flanagan said as he spooned dressing over his salad. "But about after ten days the milk is all gone and the eggs are used up and the spuds get soggy and go rotten. Powdered eggs for breakfast aren't my idea of the real thing, let me tell you."

"I always get a kick out of watching you people go for the oranges and apples when you get in," Wilson said.

"I never ate salads before the war," Flanagan replied. "Now I do. The Pharmacist's Mate aboard *Eelfish* told me that I got plenty of sunshine in peacetime. At sea we never see daylight except the first few days out and the last few days coming in. Now I find myself wanting to eat salad, lettuce, tomatoes, stuff like that." He pushed his empty salad plate to one side as the messcook came back pushing a cart on wheels and put a steak with two fried eggs on top of it in front of each man.

"I didn't think you'd make it here for chow," Wilson said slyly. "This Aussie beer is mighty powerful, and the ladies are more so. The combination of the two could make a man forget all about a torpedo tube."

"I took it easy," Flanagan said. He speared a piece of steak, put it in his mouth, and chewed it slowly. "Ate dinner at the hotel, had a couple of beers in the bar, and then I watched the Shore Patrol bring my crew back. Most of them had to be carried in by the Shore Patrol, but there weren't any charges. Kind of unusual.''

"They've got orders to treat you war heroes with velvet gloves,'' Nuthall said. "If the drunk is off a boat in from a war patrol they'll treat him nice and gentle and take him back to his hotel. If he's a tender man, doing duty on this ship or the base, they'll bend a nightstick over his head and throw him in the brig. War is hell, they tell me.''

Flanagan looked with approval at a piece of apple pie with a mound of ice cream melting beside it.

"Mighty fine meal, and I thank you. If you come ashore I'd like to repay you and throw in some beer as well. Now, you got any idea when that outer door will be here? I got to give the word to the Old Man.''

"Nothing definite,'' Wilson said, lighting a cigaret. "We got an acknowledgment this morning that they had the order in New London, and for once the yeoman must not have fucked up because they didn't ask for the requisition to be resubmitted, which is something they do almost all the time when we ask for something.''

"What that means,'' Nuthall said, "is that they will now begin trying to find a door that belongs to some boat that's on the building ways. Once that's done they got to cut orders to get it shipped. Then they got to cut a set of orders to ship it to the West Coast. Once it gets there someone there has got to cut orders to get it flown out to Pearl Harbor.

"When it reaches there they got to cut orders to send it here by air—if some Supply Officer who's queer for having an outer door doesn't grab it and hide it—and when it gets here they got to write up a letter to tell us it's here. Then we have to requisition the door.

"Once they acknowledge the requisition we have to requisition a small lifting crane and a truck and some men and go and get the thing. Then we can hang it for you.''

"Good God!'' Flanagan said.

"You asked me, I told you,'' the submarine tender Chief said. "You can figure about a month to get it, nothing under three weeks. Then, if we're lucky, we'll get you into dry dock, hang the door, and out again in two, three weeks. We can't ask for dry-dock space until we get the door, and if we're unlucky the dry dock will be tied up. But we might be lucky. You never know.''

"It ain't anything to bitch about,'' Wilson said. "The beer is good and the women, well, there just isn't any Aussie men around who aren't all shot to hell or old. They're all fighting somewhere. If you aren't married or even if you are, I've got a broad ashore who's got a cousin who's better lookin' than my broad and willing.''

"I'm not married," Flanagan said. "I tried it once. All she ever did was bitch, bitch, bitch. Got rid of her years ago. Never again."

"I'll drop by your hotel about sixteen thirty, maybe a little before," Wilson said. "I'll take you home and tell the broad I live with to call her cousin."

CHAPTER 11

For most submarine men the two weeks of rest and relaxation the Navy provided in a hotel ashore, the "R & R" period, was a time to unwind, settle minor differences that had grown to major irritations during the long weeks on war patrol, get gloriously drunk, and find a woman to engage in the act of procreation. That act was, of itself, a gesture of defiance to the death all submariners faced when they returned to sea.

Submarine officers were quartered separately from their crews. The Navy's High Command recognized that some of its officers—after all, so many were non-career Reservists—might forget themselves and act in a manner unbecoming an officer and a gentleman. The Navy felt that it was better if enlisted men did not see an officer in his cups or in pursuit of female companionship.

The port Shore Patrol teams that roamed the city day and night were instructed to treat submariners gently, to keep them from making a disturbance, and if need be, take them back to their hotels, where they were turned over to the hotel security guard.

Not all submariners spent their R & R time drinking or searching for women. Some explored the city, walked in the parks, sampled the Australian specialty of a steak topped with two or more fried eggs. Others, who chose to be quartered with hospitable families, fell happily into the family's routine and more often than not smuggled a case of Nestlé Instant Coffee out of the submarine base as a reward for their generous hosts.

Chief Monk Flanagan came down to breakfast a week after the R & R period had started. He had a dull ache in the back of his head, the result of some solitary beer drinking in his room the night before. Paul Blake saw him and waved. Flanagan walked over to his table and sat down.

"Morning, Chief," Blake said. "I don't know what this cold yellow fruit is, but it sure is good. I've had some for breakfast every morning."

"It's sliced mango," Flanagan said. "Tropical fruit. We used to buy mangoes from kids in Manila, before the war. Cost five centavos each, that's two for a nickel, our money."

The waitress, a tall, bosomy woman in her fifties, came to the table with a pot of steaming coffee and a tall glass of creamy yellow liquid. Flanagan smiled his thanks and drank the glass of liquid down in three long swallows.

"What's that stuff in the glass?" Blake asked. "Every morning when I eat breakfast I notice the waitresses give it to most of the guys but they never give me any. I don't know what it is so I don't know what to ask for."

"It's a Dutch drink, I think its name is Advocat or something like that. It's made of brandy, egg yolks, and heavy cream. Best thing in the world for a hangover. These waitresses have had sub crews in here before. They know who needs a glass of that stuff and who doesn't. You don't drink, do you?"

"No," Blake said. "My mom asked me not to drink when I enlisted, so I don't." He drained his glass of milk. "You know, I kind of like the idea of having a bowl of fresh fruit on the table for breakfast. Back home in Kansas my mom thought you had to have meat and potatoes and vegetables and even pie for breakfast before you went out to work in the fields."

"You grow up on a farm?"

"My pop has six thousand acres of wheat," Blake said. "The harvest crews, some of the men, used to drink pretty heavy, and maybe that's why my mom asked me not to."

"What's a harvest crew?" Flanagan asked.

"People who come around every year at harvest time. They have their own equipment, big stuff. They're something like submarine men, Chief. Real professionals. They stick together. They go from farm to farm during harvest—all through the wheat belt, all the way up to the Dakotas. My mom used to go over to the other farms when they'd be working those farms and help with the cooking. The other farmers' wives would come to our farm when the harvest crew was at our farm. If you think a submarine feeds good you should see what a farm puts on the table for the harvest crew!'' The waitress walked up to the table.

"You feel like food this morning, Chief?''

"Bring me about four eggs, sunny-side up, please. And a stack of toast.'' He reached into the bowl of fruit on the table, took a passion fruit, cut through the tough outer skin, and scooped out the mass of purple seeds.

"What are you doing with your time?'' he asked Blake.

"I've done a lot of sightseeing,'' Blake said. "I've been to a couple of movies. The Australians call movies 'flicks,' did you know that? And the girl who works with the Red Cross, the one I met when we were in port last time, she left a note for me. I took her to lunch a couple of times and to a movie, and this afternoon we're going out to her house for dinner with her folks.''

"Makin' out, huh?'' Flanagan asked.

Blake blushed, the crimson line crawling up his boyish face to his blond hair.

"She's a nice girl, Chief. Her folks took my picture last time and sent it to my folks, and now I guess they're writing to each other.'' He rose as Steve Petreshock and Jim Rice came up. "See you fellas later,'' Blake said. Rice and Petreshock sat down.

"What'd we do, scare the kid away?'' Rice asked.

"You'd scare away a bear with that beard and those eyes,'' Flanagan said. "You look like something the cat dragged in.''

"You hit it, Chief,'' Rice said happily. "A regular wildcat got me yesterday afternoon. I was standin' on a corner near St. George's Square, and this nice looking broad walked up to me and asked me how long it's been since I had a good home-cooked meal. I allowed as it had been quite a time, and she invited me to go home with her and she'd cook me a good dinner.

"Hell, I thought maybe I was going to meet her old man and her kids. You know how nice these Aussies are, always trying to feed you or buy you beer or do things for you.

"But she doesn't have any kids and her old man's been missing in action in Crete or someplace for about a year or more. She cooked me a damned good meal and then she just damn near dragged me into the bedroom by my beard, and once we got into the sack she turned out to be a regular wildcat! Man, I ain't had anything like that in my whole life! I told her I had to get back here early this morning. A man's got to regroup and reload after a night like that, but I'm sure as hell going back and see if her convoy needs another torpedo attack.''

"Convoy?" Flanagan said. "I've heard that thing called all sorts of names but I never heard it called convoy."

Rice grinned. "She didn't have a shower at her house so I got in the tub and she got in with me and she saw old Herman at attention in the suds and she started to laugh and told me it looked like a torpedo. Which I had to admit is about right. So we started playing a game. She was the convoy and I torpedoed her." He drained a tall glass of milk the waitress had put in front of him. "Man, that was some night!"

"What's your excuse?" Flanagan said to Petreshock.

"Who needs an excuse? I walked into a joint called the Silver Slipper and there was a bunch of wounded Aussies in there. They were trying to big-deal the bartender into giving them each a beer and he wasn't budging. From what they said they'd busted out of the hospital and they didn't have a florin between them. So I popped for a few beers. I don't remember comin' back to the hotel, don't know how I got here, but when Jim walked in and woke me up this mornin' I checked my wallet, figured they'd take me for every damned pound in it, but as far as I can tell there ain't a sixpence missing."

"Aussies are good people," Flanagan said. "I looked at the security logbook this morning. They checked you in at twenty-three hundred hours. Shore Patrol brought you back to the hotel."

"Any charges against me?" Petreshock's face was suddenly concerned.

"No charges."

"Nice people," Petreshock said. "Not like the Shore Patrol back in Pearl. Those bastards will hammer you on the head with a nightstick and then write you up on charges of damaging the club."

Paul Blake walked out of the hotel into the early morning heat. He smiled to himself. Everything was backward in this country. They ate eggs for supper, on their steak. It was January and full summer. He looked at his wrist watch. He had several hours to kill before Constance Maybury would be off duty at the Red Cross. The zoo was down the avenue, he remembered. He began to walk, smiling broadly at the people hurrying to work, all of whom smiled at him. As he walked he saw the open door of a church, and without thinking he turned and went inside. He stood in the cool gloom at the back of the church. Then he knelt on the padded kneeling board that was fastened to the back row of seats.

Listening to the words of the Twenty-third Psalm that had been sent by the sonar operator on the U.S.S. *Mako* as that submarine sank slowly into the 30,000-foot depth of the Philippine Trench had driven into Paul Blake's consciousness the fact of his own mortality, a recognition that few 22-year-olds know. He bowed his head as he knelt, and he wondered how it would feel to know you were going to die very soon, that there was no way to avoid death or delay it? How would it feel to wait, as the men of the *Mako* had waited, for their ship to sink deeply into the sea, until the terrible pressures of the sea crushed the ship like an eggshell? He said an awkwardly phrased prayer under his breath, rose to his feet, and saw the Anglican priest standing near the door. The clergyman's eyes went from the blue submarine insignia on Blake's right sleeve to the silver Submarine Combat Pin he wore above his breast jumper pocket.

"You are welcome, any time," the clergyman said.

"Thank you, sir," Blake replied. "Is the zoo down this street?"

"Four blocks to your right as you go out the door. You'll see the entrance to the park, and the zoo is inside, to the left." Blake nodded and stepped out into the morning sunshine, squaring his white hat carefully on his head. The clergyman watched him walk away.

"So young," he said to himself. "So very young."

Flanagan made his way to the Chief Petty Officers' Club shortly before noon. He walked down the long graveled path to the two-story building on the riverfront and climbed the white stairway outside the building to the dining room and bar. He found a table overlooking the Swan River.

The club began to fill at noon. Flanagan noted that there were a number of submarine Chiefs in the crowd, their pale faces standing out in contrast to the tanned faces and arms of the submarine tender and base Chiefs. He nodded at Nuthall and Wilson, who sat down at a table next to his in company with two other Chiefs.

"Any word on my outer door?"

"It's on the way, that's all I can tell you," Wilson said. "You get the word on the overhaul, the refit?" Flanagan shook his head.

"Since you got to wait for the door and because there's a lot of boats in port the people in the Squadron decided you would have to do your own refit."

"That's gonna make a lot of people happy when they get back from the hotel," Flanagan said. He turned his head as a burly Chief Boilermaker standing at the bar raised his voice.

"Too damned many heroes in this club," the man said. "Too fucking many Feather Merchant Reserves wearin' the Chief's hat because they're on some fucking submarine!"

"Who's that character?" Flanagan asked Wilson.

"Chief Boilermaker named Scott," Wilson said in a low voice. "He got kicked off the boats years ago, before the war. Changed his rate from Machinist's Mate to Boilermaker. Hates all submarine sailors. Likes to make trouble, and he's a nasty bastard in a fight. Strong as an ox. Trouble is, he's a hell of a good man at his trade. But the way he's drinking these days I think his liver has got to go."

Flanagan raised an arm as he saw Doc Wharton and John Wilkes Booth, newly promoted to Chief Yeoman, come in the door of the club and stand surveying the room. They saw him, and moved to his table and sat down.

"How about letting me celebrate getting the hat and buy a beer before lunch?" Booth asked. Flanagan nodded, and Booth went to the crowded bar. He wedged himself in next to the Chief Boilermaker and tried to get the attention of the busy bartender. "Three beers," he called out.

"Didn't know you submarine pukes drank beer," the Chief Boilermaker said in a loud voice. "Thought all you fucking heroes drank champagne. Ain't beer just a little bit too common for you shitheads?"

"So?" Booth said. He measured the other man's bulk with his eyes as he moved away from the bar.

"So?" the Chief bellowed. "So? So I think all you submarine fuckheads are fuckheads. That's what's so, you shithead!" He stepped away from the bar holding his empty beer stein in his right hand. The conversation in the club died away. Wilson leaned over and half-whispered to Flanagan.

"Better get your Chief away from that dude or there's going to be a lot of trouble. Old Scott has had too many and he's looking for trouble." Flanagan nodded and got to his feet. Doc Wharton followed Flanagan toward the bar.

"I don't like the way you talk, Chief," Booth said in a soft voice. "That is, if you're really a Chief Petty Officer. Maybe you stole your hat off some real Chief."

"You callin' me a thief?" the burly man moved away from the bar, his red-veined eyes glaring at Booth. "You know what I think you are? I think you're some kind of a Reserve jackass and you know how you get the attention of a damned jackass? You hit the son of a bitch on the head!" He swung the heavy beer stein up and around and smashed it toward Booth's head. The Chief Yeoman jerked his head to the right but not quickly enough. The chipped glass bottom of the stein sliced downward against his left ear. Booth reeled away, his hand going to his torn ear as Flanagan moved past him.

"You want some of the same medicine, you fucker?" the Chief Boilermaker bellowed. He swung the beer stein upward, and Flanagan moved in, his right fist traveling in a low arc, smashing into the other man's crotch. The Chief Boilermaker gagged and then he doubled over, retching. He staggered a step or two and went down on his knees, his hands clutching at his genitals, his face agonized. Flanagan moved over a little, took aim, and then kicked out hard with his right foot, slamming the heel of his shoe into the other man's head. The man toppled on his side, his breath whistling between his teeth, his hands still grabbing at his crotch.

"Will you damned people keep it quiet?" a submarine CPO said in a loud voice. "Man can't hardly hear himself eat his soup."

"How badly is he hurt?" Flanagan said to Doc Wharton. The Pharmacist's Mate was pressing a bar towel against the side of Booth's head. A steady stream of blood was running down the side of Booth's neck, staining the collar of his new khaki shirt.

"Looked like his ear was torn off about half way down," Doc said. He motioned to the bartender, who gave him another clean towel. Wharton took the bloodstained towel from the yeoman's head and looked at the ear closely. He pressed the clean towel against Booth's head.

"He's gonna need a lot of stitching," he said.

"Hospital?" Flanagan asked.

"He should go there, but if we take him there they'll hold him for God knows how long to check for concussion. Any time someone gets hit in the head they worry."

"If that happens we'll lose him off the boat, sure as hell," Flanagan said. "What with charges and God knows what being brought. Best damned yeoman we ever had. Good man on the twin twenties, too." He looked at Wharton. "You think you can take care of him?"

"I could sure as hell try," Wharton said. "My kit is at my girl's flat. We can do it there. If it works, fine. If it doesn't we can always send him to the hospital."

Flanagan turned and faced the Chief Petty Officers in the restaurant and bar. He looked down at the unconscious Chief Boilermaker and then at the seated Chiefs.

"My name is Flanagan, Chief of the Boat of the *Eelfish*," he said in a flat tone of voice. "If this dude or any of his friends wants to see me they can come around." He turned and saw that the two relief-crew Chiefs, Nuthall and Wilson, were helping Wharton move Booth toward the door. At the end of the gravel path Nuthall left and trotted down the street.

"We've got a Squadron car parked down the street," Wilson said. "We'll drive you wherever you got to go with this guy."

"You're good people," Flanagan said. "Doc is going to try and sew him up over at his girl's place."

Nuthall drove up and the three men got into the car. Ten minutes later they were in the sitting room of a modest flat. A buxom young blonde went hurrying into the kitchen for a basin of warm water in response to Wharton's order.

"Her name's Sheila," Wharton said. He sat Booth down on a kitchen chair that Nuthall had brought out and carefully moved the bloody towel from the side of Booth's head. The left ear was hanging, torn away from the scalp skin down half the length of the ear. Wharton gently bathed the area with warm water and soap. He turned to the girl.

"Get me that bottle of rum I bought yesterday. Pour out a big glass. I'm gonna have to hurt this bastard, and a little rum will make it easier on both of us. Not as good as a shot, but I don't have any morphine." He handed Booth the glass of rum, and he gagged as he took a swallow.

"Get it down, fella," Wharton said. "Soon's you begin to feel brave and happy lemme know, and I'll go to work."

Booth smiled wanly. "Fucker sneak-hit me. You fix me up and I'll go back and cold-cock that son of a bitch so hard he won't wake up for quarters." He drank the rest of the rum, shuddering as the powerful liquor bit at his throat. Flanagan held a towel against the damaged ear while Wharton laid out a curved needle and sutures. He threaded the needle and dipped needle and suture in a vial of alcohol. He pulled on a pair of rubber gloves, picked up the needle, and moved in beside Flanagan. Flanagan took away the towel, and the upper half of the ear flopped down as the blood began to run.

"Can't work on that damned thing with him sitting up," Wharton said. He turned, looking at the furniture in the room.

"Sheila," he said. "You sit at that end of the couch. We'll lay him down on the couch, put his head in your lap. I can kneel beside the couch and sew him up. That way the damned ear won't flop around."

"Gimme 'nother drink," Booth said. Flanagan filled the glass half full of rum and handed it to Booth, who drank it down in three long swallows. Sheila sat down at the end of the couch, and Nuthall and Wilson helped lay Booth on the couch with his head in the girl's lap. She curled one arm over the back of his head and pressed his face into her bosom. Wharton knelt on the floor and turned to Flanagan.

"Drape that clean towel over his face. I'm gonna start sewing at the bottom part of the ear and go up and around the top. One of you other guys get some ice out of the icebox in the kitchen. You'll find an icepick in the drawer. Wrap the ice in a towel and maybe we can slow down this damned blood a little. Bastard bleeds good. Monk, if you'll get some of that gauze out of my kit, give it to me so's I can keep the work area clean."

He bent to his work, his whole being intent on what he was doing as his rubber-gloved fingers gently inserted the needle through the skin of the ear and then through the scalp skin, pulling the edges together. He tied off the knot expertly, clipped the suture with a pair of small scissors, and began the second stitch. He finished the third and fourth stitches, and Sheila began to moan.

"What the hell's eatin' you?" Wharton grumbled. "He's the one gettin' hurt, not you." He stitched expertly, working his way up around the curve of Booth's ear. Sheila moaned again and suddenly crossed her legs, moving Booth's head.

"Damn it, woman!" Wharton snapped. "Don't move his head sudden like that. I might put this damned needle in his eye, for Christ's sake! And stop moaning." He stopped his suturing and stared, and then he yanked the towel. He rocked back on his heels.

"Why you damn woman!" he roared. Wilson and Nuthall, standing at the end of the couch, began to laugh.

Sheila's head was thrown back against the couch, her eyes closed, her shoulders quivering. A low moan escaped her lips. Flanagan moved so he could see what had upset Wharton and he grinned. Under the cover of the towel draped over his face Booth had unbuttoned the girl's blouse and had fastened his mouth on the nipple on her breast.

"Don't get mad, Doc," Flanagan said. "Rum or a tit, no difference, so long as the bastard keeps his head still and doesn't holler."

"I keep telling this broad she should wear a brassiere," Wharton said. "I never ran into anything like this before, damn it." He ground his teeth and went back to work, pulling the needle through the flesh with little regard for the pain he was giving to Booth. Finally he stood up and reached for a wad of fresh gauze. He smeared Vaseline on the gauze and then sprinkled a heavy layer of sulfa powder on the Vaseline. He fastened the gauze over the damaged ear and strapped it down with adhesive tape.

"Uncouple from that tit, you bastard," Wharton said. "Sheila, you bitch, get that man's mouth off'n you. Jesus Christ! I never seen the like of this in all my life!"

Booth sat up on the couch, his eyes squinting shut. "Man, you are sure some kind of doctor," he said. "And who's this lovely creature who held my poor old Alabama head?"

"Never mind who the hell she is," Wharton snapped. "What the hell kind of thanks is that? I sew you up and you go to sucking on my girl's tit?"

"Is that what I was doing?" Booth said. He touched the gauze over his ear tentatively. "Well, I don't rightly remember doing that, but if you say I did then I must have done it. My pappy would tan my ass he caught me doing that to your girl. But my pappy ain't here, he's on the farm in Alabama. You know where is Alabama, honey?" he turned to the girl.

"No, she don't know where Alabama is and she don't have to know," Wharton said. "Just get your ass out of here." He turned to Flanagan.

"Take him to the hotel and keep him there. I'll come by tomorrow morning if I can get a doctor on the tender to come out with me." He took some pills out of his kit and gave them to Flanagan. "Give him two of these soon's you get him back to the hotel. Two more in four hours. Should knock him for a loop, loaded with codeine." He stripped off the rubber gloves and looked at Wilson and Nuthall.

"Appreciate your help but don't go talking about this damned caper or I'll wind up with my ass in the brig."

"Us, too," Wilson said with a grin. "We'll take the patient back to the hotel, Doc."

Flanagan was waiting in the lobby of the hotel the next morning when Wharton came in with another man. He was short, not over five feet three, and he walked briskly, the small gray goatee on his chin leading the way with a belligerent firmness.

"Doctor Silver," Wharton said to Flanagan. "Doctor, this is the Chief of the Boat, Chief Torpedoman Flanagan."

"If you haven't eaten breakfast yet, sir," Flanagan said to the small Commander. "They serve a mighty fine meal in this hotel."

"I haven't eaten and I might as well," the doctor said. "All this *tsimmes* because of this Navy's stupid rules. A man is sick or hurt I make him well if I can. That's what I am, a doctor, not a robot with rule books in my eyes and cotton in my ears. I am a healer. So I risk a court-martial. Maybe they'll throw me out and I can go back to civilian life.

"This man here, my friend, you know he was a dancer in civilian life? So they make him an assistant to a doctor, me. The Navy is crazy. We'll eat and then see if this man I call friend learned anything from me before he got the itch in his ass to go to sea on a submarine." He looked at Flanagan shrewdly.

"Ah, you are the one who hit the other man in his testes. I treated him, you know. They brought him in to me yesterday. You hit him very hard. Had cause, I am told. Hitting a man in the testes is a good thing to do to put him out of combat. Makes him reflect on his lost youth." He sat down at a table with the two Chiefs and helped himself to some slices of chilled mango.

"This friend of mine, here," the small doctor continued, "he tells me a story of how effective a woman's breast, her nipple, is as an anesthetic. He should write an article for the *New England Journal of Medicine*." He shook his bald head. "You never know what will work. If the patient had been a homosexual you might have put him into shock."

In Booth's hotel room Dr. Silver stripped off the adhesive tape with a gentle touch and removed the dressing. He looked at the suturing Wharton had done with a critical eye.

"For a *goy*, not bad," he said. "Now I want you to go downstairs and do something for me.

"When we came in through the hotel garden I saw some very big aloe vera plants. You know what is an aloe vera, dancer? No. You would not know that.

"The aloe vera is a sort of big cactus but it has no spines. It has very wide, very thick leaves filled with a healing gel. Ask the hotel gardener to cut off one large leaf for me and bring it here. Cut it off at the base of the leaf.'' Wharton left and the doctor busied himself taking Booth's pulse. Wharton returned with the thick leaf of the aloe vera plant, holding it away from him so the thick, sticky gel dripping out of the cut area of the leaf wouldn't soil his uniform.

"This plant is called the medicine plant down in the tropics,'' Dr. Silver said. "You can find reference to it in the Bible, Old Testament, of course. You can find reference to this plant in the old Egyptian writings.

"Now, you cut off an inch or so from the bottom of this cut end of the leaf.'' He sliced through the fleshy leaf and a thick, sticky, colorless gel oozed out. "You spread this on the wound. It heals. If you burn yourself and spread this on, it will stop the pain almost at once, and the burn will heal without scarring or blistering.'' His gentle fingers spread the sticky gel over the entire wounded area.

"You see, how it is absorbed almost at once. Now a little more, so, and a new dressing.'' He turned to Wharton.

"I want this done three times a day. Keep the aloe vera leaf in a refrigerator or an icebox here in the hotel. Take his temperature each time you dress the wound. If he runs more than one degree above normal, call me. If he feels nauseous call me.'' He went to the sink in the room and washed his hands.

"For you, patient,'' he said to Booth, "no alcohol. Lots of rest. No anesthetic like you used yesterday. It could raise your blood pressure, make your other ear drop off.'' He left the room followed by the two Chiefs.

"Let's have a little more of that excellent coffee in your hotel dining room, and then I must go back to the ship and lecture Navy officers on the treatment of sailors who must be considered to be human beings and not enlisted men.'' Seated at the table he grinned at Wharton.

"A creditable job of suturing, my friend. What I taught you must have taken hold. But if I have to criticize, and I must, the suturing at the top of the ear is not as neat as at the bottom part of the area. You didn't have to go as far away from the cut at the top to find tissue strong enough to hold the sutures.''

"That part was done after he had seen Booth, ah, sir, sucking on his girl's breast,'' Flanagan said.

Dr. Silver shook his head. "You have to learn never to let all your emotions show. You can show sympathy, empathy, joy. Never distress or sorrow. It upsets the patients. Worse, it upsets their relatives. Patients should never have relatives. It is unfortunate they do. They get in the way of the healing process. They expect miracles. The patient hopes for a miracle but he'll settle for less. I'll come back tomorrow at lunch, my friends." He left, walking with swift strides on his short legs.

"He's one hell of a man," Wharton said. "He fights with the Navy brass all the time. He knows more about medicine than all of the doctors on the tender put together, and he lets them know that every day. Those who listen to him learn. Those who don't listen don't get over it for a long while. He works a lot at the Australian military hospital on his off time. Sort of a consultant. Most of the medical people in the hospital think he's God Himself."

"Well," Flanagan said, "he's the right race, isn't he?"

CHAPTER 12

The crew of the *Eelfish* piled their sea bags and ditty bags around the forward deck gun and fell into line for quarters on the afterdeck. Some of them looked refreshed and fit after the two weeks of rest and relaxation. Others looked totally exhausted.

"Looks like the relief crew is running behind schedule," John LaMark said to Jim Rice. "They ain't painted the topside yet."

At quarters John Olsen gave the crew the bad news. They would have to do their own refit because they had to wait for the torpedo-tube outer door. After the groans had died down Olsen pointed out that they'd have at least three more weeks of liberty.

"Thing that pisses me off," Fred Nelson said to Chief Flanagan two weeks after the crew had returned to the ship, "the thing that really pisses me off is that they keep us outboard of all the submarines alongside. Every damned thing I've had to bring aboard I've had to carry it over the decks of five other boats. The least the bastards coulda done is to leave us inboard."

"Two ways to do things," Flanagan said. "The right way and the Navy way. You know that. When you going to be through painting your room?"

"Tomorrow. We finished scrubbin' it down today. We'll be done by fifteen hundred tomorrow. All the rest of the work is done. We reshimmed the rollers in the tubes and on the skids. We worked on damned near everything that could be worked on in that fuckin' room. People back there been workin' their asses off. Me too."

Flanagan took a small notebook out of his shirt pocket and made some notes on a page. "Same thing all over the ship. There ain't a piece of gear on this ship that hasn't been taken apart, cleaned, adjusted, and put back together again. Everything is working so good you'd think we just came out of the Navy Yard."

"It's workin' better than it would if we'd been in the Yard," Nelson growled. "What's the word on the new door?"

"Last word I get is that it's in Pearl now and it'll be here a week from Friday. That's in ten days. We can't go in the dry dock on Saturday so we'll probably go in on the following Monday. Then they got to hang the door. They didn't send any hinge pins for the door, but the shop on the tender had the machine shop make up some bronze pins from blueprints. I figure they'll fuck around with them for half a day, honing them to fit.

"The Squadron wanted ship's company to scrape and wirebrush the bottom and paint it, but the Old Man screamed so loud that the relief crew is going to do that. That will probably take three, four days. Once that's done we'll go alongside and take fish aboard and take stores and get the hell out of here."

"I ain't mindin' it too much here," Nelson said. "Found me a woman who likes big noses."

"She must like the hell out of you!" Flanagan said.

"She even wanted to cut my toenails," Nelson said with a grin. "How about you, you make out?"

"Chief on the tender wanted to fix me up with his girl's cousin, but I backed off. Every time I look at a broad I start thinking about the one I was married to once, and it turns me off."

"Didn't know you were ever married," Nelson said.

"Did it when I was second class. Made first class and all she did was bitch about why didn't I make Chief, why didn't I try for Warrant. Spent so much money that I was working as a bartender when I had the liberty so I could pay the bills.

"We went out to sea for a month on maneuvers, and when I got back I found that she'd taken about half of the furniture and moved in with some damned civilian. Then she ran up about fifteen hundred clams worth of bills in Sears and Sawbucks. Took me two years to get that paid off."

"Where was that?" Nelson said.

"Key West," Flanagan said.

"She marry the civilian?"

"Don't know, don't care," Flanagan said. "All's I know is he paid for her divorce." He studied his notebook and then put it back in his pocket. "Old Man's due aboard. I got to see him."

Nelson watched Flanagan's slope-shouldered figure walk up the length of the deck, thinking that he had learned more about his Chief of the Boat in the last ten minutes than he had known in the two years they had served together.

Eelfish came out of the dry dock and was moved directly to the tender to an inboard position. The torpedo loading hatches were opened, and in the two torpedo rooms the men were preparing to take aboard their torpedoes. On deck Chief Flanagan and two seamen were greasing the loading skids down which the torpedoes would be slid. Captain Brannon walked up and stood watching the preparations.

"We put the finals on the fish ourselves," Flanagan said to Mike Brannon. "Did that yesterday, up in the shop. I stopped liberty for all hands in both rooms until we get the fish aboard and stowed. Cook told me he's taking stores aboard tomorrow, and I want all hands available for that."

Brannon felt a shadow block out the sunshine. He looked upward and saw a torpedo hanging from the crane right over his head. He moved hastily to one side and then went over to the tender and out on the dock where John Olsen was waiting for him with Admiral Christie's car and driver.

"What's this meeting about?" Olsen asked.

"The usual thing, I guess," Brannon said, as he settled himself in the car's back seat. The driver closed the door and got in behind the wheel, and the car moved away.

"I guess they're going to talk about our next war patrol area. I hope they give us a good one."

The two officers walked into the cool foyer of the Bend of the Road. The Marine sentry checked their ID cards and waved them toward the long hallway that led to the conference room. As they walked toward the hallway they saw an officer dressed in khakis that glistened with a starched sheen, the creases in the shirt and trousers standing out like knife edges. The officer wore the silver eagles of a captain on his collar tabs. He stood with his feet slightly spread apart, his hands clasped behind his back. As Brannon and Olsen passed by him he stared at the men with cold, pale blue eyes. His harsh face gave no evidence of welcome.

"Boy, I'll bet he's a tough one," Olsen half whispered to Brannon as they walked down the hall. "That four-striper back there, did you see those eyes? I thought they were going to bore a hole right through me.''

"His face is familiar, damn it,'' Brannon said, "but I can't put a name to him. I should be able to. Not that many four-stripers wear a white mustache.'' The sentry at the door of the conference room checked their ID cards and opened the door and closed it behind them.

"Good to see you, Mike, Olsen,'' Admiral Christie said from the head of the table. The members of the Admiral's staff were sitting on both sides of the table, and Brannon noticed an empty chair next to the Admiral. He and Olsen moved toward two empty chairs farther down the table.

"I want to congratulate you, Mike, on the job your people did on *Eelfish* on that refit. I had a few minutes last evening and went down there with Sam Rivers. You were on the tender having chow, and we didn't want to bother you. No offense, I take it?''

"Of course not, sir,'' Brannon said. "You're welcome aboard *Eelfish* any time, you know that.''

"You're getting your torpedoes today?'' Christie asked. Brannon nodded.

"You'll get stores tomorrow, and you'll shove off day after tomorrow at zero eight hundred. You'll be fueled after stores are aboard,''· Admiral Christie said. He nodded his head at the empty chair beside him.

"We have a guest with us from Pearl Harbor. And we have a special mission for *Eelfish*.'' He nodded at one of the junior staff officers, who rose and left the room. He came back in a few minutes with the officer Brannon and Olsen had seen in the foyer. The Admiral rose.

"Captain Brannon, Mr. Olsen, this is Captain Arvin Mealey. Arvin, you've met my staff. This is Captain Mike Brannon, C.O. of the *Eelfish*, and his Executive Officer, Lieutenant Commander John Olsen.'' The dour-visaged four-striper came around the table and shook hands with Brannon and Olsen, who had risen to their feet. His handshake was brisk and powerful. His pale blue eyes bored into each man, and then he went to the head of the table and sat down beside the Admiral.

"Since this is Captain Mealey's operation I'm going to let him brief you, Brannon, Olsen. If you will, sir?'' Captain Mealey got to his feet and stood, as Brannon and Olsen had seen him earlier, with his feet spread a little apart, his hands clasped behind his back. The cold eyes looked down the table.

"Ever since the war in Europe started," Mealey began, "the German U-boats have been operating in what they call wolf packs. As few as two submarines or as many as twenty will operate with each other. They ambush convoys. The tactic has been very successful for them. Very successful.

"For some time, quite a long time, some of us have been trying very hard to get approval of the wolf-pack tactic for our own operations. Up until now the powers that be in Washington, the High Command, have not given approval.

"Now we have it.

"I might say at this point that we don't have any real information on how the Germans carry out their wolf-pack operations. The only information we have comes from the victims, officers and men who have been sunk and then rescued or whose ships managed to get away while others were sinking all around them.

"We know that in some cases the Germans, who seem to have excellent intelligence, form up on each side of the convoy course. They wait, submerged, in a long row. As many as ten ships on each side of the convoy route. When the convoy comes abeam, the submarines on one side will all fire at one time. A broadside of torpedoes. Then they'll go deep, and the submarines on the other side will fire their broadside. Then both sides will surface and run among the convoy shooting with deck guns. In a large convoy of fifty or sixty ships traveling in lines there is bound to be a great deal of overlap, and most torpedoes seem to find a target." He paused.

"When they use a smaller number of submarines, down to as few as two, the tactics vary. But always they are bold and very aggressive. The loss of lives and ships in these attacks has been enormous. In many cases the Germans seem to prefer to attack at night. The reason for that is quite obvious. Merchant-ship captains are not used to maneuvering radically at night in company with other ships, and they get confused. The submarines which surface go among them like a pack of wolves among sheep. Hence the term wolf pack.

"One thing we must recognize, and we often fail to do so, and that is that we must recognize the brilliance of the enemy when it is warranted. Admiral Doenitz is a brilliant tactician. We are now going to use his tactics, so far as we are able. I have been sent out here from Pearl to command the first wolf-pack patrol.

"I have chosen to put my flag in the *Eelfish*, if Captain Brannon has no objection. We will not have a large number of submarines to work with, only two others, the *Hatchet Fish* and the *Sea Chub*." He stopped, his cold eyes looking at Mike Brannon.

"The decision to put my flag aboard *Eelfish* rests, sir, with you. Your decision will be heard without prejudice, I assure you. I could sail aboard either of the other two ships if you would rather have it that way."

"I have absolutely no objections, sir," Brannon said. "If I may, sir, I look forward to the experience, to learning whatever I can from the man who took the *Mako,* my old ship, under a twelve-destroyer screen to attack a battleship."

"And who got the living hell depth charged out of him," Captain Mealey said with a wry smile. "Don't forget that part, Captain Brannon. Audacity in war always extracts a price. We paid heavily on *Mako* for that attack."

"And don't forget that while the Japs were, as the Captain says, depth charging the hell out of him he came up to periscope depth and blew one of the attackers to pieces with one torpedo," Admiral Christie said in a booming voice.

"Arvin, you're going to put your flag in the smartest, cleanest, best-run ship in my command. You and Mike and Olsen can go to lunch if you wish. You're welcome to eat here. We've got so much work to do we'll eat and work at the same time."

Captain Mealey and the two *Eelfish* officers found a table shaded by a huge hibiscus bush on the patio. They ordered from the menu, and when the waiter had left Mike Brannon cleared his throat.

"Sir, if I may, can I ask a few questions?"

"Go right ahead," Mealey said.

"First, you're welcome to my stateroom."

"I'll share it with you, if you don't mind," Mealey said. "I went aboard last evening with the Admiral, and I noticed that the top bunk wasn't made up. I like top bunks."

"Fine," Brannon said.

"What else?" Mealey asked.

"The only other things I am curious about—I guess John, who's my navigator, is equally curious, sir—is how the three submarines will travel to the patrol area, wherever that area is—they haven't told us as yet. And how you'll deploy your force in the patrol area, how you will attack."

"Our area is Luzon Strait," Mealey said. "The Strait is the crossroads for shipping going north and south to and from the Empire of Japan.

"*Hatchet Fish* and *Sea Chub* are leaving this afternoon for Exmouth Gulf. They'll top off with fuel there and wait for us. We have a long way to go to get on station, so we'll run in line, with the Flag leading the column, and run as economically as we can to the patrol area. I haven't checked the charts closely, but I estimate it will take us a good thirteen or fourteen days to get on station.

"I don't plan to try for German efficiency and make each of our pack cruise in a rigid formation in the patrol area. It's a big area, and what I plan to do is to station the other two ships so as best to cover the sea routes the Japs are using. When one of us sights a target or targets he'll notify the others. If that sounds loose and haphazard, perhaps it is. At the moment that's the way I see it.

"Now a word on why I chose *Eelfish* for my flag. I have studied your patrol reports, sir. I am satisfied that you are an aggressive, efficient Commanding Officer. I am confident that we will work together very well as a team."

"If I may, sir," Olsen said. "You must know that we, all of us in submarines, have studied your patrol report on the attack on the battleship at Truk. Those patrol reports were circulated to the whole submarine force, sir. And if I am not out of order, that attack was one of sheer, cold guts!

"I talked to a Chief in the relief crew here who said he was in Pearl Harbor when you came back to port, and a Chief on the *Mako* said that as scary as that whole operation was, no one was really afraid because you were in the Control Room. I mention that because if you didn't know it I think you should, sir."

Mealey looked at Olsen, and the smile appeared briefly under his white mustache. "That sailor didn't know how scared I was during that depth-charge attack. I had a fine ship, a well-trained crew. Part of that was due to you, Captain Brannon. You were the Executive Officer aboard the *Mako* before I took over. And let that be the last of the mutual admiration society. We have a lot of work to do once we get under way." The waiter appeared with three chilled cups of vichyssoise.

"When did you arrive in Australia, sir?" Brannon asked.

"I arrived in Brisbane two weeks ago," Captain Mealey said. "I flew over here five days ago."

At the end of the meal Mealey pulled out a pipe and a worn tobacco pouch. "I see no need to disturb you aboard ship any more than necessary," he said as he filled his pipe. "I'll report aboard at zero seven hundred, day after tomorrow."

*   *   *

Back aboard the *Eelfish* Brannon gave Pete Mahaffey orders to
draw bed linen for the unused bunk in his stateroom. He listened
to the noise of the people in the Forward Torpedo Room
finishing their work. He closed the cloth drape that served as a
door and sat on the edge of his bunk.

Captain Mealey was a fire eater, and he was a master at
surviving prolonged depth-charging attacks. How would Lieutenant Commander Michael P. Brannon measure up against the
standard that Captain Mealey had set and would undoubtedly
expect him to equal?

He wondered, as he had wondered so often about the late
Captain Hinman, did men like Mealey ever really feel the fear
that he felt when he went into action? At lunch Mealey had said
he was frightened during the depth charging at Truk. Did he say
that to make him and Olsen feel better, to show himself as no
different than they? And why had Captain Mealey chosen the
Eelfish for his flagship? The Captains of the *Hatchet Fish* and the
Sea Chub were both senior to Brannon. Both men were close to
promotion to four-stripe Captain.

There was the point John Olsen had raised; what was Captain
Mealey doing in Brisbane for over a week? And even more
importantly, why had he been sent to the Australian command to
take command of a wolf pack when he could just as easily have
formed a wolf pack with Pearl Harbor boats?

There must be a reason, he mused, a reason for all of this. He
got up and combed his thick black hair in front of the small steel
mirror above the washbasin. The next six to eight weeks could
determine the fate of his entire Naval career. If he failed in any
way with those cold blue eyes watching him he could figure on
being relieved of command and relegated to a desk job ashore
until he had his time in for retirement.

CHAPTER 13

Captain Mealey stood quietly on the cigaret deck of the *Eelfish*
as Mike Brannon eased his ship out from between the submarine
tender and another submarine. Once clear of the submarines

alongside the tender Brannon maneuvered through the harbor toward the open sea.

On the main deck Chief Flanagan was securing the topside for sea. He could feel the cold eyes of the grim-faced Captain on the cigaret deck watching his every move. When he had finished he patiently double-checked his work and asked the Bridge for permission to go below. He climbed to the cigaret deck and murmured a polite "Good morning, sir" to the austere Captain in his heavily starched khakis. Captain Mealey nodded, raised the binoculars hanging around his neck, and studied the submarines that were jostling back into position alongside the tender. Flanagan went below to the Crew's Mess, where Scotty Rudolph put a cup of hot coffee and a freshly made doughnut in front of him.

"Gonna be something different this time, huh?" the ship's cook asked. Flanagan bit into the doughnut and nodded. He chewed slowly and then washed the doughnut down with a swig of coffee.

"Wolf-pack operation with the *Hatchet Fish* and the *Sea Chub*," he said. "They're waitin' for us in Exmouth Gulf. The three of us will operate in a wolf pack, like the Germans do. Only they do it with ten to twenty submarines in one pack. This four-striper who's ridin' with us, Captain Mealey, he's the Flag."

Rudolph sipped at his coffee. "Don't envy our Old Man having to operate under his eye. I knew him in Panama, years ago, when he had an R-boat. Tough son of a bitch. Hell of a seaman."

"Tough fighting man, too," Flanagan said. "There's a mustang in the relief crew, name of Botts. I knew him when he was a Chief Torpedoman before the war. He was on the *Mako* when Mealey took the *Mako* out and dove under twelve destroyers at Truk and slipped about eight fish into a battlewagon

"Botts told me that this guy is made of ice water and chilled steel. Went through the most hellish depth charging any submarine ever took, came up once and sank a big Jap destroyer with one fish, and then went down again to seven hundred feet, get that, seven hundred feet, and got away from the other eleven tin cans."

"Too damned bad they didn't keep him on the *Mako*," Rudolph said. "Maybe if they had done that the *Mako* wouldn't have got sunk."

"Could be," Flanagan replied. "But he made four stripes

while he was on that patrol run, and they don't keep four-stripers on submarines. Only way he could get back to sea, I guess, is to do something like this, take out a wolf pack of submarines.

"But like you said, I wouldn't want to be the Old Man with him looking over my shoulder. I don t know how many times in my life I got the topside of a submarine ready for sea, and when I was doing it a little while ago, with that dude standing on the cigaret deck, I felt like a seaman deuce. I double-checked everything, and then I began to worry that I'd missed something and started to do it all over again. He can sure make you feel funny when he looks at you with those eyes."

During the 800-mile trip north to Exmouth Gulf along the west coast of Australia Captain Mealey made several trips through the *Eelfish,* stopping to talk when he saw a face he knew from other submarines, other duty stations prior to the war. In the Wardroom he was a pleasant enough visitor, listening far more than he spoke. He unbent only once, the evening before *Eelfish* was due to arrive at Exmouth Gulf to top off her fuel tanks.

Sitting at the Wardroom table after dinner, Lieutenant Bob Lee suddenly asked Captain Mealey to tell the officers seated around the table about his strategy in attacking the battleship that was guarded by twelve destroyers and aircraft. Mealey looked at Lee for a long moment and then asked Pete Mahaffey to bring him a plotting board and a fresh cup of coffee.

With the plotting board in front of him he marked in the position of the battleship and the twelve destroyers guarding it and the position he had maneuvered *Mako* into before the attack began. Then, as he penciled in each stage of the attack, he paused to fire pointed questions at Bob Lee, Perry Arbuckle, and Jerry Gold, asking them to tell him why he had done this, why he had done that. Mike Brannon and John Olsen sat quietly, saying nothing, watching their junior officers squirm under the sharp questions. At the end of an hour's give and take Captain Mealey sat back, stuffed his pipe with tobacco, and lit it. When it was drawing to his satisfaction he let a small smile show under his white mustache.

"All three of you seem to have a good grasp of the fundamentals of the attack problem," Mealey said. "I will credit Captain Brannon and Mr. Olsen for that. The knowledge you have gained will stand you in good stead in your careers. Assuming, of course, that you are Regulars?"

"No, sir," Lee said. "All three of us are Reserves. I'm a lawyer, that is, I passed my bar exam in California before I enlisted for the duration. Perry is an architect." Mealey nodded and looked at Jerry Gold.

"And you, sir? I noticed that when we made our first trim dive out of Fremantle that the ship was in almost perfect trim. That is quite a feat, sir, after weeks in port, after dry-docking. What is equally commendable is that I noticed in my walks through the engineering compartments that everything there is spotlessly clean and in excellent condition."

"I thank you, sir," Gold said with a grin.

"What are your civilian credits?" Mealey asked.

"I finished dental school and was getting ready to sit for my license when the Navy reached out and grabbed me," Gold said. "I think being a diving officer is good training for a dentist. I fill and empty variable ballast tanks as a diving officer. When I get out and open an office I'll be filling cavities and emptying abscesses." Mealey's frosty smile came and went.

"I have been in the Navy for eighteen years," Mealey said. "I never cease to marvel at the way the Navy works. In time of war they seem to act without any thought when it comes to the assignment of personnel, and yet what they do seems to work out for the best. I had an Executive Officer aboard the *Mako*, a Reservist. The first, I believe, to ever be an Executive Officer. He was an engineer in civilian life, mechanical engineer I believe. He was an absolutely superb Naval officer. And a first-rate navigator as well." He turned his pale blue eyes on Olsen.

"Your navigation on this patrol will be tested, sir. We are going to run Sibutu Passage between Tawi Tawi and Borneo and then run the Balabac Strait, south of Palawan, and then go north along the west coast of Palawan to our area."

"Mines!" Olsen said suddenly. "Isn't Balabac Strait heavily mined, sir?"

"It is," Mealey said calmly. "But there are several passages through Balabac. The Japanese periodically sweep up their mines in one passage and then mine another. The Ultra decoders in Pearl Harbor have been very successful in keeping up with that information. Over thirty submarines have made a transit through Balabac Strait without incident, following the Ultra information. We will get the latest information on the mined and cleared areas the day before we make the transit." He turned to Mike Brannon.

"While Mr. Gold is topping off our fuel tanks tomorrow we'll have a conference aboard this ship with the Captains of the *Hatchet Fish* and the *Sea Chub* and their Executive Officers. If

Mr. Olsen will oblige me, Captain Brannon, I'd appreciate it if he'd lay down our course to Sibutu Passage. Give me an ETA, Mr. Olsen, bearing in mind that we will be cruising at our most economical speed while on the surface at night. It's a very long way to Luzon Strait, and longer coming home, if you run out of fuel oil. You'll find two extra sets of charts in your chart locker, Mr. Olsen. When you have laid out our course I would appreciate it if you would mark the other two charts similarly for the benefit of the other members of the wolf pack." He rose.

"If I may, Captain Brannon, I'll go topside. I want to have a few words with young Michaels about radar and sonar. He has the OOD watch, I believe?"

"Yes, sir," Brannon said. The younger officers around the table filed out of the Wardroom as Mealey left. Olsen came back from the Control Room with his charts and spread them out on the table.

"I was wondering," Olsen said as he spread a chart out flat, "I was wondering why we didn't do this in Fremantle? Sit down, all of us, and figure out the navigation, the courses and speeds, and all the rest of it?"

"I wondered, too," Brannon said. He looked at the chart in front of Olsen. "Going through Balabac and then north, that's quite a bit shorter than the easy way, across the Celebes Sea and out into the Pacific and then north, isn't it?"

"Looks to be quite a bit shorter," Olsen said. "But that's a damned dangerous area to navigate in, where we're going. Maybe that's why he waited until now before he told us which way we'd be going. Maybe back in Fremantle the other skippers would have raised some heat about going this way. Out here they can't do anything except bitch a little."

"He's a strange man," Brannon said slowly. "He makes me feel like I'm a snot-nosed Ensign again. When I was backing out of the nest alongside the tanker I kept expecting him to walk forward and take the Conn away from me."

"That's why you didn't let me take the ship out, huh?" Olsen said with a grin. "Afraid that if I made even one small mistake old Mealey would come down on me like a ton of bricks."

"I wasn't afraid of him gigging you," Brannon answered. "I was afraid he'd come down on me for not training you well enough. I just figured if he was going to gig anyone it might as well be me for something I did." He chewed his lower lip.

"I wonder how this damned operation is going to work out. Chet Marble in *Hatchet Fish* and Jim Shelton in the *Sea Chub* are both damned senior Commanders. They're about ready for four stripes themselves, and neither of them has the reputation of being easy to get along with.''

"Neither one of them has ever sunk a ship," Olsen said, his eyes flicking to the door opening of the Wardroom to make sure no one overheard him. "I talked to their Executive Officers in Fremantle before they got under way, and both of them told me they'd put in for transfers."

"That's odd," Brannon said. "With both their skippers ready to be promoted they'd fleet up to command. Why would they put in for a transfer?"

"The polite way to put it, Skipper, is that Captain Marble and Captain Shelton are not quote aggressive unquote submarine Captains. Both the Executive Officers are aggressive. The result is that neither Executive Officer has been recommended for command by their Captain. And that makes living aboard both ships very rough for the two Execs." His right eye blinked almost imperceptibly and he bent over the chart as Captain Mealey passed by the Wardroom door opening on his way to the Forward Torpedo Room.

The crews of the *Hatchet Fish* and the *Sea Chub* greeted the *Eelfish* with shouts of derision as John Olsen eased his ship delicately into place alongside a fuel barge. Two days of waiting for the *Eelfish* to arrive, waiting in the hot, arid waste of Exmouth Gulf with only a small supply of warm beer available in a tin hut on the beach, had not been pleasant for the crews of the other two submarines.

The meeting in the *Eelfish* Wardroom began pleasantly enough. There was the usual heavy-handed badinage from the two senior Captains about *Eelfish* getting lost on the way north. Pete Mahaffey served a platter of sweet rolls and two carafes of coffee and withdrew. As a Lieutenant Commander, and a junior one at that, Mike Brannon elected to stay silent unless spoken to, to let Captain Mealey do all the talking.

The joviality in the Wardroom faded abruptly when Captain Mealey handed a set of charts to the Captains of the *Hatchet Fish* and the *Sea Chub*. Captain Marble of the *Hatchet Fish* traced the course line to the top of Makassar Strait, where it ended with a small arrow pointing at the Sibutu Passage.

"Not going east across the Celebes and out to the Pacific?" he asked. "Look." His finger traced a course to the Pacific across the Celebes Sea.

"We could follow this course and have good deep water all the way, sir. No danger of mines, damned little need to even dive during the daylight hours, once we'd cleared the Makassar Strait." Mealey listened quietly, his right forefinger rising to touch his mustache.

"I could give you the standard Navy answer, Captain Marble," he said. "I could simply say we are going to follow the course I have laid down because I said we are going to follow that course, and that would be the end of it.

"But since we are going to be working as a team in an operation the people at Pearl Harbor see as a very significant operation, I will explain my reasons.

"The course you indicate is several hundred miles longer than the one I have laid down. That means that we will use more fuel. We may need every drop of fuel we have in our tanks before we get home to Fremantle.

"Now, as to how we will proceed. *Eelfish* will lead the way. *Sea Chub* will follow at three thousand yards' distance. As the senior of the two, *Hatchet Fish* will follow astern of the *Sea Chub* at three thousand yards' distance. Orders to dive and time of surfacing will be issued by me daily. They will be followed to the letter.

"Should we see anything in Makassar Strait that can be attacked I will issue instructions via voice radio, the same as I would do once we are in our assigned patrol area. Once we reach our area of patrol you will be assigned to positions and patrol courses with the area in conformity with information we receive from Ultra in Pearl."

"I've heard reports, Captain Mealey," Captain Marble said, "reports that there are elements of the Japanese battle fleet in the anchorage at Tawi Tawi. Your course takes us right past that anchorage, to the south. The water is very shallow there for a submarine if we run into some Jap destroyers."

Mealey's eyes seemed to protrude slightly, their cold blue gaze fastening on Captain Marble.

"You seem to be very concerned about deep water, sir," he said in a low voice. "Correct me if I am wrong, but if I recall correctly you have on several occasions decided not to attack enemy shipping because the enemy ships were in water you decided was too shallow for an attack."

"I think of my ship, sir." Captain Marble's voice was harsh. "I think it is madness to attack a target guarded by escort vessels in water that is too shallow to go to deep submergence to evade.

Admiral Christie has not seen fit to question my judgment, sir. I see no need to defend my judgment now."

"There is no need, Captain," Mealey said softly. He filled his pipe and lit it. "But if we do see elements of the Japanese battle fleet, sir, why then we shall attack. As long as they have sufficient water under their keels to keep them afloat then there is enough water for me to attack!

"We will communicate by voice radio once we leave this port," he continued in a calm voice. "Radio silence will be preserved unless you sight a target. Radar will not be used unless I so order.

"Our code name for this operation will be Mealey's Maulers. We will begin using that designator as soon as we leave. *Hatchet Fish,* as the senior Captain, will be Mauler One. *Sea Chub* will be Mauler Two." His cold stare froze the slight smile that started to form around Captain Shelton's mouth.

"We are a very small wolf pack, only three of us. What we will do, how we will attack, are decisions I will make when we have targets. If possible I intend to attack on the surface at night." He looked at Captain Marble.

"I recall your rather strenuous objections to that tactic when I mentioned it in Fremantle, sir. I trust you have changed your mind?"

"In all truth, sir, I have not," Marble said. His heavy face was flushed, his mouth set in stubborn lines.

"We've lost too many submarines in this war, far too many. It is my judgment we lose submarines because we take unnecessary chances, reckless chances. *Mako,* as Captain Brannon here knows very well, the *Mako* was lost because it attacked a convoy on the surface at night. If I remember Captain Brannon's patrol report, *Mako* was raked by heavy gunfire, went down, and was lost. And I point out, sir, with all due respect, that Captain Brannon's brilliant attack on the two Japanese destroyers that killed *Mako* was conducted while *Eelfish* was submerged. At night."

Captain Shelton saw the gathering storm in Captain Mealey's face and cleared his throat.

"We will, of course, sir, follow your orders as you give them. To the very best of our ability. Where you lead, sir, we will follow. Never doubt that."

Captain Mealey looked at the officers around the Wardroom table.

"Let me say this, gentlemen. When Captain John Paul Jones

was put in charge of a small battle fleet in our Revolutionary War, he said, if I can recall, quote: I wish to have no connection with any ship that does not sail fast, for I intend to go in harm's way.

"I cannot ask for ships that sail fast because we must conserve our fuel, but, by God, *we will go in harm's way!*"

Sitting in the Wardroom after the other Captains and their Executive Officers had left, Captain Mealey turned to Mike Brannon.

"We have our work cut out for us, sir. I am going to break one of my own rules. I am going to take you into my confidence. If I had been able to overcome the politics we would have other ships, other Captains with us for this first wolf-pack operation. But I could not."

"Politics?" Brannon said.

"Politics," Mealey answered. He drew a small circle on the green-baize table covering with the stem of his pipe.

"Both the Commanding Officers of the other submarines are very close to being promoted to four stripes. Neither has a good war-patrol record. Both have very powerful friends in Washington. That's the background.

"When word got out some weeks ago that we were going to mount a wolf pack, both of them were told about it by their friends. The pressures from Washington to put one of those two in charge of the wolf pack were very strong. I cannot tell you how strong." He turned his bleak face to Brannon.

"That's why I am here, why my flag is in *Eelfish*. This wolf-pack operation must be successful. My boss in Pearl Harbor, Captain Rudd, and I share the opinion that if either Marble or Shelton led the wolf-pack operation it would not be successful."

"I may be pretty dumb," Brannon said slowly. "But I don't make the connection at all."

"I'll try to explain," Mealey said. "If either one of them led the wolf pack and if they ran true to form, which is to say that the wolf pack operation would fail, the black eye for that failure would be painted on Captain Bob Rudd. This is his idea. He's fought for it for months and months. He's made a lot of very powerful people in Washington very unhappy.

"Captain Rudd became controversial when he began backing submarine captains in their complaints about the Mark Six exploder. He did a lot of research on that exploder.

"One of the things he found out was that the Mark Six exploder was developed by the United States in the mid-nineteen twenties. The British and the Germans developed an almost identical version shortly afterward. The British and the Germans began using their magnetic exploders as soon as their sea war started. They found them to be extremely unreliable, just as our submarine Captains found. They stopped using them and went back to contact exploders.

"We knew this. Bob Rudd also found out that our Mark Six exploder had never once been fired from a submarine at a target. Never once tested! Not from a submarine."

"I didn't know that," Brannon said.

"Few people do," Mealey said. "What's more, you won't find a single piece of literature on that exploder which tells you how to maintain it, test it, or use it. That literature was drawn up, but the Gun Club Admirals who developed the exploder decided that the literature was too secret to be disseminated, so they locked the original copy up in a safe.

"It took Captain Rudd a solid year of work and, I have to say this, of politics to break that logjam and modify the exploder so that it will work on contact. That was one major political battle that was won. Now Captain Rudd is in the middle of another political battle, the wolf pack.

"He's won the first round. We will try a wolf-pack operation. Just one. If it's successful Captain Rudd will be riding high. If it fails he'll probably lose his job, will probably be relieved and sent to a desk somewhere where he'll rot away. That would be one hell of a loss, in my own opinion. He's made a lot of very powerful Admirals angry with his work in exposing that Mark Six exploder. He rammed it right down some very sensitive throats, and if this wolf pack fails they'll nail his hide to the door."

"You'll just have to forgive me, sir," Brannon said. "I don't get the connection between Captain Rudd's unpopularity with some Admirals and the assignment of Captains Marble and Shelton to this wolf pack."

Mealey bared his teeth in what was more of a grimace than a smile.

"Captain Rudd checkmated the effort to put Marble or Shelton in charge, knowing they would fail. He managed to get me assigned to run the first wolf-pack operation. The opposition countered, sir, countered very well. They've given me two weak sisters, Mister! All I've got, all Captain Rudd and I can depend on, is the *Eelfish* and the two of us. Let's pray to God that the *Eelfish*, you and I, will be enough. Because I mean to be successful! Each night before I go to sleep I pray, Captain Brannon, I pray that if I do not measure up to what is expected of me that the Lord will take me before I get back to port and have to face people I respect, have to face myself for the rest of my life!''

Brannon sat quietly, his hands slowly turning a pencil around and around on the table top. He was stunned by the intensity of the older man. *I'd better start praying myself, he thought, praying that you do everything you expect you should do, because if you don't and your prayer is answered that you die, the* Eelfish *dies with you.*

The three submarines, following the courses advised by the Ultra code breakers, eased through the Sibutu Passage and timed their arrival at Balabac Strait so that that dangerous area could be run through during the night. They twisted and turned their way through the maze of small islands and turned north to begin the run up the west side of Palawan Island, through the justly feared Palawan Passage.

The water along the 300-mile length on the west side of Palawan Island is called "foul ground" by sailors. It is shallow and treacherous. Barely twenty miles to the west of Palawan's foul ground there is a vast area that is marked on the charts with the name "Dangerous Ground." Ships going north and south to the west of Palawan used a narrow alley of deep water between the foul ground and the Dangerous Ground. But even that narrow alley of water is not safe. Dangerous reefs bearing the names of sailing ships that foundered on them many years ago thrust skeletal fingers out into the deep-water alley.

Mike Brannon, who had permitted himself no more than cat naps during the time the *Eelfish* was making its twisting run through Balabac Strait and up the Palawan Passage, relaxed when John Olsen brought cups of hot coffee to the cigaret deck where Mealey and Brannon kept the night watch and announced that the *Eelfish* had cleared the Passage.

"So far, so good, sir," Brannon said to Mealey. "From here on it's a clear run to our patrol area." He turned as he heard the rasp of the bridge speaker.

"Bridge," the voice over the speaker said. "Notify the Captain that we have an Ultra message coming in."

"Bridge, aye," Lieutenant Lee said. He turned as Mike Brannon slid between the periscope shears and the cigaret deck railing and came into the tiny bridge space.

"I have it," Brannon said. He turned and spoke to Captain Mealey. "Would you like to decode with me, sir? We're going to dive in an hour or so. The baker should have some fresh pastry about now." Mealey came forward into the bridge, and the two men went below.

Brannon read the decoded message and shoved it across to Captain Mealey, his eyes glistening. Mealey read the message and smiled, his right forefinger creeping up to touch his white mustache.

"Alert *Hatchet Fish* and *Sea Chub* to form up on us after surfacing this evening," he said. Brannon nodded and went to the radio shack. He came back and sat down at the table and reread the message.

"My God!" Brannon said. "Troop transports, two oil tankers, freighters, a heavy cruiser, destroyers, and a small aircraft carrier! That's a regular task force, Captain! What in the hell is the Jap doing sending that kind of a force out of Manila to Mindanao?"

"How much of a briefing did they give you about the Navy-Army move northward from New Guinea?" Mealey asked.

"Not very much at all. They told me the Army was going to move north, but that's about all. They seldom tell us much."

"General MacArthur is going to make good his promise to return to the Philippines and free them," Captain Mealey said. "With the Navy's help, of course. He'll make good his promise to return before the end of this year, probably late in October. The first major step toward an invasion of the Philippines was taken last week. If I can recall my briefings in Pearl Harbor, the plan was to invade a small group of islands to the north and east of New Guinea called the Admiralty Islands.

"That group of islands will make an ideal cornerstone for air control all the way to Saigon and Truk and to the Philippines. From what I know of the Japanese defense in the Admiralty Islands, we'll have a tough job with the invasion, but they're committing the men to do the job.

"Once that invasion operation is over we'll have an excellent airfield and several good deep-water harbors. What's more important is that this move and the ones to follow will leave about one hundred thousand Japanese troops massed in Rabaul rotting on the vine. They'll be bypassed. After we secure the Admiralty Islands, the next move, if you look at a chart, is a series of steps north and west to Morotai, Peleliu, Yap, Ulithi—and then the Philippines."

"Where will MacArthur hit the Philippines, sir?"

"I don't know," Mealey said. "I would think he might land at Mindanao Island. Apparently the Japanese think it will be Mindanao. The Ultra message says that Mindanao is the destination of this task force." The frosty smile came and went under the white mustache.

"When they get out of Manila Harbor they'll find that we stand between them and their destination, and by God, we'll draw blood!"

CHAPTER 14

Captain Mealey bent over the chart on the Wardroom table. Mike Brannon and John Olsen sat across the table from him. Mealey's long forefinger traced a line out of Manila Harbor

"If I were commanding that task force I'd take them out of Manila Harbor, come inside of Lubang Island, and then go through this passage between Luzon and Mindoro, across the Sibuyan Sea to Ragay Gulf, down to San Bernardino Strait and out to the Pacific. From there down the east coast of Mindanao Island to Davao Gulf and to Davao. The Japs have a big base at Davao. That's the most practical route." He looked at Brannon and Olsen.

"Anything else means more sea miles, more time. Do you gentlemen agree?"

"There is an alternative," Olsen said quietly. "They could go outside of Lubang Island, to the west, and then go down the west coast of Mindoro Island and east to San Bernardino Strait."

"Too far," Mealey said flatly. "Too far. No. I'll gamble they're going to take the shortest route. The Ultra people said the Japanese message they intercepted which formed this task force carried a 'most urgent' on it. They're in a hurry. They'll take the shortest route." He rubbed his nose with the bowl of his pipe.

"Our problem is where do we choose to meet them, where do we attack? I want deep water if I can get it. I want sea room if I can get it. But if I can't have both or one we'll attack anyway."

Mike Brannon touched a small space on the chart between the northern tip of Mindoro Island and the southern tip of Luzon. "That's a pretty narrow strait there, isn't it, sir?" Mealey measured with the dividers.

"Two miles, little less. Would you attack there?"

"No, sir," Brannon replied. "But I was thinking. You've got a mix of ship captains in this task force, some Merchant Marine and some Japanese Navy captains. I think that when they come to go through that strait, it's so narrow, they'll string their task force out like a bunch of elephants in a circus parade, one ship following another. That would give them maximum sea room for navigational or maneuvering errors. I wouldn't attack there. We wouldn't have much room for maneuvering ourselves. I'd hit them a little east of the narrow gut, just after they go through it."

"I agree," Mealey said. "We can wait until they re-form their convoy so we'll know what we've got to shoot at, where they position the carrier." He touched the chart with the sharp points of the dividers.

"If we station *Sea Chub* here and *Hatchet Fish* here, to the east of our position, one of them a little north of the convoy course the other a little south, they'll be in position to pick up anyone who tries to run away from our attack. I can't see any of those Japanese ship captains risking a reversal of course and a return through that narrow gut." He looked at the Ultra message, picked up a pencil, and did some rapid figuring.

"If the Ultra people are accurate about the time they are to get under way, if we allow a couple of hours for them to form up in a convoy leaving Manila Bay, if they follow the course I think they will follow, they should be clear of that narrow gut about forty-one hours from now." He looked at the clock on the bulkhead.

"It's zero seven hundred, Tuesday," he said. "I figure they should be in a position where we can best attack about midnight tomorrow night. We'll have a quarter moon at about that time. It will help us see but it won't help them see us. A submariner's moon."

"How about target priorities, sir?" Brannon asked.

"Difficult," Mealey said. He stuffed his pipe with tobacco and then laid it in an ashtray.

"An invasion force, any invasion force, must control the sea and the air. If it does not, its landing craft, its support vessels are all sitting ducks. So I'd say the aircraft carrier is the number one priority. But the two troop transports are also high on the list. The more Japanese troops there are to oppose the landings the more costly the invasion becomes.

"The tankers are important. They'll be carrying fuel for aircraft and for the tanks and other vehicles already there. I presume the freighters will be loaded with ammunition and stores, and they're important." He picked up his pipe and lit it, his eyes looking at Mike Brannon through a cloud of pungent smoke.

"Our problem is that we have too many high-priority targets and only three submarines. I confess that if that heavy cruiser comes across our bow I would set up and shoot at it just because it's a cruiser!" He picked up a pencil and pulled the chart in front of him.

"One thing we can be sure of: Admiral Christie will be sending every submarine he's got within steaming range of Davao Gulf in that direction. The concept of a wolf pack is going to be tested, damned hard, too! We're the first fist to hit at this convoy, and we've got to smash them, sink every damned ship we can. I don't want to give the submarines that Christie sends to Davao Gulf anything more than one or two crumbs." He made three small marks on the chart.

"John, these two marks to the east are where I want *Sea Chub* and *Hatchet Fish* to take station. *Sea Chub* will take the northernmost station of the two. This other mark, to the west, is *Eelfish*.

"I want you to determine exact latitude and longitude for those positions and have that information encoded before we surface tonight. Captain Brannon, I want you to draw up our plan of attack as we have talked about it here and have it encoded. We'll send that message tonight when we surface.

"If Mr. Olsen is right and the task force goes down the west side of Mindoro, we'll be close enough to take up the chase. Include that possibility in your message. If that is what happens we will then dispatch *Sea Chub* and *Hatchet Fish* south to ambush the task force when it turns east to run for San Bernardino Strait.

"I don't expect that to happen, but I want it included in the message as a contingency. Emphasize that the carrier is the number one priority. Then the troop transports, the oil tankers, the freighters, in that order.

"The code word we will broadcast to let *Sea Chub* and *Hatchet Fish* know that we have started the attack will be..." He paused and thought a long moment.

"How does 'Mealey is mauling' sound to you?"

"Succinct, sir," Olsen said with a wide grin. "I can just hear some Jap radio officer telling his skipper that 'Meary is mauring.' It isn't going to be easy for them."

Mealey's smile came and went. He pushed the chart toward Olsen and turned to Brannon.

"I'd suggest, Captain, that we take a tour through the ship, let the crew know what we're planning. I have learned that when a ship's company is taken into the Wardroom's confidence, morale is increased and we are likely to get a better standard of performance."

Steve Petreshock had finished topping off the charge in the air flask of a reload torpedo and was struggling to coil the copper charging line when Captain Mealey and Mike Brannon came into the torpedo room.

"Have to anneal this bastard again," Petreshock said to Jim Rice. "The fucking thing is getting as stiff as a damned board." He sensed the presence of someone else in his torpedo room and turned and saw the two officers.

"Sorry, sir," he said.

"Nothing to be sorry about," Mealey said. "I know how troublesome a stiff copper charging line can be. You're Petreshock?" The torpedoman nodded, and Brannon saw the muscles in his shoulders bunch slightly.

"The man over there behind all that beard is Jim Rice, Captain," Brannon said. Rice nodded, his eyes on Mealey.

"I'd like to talk to both of you," Mealey said. Jim Rice moved over next to Petreshock.

"We've been diverted from the patrol area Captain Brannon announced when we left Exmouth Gulf," Captain Mealey said. "A Japanese task force consisting of an aircraft carrier, a heavy cruiser, two oil tankers, two troop transports, some freighters, and a number of destroyers is under way going south.

"We intend to intercept them tomorrow, about midnight. We will attack on the surface." He heard the stir in the bunks as men who had stood the night watches, eaten breakfast, and then turned in leaned over the bunk rails to listen.

"*Eelfish* will have the first crack at the task force," Mealey continued. "We face a problem. We will be attacking at night on the surface. There will be numerous targets. I will require that reloading of fired torpedo tubes begin as soon as those tubes are fired. A faster reload than you have ever attempted, I believe." He paused a moment and turned his head as he caught a murmured "Dear Jesus!" from one of the bunks.

"When I had the *Mako* at Truk we had a torpedoman in the

Forward Room who was named Ginty,'' Mealey said. ''Did either of you know him?''

''I knew Ginty when I was on the Asiatic Station,'' Petreshock said. ''Before the war, sir. Big brute of a man. A real good torpedoman.''

Mealey nodded. ''He was all of that and more. When I started shooting from the Forward Room, Ginty started the reload. What I want to know is can you do that?''

''Captain, sir,'' Petreshock said. ''I've drilled my people who work in this room and the reload crew harder and longer than any other torpedo room in the whole fleet except for our own After Room.'' Mike Brannon saw that Petreshock had assumed an almost belligerent stance, his legs braced, his head thrust forward, fists knotted at his sides.

''Soon as you or Captain Brannon start shooting, sir,'' Petreshock said in a flat, hard voice, ''soon's you start shooting we'll start a reload. Don't worry about a fish gettin' away if you have to dive sudden. We know our jobs, sir.'' The last word came out bitten off, sharp.

''Very well,'' Captain Mealey said. ''I did not mean to imply you don't know your job. I wanted you to be perfectly clear on the problems the Bridge will face in this action. We will have lots of targets. Some of those targets are more important than others, the carrier for example. We won't have time to pick and choose so we're going after the most important target of the lot and then just keep shooting until we have no more torpedoes. Once we're in the middle of that task force I won't be able to wait until someone untangles a block and tackle.''

''I understand, sir,'' Petreshock said. ''We'll give you two reloads on Tubes One, Two, Three, and Four. No sense in trying to reload Five and Six if you're in a hurry because we have to take up the deck plates to get at those reload torpedoes. That gives you fourteen fish up here and all you or Captain Brannon's got to do is tell us when. Ginty was one hell of a man, but he wasn't any better than my people.''

Captain Mealey and Brannon worked their way aft, stopping in each compartment to explain the attack they were going to make. The crew accepted the news with almost a total lack of concern. There were a few guarded attempts at wisecracks, which Mealey pretended not to hear. When they were back in the Wardroom Mealey looked at Brannon.

''I like the mood of the crew, Mike. They're confident. That's a good sign. They'll perform. But I touched a nerve in that man Petreshock, up forward.''

"You did, sir," Brannon said. "I served with Ginty when I was in *Mako*. He put the ship in commission, as I did. Petreshock isn't as large as Ginty was, few men are, but he's every bit as good a torpedoman as Ginty was. Steve is a fussbudget, a perfectionist. So is Fred Nelson, back aft.''

"One other thing," Mealey said. "When I went in on the battleship at Truk I sent the Chief of the Boat to the Forward Room and the Torpedo Officer to the After Room to supervise the reloads. What do you think of that idea?"

"I think it's a good idea," Brannon said. "But I'm short one officer as you know. The Chief of the Boat is the Assistant Diving Officer and in charge of the Control Room during General Quarters. Mr. Lee, the Gunnery Officer, is the number two man on the plot under John Olsen. He takes over the plot if I use John Olsen on the bridge.''

"Understood," Mealey said. "Forget it." He thanked Pete Mahaffey for the fresh cups of coffee, reached for the chart on the table, and unfolded it. Olsen had drawn the projected course of the task force as Mealey had said he thought it would be. He had also drawn in the alternate course, down Mindoro Island's west coast.

"Your Executive Officer is a careful man," Mealey said as he studied the chart. "I think they'll come to us."

Eelfish surfaced an hour after dark and circled slowly south of Lubang Island, waiting for *Hatchet Fish* and *Sea Chub* to join up. An hour later all three submarines were close together. The coded message was sent informing each of the other Commanding Officers of the battle plan and their positions. Captain Mealey stood on the cigaret deck as the other two submarines disappeared in the dark, heading east.

"Now all we have to do is wait until they think about the message and see if they have any objections," Mealey said.

"I don't see why there would be," Brannon said, picking his words carefully. "It's a very large task force. There's enough to go around for everyone."

"They'll have to exercise initiative," Mealey snapped. He turned and moved closer to Brannon, so closely that he was standing shoulder to shoulder with him. When he spoke his voice was so low that only Brannon could hear him.

"Tell me, sir," Mealey said. "Do you ever feel fear?"

The sudden question, the intensity in the low-pitched voice, caught Mike Brannon off guard. He hesitated a moment and then said, in a very low voice, "Yes, sir, I do. Every time we go to General Quarters. I used to worry about that. I still do, even though once Captain Hinman told me that he felt the same way. He said that before a wrestling match—he was a champion middleweight wrestler at the Academy—before a wrestling match he would be so afraid he'd throw up. I guess fear is normal."

"It is normal," Mealey said. "Admitting you are afraid is a bit abnormal. The man who does not fear takes unnecessary risks. The man who is afraid to admit his fear often takes even worse risks, just to prove he is not afraid. Both of those types get themselves killed.

"There are no heroes, you know, not in this day and age. It was different in the old days. The mothers of the Spartan warriors told their sons to come back carrying their shields or borne on them, dead.

"All we can hope for today is to have superbly disciplined men who will do what they have to do when they have to do it, regardless of the consequences.

"We have to understand that the people we command are afraid, that they feel fear as we do. That is one of the burdens of being a leader."

He turned his back on Brannon, went to the other side of the cigaret deck, and began to study the horizon with his night binoculars. Brannon kept his distance, wondering what had moved this strange and distant man to talk about fear. Captain Mealey had been awarded the Congressional Medal of Honor after his attack on the battleship at Truk. Everyone Brannon knew believed he had earned that honor. And yet, without reason or cause, he had spoken about fear. Brannon shrugged. If Captain Mealey was afraid going into action, then that made two of them.

The next night and day passed slowly. In the two torpedo rooms Petreshock and Nelson routined each torpedo, making sure that it would run properly when fired. The reload crews were summoned to go through simulated drills of a fast reload, working in the dim light of battle lanterns to simulate the loss of lights during a depth-charge attack.

Captain Mealey sat with the officers of the *Eelfish* after dinner, six hours before he estimated that the attack would begin. Mike Brannon, sitting at his right hand, realized that the atmosphere in the small Wardroom had subtly changed. Without a word being spoken, full command had slipped from him to Captain Mealey.

"Here is how we will operate, gentlemen," Mealey said. "The Battle Station assignments you are familiar with are not altered, with one exception.

"Mr. Olsen will run the plot until just before we go to the attack. Then he will go to the Conning Tower and man the battle periscope. At that time Mr. Lee will take over the plot. Mr. Arbuckle will run the TDC. Mr. Michaels will handle radar and sonar. Mr. Gold will stand by to dive." He looked at Jerry Gold.

"You will have your work cut out for you, sir. I intend to fire every torpedo we have in the tubes and to begin a reload as soon as we begin firing.

"We will be attacking on the surface. If we have to dive it will be a crash dive. I want a safe trim on this ship.

"Bear in mind, Mr. Gold, that during a hasty reload operation a good torpedoman is not likely to wait until he has blown his fired tube down to the WRT tank and vented off the tube before opening the inner door and beginning the reload. He will, I am sure, stop blowing, vent, and open the inner door while there is still considerable water in the tube. That water will go into the forward bilge, and it will affect your compensation for a good trim. You are going to have to be very sharp, sir."

"I talked about that with both torpedo rooms, sir," Gold said, his voice a slow drawl. "I've got a fairly good idea of how quick they're going to be opening those inner doors, about how much water they're going to take in the rooms." He tapped a leather-covered notebook in his shirt pocket. "Got nearly every contingency you can think about all worked out here. We'll make it, sir." Captain Mealey stared at Jerry Gold for a long moment. Gold grinned back at him and Mealey turned to Lieutenant Perry Arbuckle.

"Captain Brannon and I will be on the bridge. Captain Brannon will have the after TBT. Mr. Olsen will be with you in the Conning Tower. Once we go into action you are going to be literally swamped with bearings from me, from Captain Brannon, from Mr. Olsen, and with bearings and ranges from radar and sonar. There will be a lot of confusion. That can't be avoided. There will be noise, too. You'll have to keep a clear head."

"No sweat, sir," Arbuckle said. A smile spread across his full lips and crinkled around his dark brown eyes. "As long as the gears in that TDC don't burn out, sir, we'll give you solutions just as fast as we can."

Mealey turned to Jim Michaels. "We are going to use your radar sparingly until we get into action. Then I want you to range on everything you see. Keep feeding the information to the Conning Tower and to me. It is vital that you give only accurate information."

"Understood, sir," Michaels said. His serious young face was flushed, and he was shifting slightly in his chair with the excitement he felt.

"Any questions?" Mealey asked.

"One, sir," Olsen said. "Bridge complement. Who will be on the bridge. We have some trained Battle Surface lookouts, sir."

"Captain Brannon and I will be alone on the bridge," Mealey said. He reached over beyond the end of the table and picked up a bulky canvas bag that made a clinking sound. He opened it and took out two metal helmets, the type used by the Marine Corps.

"I took the trouble to find out your hat size, Mike," he said. "This one is yours. We'll wear these topside in case the Jap begins throwing shot at us. Mr. Michaels, see to it that the galley has plenty of hot coffee and sandwiches. If we get driven down—there are a number of destroyers in that task force—if we are driven down we may be down for a very long time." He turned to Brannon. "I'm going to lie down for a while, Mike. Call me in two hours. No sense in not getting some rest before the music starts to play."

Sitting in the Wardroom after Mealey had gone to his stateroom, Olson looked at Brannon.

"What did he say? 'Before the music starts to play'? Some concert!"

"It's going to be one hell of an operation if he pulls it off," Brannon said. "No one has ever seen a task force this big. No submarine has ever seen one. That attack we made on that baby convoy in Leyte Gulf, that was peanuts compared to this operation. He's going to pull a first."

"He's done things like this before," Olsen said. "No one had ever tried to get at a battleship guarded by a dozen destroyers with aircraft overhead. He did it. Did it damned well, too."

Lying in his bunk Captain Mealey composed himself for sleep. So far everything had gone well, he reflected. Everything except the one mistake he had made. It had been a mistake to talk to Mike Brannon about fear. There was only one person that he should talk to about things like that, his wife. He remembered that after he had brought *Mako* home from Truk he had told her how scared he had been during the long, long hours of depth charging. She had looked at him with a smile.

"We are all afraid of what we don't know," she had said. "And often more afraid of what we think we know.

"When young Arvin was born, when he was due to be born, I was paralyzed with fright. You were gone, on that awful little S-boat. All I could remember, all I could hang on to, was what you had once told me, that a good sailor does what he has to do when he has to do it and that nothing else matters.

"Well, young Arvin didn't give me any choice. He decided it was time to be born, and when it was over I remembered that I'd been afraid but that once it was over it didn't matter."

He wriggled in his bunk, trying to get comfortable, and then, suddenly, he drifted off to sleep, thinking again that it had been a mistake to talk to Brannon about being afraid.

CHAPTER 15

The *Eelfish* surfaced after dark, creeping along the northern coast of the island of Mindoro, certain that any enemy radar would fail to detect the ship against the background of mountains. The night air was like warm velvet on the skin, the humidity so high that drops of moisture formed on the flat surface of the teak bridge railing. Overhead a canopy of stars blazed in the clear sky, but off to the east, where the *Hatchet Fish* and the *Sea Chub* were waiting, a line of clouds obscured the horizon. Lieutenant Jerry Gold stood in the bridge space, periodically sweeping the horizon with his binoculars.

Captain Brannon paced the starboard side of the cigaret deck from the periscope shears aft to the rail, waiting. Captain Mealey had taken up his position on the port side of the cigaret deck. He paced fore and aft, stopping occasionally to examine the horizon over which he hoped the task force would come. *Hatchet Fish* and *Sea Chub* had reported themselves on station shortly after *Eelfish* had surfaced, advising that in order to present less of a silhouette they would cruise with decks awash.

Down in the Control Room John Olsen had laid out the tools of the plot on the gyro table. He looked over at Jim Michaels.

"What's the extreme range you could expect to get a solid contact on radar, Jim?"

"We'd get good clutter at about eighteen thousand yards, sir. But in this area, where we are with mountains on both sides of that pass those ships will come through, I'd rather say fifteen thousand yards. At that range we could be accurate."

Olsen looked at the plotting board and the chart and did some quick calculations. "That would be in about another fifteen minutes," he said.

Jerry Gold's voice from the bridge sounded over the Control Room speaker.

"Bridge requests a radar sweep."

"Order received," Olsen said. Michaels and Rafferty studied the radar scope as the beam swept around.

"Bridge," Michaels said, "I've got a lot of clutter. I'm sure there's ships in there but I'd rather wait another ten or fifteen minutes. I think I could give you an accurate reading then."

Ten minutes went by, and then the port lookout coughed loudly and spoke.

"I see a rocket or something like a rocket bearing two six five, almost dead abeam to port, Bridge."

Mealey raised his binoculars and saw the sputtering flare arcing and then descending to vanish. Mike Brannon, who had moved to the port side of the cigaret deck when the lookout reported, said, "A rocket, sir? Strange."

"Yes," Mealey said. "Strange, but perhaps not too strange. You mentioned earlier that this task force has a mix of Merchant Marine and Navy captains. It could be that the Flag Commander fired the rocket to signal a change of course to his sheep or to order them to form up. They should be almost through that narrow gut by now. Mr. Gold, tell Mr. Michaels what we saw up here and get a radar sweep."

The radar antenna turned to the bearing the lookout had given and then began to search on either side of the bearing.

"Contact!" Jim Michaels's voice was loud enough to be heard clearly on the cigaret deck. "We have a lot of pips bearing two six nine. Range is one six zero zero zero yards. Repeat, sixteen thousand yards, Bridge."

"Plot, give me a course to our attack position," Captain Mealey snapped. "Make turns for eighteen knots."

"Recommend we come right to zero nine one, Bridge. Making turns for eighteen knots, sir." Olsen's voice was calm.

"Secure the radar," Mealey said. "Plot, I want to run on this course for fifteen minutes, and then we'll take another radar sweep on the targets."

"Sir," Olsen said. "If I may, sir, an observation."

"Go ahead," Mealey said.

"At this speed we're running away from the targets, sir. We're on a course that will take us into their base course, but I don't think they're making more than fifteen knots, sir. We're opening the range. Recommend we slow to ten knots on this course. Let the task force come closer to us. Intersect time should be a little under two hours, sir."

"Very well," Mealey said. "Make turns for ten knots. We'll take another radar sweep when your plot shows the targets to be within fourteen thousand yards." He turned to Mike Brannon.

"They're coming to us, Mike. They're coming right to us!"

The minutes crept by slowly as *Eelfish* headed away from the coast toward a spot on the dark sea where it would intersect its course with that of the task force. Overhead a pale quarter moon blinked through the low, scudding clouds that had blown in from the east. Mealey studied the sky.

"I hope it rains," he said to Mike Brannon. "Rain would give us a big advantage." He looked at the dial of his wrist watch and then began to study the horizon through his night binoculars.

"Bridge," Olsen's voice came over the speaker. "Radar requests permission to make a sweep. We should have the task force well within accurate radar range by now."

"Permission granted," Mealey answered.

"Contact bears two zero five, repeat two zero five. Range is one two zero zero zero yards. Repeat. Twelve thousand yards. Target course is one four one. Repeat. One four one. Target speed is one four knots. Repeat. Fourteen knots, Bridge."

"Very well," Mealey said. He turned to Jerry Gold. "We'll maintain the topside watch for a little while. When we reach our attack position we'll secure the lookouts and the bridge watch. Please notify the galley to serve coffee now." He turned to Mike Brannon.

"Let's go below and look at the plot." Brannon followed him down the hatch to the Conning Tower where Perry Arbuckle was standing with Bill Brosmer, the Quartermaster.

"When do you give the downbeat for the music to begin, Captain?" Arbuckle said to Mealey.

"I'd say two hours, little less. Stand easy. If you want coffee get it now. Send the cups back below when you're through. I don't want anything adrift in this Conning Tower when we go into action." He went down the ladder to the Control Room. Brosmer turned to Lieutenant Arbuckle.

"That old S.O.B. doesn't forget anything, does he? Send the coffee cups below so nothing will be adrift."

"He's all Navy," Arbuckle said in a low voice. "And that might not be a bad thing on this night."

Standing in the small bridge space Jerry Gold put his binoculars to his eyes and began a 360-degree search of the horizon. *Eelfish* was running out to sea now, away from the bulk of the mountains on Mindoro. He could see flickering pinpoints of light in the lowlands. The lookouts had reported those lights earlier, and Captain Mealey had decided they were the lights of cooking fires. Someone over there on the land, Gold mused, was living in complete ignorance of the fact that in a matter of two hours or so a battle would be joined within miles of them. A battle in which men would die. Some in the searing blasts of torpedo explosions, others more slowly in the dark waters where they would drown or be torn to bits by sharks. *Better you should be a dentist in Chicago, Gold, he said to himself. Copping feels off patients who hope you will do just that when they're stretched out in the chair.*

In the Control Room Captain Mealey studied the plot and the chart. He picked up a pencil.

"We'll take up position here, a little west of where we had originally planned. I want to hit them while they're still close enough to that narrow gut between Mindoro and Luzon so they won't think about reversing course and heading back the way they came. It would take damned good seamanship to try that at night while they're under attack, and they should figure that there's another submarine in back of them waiting for them to do something like that." He looked at the chart.

"I reason that when we start shooting and then get in among the convoy the ships will break out of their formation. The instinct of men under attack is to move in another direction. In this case I think they'll move forward, and they'll also veer north and south. That should put them in line with *Hatchet Fish* and *Sea Chub*."

Mike Brannon studied the chart. "Sir," he said. "We are going to be west of where we had intended to be, and that puts *Hatchet Fish* and *Sea Chub* farther east of us than before. Do you think we should move them in a little, say two or three miles?"

Mealey looked at the chart a moment and then nodded his head. He turned to Jim Michaels.

"Are we close enough together for voice communication?"

"Yes, sir."

"Tell Mauler One and Mauler Two to shift position. Mr. Olsen will give you the exact coordinates." He waited until Olsen had worked out the precise positions and given them to Michaels.

"How long until the music begins, John?" Mealey asked. Olsen worked at his plotting board.

"We'll be on station in thirty minutes, sir. The task force should be on our port bow at that time, moving to cross ahead of our bow about ten minutes after we are on station."

"Inform Mauler One and Mauler Two that the music will begin in forty minutes," Mealey said to Michaels. "Tell them that once the music begins there will be dancing and we'll ask them to the ball." He leaned down and picked up the canvas bag that held the two steel helmets he had brought aboard. He gave one to Mike Brannon. He fitted the other on his head and buckled the chin strap. He went to the ladder and began to climb to the bridge, followed by Mike Brannon.

"Clear the bridge, Mr. Gold," Mealey ordered. He waited until only he and Brannon stood in the bridge, and then he bent to the bridge transmitter.

"Sound General Quarters!"

Eelfish waited.

CHAPTER 16

Mike Brannon, standing on the port side of the bridge, turned to speak to Captain Mealey and saw that the older man was standing head bowed, his hands clasped in front of him. He lifted his head and raised his binoculars to his eyes.

"Captain Brannon, take the After TBT, please. As soon as the radar gives us the disposition of the task force we can plan how we'll go in among them." He bent to the bridge speaker.

"Radar check, Control."

"Bearing on the biggest target is three five five. Repeat. Three five five. Here is the disposition as we see it, sir.

"There are two smaller pips one thousand yards in front of the mass of ships, sir. We take those to be destroyers sweeping out ahead.

"One thousand yards astern of those two contacts there is a very large pip. Very large. We take that to be the aircraft carrier. Then we have two more ships abreast, one thousand yards astern of the large pip. Two more ships back of those two, range about seven hundred fifty yards aft of the first two.

"There are three other ships back of those five and they are maneuvering. Mr. Olsen assumes they are forming up after coming out of that narrow gut. Far back of this mass of ships there is one large pip. Mr. Olsen assumes this to be the cruiser.

"There is one small pip on the starboard after quarter of the convoy. We assume that to be a destroyer. Range to that destroyer is five zero zero zero yards. Repeat. Five thousand yards.

"Range to the largest ship in the task force is two zero zero zero yards. Repeat. Two thousand yards, sir. Bearing on that ship is three five seven. Repeat. Three five seven. On the far side of the task force there are several small pips maneuvering. Assume these to be destroyers, sir."

"Open all torpedo-tube outer doors," Mealey said. "Set depth all torpedoes four feet. Repeat. Four feet. Light off numbers three and four diesels. Make the following message to Maulers One and Two.

"Mealey is mauling!"

The word came up from below. All torpedo-tube outer doors open. Depth set all torpedoes four feet. Making turns for full speed.

"All ahead flank! Stand by to shoot at the largest target. We have him in plain sight. That's a carrier, by God!"

Eelfish shuddered as Chief Ed Morris threw all the power generated by the four big diesel engines into the generators that drove the big electric motors. In the Forward Torpedo Room Steve Petreshock eased between the two banks of torpedo tubes, his hand hovering over the safety bar for Number One tube's firing key.

"Olsen, start the problem on that big target," Mealey rasped. John Olsen flicked the focus handle on the battle periscope and steadied the periscope on the target. Brosmer sang out the bearing to Arbuckle. John Wilkes Booth, the Chief Yeoman, settled himself on his stool next to Paul Blake, at the sonar, and prepared to take down in his notebook every word that was said.

"Request desired shooting range, Bridge," Arbuckle called out.

"One thousand yards," Mealey answered. "The escort back on the task force starboard beam still hasn't seen us. Angle on the bow of the first target is zero six zero, starboard. Here we go!" He stood in the center of the small bridge, his fierce eyes glaring at the dark bulk of the aircraft carrier that was sharp on his port bow.

"Range to the first target is now eleven hundred yards, Bridge." Michaels's voice floated up to the bridge. In the Conning Tower Arbuckle cranked in the range on the TDC. He spoke softly into the battle telephone that hung around his neck. "Stand by forward . . ."

"You have a shooting solution, Bridge," Arbuckle sang out.

"Fire one!" Captain Mealey yelled. He felt the thumping jolt in his legs and feet as a fist of compressed air and water hurled the 3,000-pound torpedo in Number One tube down the length of the tube, its steam engines screaming into life as it passed through the tube. Mealey counted down from six to one.

"Fire two!" He felt the second torpedo leave.

"Fire three! Begin the reload forward!"

"All torpedoes running hot, straight, and normal, Bridge," Paul Blake called out from the Conning Tower.

A booming roar echoed across the surface of the water, and then another explosion shattered the night. Mealey saw two orange and red explosions against the dark bulk of the target. A siren began to wail in the night.

"Two hits!" Mealey yelled. "Two hits in the first target!"

Brannon's voice came from the after end of the cigaret deck. "Escort on our port quarter has a bone in its teeth. He's seen us!"

"Very well," Mealey said. "Left fifteen degrees rudder." *Eelfish* heeled over into the turn, its bow swinging away from the stricken aircraft carrier. Mealey glanced briefly at the target and saw a huge explosion of flame gush out of the carrier's midsection.

"Meet your helm right there!" Mealey yelled. "Steady on that heading, Plot. Next target is the ship on my port hand. Angle on the bow is twenty port. Target is beginning a turn away. Make that angle on the bow thirty port. Give me a solution!" He heard Olsen's voice calling out the bearing and Michaels giving the range.

"Solution!" Arbuckle yelled.

"Fire four!" Mealey counted down carefully, watching the ship out to starboard beginning to turn away from him.

"Fire five!"

"We're getting company." Michaels's voice over the bridge speaker was calmer than it had been. "The escort vessels out ahead of the task force are now coming this way."

"Fire six!" Mealey roared.

"Torpedoes running hot, straight, and normal," Blake reported. On the cigaret deck aft of the bridge Mike Brannon crouched over the TBT, lining up the pointer on the TBT with a destroyer that was plunging toward them.

"Escort astern is coming up on us fast," he yelled.

"Right ten degrees rudder," Mealey ordered. He saw a sudden blossom of flame near the second target's bow and heard the roar of the explosion. Another burst of flame in the midships section of the target lit up the sky.

"Two hits in the second target!" Mealey yelled. "Reverse your helm! Steady on this heading. All ahead flank! Maneuvering, give me every turn you can."

He stood in the small bridge space, his hands gripping the teak rail, his seaman's eyes judging the speed of the escort that was swinging into a wide turn around the bow of the sinking ship he had hit in the second attack. He looked at his second target. He could see hundreds of men leaping from the decks into the water. "Troop transport," he said to himself. He raised his voice.

"Brannon! Set up on that escort when he's broadside, before he makes his turn to come down on us. Conning Tower, give Captain Brannon some help!"

Eelfish raced down the side of the sinking troop transport as the escort vessel swung wide of the bow of the troop transport. Mealey heard Brannon's voice giving the Conning Tower the angle on the bow of the destroyer, heard him yell,

"Fire eight!

"Fire nine! Begin reload aft!"

Mealey forced himself to look away from the action astern. He searched the dark sea ahead of him, looking for his next target. Behind him he heard the familiar sound of a torpedo exploding against a ship and heard Brannon's exultant cry.

"Hit! The destroyer is down by the bow! He's sinking!"

In the Forward Torpedo Room the incredibly intricate choreography of a reload had begun as soon as the first torpedo had been fired at the aircraft carrier. Petreshock whirled the big Y-wrench that was used to open and close the outer torpedo tube door and shutter in a spinning arc as he closed the outer door to Number One tube. As the door slammed shut he tossed the wrench to a member of the reload crew, who put it in an upper bunk. Petreshock opened the drain valves for the tube and twisted an air valve to put pressure into the tube to blow the water in the tube down into the WRT, the Water 'Round Torpedo tank. He counted to himself, listening with one ear to the flow of orders the telephone talker was hearing and repeating aloud. He closed the air valve and vented off the pressure in the tube, and a reload member gave him a wrench. He slammed the wrench on the stud that turned the locking bayonet joint on the inner door and heaved on the wrench. The door came open with a jolt and a stream of water poured out into the room. Petreshock struggled through the water pouring out of the tube and ducked down as the reload crew, hauling mightily on a block and tackle, began to move the reload torpedo into the tube. As he crouched below the moving torpedo Petreshock opened an air valve to recharge the impulse firing tank for the tube. He raised a hand as the tail of the torpedo cleared the forward end of the roller stand. The reload crew stopped hauling and Petreshock threw off the block and tackle and began to push the torpedo the final few inches into the tube, easing it in until he felt the guide stud on top of the torpedo come up against the stop bolt in the tube. He yanked the brass propeller guard off the torpedo's screws and tossed it up into a bunk, then closed the door and carefully adjusted the tail buffer to make sure the torpedo was held firmly in the tube. He opened the tube vent, stooped and closed the air valve to the impulse tanks, and began to open the outer tube door. In between the tube banks Jim Rice carefully engaged the gyro spindle, engaged the depth spindle and set the depth at four feet, and disengaged the depth spindle.

"Report Number One tube reloaded, depth set four feet. Gyro spindle engaged. Outer door open." He ducked back between the tubes to avoid being hit by the Y-wrench Petreshock was spinning as he closed the outer door to the Number Two tube.

"Right ten degrees rudder," Mealey roared. *Eelfish* was twisting and turning in the midst of the task force. Ahead of him Mealey could see the dark bulk of ships moving in different directions. From one of the ships rockets were being fired to explode far overhead, bathing the ocean in an eerie red light.

"Reload completed on Number Two tube. You have Number One and Two tubes forward ready to shoot." Flanagan's voice over the bridge speaker was calm.

"Next target bears zero eight zero. Meet your helm right there," Mealey yelled. He looked around swiftly. Astern he could see the bulk of the first target, lit now by a roaring column of flame that seemed to reach hundreds of feet into the air. On his port quarter the second target was down by the bow, sinking, its whistle bellowing hoarsely to indicate the ship's plight. The destroyer Mike Brannon had hit was gone, nowhere in sight.

"I've got three fast ships coming at us from ahead, four from our starboard bow," Michaels's voice came over the speaker.

"Reload on Three and Four completed, Bridge. Reload on Seven and Eight completed." Flanagan reported.

"Very well," Mealey said. Ahead of him to starboard he saw the long outline of an oil tanker.

"Come right five degrees, Helm," he yelled. "Next target is the ship bearing dead ahead and moving to our starboard bow."

"Bearing is zero zero nine," Olsen yelled from the battle periscope. "Range is nine hundred yards."

"Angle on the bow is one one zero starboard," Mealey called out.

"Solution!" Arbuckle yelled.

"Fire three!

"Fire four!" Mealey looked around quickly. He could see the closest of the four ships Michaels had reported coming at the *Eelfish,* a destroyer, its bow wave curling high and white in the moonlight. He turned and looked astern. In the light from the burning aircraft carrier he could see three ships coming at him, all destroyers. He turned back and saw a huge explosion of flame in the tanker.

"Hit!" he screamed. "Ten degrees right rudder. Pour on all the coal we've got. Maneuvering!

"Michaels. Call up Maulers One and Two. Invite them to the dance at all possible speed." *Eelfish* was swinging to the right, running toward the burning tanker. Mealey looked at the closest destroyer, gauging the distance between the destroyer and the burning tanker.

"Meet your helm right there. Give me more speed, damn it!" he yelled down the hatch. "More speed or we're going to be rammed!" He ducked instinctively as a shell from the onrushing destroyer screamed above the periscope shears.

"Get behind the damned shears, Brannon!" Mealey yelled. "That son of a bitch is going to open up with small stuff in a minute!" Brannon scrambled forward from the TBT and crouched behind the heavy steel structure of the periscope shears.

Captain Mealey stood in the center of the open bridge, judging distances, judging his speed, the slowing speed of the burning tanker and the speed of the destroyer racing toward the *Eelfish*. *Eelfish* was closing on the burning tanker, racing to cross its bow before the destroyer coming up the tanker's starboard side could ram. Brannon, crouched behind the periscope shears, looked at Captain Mealey and saw him raise both arms and shake his fists as the destroyer raced toward *Eelfish*, its bow guns firing continuously. In the red glare of the burning tanker Brannon could see that Mealey's face was set in a demonic grin.

"My God!" Brannon muttered to himself. "He's Captain Ahab and this is his white whale!"

The *Eelfish* cleared the bow of the burning tanker by a scant fifty yards and heeled in a sharp left turn in response to Mealey's barked order.

"Shoot that son of a bitch coming after us when he makes his turn," Mealey yelled back at Brannon, who sprang to his feet and ran aft to the TBT.

"You've got all tubes, all tubes," Flanagan's voice roared out of the bridge speaker. "You've got ten tubes, outer doors open, depth set four feet."

"Very well," Mealey answered.

The next twenty minutes, as Brannon was to recall later, were the wildest he had ever experienced. *Eelfish*, the target of seven destroyers, twisted and turned through an ocean lit by the glare of the burning ships. Sirens on the stricken ships moaned and wailed as Captain Mealey dodged and twisted, using the sinking ships as shelters to dodge behind as *Eelfish* raced at top speed through the sea.

Brannon remembered later that at one point *Eelfish* had plowed through hundreds of troops swimming in the water. He had heard the screams of the men in the water as the bull-nosed bow of the *Eelfish* cut through a life raft loaded with men and then sideswiped a lifeboat, turning it over and spilling everyone in it into the water.

Dodging and twisting, *Eelfish* cleared the bow of a sinking troop transport, and Mealey saw a freighter heading for him, its whistle blowing steadily.

"Target is dead ahead!" Mealey yelled. "Angle on the bow is zero."

"You've got all tubes forward and aft," Flanagan repeated from the Control Room.

"Down his damned throat. Stand by forward!"

"Fire one!

"Fire two!

"Fire three!"

The first two torpedoes missed ahead of the freighter's blunt bow. The third torpedo exploded with a roar against the side of the ship's bow, just below the hawse pipe, and the ship slowed and began to plow its way into the sea.

"Hit on that target!" Mealey yelled. "Give me fifteen degrees right rudder." *Eelfish* twisted away as the freighter exploded with a gigantic roar.

"Ammunition ship!" Mealey yelled. "Set up on this destroyer coming in from behind that last target. Angle on the bow is nine zero port!"

"Solution!" Arbuckle yelled.

"Fire four!

"Fire five!"

Mealey saw the destroyer heel sharply to put its squat stern to the oncoming torpedoes. "Bastard!" Mealey yelled as he saw the phosphorescent wakes of both torpedoes race past the destroyer. He turned and saw another destroyer astern, heard Brannon chanting bearings and an angle on the bow, heard him give orders to fire tubes Seven and Eight. And then Brannon's exultant yell.

"Hit! Hit on that destroyer! He's broken in two!"

Mealey looked around him. The last ship he had hit was disintegrating in a series of violent explosions. Beyond that ship the destroyer he had fired at and missed was turning to come back toward him.

"Right full rudder," Mealey yelled. "Brannon, take that bastard coming at us! Eyeball it!"

"Fire nine!

"Fire ten!" Brannon's voice was a scream. Mealey, watching, saw the destroyer swing wide to one side. "That bastard's got a charmed life," he muttered to himself. He yelled at Brannon to come forward to the bridge.

"We're being boxed in," he said, ducking with Brannon as a shell screamed over the forward deck of the *Eelfish*.

"That bastard in charge of those tin cans knows what he's doing. He's closing us in. Let's get down and out of here. Dive! Dive!" His fist hit the diving alarm and he followed Brannon down through the hatch, grabbing at the toggle on the end of the short bronze cable that hung from the center of the hatch, hauling downward on the cable as Brosmer pushed by him on the ladder to spin the dogging wheel and close the hatch tightly.

"Four hundred feet," Mealey called down the hatch to the Control Room. "Make it fast! Rig for depth charge. Rig for silent running." He slid down the ladder to the Control Room.

"How's your trim?" he said to Jerry Gold.

"Can't tell," Gold replied offhandedly. "We've got a fifteen-degree down bubble. Seems to be all right. I'll know when we try to stop her at four hundred feet."

Mealey glared at Gold's broad back and then turned his eyes to the long black needles of the depth gauges.

"Screws coming fast," Blake reported from the Conning Tower. "Bearing one four zero, sir, coming very fast." Mealey raised his head and listened as the thunder of the destroyer's propellers filled *Eelfish*'s hull. The people in the Control Room saw him wince slightly as two sharp cracks could be heard.

"Here it comes," Mealey said in a low voice, and then two tremendous explosions shook the *Eelfish*. Jerry Gold was spun away from his position by the ladder to the Conning Tower. He tried to catch his balance and slammed into Mike Brannon, knocking him off his feet. A light bulb burst with a sharp noise.

"Two sets of twin screws coming fast, bearing one five eight and one four seven," Blake called from his place in the Conning Tower.

The thunder of the destroyer's screws reverberated through the hull of the *Eelfish* as the attackers raced overhead. The *Eelfish* reeled and twisted as the depth charges exploded in what seemed to be a continuous roar of sound, the ship's thin hull creaking under the force of the underwater explosions. Captain Mealey stood at the gyro table, his hands clutching at the edge of the table for support, his eyes on the line on the plot that Bob Lee was drawing.

"They're dedicated bastards," Mealey said dryly. He raised one hand from the edge of the gyro table and put a finger on the plot. "We're here, and that's almost the exact spot where we ran through all those troops in the water. Those bastards are dropping charges with their own people there. They're killing their own damned people!" He looked over at Jerry Gold.

"I asked you for a report on your trim."

"Slightly heavy by the bow, sir," Gold said. "Next time they make a little noise I can correct that, sir."

"Five hundred feet," Mealey said. Gold turned his head and looked at Mealey. He nodded and touched the bow and stern planesmen on their shoulders.

"The man wants five hundred feet. So go to five hundred feet. Smartly."

A sharp ringing noise sounded throughout the hull of the *Eelfish*. It sounded again, and Paul Blake called out, "He's pinging on us with sonar, Control."

"Very well," Captain Mealey said. He looked upward toward the Conning Tower hatch. "Advise me the minute you hear his screws pick up speed, sonar."

The pinging went on for several minutes, and then Blake called out, "Three sets of screws picking up speed, Control. Bearings are from one six zero to one eight zero."

"Six hundred feet, fast!" Mealey snapped. *Eelfish* took a steep down angle and slid deeper beneath the sea. Gold leveled the ship off at 600 feet as *Eelfish* reeled under a barrage of depth charges exploded around and above the submarine.

"Get ready for a long siege," Mealey said calmly. "We're going to be getting hell for a long time. We've made those people pretty angry. I want damage reports from every compartment after every attack. I want reports of leaks, no matter how small. We may have to go deeper than where we are now." He wiped perspiration from his face and neck with a towel and studied the chart and plot.

CHAPTER 17

Three miles to the east of where *Eelfish* was being pounded by the Japanese destroyers the bridge crew of the *Hatchet Fish* could see the fires of the burning ships and hear the thunder of the depth charges. Captain Chet Marble leaned toward his bridge transmitter.

"Give me a radar check. I want to know how many ships there are out there."

"I read seven ships maneuvering radically, Bridge. Range to the mass of ships is six thousand yards."

"Very well," Captain Marble said. His Executive Officer, a

tall, lean, dour man named Abe Wilkinson, looked at his commanding officer.

"We're going over to help *Eelfish*, aren't we?"

"No," Captain Marble said. "Captain Mealey gave us our orders. He was specific. We are to wait here and intercept and sink any shipping that comes our way."

"I understand, sir," Wilkinson said patiently. "But at the time he issued those orders to us nothing was said about one or the other of us being attacked with depth charges. I would assume that if we were being pounded, as *Eelfish* is being pounded, that Captain Mealey would come to our rescue."

"Don't assume," Chet Marble said, the acid in his voice apparent to everyone within earshot on the bridge. "Captain Mealey would come to our rescue if he could see another Medal of Honor in it for him. We will follow our orders, sir." His Executive Officer stared at him for a long moment.

"Permission to go below, sir?"

"Granted," Captain Marble said. "Send me up a cup of coffee when you get below." He turned and leveled his binoculars at the fires on the horizon. His Quartermaster turned his back on his Captain and stared to the eastern horizon.

On the *Eelfish*, twisting and turning 600 feet below the surface, the temperature had climbed to 120 degrees. The humidity was 100 percent. Puddles formed on the deck, on level surfaces, and re-formed as rapidly as they were wiped up. The continual barrage of depth charges had long since broken all the lights and most of the gauge glasses. The interior of the *Eelfish* was lit by battery-powered battle lanterns equipped with heavy glass fronts that could not be broken by anything less than a direct blow with a sledgehammer. The interior of the *Eelfish* reeked with the fetid odor of stale air and sweating men and the stench of fear.

The hours wore on. Up above, on the surface, the Japanese destroyers had established a pattern. Two of them searched for the *Eelfish* with sonar beams, and when they found the submarine they took up position on either side of the *Eelfish*, while the other five destroyers made their runs between their two sister ships, dropping depth charges off their sterns, firing them out to the sides with Y-guns.

The *Eelfish* responded to the attacks, speeding up when Paul Blake reported that an attack run had started, turning in half circles, changing depth upward and downward to throw off the gunners on the Japanese ships who were setting the depth-charge explosion depths. Captain Mealey stood at the gyro table, a soggy towel draped around his neck. Mike Brannon stood beside him. Mealey peered at the luminous dial of his wrist watch, barely visible in the gloom of the Control Room.

"It's daylight up above," he said. "They've been at it for over eight hours." He wiped his face with the end of the towel as Paul Blake reported that another attack run had begun.

"Right fifteen degrees rudder," he snapped. The two men stationed at the helm grunted with effort as they turned the ship's rudder by hand power.

"Rudder's fifteen degrees right, sir," one of the men gasped. He hung on the brass wheel, sobbing with his effort, gasping for air in the oxygen-depleted atmosphere.

"Very well," Mealey said. "Seven hundred feet, Mr. Gold. Smartly, if your people can do it." At the bow and stern planes the two Battle Stations planesmen gasped and grunted as they fought to tilt bow and stern planes downward by hand power alone. *Eelfish* slanted downward as the crashing explosions of the depth charges shook the submarine and twisted it in a vortex of water until the hull rivets creaked and groaned under the strain.

In the Forward Torpedo Room Steve Petreshock had organized his torpedomen and the reload crew into four groups. Two of those groups worked at the job of turning the sound heads by hand power while the other two groups rested.

"Son of a bitch can go back to hydraulic power any time he wants," Rice grunted. "Fucking Japs know where we are anyway, so why make us do this shit, go to hand power on the helm, the planes and the sound heads?" He staggered away from the sound head shaft and sagged against a torpedo skid. "Bad enough you wear your ass out reloadin' all the fish in this room, including that fucking Numbers Five and Six, bad enough you got to do that without puttin' up with this shit."

"Save your breath," Petreshock grunted. He looked at the pressure gauge and tried to whistle and failed. "My God, we're at seven hundred feet! What the hell does he think this damned submarine is?"

In the Control Room Mealey stared at the plot and then looked at Jim Michaels.

"What was the last contact you had with Maulers One and Two?"

"They receipted for our message that we were beginning the attack, sir. Mauler Two receipted for the message inviting them to take part in the action. Mauler One did not receipt for that message, sir."

"Bastards!" Mealey growled out the word from between clenched teeth. "If one of them would get over here and fire at one of those tin cans up there it might help out a hell of a lot. As long as they think they've got only one submarine here they might stay here all day and night." He looked at Flanagan.

"How many torpedoes do we have, Chief?"

"Three, sir. One in Number Six tube forward. Two back aft. In Nine and Ten tubes, sir."

"Three fish, seven destroyers. Bad odds," Mealey grunted. He looked up as Paul Blake's voice came down from the Conning Tower.

"Here they come again, Control. Three destroyers coming at us from dead ahead, sir."

"Rudder amidships. All stop." Mealey snapped. "We've been turning away from his attacks. Last three runs he peeled off on each side to catch us. We'll see if this does any good, staying almost still." The crew braced, hearing the thunder of the destroyer screws, wincing as a man at the sharp crack of the depth-charge exploder mechanisms going off, and then the shattering roar of the exploding charges shook the *Eelfish* like a rat in the jaws of a terrier. In the After Torpedo Room Fred Nelson was thrown from his feet in front of the torpedo tubes. He hauled himself erect by grabbing at the torpedo roller stand, blood gushing from his hooked nose.

"One more like that, you fucker," he growled, "and I'm puttin' in for a transfer from this fuckin' submarine navy." He moved down the length of his torpedo room, patting men on the shoulders and backs.

"Don't none of you people start pukin'," he said, "because I ain't got the patience to clean up after you. Last time I looked at the depth gauge that S.O.B. up there in the Control Room had us at seven hundred feet. No wonder the damned room's beginning to leak."

"You want to report leaks?" the telephone talker stammered, his chin wobbling with fear.

"No I don't want to report no damned leaks," Nelson growled. "That S.O.B. in the Control Room has got enough on his mind without me adding my share of shit. As long as I ain't worried about a little water comin' in you don't have to worry."

In the Conning Tower Paul Blake clung to the edge of the shelf on which his gear was mounted. Lieutenant Perry Arbuckle, who was hanging on to the periscope cables for support, saw the effort that Blake was making to stay calm.

"Must be hell up in the Forward Room, turning those two sound heads by hand," Arbuckle said, trying to keep his own voice conversational. Blake nodded and bent his head, listening. His head came up suddenly, his eyes wild.

"Control! I can hear torpedoes running, three or four of them! Control!" He cried out in pain as a tremendous noise crashed through his earphones and the hull of the *Eelfish*.

"Where did you hear torpedoes?" Captain Mealey was half-way up the ladder to the Conning Tower. "What bearing?"

"I was tracking a ship bearing one six zero, sir," Blake said. "The screws I heard, very fast, high-pitched, just like our own torpedoes, sir, came from aft of that bearing. They ran right into the bearing of the ship I was tracking."

"Left full rudder," Mealey snapped. "Mr. Gold, don't let this ship get one foot above seven hundred feet. I've got to sort this out." He turned as the sound of two depth charges echoed through *Eelfish*'s hull, depth charges dropped at some distance.

"Will your torpedoes stand being fired at one hundred feet, Chief? Yes or no?"

"I Tacki-waxed the exhaust valves myself," Flanagan said. "They won't leak through the valves. Yes."

"One hundred feet, Mr. Gold. Give it one big effort, men." He joined Jerry Gold on the planes, Gold helping the stern planesman, Captain Mealey throwing his stringy muscle against the bow plane wheel.

"Set depth on torpedoes Nine and Ten at zero feet," he called out. "Set speed at low. Repeat, torpedo depth on numbers Nine and Ten tubes at zero feet. Speed on the low setting." He watched the black needles on the depth gauges moving toward the one-hundred-foot mark.

"Sonar! Give me an accurate bearing at the ships you have." He waited.

"Bearing on the depth charging is one seven zero, sir."

"Left five degrees rudder," Mealey said. "Stand by aft." He turned to Brannon. "I'll shake those bastards up, when they see fish plowing toward them!"

"Targets bear one eight zero, sir," Blake cried.

"Meet your helm. Stand by aft . . .

"Fire nine!

"Fire ten!"

The two torpedoes burst out of the tubes at a depth of 95 feet,

planed upward to the surface, and streaked across the sunlit
water, splashing and throwing spray. A siren sounded on a
destroyer, ululating. The pack of destroyers scattered, their squat
sterns dropping into the water, their bows rearing high as their
engines went to full speed.

"They're going off in all directions, sir," Paul Blake reported.
"All the screws I can hear are turning up very high revolutions."

"Very well," Mealey said. "Maintain depth at one hundred
feet, rudder amidships. Now we'll wait and see if that did any
good." He mopped his face and neck with the wet towel.

Blake reported that he had lost all the high-speed screws five
minutes later. Mealey nodded and looked at the two men on the
helm. Both were hanging on to the big brass wheel for support,
physically exhausted.

"Shift to hydraulic power on the sound heads, bow and stern
planes, and the helm," Mealey said.

"I can hear a slow twin screw beat bearing one seven zero,"
Blake reported. "Sounds like one of our submarine screws, sir."

"Any guess, son, on how far away he might be?"

"No, sir, but he's not too far."

"Make a recognition signal by sonar," Mealey ordered.

Blake keyed the sonar transmitter slowly and carefully and
waited. The entire crew of the *Eelfish* heard the answering
message beat against the hull.

"Mauler Two reporting for duty. Mauler Two reports two
torpedo hits in a destroyer and observation of the destroyer
breaking up. Mauler Two at periscope depth and can see no
enemy. Over."

"Tell Mauler Two many thanks and that we will surface on
heading three five zero," Mealey said. He looked at Mike
Brannon, and a faint smile showed under the white mustache.

"The Lord provides when you need it most. Stand by to
surface." The surface klaxon squawked and the *Eelfish* surged
upward in a long slant. Captain Mealey climbed the ladder to the
Conning Tower and looked at Lieutenant Perry Arbuckle and
Paul Blake.

"Damned fine work, you two. Dàmned fine."

Eelfish burst through the surface of the water as Mealey fought
his way upward through the bridge hatch, ignoring the residual
water that poured in as he pushed the hatch open. Mike Brannon
followed him to the bridge and jumped out of the way as the
lookouts and Bob Lee came scrambling topside.

"Submarine surfacing bearing one five zero," the starboard

lookout bellowed. Brannon ran aft to the TBT and then relaxed as he saw the familiar shape of a U.S. Navy fleet submarine. Blake's voice floated up the hatch.

"Mauler Two requests permission to close and speak to Captain Mealey, Bridge."

"Answer affirmative," Mealey called down the hatch. "Tell him to come up on my starboard side." He leveled his binoculars at the *Sea Chub* as it slid into position barely fifty feet off the starboard side of the *Eelfish*.

"Hold your course steady," Mealey called down the hatch. "Make turns for one third ahead. Start the battery charge. He leaned his elbows on the bridge rail and cupped his hands around his mouth.

"Many thanks for your attack, sir. They were a very persistent bunch."

"We appreciate your getting them off our backs, sir," Captain Shelton sang out in a loud voice. "We could hear those fish of yours thrashing along; my sound man thought you fired your torpedoes at a low speed setting. That right?"

"Affirmative," Mealey called out. "We fired from one hundred feet, depth setting zero, low speed. Figured they would see them and get panicky."

"Mauler Two reports sinking one troop transport, sir. We have two prisoners from that ship. What was your bag?"

"One small carrier, one troop ship, one tanker, one freighter, and two destroyers," Mealey called out. "How many torpedoes do you have left?"

"Fired four at the transport. Fired four at the destroyers that were clustered over you, sir. We have sixteen fish left, twelve forward, four aft."

"We have one left forward," Mealey called out. "Have you heard from Mauler One?"

"Negative, sir. Advise you inspect your topside. From here it looks as if you've lost most of your main deck. Congratulations on one hell of an attack, sir."

Mealey and Brannon looked at the decks. The area forward of the bridge was a mass of twisted wood and steel supports. Aft of the deck gun on the afterdeck there was no deck at all.

"They have some big sea lice in this part of the world," Mealey yelled across to the *Sea Chub*. "Where did you pick up the troop transport?"

"Picked him up when we headed for your fireworks, sir," Captain Shelton yelled back. "He came right across my bow.

Stopped to get two prisoners hanging on to a life ring. Went under far enough to submerge our decks and used radar to sort out what was happening to you. Couldn't get into your mess until you had gone under and the destroyers had established an attack pattern that we could take advantage of.''

"Took him a hell of a while to do that," Mealey said in a low voice to Brannon. He raised his voice and faced the *Sea Chub*.

"Our thanks to you. Haul off now and take up position five hundred yards on my starboard beam. We'll wait for Mauler One to show."

An hour later Jim Michaels reported that Mauler One was requesting contact with the pack leader. Mealey looked at Mike Brannon. "I'll talk to that gentleman myself," he said and went down the hatch.

At the door of the radio shack he motioned to Jim Michaels.

"Ask the radioman to step out here please," he said. "I'll talk to Mauler One and I'd like to keep the door closed, if you don't mind."

The radioman closed the door after Captain Mealey had gone into the radio shack. He grinned slyly at Jim Michaels. "I don't think my gear is going to stand up under what the S.O.B. is likely to say," he half whispered to Michaels. "Did you see those eyes? He's mad enough to bite the damned mike off'n the stem."

Mealey sat in the radio shack and pushed the transmit button.

"Mealey to Mauler One. Mealey here."

"Mauler One affirmative."

"Report your position," Mealey said.

"Mauler One is on station as ordered, sir."

"Is this the Captain speaking?" Mealey asked.

"No, sir. Captain is in the radio shack. This is Harold Crippin, Chief Radioman, sir."

"Please put Captain Marble on the microphone," Mealey snapped.

"Marble here." The voice was a slow drawl.

"How many torpedoes do you have left?" Mealey asked.

"Mauler One reports all torpedoes aboard, sir."

"Were you aware, sir, that we were under heavy attack?"

"We saw your fires and heard what we took to be some depth charging, sir." Captain Marble's voice over the air was almost frosty. "We received no orders to contradict those you issued with commendable firmness, sir, to stay on our station."

Mealey stared at the microphone. He drew a deep breath and thumbed the transmit button.

"Stand by to copy your orders, sir.

"*Eelfish* is returning to port with only one, repeat one torpedo. Mauler Two has sixteen torpedoes. Mauler One will proceed in company with Mauler Two to original patrol area. Advise Mauler One, as pack commander, that the rest of that task force is steaming back toward Manila. There is a heavy cruiser in that lot and at least six destroyers. Over and out."

"Thank you, sir. Mauler One will assume pack leadership and proceed to original patrol area. Over and out." The circuit went dead and Captain Mealey pushed his chair back from the radioman's small table.

"You son of a bitch!" he whispered to himself, "you damned cowardly son of a bitch! I'll hang you, Marble, I'll hang you so high you'll get airsick reading the charges!" He went out into the Control Room and climbed wearily to the bridge. Jim Michaels's voice came up through the bridge speaker.

"Mauler Two reports reading message to Mauler One and wishes *Eelfish* a safe and speedy return home."

"Tell them Godspeed," Mealey said. He turned to Mike Brannon.

"I'd appreciate it, Captain, if you'd take back your ship, sir. I suggest you secure from General Quarters, set the regular sea watch, and have Mr. Olsen lay down the most direct course to Fremantle. I would like to see you in the Wardroom in ten minutes." He turned and began to climb down the ladder. Brannon, watching him, wondered at the slowness of his movements and then realized, as Captain Mealey looked upward, that the older man's face was haggard with exhaustion.

CHAPTER 18

Mike Brannon walked into the Wardroom and found Captain Mealey sitting there, a cup of coffee in front of him. The Captain reached for his pipe and tobacco and began to fill his pipe with slow, deliberate motions.

"As part of my last duties as the wolf-pack commander," he said, "I think we should get off a report at once telling Pearl

Harbor and Fremantle what ships we sank and what the *Sea Chub* sank and advise Fremantle that we are returning to port because we have only one torpedo left. Advise Fremantle that *Hatchet Fish* and *Sea Chub* have been sent to the original patrol area by my order. That's the only mention I want made of *Hatchet Fish* in this message. Advise Fremantle of our course and ETA. I don't want some trigger-happy submarine skipper shooting at us on our way home because he doesn't know we're supposed to be going through his area.''

Mealey stopped and sipped at his coffee, and then he lit his pipe. "I don't know how you go about getting ready to write a contact and action report, Mike. But if I may make a suggestion: So much was going on during our action, so damned much, that rather than leave something out it might be a good idea to get everyone in here and get the benefit of their recollections. With the plots, of course. I think if we do that we'll have a very comprehensive report, and that's what Captain Rudd is going to need. We can do that right after the noon meal.''

"If I may suggest it, sir . . .'' Brannon's face was concerned. "You look awfully tired.''

"I know how I look,'' Mealey said. "I washed my face when I came below. I am not that tired, sir, nor that old. I am forty-one years old this past birthday. This is supposed to be the prime of my adult life, at least intellectually. What you see in my face, sir, is not weariness. It is disgust.

"I am sick to my stomach, sir. Sicker than I have ever been in my life, and the sickness is not due to anything I ate.''

"I understand, sir,'' Brannon said softly.

"Do you?'' Mealey's eyes were boring into Brannon. "Yes. You probably do. You're Irish. You would understand.'' He looked up as Pete Mahaffey came into the Wardroom with a carafe of coffee.

"Captain,'' Mahaffey said to Brannon, "cook wants to know if he can feed steak for the noon meal. Cook figures Captain Mealey needs some more red meat.'' His cheerful face split in a wide grin.

"Absolutely,'' Brannon said.

"One steak or two for you, sir?'' Mahaffey said to Captain Mealey.

"One. Very rare.''

The contact report from the *Eelfish* arrived at the Bend of the Road while Admiral Christie was holding a staff meeting. He read the message and bounced to his feet, waving the message flimsy in the air.

"Mealey smashed that task force to bits!" he shouted. "He sank, let me see, it says here he sank one small aircraft carrier, a tanker, a freighter loaded with ammunition, a troop transport—he says he saw hundreds of troops in the water—and two destroyers! My God!"

"He says the rest of the task force hauled ass back toward Manila Bay. Call General MacArthur right away, Sam. This can make a hell of a difference to his plans." He sat down in his chair, holding the message in front of him.

"Oh, this makes my day? My whole week! That crusty old S.O.B., he was right. The wolf pack idea is a good one."

"How many Captain Mealeys do we have in our skipper locker to run wolf packs?" Sam Rivers said dryly. "And what about *Hatchet Fish* and *Sea Chub*?"

"Let me see, I didn't even read the whole thing. Oh, he says that Shelton in *Sea Chub* got a troop transport and has two prisoners and that he got a destroyer." He read through the message again. "That's strange, not one word about *Hatchet Fish*'s part in the action. The only time he mentions Captain Marble and *Hatchet Fish* is at the end where he says he ordered the other two boats to proceed to the original patrol area under command of Chet Marble. That's very strange."

"Not to me," the Operations Officer growled. "Old Chet Marble was probably hunting for a way to get away from that action if I know him. Either the water wasn't deep enough or it was too deep or the Japanese destroyers were vicious. He'd find some reason not to put his ass in danger."

"Now wait a minute, Sam," Admiral Christie said. "We don't have Chet's side of the story. Maybe he lost touch with Mealey, maybe his communications got fouled up. Maybe Mealey deployed him way out in left field and he couldn't get into the fight. We just don't know."

"I know one thing," Sam Rivers growled. "Being with Mealey must have done something for Shelton in *Sea Chub*. If he got two ships he must be creamin' his shorts! He's never hit a ship up until now, and he's made three war patrols."

In Pearl Harbor Captain Mealey's boss, a tall, beefy, red-faced four-striper named Bob Rudd, was eating dinner in the Officers' Club when a Marine Sergeant came up to his table and handed him a sealed envelope. He opened the envelope by running a thick index finger between the flap and the back of the envelope, pulled the message out, and read it. His eyes widened, and he read the message again; then he leaped to his feet with a whoop that startled the other diners, grabbed a roll and stuffed it in his pocket, and ran for the door. Back at his office he sat down at his desk and began dialing telephone numbers. When his staff had assembled in a cluster in front of his desk he held up the message he had received in the O-Club.

"I didn't drag you away from your dinners for nothing, fellas. Listen to this." He read the message slowly and then reread it.

"That old bastard did it again! He purely knocked the living shit out of those people and sent them running back to Manila Bay! Christ, he even got Jim Shelton to bust his cherry. He isn't a virgin any more, he got two ships. But he doesn't say anything about the other boat in the wolf pack. Chet Marble in *Hatchet Fish*. Must be Marble is still a virgin. Something funny there, but we'll know about it soon enough." He turned to his Operations Officer.

"Walt, make a copy of this and hand deliver it to those people in Ultra. Read it out loud to the whole damned bunch. They did an absolutely superb job of pinpointing the assembly and the departure of that task force, and we owe them one hell of a lot of thanks. So let them know how we feel."

"Maybe if I go down into that damned cubbyhole of theirs with something like this," the Operations Officer said with a small grin, "maybe if I give them something like this that weird guy in charge who walks around in a damned smoking jacket and slippers will finally give me the time of day. Every time I've had to talk to him he just looks right through me and grunts."

"I don't give a damn if he grunts or if he wants to wear bathing trunks and a diver's helmet. Mr. Rochefort is a damned genius, that's what the son of a bitch is.

"Now, the rest of you: First thing tomorrow morning call a meeting of all Squadron Commanders. I'll have copies made of Mealey's message by then.

"We are going to wolf pack, fellas. Mealey's proved it can be done and by God, we'll do it!" He reached for the telephone. "You people can go back to doing what you were doing when I called you. Breakfast staff meeting at zero seven hundred tomorrow." He put the phone to his ear and spoke to the yeoman outside his office.

"Get me Admiral Nimitz, son. Get him no matter what he's doing, even if he's in the sack with some broad." He waited, drumming his fingers on the desk.

"Sorry to take you away from dinner, Admiral," he said, "but I knew you'd want to know this." He began to read the message from Captain Mealey.

The arrival of the *Eelfish* in Fremantle was a celebration. A fire tug, its fire nozzles spouting great arcs of water, accompanied the *Eelfish* into the harbor, where ships responded with congratulatory blasts of their whistles. The *Eelfish* slid in alongside the outboard submarine of the clutch of submarines nestled alongside the submarine tender. A crew of ship's carpenters was waiting with a section of wooden platform to lay over the torn deck near the afterdeck gun. The gangway was run over when the carpenters had finished, and Admiral Christie raced down the gangway, his hand outstretched to Captain Mealey.

"Just absolutely damned great, Arvin!" Christie boomed.

"Thank you, Admiral," Mealey said. He released the Admiral's hand and stood to one side so the Admiral could pump Mike Brannon's hand. The Admiral looked up and down the deck. "If this is all that's busted up we can take care of that in no time. No leaks? You must have taken a hell of a pounding."

"Nothing major, sir," Brannon said.

"Good," Christie said. "Staff meeting at fourteen hundred hours, gentlemen, at my headquarters. Captain Mealey, Captain Brannon, your Executive Officer." His bright eyes fastened on Captain Mealey.

"I'm told that Admiral Nimitz is so damned happy that he's turning cartwheels, or so Bob Rudd says. I'd be doing the same thing if I could turn cartwheels. Mike, the buses will be here at eleven hundred thirty hours. Dress blues, white hats, shined shoes. It's winter here now. Gets a little cold in the evening and at night. Noon meal will be served at the hotel. Paymaster will be in the lobby after the noon meal. See you this afternoon." He turned and bounded over the gangway, followed by his staff. A Lieutenant and three Chief Petty Officers who had been standing patiently on the submarine alongside came over the gangway. The Lieutenant saluted Mike Brannon.

"I'm Lieutenant Pinter," he said. "We're the relief crew people. I guess we'd better meet in the Forward Torpedo Room, sir. Not much room up here."

Mike Brannon looked at the shattered decks of his ship. His crew was perched in the wreckage, eating apples and oranges and reading their mail. He turned to John Olsen.

"Tell Chief Flanagan to get the other Chiefs up in the Forward

Room. Round up the Division Officers. Tell Flanagan that uniform of the day is dress blues and white hats. Buses will be here at half hour before noon. Noon meal in the hotel. Payday after that."

Brannon noticed a difference when he got out of the car Admiral Christie had sent for them. The Marine sentry at the gate wore a broad smile. An aide of the Admiral's was waiting in the lobby to lead them down the long hall to the conference room. Walking behind Captain Mealey, Brannon whispered to Olsen.

"Makes a difference when you've had a real good patrol. Those people didn't know we existed the last time we were here. Now they're all smiles." Olsen nodded and grinned.

Admiral Christie and his staff were waiting in the conference room. Christie shook hands again with Mealey and Mike Brannon and with John Olsen. The staff lined up to offer their congratulations.

"Get yourselves some coffee and sit down, gentlemen," Christie said. He shuffled a stack of papers in front of him. "We've all read your patrol report, Captain Mealey, Captain Brannon. So this debriefing shouldn't take too long." He looked at Mealey.

"Arvin, I've got to say that what you and Mike Brannon did on that night must have been one of the wildest sixty minutes in the history of submarine warfare. I've read God only knows how many patrol reports and ship action reports, and I've read widely in the history of submarine warfare, the reports from British ship captains in the Atlantic Theater. Nothing comes close to your report."

"We should have done better," Mealey said in a dry voice. "I missed with too many torpedoes. Captain Brannon missed with some of his shots, but that was mainly my fault. I had the conn and I was maneuvering radically, and he didn't know which way I was going to go." His right forefinger crept up and touched the right side of his white mustache.

"I will say those torpedoes we missed with did serve a purpose. They kept two or three Japanese destroyers from ramming us. They turned away when they saw the torpedo wakes."

"They could see your torpedo wakes at night?" Sam Rivers said.

"Yes, Sam, you can see torpedo wakes at night. There's a lot of phosphorescence in that water. The wake stands out like a chalk mark in the black water," Mealey said.

"Didn't know that," Rivers muttered.

"The hits you did get, and there were plenty of them," Christie said, "all good solid explosions? No low-order detonation?"

"Excellent warheads and exploders," Mealey said. "Rather astounding results on a couple of them. We apparently hit the aviation fuel tanks in that small carrier, because she burned like a big torch. The one freighter I hit started to explode like a Fourth of July display at a county fair. It must have been loaded with ammunition. I've been told that their tankers are often hard to sink because of their excellent compartmentation and watertight integrity, but the one we hit simply went up with a big roar." He looked at Admiral Christie.

"Any word from the rest of the wolf pack, sir?"

"Yes," Christie said. "Jim Shelton in *Sea Chub* went after the rest of the ships of the task force that had turned back to Manila Bay. He confirmed that they did return, as did an Ultra message two days later. The Ultra people also confirmed every one of your ships, gentlemen. Higher tonnages than you had estimated on the tanker and the freighter. I have a copy of the Ultra report here for you. *Hatchet Fish* and *Sea Chub* are on their way back here. They'll be in day after tomorrow."

"Why didn't they go on to the patrol area?" Mealey snapped. "Those were my orders."

"Admiral Nimitz ordered four submarines that were in the area just north of your patrol area to form up as a wolf pack and take over that spot," Christie said. "All four of those skippers had the benefit of some long discussions, or so I gather, with Bob Rudd and Nimitz about wolf-pack operations. So they won't be going in cold, so to speak. They know what they want to do." He looked at Mealey.

"Where did you station *Hatchet Fish* and *Sea Chub*, Captain?"

"As I mentioned in our action report and our patrol report, sir, we stationed *Hatchet Fish* three miles to the east of the proposed attack area and slightly to the south. *Sea Chub* was stationed three miles east and slightly north. I thought it reasonable from a seaman's point of view, and Captain Brannon concurred, that the task-force captains would not attempt to reverse course and go back through that narrow gut between Luzon and Mindoro.

"I reasoned that when they came under my attack they would bolt the task-force formation and go east, breaking off to the north and south. *Sea Chub* got the troop transport when the captain of that ship did precisely that. He slanted off to the northeast in an effort to get away from the attack. *Sea Chub* stopped to pick up two prisoners and a life ring. I think that was good thinking on his part." Mealey's long forefinger rose and touched the side of his mustache.

"Speaking for myself alone, Admiral, I deeply appreciate the attack made by *Sea Chub* on the destroyers that had pinned us down for some nine hours, but I submit . . ." His face hardened, and the pale blue eyes bored at Admiral Christie. "I submit, sir, that they took one hell of a long damned time to make up their mind to attack!"

"That's a grave charge, Captain Mealey," the Admiral said. "We haven't been told his side of the story. He may have had some problem in materiel. We don't know."

"Granted," Mealey said, his voice dry.

"And *Hatchet Fish*?" Admiral Christie's voice was almost silken in tone.

"I intend to prefer charges of cowardice against that man!" Mealey snapped. "He lay out there, six thousand yards from the action, safe and sound. He could see the fires of our targets—*Sea Chub* saw them. He could hear the Japanese destroyers giving us hell—*Sea Chub* heard them. He made no effort to come to our assistance. I demand, sir, that he be relieved of command, and if there is any way I can do it I am going to have that man hung!"

There was a dead silence around the conference table. Mike Brannon moved restlessly in his chair. John Olsen sat very still, his eyes on Captain Mealey. The silence was broken at last by Captain Sam Rivers, the Operations Officer.

"Captain Marble has informed us that you gave him very strict orders to maintain his patrol position. He says you sent him no orders to join in the action, as you say in your action report you did. If, sir, I may say this without prejudice on my part, I am merely reading what Captain Marble has said—he charges you with hogging the action. Those are his words, hogging the action so that you could attack the targets and get, ahem, another medal." He sat back in his chair, his powerful chest and shoulders rigid.

Captain Mealey turned to Admiral Christie. "A moment ago, sir, you said I had made a grave charge against the Captain of the *Sea Chub* when I said he took too damned long to come to our aid. Captain Marble has made a heinous charge against me, and I demand satisfaction." He paused, and Mike Brannon could see him fighting for composure and control.

"I demand, sir, with all due respect to you, that the commanding officers of the *Sea Chub* and the *Hatchet Fish* face me in this room, before you and your staff, sir, and we'll find out who the damned liars are!''

Admiral Christie stared at the table in front of him for a long moment and then raised his face.

"Unfortunately, or perhaps fortunately, Captain Mealey, I cannot grant your legitimate request.

"Admiral Nimitz has ordered you home to Pearl by the fastest possible means. A plane is available tomorrow morning. I must insist that you be on it." His normally jovial face was grim, almost sad.

"If I were you, sir, I would thank Captain Rudd when you get back. He received a copy of your action report. He has been informed of Captain Marble's charge. I think he anticipated your reaction, and he has added his own urgent request for your immediate return. His exact words in a cable to me are . . ." He shuffled in the papers in front of him. "He said, and I quote, tell the S.O.B. that we've won a little war and there is no reason to risk another battle, unquote. You undoubtedly know what Captain Rudd is referring to, sir. Now . . ." His face brightened.

"I cannot recommend you for another Congressional Medal of Honor, as much as I, all of us here, want to. So we have settled for a Navy Cross. Captain Brannon is to get a Navy Cross also, and Mr. Olsen, for his sterling work as the Executive Officer of the *Eelfish* in what will go down in our history sir, as the Battle of the Sibuyan Sea.

"We have also decided to award every member of the Wardroom a Silver Star. We've never done that before, but we think they deserve it." The Admiral stood up, and the people around the table rose in response. He looked at Captain Mealey and Mike Brannon.

"Gentlemen," he said softly, "if we had an Arvin Mealey and a Mike Brannon on every submarine and if every submarine we had was an *Eelfish* this war would be over now. Please accept my heartfelt thanks and congratulations."

Later, standing in the lobby waiting for the car to take them back to the *Eelfish*, Captain Mealey turned as Captain Sam Rivers walked up. He looked up at the taller man and put his hand on Mealey's arm.

"Chet Marble is being relieved of command with prejudice, sir," he said in a low tone. "The Admiral has decided to give Jim Shelton another chance, now that you've shown him how to sink ships."

"With prejudice?" Mealey said.

"He's going to the Navy Yard in San Diego," Rivers said. "That, sir, is prejudice, and it won't look good in his service jacket. Be content." He turned and walked away, his short, squat figure rigid.

Mike Brannon sat astride a chair in his stateroom, resting his arms on the chair back, and watched Captain Mealey pack.

Mealey turned to him, holding his razor in his hand. "You should understand a little more about politics by now, Mike. For a minute or two I forgot what I'd learned at Pearl Harbor. Captain Rudd never forgets. He knew I'd blow my stack about Chet Marble. So he's getting me back there where he can keep a tight rein on my big mouth." He smiled briefly. "Captain Marble has very powerful friends in Washington. Admiral Christie will have to run the risk of those people."

Brannon shifted on his chair. "I want to say something, sir, but I don't want it to come out the wrong way. If you ever command another wolf pack I'd be honored to serve under you, sir."

"You would?" Mealey said. "You know what Bob Rudd called me, the S.O.B.?"

"Oh, sure," Brannon said. "Everyone knows you're the S.O.B. I heard a fireman in the engine room one day before we started this patrol run say to an engineman that the old S.O.B. was sailing with us. He was proud you were aboard. We all feel that way, sir. If a man can sail with you he could sail with the devil himself." He flushed. "I didn't mean it to come out that way, sir."

Mealey stared at Brannon. "You're a little bit too sentimental, Captain. That could be a weakness unless you keep it under control." He picked up a suitcase and moved toward the door of the stateroom.

"You're a damned good seaman, Mike, and one damned good fighting man. Don't change."

Brannon watched as Pete Mahaffey picked the bag Mealey had been carrying out of his hand and went into the Forward Torpedo Room. John Olsen stuck his head in the stateroom.

"We have to come back to the tender tomorrow to get paid, sir."

"Oh, hell," Brannon said. "I was going to invite you to a good dinner downtown, on me, to celebrate your Navy Cross.

Not every day that the Executive Officer gets a Navy Cross. But I'm broke."

"I'm a single dude," Olsen said. "I've got some money."

"Good," Brannon said. "I was hoping you'd say that."

"You can pay me back tomorrow," Olsen said.

CHAPTER 19

The two weeks of R & R passed swiftly for the *Eelfish* sailors. Paul Blake left the hotel on the second day, took his seabag to the house where Constance Maybury lived, and spent his leave time with her family. Bob Lee disappeared on the third day from the house where he was quartered with Jerry Gold and Perry Arbuckle. He was seen several times in the company of a tall, lissome brunette who towered over him by several inches. Jerry Gold, curious to know what was going on, sought out Chief Flanagan.

"The word I get," Flanagan said, "is that Mr. Lee is going with a lady he met two rest periods ago. She's a widow, husband was killed while serving with the Ninth Division, that's the famous Aussie fighting division. I heard that her husband was a captain in the Aussie Army. From everything I hear Mr. Lee is pretty serious about her."

"Know anything about what sort of a lady she is?" Gold asked.

"Solid, from what I've been told," Flanagan said. "She works in some bank in town. No children. You got to be careful with those quiet ones like Mr. Lee is." He grinned at Lieutenant Gold. "Chief Yeoman on the tender told me that Mr. Lee has put in for a permit to marry the lady. Chief on the tender says he's made out all the papers and has been talking with the Squadron legal officer."

"Mr. Lee is a lawyer," Gold said.

"I know," the Chief answered. "He's not the only one. Paul Blake is going through the same routine. Mr. Lee helped him file his papers."

"Does the skipper know about this?"

"I doubt it," Flanagan said. "Might be a good idea if he did."

"He wouldn't try to stop either man, you know," Gold said. "The Old Man's got a real good marriage, and he thinks everyone should be married."

"I could tell him different," Flanagan growled. Jerry Gold shrugged.

"Look, Chief," he said, "I know that the Australian people are about the nicest people in the world, but what's the big attraction, why do Mr. Lee and Paul Blake want to get married?"

"Mr. Gold, it ain't only Mr. Lee and Paul Blake. From what I hear half of the single dudes on the tender and in the relief crews, they're lining up to get marriage forms. Lots of the people on other submarines want to get married.

"You see, if you've done duty in Pearl Harbor you'd know that you haven't got a chance to meet a broad there. There's about a thousand men for every woman in Pearl. And if you do score and make a date with some broad the odds are that in a half-hour your stomach will be turned because she's so damned spoiled that you can't stand it. Hell, some of the worst-lookin' broads you ever saw act like beauty queens in Pearl, and they get away with it because a woman, any kind of woman, is in damned short supply there.

"In Australia it's the other way around. How many men you seen on the streets lately who are young, say between twenty and forty, how many civilians you seen who have all their arms and legs?"

"Come to think about it, I can't say many," Gold said. "I've even seen some Australian soldiers in uniform with an eye patch."

"That's right," Flanagan said. "The Chief Storekeeper who runs the CPO Club in Perth told me the British use the Aussies as shock troops, throw them in with rifles and bayonets against General Rommel and his tanks in Africa, do the same thing up in the Islands. Australia has lost most of its young men in this war.

"So the country is full of women, good-lookin' women who got to figure they don't have much chance of ever gettin' married to an Aussie near their own age. And they look around and there's all our guys. Young guys. Healthy guys with all their arms and legs. If you've been out with any Aussie girls you got to know that they treat you like some kind of a king. Nothing's too good for you, that right?"

"I've noticed that," Gold said, "but I thought it was just my irresistible charm. Go on, Chief."

"Not much more to say. I was told Mr. Lee walked into a bank downtown to try and get the name of a reliable guy to appraise some opals he wanted to buy for his mother. Opals are mined here, and they're cheap if you don't get cheated.

"The manager of the bank is a tall, good-lookin' woman. That's the lady he wants to marry. Her husband was killed about a year ago. I heard he was an Aussie Army officer. Anyway, she's a four-oh lady. She's maybe four, five inches taller than Mr. Lee, but if she can manage a bank then she's got to have a lot of smarts. And if she is around Mr. Lee for an hour or two she's got to know that he's got all the smarts there is. Besides, he's a hell of a nice dude. He ain't your big sturdy type, but he's wiry and he's got all his arms and legs and eyes. So I guess the lady liked what she saw and sure as hell Mr. Lee likes what he saw and that's it."

"You disapprove, Chief?"

"Hell, no, Mr. Gold. Mr. Lee's a grown man. He's got a good head on him. No disrespect, sir, but a guy who ain't as tall as some has got to feel pretty chesty with someone as good lookin' as his girl hanging on his arm. Make a lot of tall dudes a little jealous, I'd think." He rubbed his chin with his hand.

"Way I figure it, Mr. Gold, it doesn't make one whole lot of difference where you find a wife or what she looks like or even what color she is as long as you hit it off and she treats you right and you can read the signs that she'll keep on treating you right."

"How about young Paul Blake?" Gold said.

"Ah! That's young love, sir," Flanagan said with a grin. "He met her when she came to the hotel with some Red Cross people, and she took him home to meet her family. She's a hell of a nice young girl and her folks are good people, very solid. If they think they love each other, the hell with it, it's their business, not mine. All's I hope for is that the damned red tape and all the paperwork they got to do takes a long time. If either of them gets married and wants off the ship to work in the relief crew they'd get an okay on their request because they've made enough war patrols to rate tender duty.

"Truth is, sir, I'm selfish. Mr. Lee is a hell of a good Torpedo Officer and Blake is the best damned sonarman I ever saw. I don't want to lose either one of them."

"I'm obliged to you, Chief," Gold said. "I hope you don't think I was being nosy?"

"No, sir," Flanagan said. He grinned. "I figured the Old Man would send someone around to find out the score. Figured it would be you. So I nosed around and found out what I had to find out." His grin broadened into a smile.

"That lady you were with a couple of nights ago, the blonde? I hear she's got some good contacts in the black market, that she's got twelve cases of Nescafé in her house. Chief I know in the CPO Club told me that. Don't know if it's true, though."

"Ten cases," Jerry Gold said. "See you around, Chief."

The day before *Eelfish* was to leave on its fourth war patrol a working party brought a large, tightly rolled burden to the submarine's foredeck. Flanagan looked at it and then at the Petty Officer in charge of the working party.

"What the hell is that, rubber boat?"

"Six-man boat, Chief. Sign these papers here to show you got the boat and this gear that goes with it, two sets of paddles, CO-two bottles to inflate it, two of those, and a compass with a battery-powered light."

"You sure this is for us?" Flanagan asked.

"Look right there, says 'U.S.S. *Eelfish*.' We rolled the son of a bitch tight enough to go down your torpedo-room hatch." Flanagan nodded and signed the papers, and told two seamen to take the boat below to the Forward Torpedo Room.

Eelfish cleared the port early the next morning and settled down for the long run to its patrol area. Captain Brannon went to the Wardroom after the sea watch had been set, sat down with John Olsen, and opened the patrol orders.

"We're in General MacArthur's submarine navy," Brannon said dryly. "Before we go on patrol we have to carry out a special mission. That's why they sent aboard that six-man rubber boat that Flanagan has been grousing about." He reached for the telephone hanging on the bulkhead and punched the button that would enable him to talk to everyone below decks over the 1MC loudspeaker system.

"Now hear this," he said. "This is Captain Brannon. We have our patrol orders. A good area just at the end of Davao Gulf, south of Mindanao Island. But before we go there we have to carry out a special mission for General MacArthur. That shouldn't take more than a day or two." He hung up the phone and looked at the chart that Olsen had laid on the table.

"Borneo," Brannon said. "Northeastern tip, that's it, right there. Hell of a name, Bum-Bum." He looked again at the patrol orders.

"There's a big mountain near there?" Olsen nodded at Brannon. "Okay, that's where these ship watchers have been hiding for the past two years. This paragraph here says that for the past six or seven months the reports from the ship watchers on Japanese shipping have been erroneous and that the assumption is they're suffering from fatigue and tension.

"So we pick them up and *Sea Chub* will drop off four more ship watchers. Shouldn't be too tough a thing to do."

"All four of those dudes might be out of their minds by now, might not be such good passengers to have aboard for a whole patrol run," Olsen said. "Hiding in those mountains and watching ships go by and reporting the ship movements and hoping the Jap doesn't zero in on you with radio direction finders, that must be a scary business to be in."

"We'll have to send in at least three people," Mike Brannon said. "One man can't handle a six-man rubber boat, or can he?" He nodded at Pete Mahaffey and sent him in search of the Chief of the Boat.

Flanagan listened as Brannon outlined the mission. "One man can't handle one of those things, Captain. Takes at least three men. One to steer, two to paddle. Six-man boat will carry ten people, you know. They're heavy."

"Any suggestions as to who would want to volunteer?" Olsen asked.

"I'll take the thing in," Flanagan said. "If I could have Booth and Charlie Two Blankets, they're good men, it should be easy."

"Would they volunteer?" Brannon asked. Flanagan nodded his head. "They'll volunteer. No sweat, sir."

Eelfish arrived off the point that was identified on the charts as Bum-Bum and patrolled up and down the ten-fathom curve, barely ten miles from the headland for two days and nights, watching.

"We'll go in tonight," Brannon said to the officers gathered in the Wardroom, as *Eelfish* cruised at 110 feet a dozen miles from the land. "We told them it would either be last night or tonight when we arrived on station. We leave the hundred-fathom curve about eight miles before we get in to the land area, and the chart shows deep water all the way in to near the beach. We can launch the boat a thousand yards from the beach. They told us to make the pickup at a sandy beach on the headland.'' He looked at his wrist watch.

"It's fourteen hundred. We'll surface at nineteen hundred hours, full dark, make a radar search and move in if we're sure we're alone. We should be able to launch by twenty hundred and have the boat back in an hour or two.''

Booth and Charlie Two Blankets paddled the six-man boat toward the dark bulk of the shore while Flanagan steered the clumsy craft with a paddle.

"I can see that sandy beach,'' the Apache said. He shifted the three rifles that lay against the seat between himself and Booth and stood up in the boat.

"Damned moon is sure bright. Yeah, that's the beach. Looks like there's a big tree or something laying in the water near the beach, Chief.''

"I can see it,'' Flanagan said. "Probably a big palm tree. There was a big storm here a week or so ago according to Mr. Michaels.'' He steered the boat toward the tree lying in the water. Booth scrambled to the forward part of the boat and grabbed the tree roots. The boat swung in behind the massive bole of the tree.

"Take a turn with the bow line around some of those roots,'' Flanagan ordered. He reached over the side of the boat and probed for the bottom with his paddle.

"Water's only about two feet deep,'' he said. "I think this is as far as I want to go with the boat. Which one of you two dudes wants to go in and make the contact?''

"I'll go,'' John Wilkes Booth said. He dropped over the side of the boat and began to wade toward the beach. Flanagan and the Apache watched the yeoman as he waded up out of the water, shaking first one leg and then the other. A man left the tree line behind the beach, followed by three other men. The man in the lead suddenly turned on a flashlight.

"Turn off the fucking light!'' Booth's order carried across the water to the rubber boat.

"Too right, mate,'' the figure said. The light was turned off and Flanagan and Charlie Two Blankets saw the man holding the flashlight spring forward and swing the flashlight at Booth's head.

The rifle shot caught Flanagan by surprise, hammering in his ears. He saw the second man coming down the beach from the tree line fold at the waist and fall. Charlie Two Blankets, his rifle resting on the top of the tree trunk, squeezed off another shot and the third man coming down the beach spun around and went down, his legs kicking. The fourth man turned and ran for the tree line.

"Turn that son of a bitch!" the Apache yelled at the two men struggling together in the sand. "Turn that son of a bitch, Booth, so I can see who's who!" He was kneeling on the seat of the rubber boat, his rifle across the tree bole.

"Don't shoot, for Christ's sake!" Flanagan yelled. He grabbed one of the rifles in the boat, jumped over the side, and started to splash around the end of the tree roots. He heard the Apache say "Ahhh!" and heard his rifle crack. One of the two figures struggling on the beach dropped, and the other one turned and sprinted for the water. He floundered through the shallow water, and Flanagan saw the flashes of rifle fire in the dark tree line. Gouts of water began to rise on either side of Booth as he labored toward the safety of the tree. Flanagan raised his rifle and got off five shots into the tree line as fast as he could work the rifle bolt. The Apache was firing steadily from the boat.

"Zigzag, you dumb bastard!" Charlie Two Blankets yelled, and Booth began veering from one side to the other. He dove forward and began to swim frantically.

"Smart," the Apache said. "The Chief Yeoman has got the smarts. They won't hit him now." He ripped two shots into the tree line, reached for a canvas bandoleer in the bottom of the boat, and jammed another clip in his rifle. Flanagan, crouching low in the water, moved out from the shelter of the massive ball of tree roots, grabbed Booth, and dragged him behind the tree and into the boat. A machine gun in the tree line began to chatter, its bullets ripping into the trunk of the tree.

"That fucker's gonna need all the machine guns on the island to make chips outa this big tree," the Apache said. He climbed out of the boat and eased up behind the tangled mass of roots, his eyes studying the tree line. Very cautiously he edged the rifle between the roots and sighted. He fired once, then again, and climbed back into the boat.

"They need a new gunner," he said. He looked at Booth. "What kind of a dance was you doin' with that dude on the beach?"

"Fucker was a Jap. Hit me so fucking hard on the shoulder I thought he'd broke it. Bastard was trying to bear hug me to death. Woulda done it, too, if you hadn't shot his ass off, old Indian."

"We're all gonna get our ass shot off if we try to leave this damned tree to go back to the ship. Listen to the fire those cocksuckers are layin' down. Must be a hellish lot of them up in those trees." He pawed over the bandoleers in the bottom of the boat. "We got maybe a hundred, hundred and twenty rounds between us. Not enough if they decide to come after us." He dove into the bottom of the boat as an express train screamed by close overhead. The express train exploded with a burst of fire and a roar against the tree line. Another express train left a banshee wail behind it as it roared by only a few feet above the heads of the men in the boat. A huge gout of sand burst upward with an orange burst of fire at the edge of the tree line. The boom of the two 5.25-inch deck guns of the *Eelfish* echoed across the water, followed by the stammering roar of the 1.1 pom-pom and the steady stutter of the twin .20mm guns.

"Old Man's laying down covering fire. Contact fuses so they burst as soon as they hit something up there in the trees," Flanagan yelled. "Let him get off a few more rounds and then we'll haul ass outa here." Booth crawled forward in the boat, untied the bow line, and held on to the tree roots, keeping the boat snugged in next to the palm tree, ducking as two more shells screamed by overhead.

"Keep your heads down," Flanagan ordered. "Shove off, Booth, let's get the hell out of here." Booth and Charlie Two Blankets, crouching on their knees in the rubber boat, paddled steadily away from the safety of the downed palm tree and toward the open sea as the fire from the *Eelfish* roared overhead toward the tree line on the beach.

Steve Petreshock was down on the pressure hull with a safety line around his waist as the rubber boat bumped alongside. He grabbed Booth and then the Apache and helped them up on the deck, and then took the three rifles and bandoleers from Flanagan.

"Scuttle the boat, Chief," Mike Brannon called from the bridge. Flanagan pulled out his sheath knife and punctured the rubberized fabric in a half-dozen places, then scrambled onto the pressure hull where Petreshock grabbed him.

"Belay firing, secure the deck party, secure all guns," Brannon barked. "Right ten degrees rudder. Make turns for full speed. Deck party below. Lookouts keep a sharp watch. Control, give me a radar sweep." He stood to one side as the deck gunners scrambled down the hatch.

"Radar reports no contacts, Bridge," the speaker on the bridge echoed.

"Very well," Brannon said. He turned to Lieutenant Gold. "Take the deck, Jerry. Maintain this speed for fifteen minutes and then make turns for two thirds. Keep the lookouts sharp. Radar sweep every five minutes for the next fifteen minutes."

John Olsen had led the boat party into the Wardroom by the time Mike Brannon got below. Pete Mahaffey was serving coffee.

"Begin at the beginning, when you left the ship," Brannon said. Flanagan nodded and recounted the operation from the time the six-man rubber boat pushed away from the side of the *Eelfish* until he had ordered it tied up to the roots of a downed palm tree in the water. He turned to Booth.

"I volunteered to go ashore and lead the ship watchers out to the boat," Booth said. "The guy who came down the beach, there were four of them, the right number, the guy in the lead had a flashlight lit and I told him to shut it off. He tried to hit me in the head with it. Damned near broke my shoulder. I grabbed him and he got me in a bear hug. I heard a rifle firing but I didn't know what was happening, that guy was squeezing me so tight and he was, kind of, grunting and slobbering on me. Then all of a sudden he made a funny sound and he just dropped. I ran like hell for the water and the boat.

"I heard Charlie yelling at me to zigzag and I tried to do that and then I dove in and sort of grabbed at the bottom and pulled myself along. Chief Flanagan came out from the tree, into the open, and got me and hauled me back into the boat."

"Charlie figured out what was going on before I did," Flanagan took up the story. "He opened fire as soon as the guy grabbed Chief Booth. I saw the second guy coming down the beach go down and then the third guy went down and the other guy, the fourth one, he ran back into the trees.

"Charlie was yelling at Chief Booth to turn the guy he was fighting with around so he could get a shot in and I yelled at him not to shoot and got out of the boat to go help Booth, and then all of a sudden Charlie loosed off one round and the guy Booth was fighting with dropped."

Mike Brannon looked at the Apache Indian. "That's sort of miraculous shooting, Charlie. To hit the right man at night when the two of them were struggling together."

"The Jap had on white shorts and a white shirt, sir," the Apache said. "Chief Booth had on dungarees. Moon was awful bright. Range was only thirty, thirty-five yards. When Booth swung the guy around so they were sideways to me I got a good sight on that white shirt and popped him with one under his left armpit. Man don't live with a thirty-ought-six slug hitting him there, sir."

"You're sure he was a Japanese?" Brannon looked at Booth.

"Yes, sir. Big fellow. Bigger than I am and I'm six feet and two hundred, sir. When he spoke to me, when I told him to put out the flashlight he had an Aussie accent. But he was a Jap, no doubt. A strong son of a bitch, too."

"When Booth was back in the boat they opened up with a machine gun, sir," Flanagan said. "If you hadn't come in with the deck guns I don't think we could have made it back."

"Lieutenant Gold heard the rifle fire," Mike Brannon said. "We were cruising in a circle from where we dropped you off."

"Captain was going to flood down forward and run the ship up on the beach and lead a boarding party to come and get you," Olsen said with a grin. Brannon shook his head. "I was afraid we were going to lose all three of you. Chief Booth, would you write up this operation? Do it in the first person with Chief Flanagan as the narrator. He'll sign it. Go to direct quotes from you and Charlie where needed." He looked at the three men.

"I'm just damned glad we got you back and I'm damned sorry that we had to do the operation. We're a submarine, not the Marine Corps."

Sipping at a coffee cup after the three men had left, John Olsen looked at his Captain.

"I wonder what happened to the Australians who were supposed to be manning that ship-watching station?"

"They're probably long dead," Brannon said. "Hey, maybe that's why their reports were so wrong. The Japs had probably killed the ship watchers and were sending phony reports to Fremantle about ship movements. *Sea Chub* is coming in here in about a week with a new crew of ship watchers and some new radio gear. Get Michaels and make a coded message direct to Admiral Christie. Tell him what happened and tell him to keep *Sea Chub* away from here."

The throat of the Gulf of Davao from its easternmost point at Cape San Agustin to the main part of the Island of Mindanao, at a small fishing village called Lais, is 30 miles wide. The port of Davao lies 65 miles to the north, up the Gulf on the east side of Mindanao. Early in the war the Japanese had occupied Davao and used it as a major naval base and a staging area for their conquest of Celebes and Borneo. Now, in mid-1944, Davao was once again a major naval stronghold for the Japanese. The elements of the Japanese fleet that had been driven out of strongholds in the Pacific islands by the relentless stepping-stone tactics of the American Naval and Army forces had concentrated in Davao, at Tawi Tawi just north of Borneo, at Surabaya and at Singapore.

Mike Brannon had been prepared for a nonproductive patrol area. Captain Mealey had made an appearance in the Officers' Club the evening before he was flown back to Pearl Harbor, and when asked about his patrol Captain Mealey had praised Mike Brannon and *Eelfish* and let it be known, in caustic words, what he thought of senior submarine commanders who lacked aggressiveness. After Mealey had been flown out of Fremantle Mike Brannon had noticed a chill in the air when he went to the O-Club to eat.

"I'm proud to have served with Captain Mealey," he said to John Olsen as the rest period neared an end. "But I wish that he hadn't been as tough on some of those senior skippers out here. They'll take out their dislike of Mealey on us, you'll see. We'll get a patrol area where there won't be any ships."

Eelfish was assigned to patrol the eastern third of the opening to the Gulf of Davao. Two weeks after the *Eelfish* reached station John Olsen came on the bridge one morning to get star sights before the *Eelfish* submerged for the day.

"*Sea Chub* reported seeing two enemy cruisers and a destroyer. They're giving chase but they're too far away, I think, to catch up," Olsen said.

"Where?" Brannon said.

"Over on the west side of the Gulf," Olsen replied.

"Son of a bitch," Brannon said. "The ships that come out of this damned Gulf aren't going to turn east, where we are. They're going west, to Tawi Tawi or to Borneo. Nothing comes this way. We've been here a little over two weeks and we haven't seen one damned ship. The Irish have no luck, John, no luck at all."

"Neither do we Swedes, sir," Olsen said.

Four days later, patrolling at the western limit of his area, Mike Brannon relieved Bob Lee at the periscope for the usual hourly periscope sweep and saw the smoke of a small freighter to the west. He watched as the smoke came closer and when the small freighter crossed his bow he fired two torpedoes at a range of 800 yards. The small inter-island freighter—Brannon estimated it to be no more than 2,000 tons—rolled over and sank. Three days later Perry Arbuckle saw an inter-island freighter with a heavy deck load and Brannon attacked. He fired one torpedo and the freighter broke in two and sank. Two days later *Eelfish* was ordered home with twenty-one torpedoes aboard.

Admiral Christie's booming assurances that the *Eelfish* had indeed had a successful patrol did little to mollify Brannon's barely concealed anger over the unproductive patrol area he had been assigned. The crew of the *Eelfish*, not unaware of the political infighting that went on constantly among the senior submarine captains to get productive patrol areas, got ready to go to the hotel for their two weeks of R & R.

Paul Blake approached Lieutenant Bob Lee on the afterdeck before the bus arrived to take the crew to the hotel.

"Do you think all the paper work is done yet, sir?"

"I don't know," Lee answered. "I did all I could before we left on patrol. Now it's up to the people on the Base and the tender. They have to make an investigation of the family and the woman, you know. The chaplain has to talk to the ladies we want to marry. I believe that Captain Brannon has to interview them also. Then, after all that's been done and everything is four-oh, the whole business goes to the Admiral for his approval."

"That's an awful lot of stuff to go through for someone to marry a nice girl," Blake said. "It isn't that Constance is a bar girl or anything like that. Her folks are just as nice as my folks."

"I know," Lee said. "You know what General Sherman said: 'War is hell.' I'll check with the legal officer on the tender tomorrow. We went to the same law school but he was about three years ahead of me. I'll be in touch with you as soon as I find out anything. You going to spend your rest period at her folks' house?" Blake nodded. "I'll get in touch with you there. Don't sweat it. Everything will come out all right."

CHAPTER 20

The night before *Eelfish* was to leave on patrol Captain Sam Rivers led a tall, thin, U.S. Army Brigadier General into the small Wardroom on the submarine. Captain Brannon, alerted by a message from Admiral Christie, was waiting, seated at the Wardroom table.

"I'd like to make the area secure, Captain," Rivers said. Mike Brannon motioned to Pete Mahaffey, who left his galley and closed and dogged the watertight door to the Forward

Torpedo Room. He stopped at the Wardroom door on his way aft.

"No one else in the Forward Battery, sir," Mahaffey said. "Forward Room won't allow anyone to come in until you give the word. I'll dog down the door to the Control Room after I go through and stand watch on it. There's a carafe of hot coffee in the galley, sir."

"I'm sorry about the secrecy," Sam Rivers said, "but we're asking you to undertake a special mission, and if word gets out there'll be all hell to pay." He nodded his head toward the Army officer.

"This is Brigadier General Dennis Connelly. Captain Brannon, General. The General will take it from here, sir." He sat back in his chair. The General put a cloth bag he had been carrying on the table in front of him.

"Briefly, Captain Brannon, General MacArthur is going to make good on his promise. He's going to return to the Philippines on October twentieth. He will land on that day, and President Osmena of the Philippines will be with the General." He paused. "One cannot underestimate the symbolism here, Captain Brannon. The General will return. The hearts of all the people of the Philippines will swell with pride.

"The invasion will be the largest of the war. The Navy is committing over seven hundred ships of all sizes."

"Including eighteen carriers, six battleships, seventeen cruisers, and more than sixty destroyers," Captain Rivers interjected.

"Yes," General Connelly said.

"What part does *Eelfish*, my ship, play in this, sir?" Brannon asked.

"It is imperative that the landing be kept secret," the Army General said. "We are realistic, however. We assume that someone, somewhere will find out about it, will add up some of the enormous logistics that have gone into this months-long planning and inform the Japanese. They will know what is coming if that happens.

"There is a guerrilla leader in Leyte, an Army Sergeant who escaped from the Bataan March. He has been communicating with us for quite a long time by radio. He commands about ten thousand irregulars, guerrillas, some trained Filipino soldiers. His main camp, his base, is near Tacloban, a place at the top of Leyte Gulf on Leyte Island."

"I know where it is," Brannon said. "Is that where the General is going to land?"

"Well, yes, of course," the General said. "We know what the enemy's strength is in that area. We want *Eelfish* to go in and send a man ashore to meet with this Sergeant's people and deliver to the Sergeant, personally deliver to him, a set of orders. Those orders will tell the Sergeant what roads to cut, what bridges to blow up so that the enemy forces in place cannot be reinforced. The landing must take place. It will take place.

"I wanted to send a trained commando team in to take these orders to the Sergeant in charge of the guerrilla force. Admiral Christie made it quite plain that you, sir, and your crew could do this job and do it right. We accept the Admiral's assessment of your capability."

"I'm sure that we can do whatever you want," Mike Brannon said. "Will this Sergeant know we are coming, will he meet us on the beach?"

"Yes. All that will be arranged for by radio. You will be informed of recognition signals, time to go in, that sort of thing." He reached in the cloth sack he had brought with him and pulled out a khaki-colored webbing belt that had a long pouch on the belt opposite the strap and buckle. The edges of the pouch were sealed with what looked to Brannon like white wax, and a red string with a red wooden knob on the end of it hung down out of the wax along the edge of the pouch.

"Your man will wear this belt. The strap goes in the back," the Army man said. "When he makes contact with Sergeant McGillivray he will turn over the belt to him. This envelope here contains the names of the Sergeant's mother and her maiden name, the maiden name of his wife and his service number. Your man will commit those to memory, and if the man he meets can answer those names correctly he will give him the belt." He stopped and fingered the red knob.

"If your man is captured or about to be captured he will pull smartly on this wooden knob. A charge of thermite inside the pouch will burn its contents to ash. If he is satisfied the man he meets is indeed the right man he must caution Sergeant McGillivray not to pull the knob, but to break the wax seals and open the pouch."

"I understand, sir," Brannon said slowly. Captain Rivers laid a thick envelope on the table.

"These are your patrol orders, sir. Orders for the special mission and for your patrol area after the mission." He rose. "You'll be pleased with the patrol area. Tawi Tawi! You should be able to indulge in your ability to sink Jap warships at that place!'' He walked to the door of the Wardroom and looked up and down the empty passageway.

"You will not divulge any of this to anyone, not even to your Executive Officer, until the time of the actual operation. At that time you will tell your Executive Officer and the man who will deliver the orders about the mission but you must not tell them the reason for the mission.'' Rivers glanced at the General, and noting that he was not looking at him, he closed his right eye in a slow wink. "Please lock your orders and this belt in your destruct pouch.''

Mike Brannon accompanied the two officers to the deck and shook hands with them at the gangway. As soon as they were out of sight he went back to the Wardroom and looked at the sealed envelope and the canvas belt. Then he asked Pete Mahaffey to get John Olsen for him and to tell the deck watch to alert him if anyone wanted to come aboard.

Olsen listened as Brannon repeated what had been told to him by the Army General and Captain Rivers.

"Who are you going to send ashore?'' he asked.

"I thought we might ask Flanagan,'' Brannon said slowly. "For two reasons, really. One is that he's damned well able to take care of himself. The other is that he has no dependents. He's an orphan, you know.''

"Charlie Two Blankets wouldn't be a bad choice,'' Olsen said. "That man knows how to take care of himself.''

"Charlie has a big allotment going to his mother and father,'' Brannon said slowly. "They depend on him for that money. I know he's a good man in a fight. He proved that when they went in to get the ship watchers, but I don't like sending a man who has dependents on a mission like this.''

"I'm single,'' Olsen said.

"Not a chance,'' Brannon answered.

The next day Brannon called Chief Flanagan in to the Wardroom and explained the mission to him.

"It's purely a volunteer mission,'' he said to the Chief of the Boat. "If you don't want to go, no sweat.''

"I'll go,'' Flanagan said. "Shouldn't be too hard. If this Army Sergeant has survived all this time in the Islands I shouldn't have anything to worry about. He must know what he's doing a whole lot better than the Japs know.'' He turned the canvas belt over in his hands.

"I'll tell you one thing, Captain. I don't like the idea of

pulling this damned knob. If there's enough thermite in there to burn up whatever paper is inside that pouch there's enough to burn me in two!''

"I thought of that," Brannon said. "Maybe John LaMark can figure out something. He's a good explosives man."

"Maybe he could cut the belt on either side of the pouch," Olsen said, "and then sew it back with kind of weak thread. Then if you fasten the knob to the other part of the belt the Chief could rip the pouch away and just throw it and the pouch would burn up wherever he threw it."

"That sounds reasonable," Brannon said. He sat back in his chair. "I hate this damned cloak and dagger stuff. I don't like the idea of General MacArthur running our damned submarine navy, doing his errands when we should be out sinking Japanese ships."

"Once he lands in the Islands, sir," Flanagan said with a grin, "he'll be so busy letting Filipinos kiss his feet that he won't even think about us."

On the night of October sixth *Eelfish* was cruising just south of Leyte Gulf, in the Surigao Strait. Jim Michaels came down from the bridge and as was his habit, stopped in the radio shack. The radioman was busy taking a coded message, and Michaels took it from him and went into the deserted Wardroom to decode it. Fifteen minutes later he climbed to the bridge and took the message back to Mike Brannon.

"Courier comes to bat at twenty-two hundred next. We need a home run." He held the message sideways and read it again in the light of the moon.

"I take it to mean that we do the operation you told us about, sir, tomorrow night. This message has a time of transmission on it of twenty-three forty-five hours, sir."

Brannon nodded his head. "When you go back down below will you have the watch wake up Mr. Olsen and tell him to notify me when he's had some coffee and has his charts ready in the Wardroom?"

When Brannon went into the Wardroom ten minutes later Pete Mahaffey was pouring fresh coffee into a cup in front of his place at the table.

"Don't you ever sleep, Pete?" Brannon asked. "I've told you before that you don't have to get up in the middle of the night to serve coffee."

Mahaffey grinned. "My poppa told me when I came in this

Navy, sir, to do my job and don't let no one ever do it better than I do it. I'll see if the baker has any fresh pastry.''

"If we submerge here at dawn, a little before dawn," Olsen said, touching the point of a pair of dividers to the chart, "if we submerge here and run up the coast at two knots—we'll run well offshore and at one hundred feet—we can be right here''—the dividers touched a small pencil mark—''right here just about an hour after dark. We can surface and make a run up the rest of the way while we charge batteries. We can come in pretty close. Water's deep all the way in to the beach almost. Be there in plenty of time to launch Flanagan at twenty-two hundred, sir.''

"No indication of currents on that chart," Brannon said with a frown. "I don't want to put him off in that damned little rubber boat and have him get pushed way off course by currents.''

"I doubt there'll be any current to amount to anything, sir. The tide in Leyte Gulf is only two, two and a half feet, high and low water. I don't think we have to worry about that.''

Eelfish surfaced after full dark that night and began the run up the coast of Leyte Island. To the port side the dark bulk of the mountains loomed against the black night sky. On the foredeck of the *Eelfish* Steve Petreshock finished blowing up the one-man rubber boat and threw the empty CO_2 cylinder over the side. He clipped a small compass with a hooded red lamp and a battery to a cross brace in the boat. He checked the spare CO_2 cylinder and fastened it in its holder under the wooden seat.

"Don't step on this, Chief," he said as he laid a thick billet of metal in the bottom of the boat. "That's a new gadget they gave us in Fremantle two runs ago. It's a Christmas tree made of aluminum. You take hold of the thick end, the butt, and you twist it with your other hand and keep pulling it out and it stretches out about eight feet with all sorts of little aluminum branches coming off of the main shaft. It goes in this clip on the back of your seat.''

"What the hell is it for?" Flanagan asked.

"No way the radar could pick you up in that little boat against the mountains," Petreshock said. "With this gadget up they can grab you right away.''

"Thanks a bunch," Flanagan said. The Chief Torpedoman was dressed in dark blue dungarees with black socks and a pair of regulation white tennis shoes that had been colored black with shoe polish. He wore a thin black jersey that covered his heavy, sloping shoulders and a black watch cap. John LaMark, the

Gunner's Mate, came ambling up the deck and handed him a .45 automatic and two clips of ammunition.

"Stick it in your belt," LaMark said. "Figured you would get all fouled up if I brought you a belt. You already got that junior fireworks belt on you now."

"Coming up on the launch point," Olsen said from the bridge. Mike Brannon climbed down from the cigaret deck, walked forward, and handed Flanagan a canvas haversack.

"That Army guy has been in the hills since right after the war started, Chief," he said. "Might be nice if you gave this to him."

"What's in it, sir?"

"Cook put in a ten-pound canned ham, and Mr. Olsen found a bottle of Australian scotch somewhere. Doc Wharton had a good idea and he put ten pounds of sulfa in the pack, and Fred Nelson contributed a big pinup of Betty Grable." Flanagan nodded and put the haversack in the boat.

"We're at launch spot, Captain," Olsen said.

"Very well," Brannon answered. Petreshock and Jim Rice eased the small rubber boat over the side as the *Eelfish* slowed to a stop and held on to the bow and stern lines as Flanagan climbed down into the boat. He picked up the double-ended paddle and looked up at the deck.

"Could be, sir, like we talked about; maybe this guy's camp is some distance away and I can't make it back before morning."

"I'll be here every damned night until the invasion force drives me away," Brannon growled. Flanagan raised his arm and Petreshock and Rice cast off the lines. The Chief of the Boat shoved away from the side, and Brannon blinked in surprise as the small rubber boat was lost to view in seconds in the darkness.

"Take care of him, Lord," he breathed softly to himself. He went aft and climbed up on the cigaret deck.

"Begin Condition Alert as per the Night Orders," he said to Perry Arbuckle. He went back to the cigaret deck, catching at the periscope shears for support as the *Eelfish* heeled to starboard to begin running up and down a course off the landing area.

Flanagan settled down to a steady beat with the two-bladed paddle, keeping his eye on the small ruby-red face of the compass. The landing area, according to information received from the guerrillas, was a dark portion of the shoreline just north of a white, sandy beach. He caught sight of a gleam of white sand in the starlight and corrected his course to aim the boat to the right of the beach. As he neared the beach he stopped paddling and eased the gun in his belt. He paddled gently toward a tangled mass of foliage at the dark part of the shoreline and felt the nose of the boat ground in soft muck. He put the paddle in the boat, took the pistol out of his belt, and pulled the slide back to put a shell in the chamber, letting the slide go home with a sharp click.

"Don't shoot, sailor," a deep voice said out of the darkness of the shore. "I'm Sergeant McGillivray, and there's four rifles aimed at you. Let my people come out of the bushes and pull your boat up on the shoreline."

Two shadowy figures came out of the dark bushes, took hold of the boat, and pulled it up toward the bushes. Flanagan sat in the boat, the gun cradled in his lap, his finger on the trigger, his thumb ready to flip off the safety. A large figure suddenly appeared, his white hair shining in the faint light of the stars.

"Glad you made it, sailor," the large man said. "When you get out of your cruise liner there's about four inches of muck. Move right on up to me and we'll get to some dry ground." Flanagan felt his shoes sink down in soft mud as he got out of the boat. He followed the figure of the large man. He looked around as he heard a scraping, sucking noise and saw the rubber boat being pulled into the bushes. He held the pistol in front of him.

"Something we have to do, Sergeant," Flanagan said. "Do you remember your service number?"

"Yeah," the man said and rattled off a seven-digit number.

"How about your wife's maiden name, your mother's maiden name?"

"Okay. My wife's maiden name was Malden, Mary Ann Malden. My mother, rest her soul, was a Shaughnessey, Mary Margaret Shaughnessey."

"Good enough," Flanagan said. "I'm Chief Torpedoman Flanagan of the *Eelfish*. I've got some orders for you."

"I know," McGillivray said. He turned and spoke rapidly in Tagalog to some men who had materialized out of the bushes.

"They'll lead the way," he said to Flanagan. "Point men. They can see in the dark like cats. I'll go ahead of you. Six men behind you. We've got a pretty long walk, all uphill. If you get winded, say so, and we'll stop. We're used to this."

Two hours later the party stopped. "Camp is just ahead," McGillivray said. "I'll give you time to get your breath, so when my people speak to you you won't be heavin' like a damned whale, the way you been heavin' the last hour.'' He grinned, and Flanagan saw his white teeth shine in the faint starlight. They moved toward the camp, and Flanagan heard the low voices of sentries challenging the party and McGillivray's answers. At the edge of the camp clearing they stopped, and Flanagan saw two or three small fires burning. He looked around and saw a smiling Filipino, rifle held at port arms across his chest, next to him.

"Pretty good security you've got," he said.

"Damned good," McGillivray said. "There's about four thousand Jap troops over the other side of this mountain. A good five thousand farther away. They can't get to us except along two trails, and both of them are guarded by my people. We're safe enough here." He moved toward a small shelter. A figure came out of the shelter with two small stools, and Flanagan saw that the figure was a girl.

"We'll have a little tea and then you can give me the stuff you brought me," the Army man said. He sat down on one of the stools and Flanagan sat on the other, placing the haversack beside the stool.

"How long you people been at sea?"

"About sixteen days."

"Going right back after this caper?"

"No," Flanagan said. "We'll go to a patrol area. We won't be back for another two months, maybe a little less."

"Figured it might be something like that," the Army man said. "Jesus! All that time in a little submarine! My people talked about that and figured you might like to have a good meal, but let's get the business over first."

Flanagan reached around his back and undid the strap to the belt. He held the belt and explained about the thermite charge inside the pouch and how to get the orders out of the pouch.

"Thermite?" McGillivray said. "I can use that stuff." He motioned at a small lean Filipino who came over to him.

"This is José," he said. "Best damned explosives man in the Islands." He spoke rapidly in slurred Tagalog to the man, who picked up the canvas belt and trotted away. He came back in a few minutes and handed McGillivray a thick packet of paper. McGillivray turned so he could use the firelight and read through the orders.

"So Old Doug is going to come back," the Army man said.

"That's going to end our nice life here." Flanagan started to reach for the haversack and then changed his mind.

"This isn't any surprise, you know," the Army Sergeant said. "Some of the older heads in my group, we call them the wise men, they said this was going to happen before the next new moon." He looked narrowly at Flanagan.

"Don't laugh at things like that, sailor. Those wise men can tell you things that would shake you right out of your submarine. They talk with the spirits and they've been doing things like that for a thousand years. When I give them the word tomorrow they won't be surprised.

"Like I said before, my people don't understand how you can live on a small submarine for so long, so they've sort of fixed up a little celebration for you. Man who lives on a submarine has to eat out of cans, so we've got some fresh roast pig. Not wild pig, good tame pigs we stole from the Japs." He leaned back, his face granitelike in the firelight.

"Any good reason I have to get off my ass and take you back down that mountain to that boat tonight? If there isn't you can stay here tonight and tomorrow and go back tomorrow night. We've got some good rum. Make it ourselves out of sugarcane. And about half of my people are girls. You'd see that if it was daylight. We live on a reverse schedule here. We stay up nights and sleep days. The Jap lives on a regular schedule. Gives us an advantage."

"Roast pig, rum, and girls?" Flanagan said softly. "You live a pretty good war, Sergeant."

"It's been a tough war at times," McGillivray said. "But I'm a Georgia boy, Chief. Sherman told us what war was like when he ripped through my home state. I decided to make the war as good as I could when I could." He turned as a woman came up to the two men.

"Chow's about ready," McGillivray said. "You need anything out of that sack you lugged up here?"

"No," Flanagan said. "All that's in it is some sulfa powder for you and some emergency rations for me in case I got stranded out in that boat waiting to get picked up."

"I can sure use sulfa," McGillivray said. "We have to steal our medicines from the Jap, and he hasn't got much that's worth stealing. Let's eat." He led the way deep into the trees where there were a half-dozen deep pits, each full of glowing coals with two pigs roasting on spits above each fire pit. Flanagan found a seat on a log, and a small, slim girl brought him a mug made from a coconut shell. She smiled at him, and he raised the shell to his lips and sipped. The homemade rum was smooth but there was a bite in it. He took a deeper swallow. The girl patted his knee, smiled, and moved away. Flanagan noted that while she was small and slight she had the powerful calves of a person used to walking in mountainous areas. She came back to him with two tin plates, one full of fresh salad greens, the other piled high with steaming yams and chunks of fragrant roast pork. She squatted in front of him holding the plate of salad greens. He reached for it but she pulled it away.

"You eat. I hold the plate for you. No forks. No table. Okay? Use fingers, like we do."

McGillivray, seated a few feet away, chuckled. "When in Rome, sailor. If you like her invite her to eat from your plate."

"I am ugly," the girl said, tossing her long black hair. "The sailor will not like me."

"Help yourself to some food," Flanagan said. He could feel the warmth of the rum in his stomach. The girl smiled at him and delicately scooped up two fingers of salad and put it in her mouth. Flanagan followed her example and was pleased by the crisp freshness of the food. He reached for the coconut shell and took a long swallow of the rum. It didn't bite as much, he noticed.

"Not too much too quick!" the girl said. She moved the coconut shell out of reach. "Too much, too quick, you go to sleep damned quick!" She giggled and tore a chunk of roast pork into bite-size pieces and held a piece toward Flanagan. He reached for it and she pulled it away.

"Open mouth. I feed you."

"You're home free, sailor," McGillivray said. "When they start feeding you all you got to do is sit there and let it all come to you."

Flanagan looked at the guerrilla leader. "One thing, Sergeant. This isn't someone's woman, is it?"

"No worry," McGillivray said. He waited as the girl went back to the fire, and then he turned toward Flanagan.

"The Japs killed her husband about a year and a half ago. She came with us right after that. She's a scout. Fastest woman with a knife you ever saw. She's clean. We don't have any venereal disease here. All you've got to worry about is if you're enough man. Most of my people are scared to death of her."

"Thanks a heap," Flanagan said. He smiled at the girl as she returned with a fresh plate of roast pork chunks.

"What's your name?" he asked.

"The sisters in the convent called me Mary," she said. "I like it better if you call me my right name. Maria."

"Give me a little squirt of that rum, Miss Maria," Flanagan said. She shook her head. "No. You go to sleep damned quick if you drink more." She shook her long black hair.

"My Inglis, my Spanish, not so good now. No practice. The big man, he speaks our tongue, Tagalog. That is good. No mistakes when everyone speak the same language. Now eat some more meat. Make you strong!" She giggled at him and bowed her head.

The party, if you could call it that, Flanagan thought to himself, was very quiet. Hardly anyone spoke out loud. He saw figures coming and going near the cooking fires, heard soft chatter from shadowy groups of men and women. When two or three of the Filipinos toppled over, the victims of too much rum, they were carried away with much soft laughter.

Later, when he had finished eating, Maria took him by the hand and led him through the thick brush to a small shelter some distance from the main camp.

"Here it is alone," she said softly. She led him inside the shelter and pushed him gently to his knees. He reached out and felt the edge of a thick mattress.

"Japanese take much good stuff from houses and we take from them," she said. He heard her taking off her clothes and then felt her hands at his shoelaces. He pulled off his socks and undressed and crawled up on the mattress. She snuggled in beside him and took his hand and guided it to her small breast. He put his free arm under her head and let his hand stray down her taut belly until he found the thick mat of pubic hair. She found his lips with her mouth and they lay close together, his hands caressing her. Then she rolled away from him and spread herself for him, reaching for him, guiding him into her as he covered her. She gasped and then pulled her legs up and clasped him, her hips smashing at him. He felt his own orgasm coming and fought against it, and then lost control as she cried suddenly in ecstasy and he collapsed on her, burying his head in her black hair.

"I'm sorry," he whispered, "it's been so long and it was never like this."

"So long, too long, for me, too," she whispered. He felt her reaching out to one side and then she was cleansing him with a towel. He felt the fumes of the rum in his head and relaxed, and was suddenly asleep.

He was wakened three times during the night by her insistent hand. The last time the early-morning sun streamed into the doorway of the shelter, and he turned his face away from the glare and slept again. She shook him awake with a coconut half-shell full of scalding tea. She put the shell down beside the mattress and reached outside and got a tin plate full of slices of cold pork.

"Eat. Drink. I must go now to my post until this afternoon. Do not go outside to walk around, only to go bathroom unless Big Man sends for you." She kissed him tenderly. "That you should love such an ugly one as me," she giggled, and then she was gone.

He finished the cold meat and the tea and crawled out of the shelter. A soft male voice said, "This way, sir. I show you shit place." He followed the slight figure of a man who had a rifle slung over one shoulder to a place in the bushes. The man pointedly turned his back, and Flanagan did his business.

"We go back, now," the man said. "Sergeant Mac wants to talk with you." He led the way deep into the bush, Flanagan following along behind.

"I don't suppose you people on the ship got a chance to read this stuff?" McGillivray asked, waving the sheaf of orders in his hand.

"No," Flanagan said.

"We've got a lot of work to do," the Army Sergeant said. "Can't have old Doug getting hit in the ass with twenty thousand Jap troops he doesn't figure on meeting." He looked at the orders. "Must be a pretty big invasion."

"Captain told me the Navy would have seven hundred ships, that's including everything, mine sweeps, LSTs, everything. Hell of a bunch of carriers and battleships."

"They must mean business, must be coming back to stay," the Sergeant said.

"They give you a tough job?"

"Nah," McGillivray said. "There's four bridges on the main road into Tacloban and three on the only other road. Bridges are over a hell of a deep valley ravine, kind of country a tank couldn't get through in a year. We can blow those bridges, mine the roads. They won't get any reinforcements in to Tacloban. Just to make the cheese a little more binding I think I'll send some of our people in the night before the invasion and steal all the distributors out of their vehicles."

"How about your own people, what have you got, about ten thousand?"

"No," McGillivray said. "About three thousand is all. Most of them are spread around the mountains here, on the routes the Jap would have to take to get at us if he knew where we were, if he was sure of where we were. We could cut him to ribbons if he tried to come after us. When he starts down those two roads to reinforce Tacloban we'll slice him up when he hits the first bridge we've blown. Mine the road, use mortars from the mountaintops."

"No other way he can get to Tacloban, only on those two roads?" Flanagan asked.

"Oh, sure. He could build new roads. Take about three years to build a road five miles long through this stuff in these mountains." He sat back on his heels and grinned at Flanagan. "Wait until old Doug gets here and we go out to meet him, and his paymaster finds out I swore all three thousand of my people into the U.S. Army and Doug's paymaster is going to have to give them all back pay! Won't there be hell to pay?" His bright green eyes danced merrily.

"The girl. Maria," he said. "She wants me to recruit you into our bunch. What have you submarine sailors got we foot sloggers ain't?"

"Couldn't say," Flanagan said. "I might join up with you if I thought I could get away with it. She's quite a woman."

Offshore the *Eelfish* cruised submerged. Mike Brannon sat in the Wardroom with John Olsen and Bob Lee.

"If anything has happened to Flanagan," Brannon said, "I'm going back to Australia and shoot me an Admiral and a Brigadier General."

"I wouldn't worry, Skipper," Olsen said. "He said before he shoved off, didn't he, that he might have a long walk and couldn't get back last night?"

"Stands to reason, sir," Lee spoke up. "That Army guy couldn't have his camp too close to the shore, too close to Tacloban or the Jap airfield there. He'd have to be way up in the mountains, where he'd be safe."

"If anyone could be safe surrounded by thousands of Japanese," Brannon said. "But I'll settle for that. I'm going to get some sleep. Wake me if you see anything at all on the periscope observations."

* * *

Darkness fell with the suddenness that is typical in the tropics. Maria disengaged herself from Flanagan's arms and stood up.

"It is time for you to go." She handed him the half-shell of coconut, and he drank deeply of the rum.

"Drink now," she said. "We have made love enough. I have your seed in me many times. I will make a strong boy to remember you by." She bowed her head, and he could hear her sobbing. He reached out and lifted her into his lap, his arms around her.

"Maria," he said awkwardly, "I'm a sailor. I have no parents, I'm an orphan. When this war is over, and I don't think it will be too long now, I'll retire and take my pension and come back here and by God, will you marry me?"

She peered at him in the darkness. "The nuns taught us never to believe a man, but I believe you.

"You come back. I will be here, near Tacloban. It is my home before the war. I will show you your son and I will carry your burdens for all of my life." She buried her face in his shoulder, crying softly. Then she got up and went outside and disappeared.

When McGillivray came for him Flanagan had drained the coconut shell of rum and a second one he found outside the door of the shelter. He lurched upright and nodded to the guerrilla leader. They started off, going down the mountain trail. At the last cluster of bushes at the water's edge McGillivray paused and Flanagan bumped into him. The Army man tossed the haversack Flanagan had brought with him into the rubber boat that his men had pushed out of the bushes.

"I took Betty Grable," he said. "Shove off, sailor. See you in Manila."

Flanagan picked up the double-ended paddle and began to move away from the shore. Then he remembered the Christmas tree Petreshock had told him about. As the boat floated on the lowering tide he fumbled with the collapsible device and finally got it pulled out and securely in its bracket. He reached for the paddle, couldn't find it, and then discovered he was sitting on one end of it.

"Took Betty Grable," he mumbled to himself. "Bastards took my compass, too." He felt for the compass and found it and with his fumbling turned on the small red light.

"Brought it back, okay?" he said to himself. He began to paddle, clumsily. Somewhere in the night he heard the snoring mutter of diesel engines.

"Come alongside, you fuckers," he muttered and kept paddling. Then he felt hands under his arms grabbing him and the familiar deck of the *Eelfish* under his feet. He sighed and closed his eyes. Petreshock and Jim Rice, helped by the strong arms of Doc Wharton and Charlie Two Blankets, hoisted the unconscious form of Chief Flanagan up over the bridge rail, where Bill Brosmer grabbed him in his arms. As he steadied Flanagan's slack body his nose twitched under his red mustache.

"Son of a bitchin' Chief's pissy-assed drunk and—" His nose twitched again. "And he smells of pussy!"

CHAPTER 21

Eelfish left Leyte Gulf with all four main diesel engines pounding, heading for its patrol area off Tawi Tawi. Mike Brannon and John Olsen sat in the Wardroom, drinking coffee.

"Should be a good patrol area," Olsen said. "If the Japanese are concentrating their naval forces at Tawi Tawi that means they've got to have oil, and their oil comes from Balikpapan. The tankers coming from there to Tawi Tawi will have to run right by us. Unless there are several other boats along the route to intercept them before they get to us."

"I don't think there will be," Brannon said. "The reassignments of patrol areas the last couple of days from Fremantle argue against that. I'd think that Admiral Christie is throwing every submarine he can get over on the Pacific side of the invasion area. If the Japs ever get wind of what MacArthur's planning I think they'd throw every damned ship they've got into battle to stop it. And one of the things they would have to smash would be the carrier fleet we'll have steaming off the east coast of Samar. If they could smash the carriers the invasion goes down the drain. So I'd assume that Christie is setting up a scouting line of submarines to detect any Jap fleet movements. We might be the only guy on the block when we get to where we're going. How far is it?"

"About seven hundred miles," Olsen said. "Three, three and a half days at the most." He grinned at Brannon. "I looked in the haversack Flanagan brought back last night. The bottle of booze was still in the sack and the canned ham. I gave the watch in the Control Room the word to have him report to me, to you, as soon as he wakes up.''

In the Crew's Mess Bill Brosmer, the leading Quartermaster, was drinking coffee, surrounded by the off-watch crew.

"I'm tellin' you," Brosmer said, "I'm tellin' you that the Chief of the Boat was drunk as a skunk and he smelled of pussy and I know pussy when I smell it!"

"I don't know about the Chief of the Boat smellin' like pussy," one of the night lookouts said. "But I helped carry him down the ladder to the Control Room, and I know one thing, old Chief was passed-out drunk. Stiff as a board. I haven't seen anyone that drunk since the first liberty I made out of boot camp."

"Which ain't been that long ago," Scotty Rudolph said as he came out of his small galley. "You assholes get out of here unless you want to volunteer as mess cooks. Gettin' to be time to set table."

Late that afternoon a freshly showered and shaved Chief Flanagan presented himself in the Wardroom. Mike Brannon sat at his accustomed place at the head of the table, with John Olsen seated outboard of the table to his Captain's left. Flanagan was seated at the Captain's right.

"Please fill us in, Chief," Brannon said.

Flanagan talked slowly, recounting the trip in to the beach, the first contact with the guerrillas, the trip up in to the mountains to the base camp, the delivery of the orders from General MacArthur.

"Very well," Brannon said. "Before you go on, Chief, will you please tell me just what in the hell happened to you?" Flanagan looked at Brannon and drew a deep breath. "I can't make any excuses, sir. It was a long hard walk up that mountainside. When we got up there the Sergeant asked me how long it would be before we got back to port. I told him maybe a month, maybe longer. He said he figured something like that and that his people had laid on a feast of roast pig and other stuff. They gave me some home-brewed rum. Awful sneaky stuff. I never drink much when I'm ashore at the hotel. You know that. The stuff sneaked up on me, and this Sergeant, he said he didn't want to make that trip down and back up the mountain again that night. They kept giving me that rum to drink, and before I knew it I was drunk.

"I woke up the next day and they told me they'd take me back down the mountain at night. They had some more chow and more of that rum.

"All I can say is that I'm sorry, sir. But I didn't take a drink until the Army Sergeant had the orders and said that he understood them and that he'd carry them out, sir."

"I'm not going to court-martial you, Chief, although I guess I could," Brannon said slowly. "You did carry out the mission. But you know and I know that you didn't set much of an example for the crew." Flanagan sat, his head lowered.

"Let's get the yeoman in here," Brannon said. "I want you to dictate a complete report, Chief, but before you do, what sort of a force does this Sergeant have? They told me in Fremantle that he had ten thousand troops."

"He said about three thousand, sir. I saw some of them. They look and act sharp. Good weapons, and every weapon I saw was clean, well cared for. Lot of his people are women. He said they make good spies and that most of them are very slick at cutting a Jap throat.

"They're well disciplined. They don't make noise. Even at that feast they put on for me, when some of them got passed-out drunk there was no noise. They even laugh in whispers. He and his people sleep days and work nights. He said that gives him an advantage over the Jap."

"Did he say he could carry out his orders to cut roads or whatever he has to do?" Olsen asked.

"Yes, sir. He told me there was one main road with four bridges on it leading into Tacloban and one secondary road with three bridges. The bridges, he said, go over valleys that a tank couldn't get through. He can blow the bridges and mine the road approaches. He said he intended to steal all the distributor caps off the Jap vehicles the night before the invasion. I got the feeling, sir, that if the Jap tries to reinforce Tacloban, sir, that this man will cut him into small slices."

Brannon nodded and sent Pete Mahaffey for Booth, the yeoman. He came in to the wardroom with his pad and pen, and Flanagan went over the entire operation from the moment of leaving the ship to his return, carefully omitting any mention of the rum he had been given. When he had finished Brannon turned to Olsen.

"John, when Michaels wakes up have him put together a mission completed message to Admiral Christie with the addition that the Army Sergeant said he would carry out his orders without fail. We'll get that off tonight when we surface."

*   *   *

Eelfish arrived at its patrol area just before dawn and dove near the edge of the 100-fathom curve, a few miles to the east of the entrance to Sibutu Passage. As soon as Mahaffey had cleared the table of the breakfast dishes Mike Brannon called a meeting of his officers.

"We've got quite a bit of latitude so far as our patrol area is concerned," he said. "We can stay out here, where we are to the east of Sibutu Passage, and wait to intercept any tankers coming up from Balikpapan. Or we can move over to the Sulu Sea and watch Tawi Tawi and hope to get something coming out of that Naval Base.

"I want to run at a hundred twenty-five feet during the day when we're submerged. Periscope observation every hour. Sonar sweep before every periscope observation. No radar unless I give the order. If there are Japanese Naval ships in Tawi Tawi, and intelligence says there are, they'll have some sharp people on watch, and I don't want radar used without my permission.

The days and nights passed slowly with no sign of any targets. Mike Brannon paced the cigaret deck all night long, straining his eyes through his binoculars. On the sixth night on station Brannon heard the Chief of the Watch's voice echo in the bridge speaker.

"Radio shack says an Ultra message is coming in, Bridge."

"Bridge, aye," Jerry Gold answered. He turned to go back to the cigaret deck to tell Brannon and saw his Captain coming forward.

"I heard," Brannon said. "I'll go below and decode."

The message was long and took the better part of an hour to decode. When he had finished Brannon went out into the Control Room and told the messenger to wake Mr. Olsen and bring two cups of coffee to the Wardroom.

"The code breakers in Pearl say there are two big battle fleets leaving a port over on the west side of Borneo, place called Brunei," Brannon said as Olsen, his eyes bleary with sleep, sipped at a cup of coffee. "They say these two battle fleets are going to follow two different routes. One of them is going up the west coast of Palawan and then over through San Bernardino Strait to the Pacific. The *Dace* and the *Darter* are up off the north end of Palawan now, and they've been alerted to intercept, inform, and attack.

"The second battle fleet is headed our way, through the Balabac Strait to the west. We've got to get into position to observe and report and attack if possible. But we don't attack until after we've sent a contact report on the task force." He

shoved a chart, dividers, and a pair of parallel rulers over to
Olsen, who read the message and then busied himself at the
chart.

"The course they give for this bunch we're supposed to find
and report on, they're heading right for Leyte Gulf!" His eyes
widened as the import of the message, the enemy's course, hit
him.

"They must know that MacArthur is going to land there!"

"If there's enough Jap ships, if they're big enough, if they get
to Leyte Gulf they can steam right up the Gulf and smash the
invasion force from the rear," Brannon said dryly.

"This other bunch, the one that's going up Palawan and then
out to the Pacific through San Bernardino Strait?"

"Probably going to go after the carriers that will be offshore a
hundred miles or so and supporting the invasion," Brannon
answered.

"Ain't good, Skipper," Olsen muttered. "We can get our ass
under way right now for Balabac Strait. We're two hundred and
sixty miles away. We can be in position before they're due to
come through the Strait."

"Give the courses and speeds to the Bridge," Brannon said.
He waited, looking at the chart, feeling the sudden vibration in
his feet and legs as the *Eelfish* picked up speed. Olsen came back
with a small tray with two fresh cups of coffee and four
doughnuts. The Control Room messenger stuck his head through
the green curtain at the door and held out a message.

"Just came in, sir," the messenger said.

"Thank you," Brannon said. He looked at the message.
"Standard Fleet code," he said and reached for the code book.

"It's to *Dace* and *Darter,*" he said after he had decoded the
short message. "All it says is 'one to look and one to play.' I
guess that means that one has to see what that task force is and
report it and the other one can go in to attack. Nice little problem
in who does which, depending on the seniority of the skippers."

"Let's see," Olsen said. "Dave McClintock has the *Darter*.
Clagget's got the *Dace*. Those are two pretty tough people, good
submariners, good fighters. I'd bet a month's pay that they'll get
off a sighting report and then they'll both attack."

The *Eelfish* arrived on station before daylight on the day the
Japanese battle fleet was to transit Balabac on its way northeast.
The *Eelfish* dove and slipped down to cruise at 125 feet to escape
observation by scouting planes that Brannon reasoned would be
out ahead of the ships as they moved through the Strait.

The hours ticked away. Every half-hour the sonar watch made a sweep, and when he reported no screws could be heard the *Eelfish* planed upward to sixty feet and the OOD raised the search periscope. In the middle of the afternoon watch Lieutenant Bob Lee raised the 'scope. His hoarse cry brought Brannon scrambling to the Conning Tower.

"Ships, lots of big ships!" Lee said as he stepped away from the periscope. Brannon put his face to the big rubber eyepiece.

"Sound General Quarters!" he said as he rotated the periscope a full 360 degrees. "Down periscope." He walked to the hatch that led down to the Control Room.

"Open all torpedo-tube outer doors. Set depth ten feet on all torpedoes. Repeat ten feet. Rig ship for silent running. Rig for depth-charge attack. Plotting party stand by." He moved to one side of the hatch as Lieutenant Perry Arbuckle scrambled to his station at the TDC. Paul Blake relieved the watch sonar man and Booth sat down beside Blake, his notebook and pen in his hands. Bill Brosmer buckled on his battle telephone set and stood by the periscope control. The subdued whine of the air-conditioning blowers slowed to a stop. The interior of the *Eelfish* was silent except for the low hum of the electric motors that drove the ship and the gurgle of water outside the hull.

"All Battle Stations manned," John Olsen said in the Control Room. "All torpedo-tube outer doors are open. Depth set on all torpedoes is one zero feet. Ten feet. Ship is rigged for silent running. Ship is rigged for depth-charge attack, all bulkhead openings closed, Conning Tower. Plot is ready."

"Very well," Brannon said. He nodded at Brosmer, who pushed the up button on the periscope control. The long steel tube slid upward, and Brannon went down on his knees and grabbed the handles as the eyepiece of the periscope cleared the deck level, snapped them outward, and rode the periscope upward, his eye at the lens.

"Mark!" he snapped, and Brosmer read off the bearing to Lieutenant Arbuckle who cranked it into his TDC.

"That mark is on a big battleship." Brannon's voice was tight. "Take this down.

"The task force is led by three very large destroyers. Followed by a big battleship. Then there's another big battleship followed by what I think is a heavy cruiser followed by a big destroyer. Heavy air cover overhead."

"Can you give me a range, Captain?" Arbuckle asked in a low voice.

"Range on the first battleship is . . . range is five thousand yards. Range to the second battleship is seven, make it sixty-nine hundred yards."

"We're on their port hand, sir." Olsen's voice came up the hatch. "Suggest we come right to zero five zero and make another obsei vation in three minutes, sir. We can get their speed and base course down pat then."

"Down periscope," Brannon ordered. "Come right to new course zero five zero. Let me know when you want another look, Control." He waited, his plump face impassive.

"Suggest you take another look, sir," Olsen said.

Brannon rode the periscope upward and steadied on the first battleship in the line.

"Mark! That's on the first battleship in line. Angle on the bow is one six zero port. Those people are making knots. Destroyer is coming this way. Down periscope. Close torpedo-tube outer doors. Make depth one hundred fifty feet, Control."

The *Eelfish* slid downward. Brannon walked to the hatch and stood, looking down through the circular opening at the plotting crew at work on the gyro table.

"We've got their speed, sir," Olsen said. "They're making twenty-four knots."

"Very well," Brannon said. "I'm going to stay on this course. There might be more ships coming. We can't risk not being sure of that." He turned to Perry Arbuckle.

"That's the first time I ever saw a Jap battleship, and when I do I see two of them and I don't dare shoot!" He looked at his wrist watch and turned to the hatch.

"Sixty-five feet, Control. I'm going to raise the 'scope now so watch your angle." He nodded his head at Brosmer, who raised the periscope. The *Eelfish* took a slightly sharper up angle as the periscope went up. Brannon searched astern and on both flanks and saw empty ocean. Far ahead, on his starboard bow, he could see the smoke of the task force.

"Booth, get down below and give your information on the task force to Mr. Michaels. Tell him that I want a message encoded at once. As soon as he's ready we'll come to forty feet and get the message off."

Fifteen minutes later *Eelfish* planed upward to forty feet and the radio mast was run up. The radioman began to pound out the groups of five numbers in the coded message. He stopped sending and his fingers delicately adjusted his receiver dial.

"Message received and receipted for," he said to Jim Michaels.

"I've got fast screws bearing one seven zero, sir," Paul Blake called out. "Pretty far away but getting a little stronger."

"Three hundred feet," Brannon ordered. "Down radio mast. Bastards probably zeroed in on the radio signal." He walked to the Control Room hatch.

"Stand easy on Battle Stations. Smoking lamp is lighted for ten minutes only. Maintain silence about the decks."

The Japanese battle fleet sighted by *Eelfish* was called, officially, the Southern Force. It was commanded by Vice Admiral Nishimura, and it was one of three task forces that were under way to smash the invasion at Tacloban. In Tacloban there were 28 big Liberty ships, hundreds of landing craft, and a vast armada of Navy supply and support ships, all concentrated around the port city. The cruiser U.S.S. *Nashville,* with General Douglas MacArthur aboard, was anchored in the midst of the invasion fleet, the command center for the vast amphibious operation that was striking both at Tacloban and a little farther south, along the shoreline.

Ashore the initial reaction to the American landing was light. As the hours wore on the resistance solidified and grew stronger as the Japanese began to close in on the landing areas. The call went out to units farther inland to come with all possible speed to reinforce the garrison at Tacloban. Those units could not reach the invasion area; the main roads had been cut.

While Vice Admiral Nishimura's force was sailing across the Sulu Sea toward Leyte Gulf, another battle force, this one commanded by Vice Admiral Kurita, moved to the north along the west side of Palawan Island. The *Darter* spotted the battle force and sent off a contact message, and then moved to the attack, calling on *Dace* to help.

Darter fired all six torpedo tubes forward at a heavy cruiser leading the battle force and then swung and fired four torpedoes from the after tubes at another cruiser. Five of the six torpedoes fired out of *Darter*'s forward tubes hit the heavy cruiser, and Vice Admiral Kurita's flagship, the heavy cruiser, *Atago,* blew up with spectacular explosions. Vice Admiral Kurita decided to go down with his ship, but his junior officers persuaded him to swim for it, and he was rescued by a destroyer.

The salvo from the *Darter*'s after torpedo tubes smashed into the heavy cruiser *Takao,* damaging it severely. *Dace,* racing to get into the fight, set upon the heavy cruiser *Maya* and fired six torpedoes at it. Four of the torpedoes hit, and the *Maya* rolled over and sank in four minutes.

The task force moved north, undeterred by the attack by the two submarines. Vice Admiral Kurita's orders were to go north and east and exit through the San Bernardino Strait to the Pacific and then run south down the length of Samar Island, turn west and north, and rendezvous with Vice Admiral Nishimura at 0430 on the morning of October 25, 1944. To make sure that the American aircraft carriers could not get into the fight at Tacloban or harass the two Japanese battle fleets racing toward Tacloban, Vice Admiral Ozawa's Northern Force was successfully decoying Admiral Bull Halsey's main carrier fleet away from the invasion area and to the north.

Farther to the southwest was yet another and smaller battle force, the Second Southern Force under the command of Vice Admiral Shima. This was a mop-up force to trap and sink any American ships that might escape the double sledgehammer blow administered by Nishimura and Kurita. The Second Southern Force consisted of two heavy and one light cruiser and nine destroyers.

The scene was being set for what historians would later call the greatest naval battle of all time between capital warships. *Eelfish,* far behind Vice Admiral Nishimura's battle force, was running on the surface at top speed in the hope that somehow, in some way, it could take part in the battle that Mike Brannon was sure was going to be joined.

CHAPTER 22

Sunset came at 1815 hours on October 24, 1944, at Tacloban. Ashore the American invasion troops were locked in an increasingly stubborn battle with the Japanese defensive forces. Before Leyte Island was declared to be secured and safely in U.S. hands, on Saint Patrick's Day of 1945, the U.S. forces would suffer more than 15,000 casualties. The Japanese would pay a much stiffer price. More than 49,000 of their troops would die in the five-month-long battle.

In the crowded reaches of San Pedro Bay, just across from the port of Tacloban, hundreds of tons of supplies were being shuttled to the shore where the beach captains supervised the moving and storage of the vast quantity of materiel coming in from the ships.

Thousands of fighting men were being ferried from the ships that had brought them to this desolate area to the various beach staging areas from which they were moved into the battles raging all around Tacloban. On board the ships in San Pedro Bay there was fear, open naked fear. The movements of the Japanese battle fleets, reported first by the Ultra code breakers and confirmed by submarines, left no doubt that the Japanese intended to strike from the sea at the invasion force.

As the sun set, Vice Admiral Nishimura, his flag flying in the battleship *Yamashiro*, steamed toward the invasion area. Ahead of him, four destroyers of the Japanese Destroyer Division Four were ranged: the *Michishio*, the *Yamagumo*, the *Asagumo*, and the *Shigure*. A kilometer astern of Nishimura's flagship the battleship *Fuso* steamed, followed by the heavy cruiser *Mogami*. The navigators on the bridge of the battleship *Yamashiro* worked at their charts, estimating the overall speed of the task force, and assured the Vice Admiral that they would rendezvous with Vice Admiral Kurita at 0430 on October 25—providing Vice Admiral Kurita was on time. Once the rendezvous was accomplished the combined battle fleets would steam up the length of Leyte Gulf and administer a smashing attack on the American invasion force.

At 2300 hours of the night of October 24 the Peter Tare boats—the PT boats—sighted the Japanese force in the eastern area of the Sea of Mindanao and hurled themselves into the attack against an enemy force so much more powerful than all the PT boats combined that the very fact of the attack was madness—mosquitoes attacking a herd of elephants.

The Japanese did not even bother to change course as the PT boats came hurtling out of the darkness to loose torpedoes and open fire with .50-caliber machine guns. Vice Admiral Nishimura thought so little of the attack he did not bother to break radio silence and notify his fleet headquarters that his ships had been sighted and were under attack.

The Japanese attack plan for smashing the American invasion force at Tacloban depended on almost split-second timing. The two forces, Nishimura's Southern Force and Vice Admiral Kurita's Northern Force were to achieve rendezvous and proceed in line of battle up the Gulf of Leyte to the attack. Hours before the

time of the rendezvous Vice Admiral Nishimura suspected that
Admiral Kurita might not be able to make the rendezvous at the
appointed time. Kurita had broken radio silence to report that he
had come under heavy air attack while approaching San Bernardino
Strait and might be delayed as much as seven hours. Vice
Admiral Nishimura, a stubborn and skilled fighter who relished
night battles, decided to carry on with the original plan, confident that his two battleships, the heavy cruiser, and his four large
destroyers were more than sufficient to do the job.

The moon set at 0106 on the morning of October 25. The sea
was glassy smooth, the night hot, airless, and humid. Occasional
flashes of lightning from a storm over the mountains of Leyte
Island illuminated the blue-black water.

Undeterred by the PT boat attacks, Vice Admiral Nishimura
swept into Surigao Strait and turned to make the run up the Gulf
of Leyte to his targets, the invasion fleet. He formed up his fleet
into line of battle, the four destroyers in the van followed by the
battleship *Yamashiro*, the battleship *Fuso*, and the heavy cruiser
Mogami bringing up the rear.

To the north of him, completely undetected by Japanese
intelligence, was one of the mightiest naval forces ever assembled for a sea battle: 27 U.S. destroyers and one Australian
destroyer; four heavy cruisers, one of them an Australian ship;
four light cruisers; and six battleships.

At 0300 on October 25 a lynx-eyed lookout on the *Shigure*,
the Japanese destroyer leading the way, reported seeing the
outlines of enemy destroyers. Nishimura ordered the big search-
lights on the bridge of his flagship turned on to sweep the ocean
ahead, but the American destroyers were too far away to be seen
in the searchlight beams. The Japanese battle fleet swept onward
through the quiet night.

Then, from both sides of the Japanese battle line, the destroyers roared in to the attack, each ship pouring a dense cloud of
smoke from its funnels, each ship's multiple torpedo tubes
trained toward the Japanese battle line.

It was, as naval historians were later to write, the classic,
time-honored attack by the hornets of the sea, the destroyers.
The small ships, vulnerable to a hit from a gun of almost any
caliber, roared in to the attack, loosing their torpedoes, their
small deck guns barking at the huge battleships and the enemy's
larger destroyers.

The first salvo of torpedoes slammed into the battleship *Fuso*,
cruising a kilometer behind the *Yamashiro*. The *Fuso* turned out

of the battle line as its crew fought raging fires below decks. No one told Vice Admiral Nishimura that the *Fuso* had been hit and was no longer in the battle line. Nishimura plowed forward, not even bothering to order evasive tactics for his ships.

The first wave of attacking destroyers peeled off and made room for the main destroyer attack. The destroyers, their thin hulls vibrating heavily as their engines drove the ships through the seas at thirty knots or more, charged in at the Japanese ships. As the attack developed, as destroyer after destroyer, funnels belching black smoke, torpedoes lancing into the air from the deck tubes to drop in the water and race toward the Japanese ships, guns blazing, raced in, Nishimura knew he had erred. A torpedo hit his flagship and slowed it for a few moments. The Japanese destroyer *Yamashiro* was hit and blown apart by the American torpedoes. A torpedo hit the *Asagumo*'s bow and blew the entire bow away, but that ship's captain, a doughty seaman, reversed his engines and began to steam backward to keep the sea from caving in the thin bulkheads back of the missing bow. He managed to reverse course 180 degrees and steamed toward the attacking American destroyers stern first, his deck guns firing.

At 0330 Nishimura broke radio silence to say that he was under heavy attack by American destroyers, that he had lost two of his destroyers but would continue to press home his attack. At this point in the developing battle Vice Admiral Nishimura still did not know that his other battleship had been hit, was, in fact, exploding internally with such massive force that the *Fuso* was broken into two huge pieces, each of which floated, burning brightly. Nishimura steamed straight ahead, preceded by two destroyers and followed by the heavy cruiser *Mogami*.

There is a classic naval strategy for war on the high seas that is known as "Crossing the T." The concept calls for catching the enemy battle fleet steaming in a straight line. The objective at that point is to cross the top of that straight line with one's own battle fleet, to cross the "T." The advantage, an enormous advantage, lies with the ships that cross the T; those ships can bring their entire broadsides to bear on the line of ships advancing toward them. The ships that make up the vertical bar of the letter T can fire only their forward guns.

The last time this maneuver had been successfully carried out was in 1905 when Admiral Togo succeeded in crossing the T against a Russian battle fleet in the Battle of Tshushima Strait, just north of Japan. Now, 39 years later, Vice Admiral Nishimura was unwittingly advancing into trouble.

Lying in wait halfway up Leyte Gulf was the greatest concentration of naval fire power ever assembled in one body of water. The four heavy and four light cruisers were the lightweights of the force. Just north of the cruisers there were six battleships, leisurely steaming from west to east across the Gulf of Leyte.

Two of those battleships, the U.S.S. *California* and the U.S.S. *West Virginia*, had been torpedoed and sunk on December 7, 1941, at Pearl Harbor. Three of the others, the *Maryland*, the *Tennessee*, and the *Pennsylvania* had also been hit and damaged in the attack on Pearl Harbor. Now, in company with the U.S.S. *Mississippi*, the five battleships, their officers and crews thirsting for revenge, waited, cruising slowly, the cross bar of the classic T as Nishimura steamed toward them.

As the destroyers finished their attacks and hauled off to the sides, the heavy and light cruisers began to bark at the Japanese fleet. Nishimura answered with his auxiliary batteries and one or two salvos from his forward turrets.

At 0351 on the morning of October 25, 1944, the radar screens in the American battleships showed the enemy line of ships to be 21,000 yards distant—11.9 miles.

The order was given to open fire. In a matter of eighteen minutes the six battleships fired over 3,200 rounds of fourteen- and sixteen-inch shells toward the Japanese ships.

Vice Admiral Nishimura, his flagship *Yamashiro* still afloat despite the terrible volume of heavy shells that had been poured into the ship, ordered the ship's captain to turn so he could bring his main battery to bear against the American ships. The *Yamashiro* made the turn and capsized. Almost all of the crew, including Vice Admiral Nishimura, drowned in the dark water.

The heavy cruiser *Mogami*, staggering under the impact of heavy shells hitting the ship, showed its teeth. It opened fire on every target its gunners could see, and as it turned to make its escape it fired torpedoes toward the American ships.

A salvo of heavy shells hit the *Mogami*'s bridge, blowing it completely off the ship, killing the commanding officer and his entire staff. The *Mogami* slowed and stopped, afire above decks and below. Somehow the *Mogami*'s crew got the fires under control and repaired extensive damage in the ship's engine rooms and got the ship under way, steering with a jury rig. With no navigator, and with hardly any officers left alive, the ship moved south away from the merciless rain of shells. The *Mogami* was to survive for another five hours. At 0900 of that day the *Mogami* came under heavy air attack, and its crew, gallant men by any standards, abandoned ship.

Meanwhile, Vice Admiral Shima's Second Southern Force was steaming toward Leyte Gulf to carry out its assignment of sweeping up any American ships that had escaped Nishimura's attack. This force, consisting of two heavy and one light cruiser and nine major destroyers, came under attack by the dauntless PT boats. The light cruiser *Akugumo* was hit by one torpedo and forced to drop out of formation. Vice Admiral Shima, operating in an informational vacuum—he had heard nothing from Vice Admiral Nishimura since Nishimura had reported he was under attack from destroyers—decided that discretion was the order of the day and ordered his Second Southern Force to reverse course and head back toward Borneo.

The battle of Surigao Strait, except for some mopping up, was over. Rear Admiral Jesse B. Oldendorf, USN, had pulled off the ultimate maneuver of naval warfare between heavy capital ships. He had crossed the enemy's T and in eighteen short minutes had smashed an enemy battle fleet to bits.

There was no one sleeping aboard the *Eelfish* as it raced through the western reaches of the Sea of Mindanao on that night. Elmer Rafferty, the ship's leading radioman, tuned in on the battle radio circuit of the American fleet in the Gulf of Leyte and patched the circuit into the *Eelfish*'s 1-MC system, the ship's internal communication system. The off-duty crewmen clustered in the two torpedo rooms and the Crew's Mess. They heard the first reports from the PT boats when they sighted the destroyers in the van of the Japanese battle force, heard their exultant messages as they hurled their fragile little torpedo boats against the larger ships.

"Fucking PT boat sailors," Fred Nelson growled in the After Torpedo Room. "They can't shoot torpedoes worth a damn! We should be there, damn it! All they'll do is get their asses shot off. Fuckers!" He turned and faced the people in his torpedo room. "But give 'em marks for guts. Lots of guts."

There was silence on the radio circuit after the PT boat attacks, and then the *Eelfish* crew heard the crisp orders from the first destroyers as they moved to the attack, heard the sharp commands to make smoke, to attack, and then the laconic reports that torpedoes had been fired, that hits had been made.

"Sounds like the little boys got in a good torpedo attack," John Olsen said as he and Mike Brannon stood in the Control

Room looking at a chart of Leyte Gulf. The radio crackled again with the word that the main destroyer attack was beginning.

"Holy cow!" Brannon muttered. "That first tin-can attack was only for openers. Now they're throwing a lot of tin cans in. You can't even make sense out of the orders, there are so many of them reporting." He listened as destroyer after destroyer reported that it was going in to attack. A cheer went up from the crewmen in the Crew's Mess and the torpedo rooms when a report came in of a hit on a battleship, that two destroyers of the Japanese force had been hit and sunk.

"That was our damned battleship," Brannon growled. "We had that bastard in the periscope and within five thousand yards and we couldn't attack! Damn, damn, damn!"

A burst of static blurred the order from Rear Admiral G. L. Weyler for the main battle line to open fire with broadsides against the Japanese. Seconds later, clear as a bell, came the report from the U.S.S. *West Virginia* that it was commencing broadside fire at a range of 21,000 yards, followed by similar reports from five other battleships.

"That's it," Brannon said quietly. "They must have the Japs in a box. Six battleships firing broadsides? My God, no fleet in the world can stand up to that sort of firepower!"

Eighteen minutes later the order to cease fire came. Mike Brannon lifted a telephone off the bulkhead and spoke to the crew.

"From what we heard, what all of us heard, I conclude that a major sea battle has been fought up in Leyte Gulf. My interpretation of what we've heard is that with six of our battleships firing broadsides for twenty minutes and then being ordered to cease fire the Japanese fleet we sighted the other day must either be destroyed, or what's left of it is in full retreat.

"We heard no reports of any of our ships taking any hits, so the odds are that the battle is over, but if we're lucky, if there are any ships left in that Japanese fleet we picked up in the Sulu Sea, maybe we can get them." He put down the telephone and motioned to Jim Michaels.

"I want a constant radar search, Jim. If anything did get away I want to go after it."

A few hours later, just before dawn, the *Eelfish* radar reported a multiple contact. *Eelfish* tracked, heading toward the contact at top speed, and got off a contact report. But Admiral Shima's Second Southern Force, then in full retreat toward Borneo, was moving too fast for the submarine to catch up.

The report from the *Eelfish* bore fruit. On the morning of October 27, 1944, Admiral Shima's ships were found by 44 bombers from the Fifth and Thirteenth Army Air Forces, based at Noemfor and Biak. The light cruiser *Akuguma,* hit earlier by a torpedo from a PT boat, went down in flames under the aircraft bombs. The rest of Admiral Shima's force scattered and evaded the bombers. After two days of fruitless search the *Eelfish* was ordered to return to its original war patrol off Tawi Tawi. The radio message from Fremantle congratulating the *Eelfish* for finding the Japanese battle force that had been destroyed in Leyte Gulf was greeted with silence by the ship's crew.

CHAPTER 23

Ten days after *Eelfish* had arrived on station, orders were received to scout the port of Brunei on the northwest coast of Borneo and report on any shipping seen in the port and then return to Fremantle.

"About six hundred miles from here," Brannon mused as he looked at the course Olsen had laid down on the chart. "Where's Jerry Gold, I didn't see a fuel oil report this morning. We've done an awful lot of running at top speed on this patrol."

Gold came into the Wardroom minutes later, wiping his hands on a piece of rag.

"Didn't know you wanted me, sir," he said genially, "until the messenger came looking for me."

"Anything wrong back there?" Brannon asked, eyeing the rag Gold was using as a towel.

"No, sir," Gold said. "Just adding to my education in how to clean a fuel injector."

"What's the fuel oil situation?" Brannon asked. "I didn't get a report this morning."

"My fault," Gold said with a grin. "Got it in my pocket, right here. Meant to lay it on your plate this morning but I just plain forgot."

"We've got to run over to the other side of Borneo and do a look-see for Fremantle and then go home," Olsen said.

"Can you give me an offhand guess about how much farther it

is from here to there to Fremantle against how far it is from here to Fremantle?'' Gold said.

"About four fifty, five hundred miles farther.''

Gold closed his eyes, thinking. ''No sweat, sir. Provided we don't do any more of that four-engine-make-turns-for-max-speed stuff. I heard once that *Flying Fish,* early in the war, had to come home burning lube oil instead of diesel because they ran out of diesel oil. Rather not do that. Gets kind of hairy when you have to start thinking about running the engine-room bilges through the fuel strainers.''

Lieutenant Gold had the periscope watch as the *Eelfish* slogged its way southward down the west coast of Borneo. He squinted through the lens and picked up the pencil-thin masts of ships almost dead ahead on the horizon, a little before two o'clock in the afternoon watch. Mike Brannon came to the Conning Tower and searched the horizon ahead of the *Eelfish.*

"You must have eyes like an eagle,'' Brannon grumbled. ''I can't see anything out there. You sure?''

"Yes, sir,'' Gold said. ''May I?'' Brannon stepped to one side and Gold took another bearing through the periscope. He stepped back. Brannon looked and saw two tiny lines sticking up above the horizon.

"Damn it, you're right,'' he said. ''Sound General Quarters.'' Gold punched the button, and the clanging of the alarm sent the crew of *Eelfish* racing to their Battle Stations. Two minutes later Olsen called up the hatch.

"We're due west of a place called Kota Kinabula, sir. Chart shows thirty-one fathoms of water, sir.''

"We can risk a fathometer reading. They're still a long, long way away. Gold has got eyes like I never saw.'' He heard the muted ping of the fathometer's sonar beam lancing down through the water to hit the bottom and return.

"Twenty-eight fathoms under the keel, sir,'' Olsen called up the hatch. ''Are they close enough to get a bearing, sir?''

"Not yet,'' Brannon said. ''Another three minutes.'' He stood, waiting, his plump face impassive. He bent toward the hatch to the Control Room.

"John, if I remember the chart, there's deep water to the west, isn't there?''

"Yes, sir. Plenty of deep water, real deep. We're a few miles east of the edge of the deep water, sir.''

"Very well,'' Brannon said, ''We'll take a look, now.''

"I've got two destroyers, moving pretty fast,'' Brannon said.

"Back of them there's a pretty big ship, looks like a tanker. There's some smoke back of that ship. Might be another tin can back there." He moved the periscope a trifle.

"Mark!"

"Bearing is three four zero," Brosmer said, and Arbuckle cranked the information into the TDC.

"Range is five thousand yards to the first destroyer," Brannon said. He watched the ships coming closer.

"Can you give me another bearing and range?" Olsen asked.

Brannon complied, and Olsen called up the hatch.

"They're making fifteen knots, sir. Closing at the rate of about four hundred fifty yards a minute. Suggest we come left to course one zero zero, sir. If you want to, you can let the tin cans pass and take the tanker, sir."

"Come left to course one zero zero," Brannon ordered. "I'll take the tanker, John. He's a good big one. He bears ... Mark! Range is now four nine zero zero yards on the tanker. Forty-nine hundred yards."

"We'll have a solution in six minutes, sir," Arbuckle said, "assuming a shooting range of under two thousand yards."

"I think we can live with that," Brannon said. "As long as his helpers don't bother us we'll shoot a spread of three at the tanker."

"Recommend you make turns for two-thirds speed, sir," Olsen sang out. "He's going a little faster than we figured."

"Very well," Brannon said. He put his eye to the lens of the periscope.

"Mark! Lead destroyer bears zero four one. Range to the lead destroyer is two eight zero zero. Down periscope." He looked at his wrist watch and waited, watching the second hand on the watch hitch around the dial twice.

"Up periscope. Stand by. Here he comes. Nice big, fat oil tanker. I'll give you a bearing on the second destroyer.... Mark! Bearing on that closest destroyer is three five zero. Range is seventeen hundred yards." He swung the periscope a few degrees to the right.

"Here's our boy...stand by for a shooting run...Mark!" Brosmer snapped out the bearing.

"Range is fourteen hundred yards...angle on the bow is zero six zero port...."

"Solution, sir!" Arbuckle said.

"Stand by forward...." Brannon's shoulder muscles were

bunching beneath his thin khaki shirt as he watched the heavy tanker move toward him.

"Fire one!" He counted down from six to one.

"Fire two!

"Fire three!" He swung the periscope, looking at the closest destroyer. He swung the periscope back and saw a gush of flame at the tanker's midsection, and then the whole of the ship was sheathed in spouting columns of flame.

"Good God! He's on fire from stem to stern! Right full rudder." He strained at the periscope, turning it as the *Eelfish* turned, watching the destroyers.

"Fast screws bearing one eight zero, sir," Paul Blake called out.

"Close torpedo-tube outer doors," Brannon snapped. "Take me down to one hundred and fifty feet. Watch the damned depth. We haven't got that much water under us."

He stood in the Conning Tower listening to the distant drumming of the destroyers grow louder, the sound penetrating the hull of the submarine.

"They're coming too fast to hear anything, John," he called down the hatch. "Give me a fathometer reading. One ping only."

He waited, and then he heard John Olsen say, "Five fathoms under the keel, sir." He chewed his lower lip with his upper teeth for a minute.

"I've got a third set of fast screws, sir," Blake said. "Bears zero four zero, sir." Brannon nodded and looked at the compass repeater.

"Rudder amidships. Rig for depth charge. Rig for silent running. Make turns for dead slow. Plot, give me a position and a heading to deep water."

"Course to deep water would be two six zero, sir, that's the closest one. Edge of the shelf is four miles away."

"Very well," Brannon said. At one-third speed it would take the *Eelfish* almost two hours to reach deep water. At dead slow, a lot longer. He jerked his head up as a sharp noise rang through the Conning Tower.

"He's pinging on us sir." Blake's voice was almost apologetic. Brannon nodded and went down the ladder to the Control Room. He looked at the plot.

"We're going to pay for that tanker," he said softly. "Not enough water here, damn it. But the target was too good to pass up. So now we pay."

"For that and I guess for everything that happened in Leyte Gulf," Olsen said in a mournful voice. Both men's eyes turned upward to the Conning Tower hatch as Paul Blake's voice sounded.

"Two sets of fast screws bearing two seven zero and two eight zero and picking up speed, sir. This sounds like an attack run!"

"Very well," Brannon said. The thunder of the destroyer screws grew louder, and then the people in the *Eelfish* heard the sharp, distinctive crack of depth-charge exploder mechanisms going off, to be followed by the thunderous explosions of the depth charges. The *Eelfish* reeled sideways to port and then rolled back to starboard as light bulbs and gauge glasses throughout the ship broke. Four more depth charges went off, and the submarine twisted, its hull groaning in the vortex of water.

"Forward Engine Room's taking water through broken welds on the outboard exhaust lines, sir," the telephone talker said. "The Chief back there says it isn't serious. Yet."

"Here they come again," Blake called out, and the thunder of the destroyer screws up above filled the inside of the *Eelfish*. A half-dozen depth charges went off in crashing explosions, shaking the *Eelfish* heavily.

"Watch your depth, damn it!" Jerry Gold's harsh order brought Brannon's head around. The depth gauge needles showed 200 feet as John LaMark wrestled his big brass wheel around in an effort to bring up the submarine's bow.

"Couldn't help it," the Gunner's Mate gasped. "Damned depth charge must have gone off right above the bow. Drove her nose right down."

"Damage reports," Brannon ordered. The telephone talker raised his head and looked at Captain Brannon.

"Forward Room reports a real bad leak around the capstan gear, sir. Petreshock says he's trying to stop it, but they're takin' some water. Forward Engine Room reports the leak around the exhaust lines isn't doing too much. No other damage reports, sir."

"Keep me advised of that leak in the Forward Room," Brannon said. "Jerry, keep in mind they're taking water up there."

"Aye, aye, sir," Gold said.

"I've got twin screws bearing zero one zero and running across our bow, Control," Blake called out. "I've got two sets of screws aft bearing one seven zero and one nine two. Target up ahead is pinging." Brannon nodded. He didn't need to be told the destroyer up ahead was pinging. The loud ringing noise echoed through the *Eelfish* in a constant, nagging vibration.

"Screws aft picking up speed," Blake called out. "This is an attack run, Control!"

The two destroyers raced toward the spot on the ocean beneath which they knew *Eelfish* was hiding. As they approached the area the gunners on the squat fantails released one depth charge after another, and the Y-guns amidships boomed as they threw depth charges out to the side to tumble through the air and then sink downward until they reached the depth where the sea pressure would overcome the spring tension cranked against the diaphragms of the exploders and fire the depth charges.

The *Eelfish* was smashed downward by the first two depth charges. There was a loud crunching noise that reverberated throughout the ship, and Brannon heard Jerry Gold curse. He whirled and saw the long black needle of one depth gauge standing at 220 feet. Another half-dozen charges went off with a tremendous roar, and cork from the hull insulation rained down over the people in the Control Room. Jerry Gold cried out in agony and Brannon saw him hopping on one leg, his face distorted with pain.

"Damned ladder like to broke my shin!" Gold moaned. Brannon looked and saw that the Conning Tower ladder was swaying, its bottom rivets snapped by the sudden bulging inward of the *Eelfish*'s hull.

"Forward Room is reporting we hit something, Captain," the telephone talker said.

"Our bow is stuck in the damned bottom! That's what we hit!" Brannon snapped. "All stop! Get me a damage report as quick as you can." He looked at the depth gauge. It now read 230 feet.

"Forward Room reports water still coming in around the capstan shaft. They've got a foot of water in front of the tubes. After Battery reports leaks around the sea valves for blowing the heads to sea. They're working on that. Both Engine Rooms report all exhaust welds are busted and taking some water."

Brannon lifted the soggy towel that hung around his neck and wiped his face. He stared at the plot.

"So damned near to deep water," he muttered. He looked over at the Machinist's Mate on the blow manifolds.

"Next time they make a run and drop on us," he said, "I want you to hit the after main ballast tanks with a high-pressure blow, hold it for ten seconds, and then hit bow buoyancy with high-pressure air for five seconds." He turned to Chief Flanagan. "Keep your eye on me as we blow. When I drop my hand I want all-astern rung up, all-astern full. Tell maneuvering to stand by to shut down power the minute I signal you." He turned to Jerry Gold.

"I'm going to try to jolt her off the bottom, Jerry. I don't want to go up more than twenty, thirty feet if I can help it. He looked upward, the sweat dripping off his chin, as the noise of the pinging echoed through the ship.

"I don't get anything out of the regular sound heads, Control," Paul Blake called down. "But I'm getting some readings through the topside JP sound head."

Brannon chewed his lower lip for a second. The topside JP sound gear, a small horizontal bar mounted on a shaft, was not nearly as sensitive as the two big sound heads that were lowered beneath the ship's forward keel. Those sound heads, he reasoned, were either broken off or buried in the bottom.

The thunder of the destroyer screws hammered through the submarine's thin hull, and Brannon craned his neck upward, waiting for the shattering explosions he knew would come. The first two charges exploded with a massive roar.

"Hit it!" Brannon yelled at the Machinist's Mate. The high-pressure air roared into the after main ballast tanks, and the *Eelfish* lurched upward a few feet.

"All astern! Hit bow buoyancy!" Brannon barked. The *Eelfish* lurched backward, its bow beginning to rise.

"Belay the blow! All stop! Gold, how does it feel?"

"Under control, Captain," Jerry Gold said.

"All ahead dead slow. Two hundred feet," Brannon ordered. The *Eelfish*, freed of the grip of the bottom, moved slowly upward, the men on the bow planes gasping for air in the oxygen-depleted atmosphere of the submarine.

"Two hundred feet, sir," Gold reported.

"Sonar," Brannon said. "Can you hear anything at all through the regular sound heads?"

"Negative, sir," Blake answered.

"Probably wiped them out on the bottom," Brannon said. He stood, staring at the plotting board, wishing that Captain Mealey were standing there with him. What would Mealey do with no sound heads to get accurate bearings on the enemy above? What sort of maneuvering would he go through without ears to hear?

He squared his shoulders and wiped his face with the sodden towel.

"Keep me on this course to deep water," he said to Olsen. "We can't risk going down on the bottom and staying there. We're too easy to find. How much farther have we got to run?"

Olsen measured with the dividers. "Little less than a mile, sir."

The destroyer captains recognized Brannon's strategy at once. Once the submarine was beyond the shallow shelf that ran along the west coast of Borneo it would be in very deep water, free to maneuver as it could not in the shallower water over the shelf. The navigator on the destroyer carrying the flag for the small convoy bent over his plotting board and looked at his chart.

"He's getting close, sir," he said tonelessly.

The destroyer captain, a small, thin man whose face still showed the shock of seeing his treasured oil tanker go skyward in a series of tremendous explosions, touched the chart with his finger.

"Once he is there we lose him. That paragon of virtue of a supply officer with his talk of water less than two hundred feet along the coastline! So he emptied his warehouses of all the old depth charges he had, charges that cannot be exploded below two hundred feet because they have the old exploder mechanisms! Continual attack! Continual attack!"

Eelfish twisted and turned, its hull racked and wrenched in a seemingly endless series of depth charges as it fought its way slowly toward the deeper water. The temperature in the Control Room had long ago passed 110 degrees. The humidity stood at 100 percent, the air saturated with moisture. The crew, gasping for oxygen in the foul air, struggled with the job of stopping leaks, working in the dim light of the battle lanterns.

"If those bastards up there don't get tired of loading depth charges pretty soon, we ain't gonna make it," Jim Rice grunted as he tried to tighten the packing gland around the capstan shaft, his beard dripping salt water from the leaky shaft.

"We'll make it," Petreshock said grimly. "Telephone talker says the Old Man is trying to get to deep water. The talker said we had about ten, fifteen minutes to go." He winced as a stream of salt water sprayed into his eyes as he relieved Rice on the wrench.

A string of depth charges exploded above the *Eelfish,* and John Olsen went to his knees at the gyro table with the shock.

He struggled to his feet, hearing Brannon order a fathometer reading.

"Three hundred fathoms, sir," the Chief of the Boat said.

"Make depth four hundred feet," Brannon ordered, his voice soft. *Eelfish* planed downward, and in the compartments where there were leaks the crewmen fought harder to stem the incoming water as the pressure outside the ship's hull increased steadily.

"Four hundred feet, sir," Jerry Gold gasped. He was hanging on to the ladder to the Conning Tower, fighting for breath. He raised his head as the steady ringing sound of the destroyer's searching sonar beams echoed through the ship. Gold braced himself for the depth charges.

The pinging continued for long minutes but no depth charges were dropped.

"You suppose he emptied his depth-charge lockers?" Olsen said.

"No," Brannon said. He walked to the Conning Tower ladder, realizing suddenly how deadly tired he was.

"Chief," he called up to Booth, "how many charges did you count?"

"Seventy-one, sir."

Brannon looked at Olsen. "Seventy-one. Each destroyer carries at least forty charges, that's what we've been told. Forty times three is one hundred and twenty. They've got plenty left. I wonder why in the hell they didn't drop?" He listened, realizing how utterly silent the ship was.

"They aren't pinging any more." He chewed his lower lip reflectively. "I wonder what sort of a trap that son of a bitch up there is setting for us. Whatever it is I'm not falling for it." He looked at his watch, turning his wrist so that the radium face caught the dim rays of the battery-powered battle lantern.

"Nineteen hundred hours, almost. Dark in another hour or less. I'm going to stay on this course for another thirty minutes. If they don't ping on us again we'll increase speed and see if that brings them to us." He looked at the men on the bow and stern planes and at the helmsman.

"Stay with it, fellas, just a little longer."

John LaMark on the bow planes turned a sweating face toward Mike Brannon.

"Hell, Captain, we can take this all the rest of the night. Just a nice workout." Brannon looked at the man's heaving chest, the soaking wet khaki shorts, and the puddles of sweat on the leather seat where the planesmen sat when they were using the ship's hydraulic power to tilt the bow and stern planes.

"I know you can, John," he said.

A half-hour later Mike Brannon ordered *Eelfish* brought up to two-thirds speed. There was no response from the sea above. He ordered *Eelfish* brought up to 300 feet at full speed. There was no indication of enemy retaliation.

"Nothing ventured, nothing gained, my mother used to say," Brannon said. "Shift to hydraulic power on the bow and stern planes and the helm." The hydraulic pumps in the Pump Room below the Control Room began to hum. A gusting sigh of relief came from John LaMark on the bow planes. Doc Wharton, who manned the stern planes on Battle Stations, looked over at LaMark.

"If you could do this all night, you peckerhead, why don't you tell the man we don't need hydraulic power?"

"Don't want to see a Chief pill pusher pass out on me," LaMark said. "You left arm rates got no stamina like us right arm rates."

A half-hour later Brannon cautiously eased the *Eelfish* up to periscope depth and ran the periscope upward. The sea, bathed in the white light of a full moon, was empty. He ordered the ship to forty feet and swept twice around with the radar.

Eelfish surfaced, and as the big diesels began to thunder, drawing a small cyclone of fresh, sweet air down through the bridge hatch and aft to the engine rooms the crew began to relax.

"That nice new deck they gave us at Fremantle," Mike Brannon said to Jerry Gold, who had the OOD watch. "Most of it's gone. What a beating this damned ship can take."

"Don't forget the beating we can take, Captain," Gold said. "All I want once this war is over is to get a Jap in my dental chair. Then we'll see who can take a beating."

CHAPTER 24

John Olsen watched the relief-crew officer, who was approaching down the deck. The seamed face and the grizzled patches of gray at the temples were far too old for the pair of silver Lieutenant's bars on his collar tabs. Probably a Mustang, Olsen thought, a former Chief Petty Officer elevated to officer's rank. The Lieutenant came up to him and gave Olsen a perfunctory salute.

"You people specialize in losing things we don't have in spare parts," he growled. "First you lose the outer door to a torpedo tube. Now both sound heads. I sent a priority message to Pearl Harbor asking for two sound heads, shafts, and associated parts. Haven't got an answer yet."

"I'd like to say we're sorry," Olsen said, "but we didn't have much choice. Three destroyers caught us in some shallow water after we sank their oil tanker and drove us down until we hit bottom."

"I know," the Lieutenant said. He eyed the gold oak leaf on Olsen's collar tabs. "I'm Arnold Lever, sir. I used to be a Chief Shipfitter before they hung the gold on me."

"John Olsen," Olsen said and stuck out his hand. "Am I out of order in asking when you expect to get the new sound heads?"

"Nah," Lieutenant Lever said. "I just don't know. I do know that I looked at a chart of where you hit the bottom. The chart showed mud and shell bottom, but that doesn't mean that maybe there weren't a few rocks. You've got to go in the dry dock to fit the new sound heads, and when you're there we'll check the hull, the screws, ballast-tank openings, the works."

"What are you talking about in terms of time?"

"Maybe five, six weeks," Lever said. "I don't know that, either. I've learned to say I don't know when I don't know. This place here is about as screwed up as a Navy base could be."

Mike Brannon scowled when Olsen told him the news about how long they might be in port.

"I don't like being around that long," he said slowly. "I'm afraid to open my mouth in the O-Club for fear some white rat will overhear what I'm saying and take it to the Admiral or someone else." He looked at his wrist watch. "I've got to see Admiral Christie in an hour. How about dinner this evening? I want to talk to you about something. I think." Olsen nodded, wondering what was on his Captain's mind.

At dinner that night he found out. Brannon made a little design on the tablecloth with his fork, his eyes intent on the fork's tines. Then he looked up.

"I made a strong pitch today to Admiral Christie that you have your own ship, John. He agreed. You'll make this next patrol with us and then you'll go back to the States, to attend Prospective Commanding Officers' School, which is a damned joke because you've had the experience, you have the intelligence, the time in rank to command your own ship. After PCO School I assume you'll be sent to new construction."

"I appreciate that, sir," Olsen said. "But I have to say that I'd just as soon stay aboard with you as your number two boy. I want you to know that."

"I'm grateful that you feel that way, John. But you're a career officer. Command will look good in your record later on. Now I've got other business.

"We're going to have two weddings in the next day or so. Bob Lee is getting married and Paul Blake is, too. I had to interview both women the last time we were in port. Both are first rate."

"So what's there to worry about?" Olsen asked. "You look as if this is something to be upset about."

"Well, damn it, both Lee and Blake have asked me to be their best man. I don't know anything about being a best man. The only wedding I ever went to was my own, and I was so scared that time that I didn't know what was going on."

"Well," Olsen said, "you can cut the load in half by asking the two of them to have a double wedding."

"That's a sound idea," Brannon said. "All right, if you don't know about the privileges of command here's a lesson. You argue the case for a double wedding with the two wedding parties and get hold of the chaplain to write out a short brief of my duties as a best man at a double wedding." He grinned at Olsen.

The wedding was held in the chapel of a church just off St. George's Square in Perth. The crew of the *Eelfish*, cold sober by order of Chief Flanagan, were in attendance. Later, at the reception in the hotel where the crew was quartered, Steve Petreshock nudged Jim Rice.

"There's ol' Bob Lee's new wife. Got himself one hell of a good-lookin' broad. She's what, five, six inches taller than he is? She's got that look in her eye. Swings her ass right nice, too. That skinny old Bob Lee is like to be nothing but skin and bones when the honeymoon is over. If he can go the course at all. He looks outmatched."

"Don't worry about skinny Bob Lee," Rice said, a smile splitting his black beard. "I was on watch one night in the Forward Room, and he took a shower in the officers' shower and forgot his towel. Came out buck-naked, and that skinny old boy is all horn, let me tell you. Don't sell skinny little guys short, because most of them ain't.''

Over on one side of the room Mike Brannon was talking with Paul Blake's new in-laws.

"Our only regret is that Constance will be so very far away," Mrs. Maybury said. "But we love Paul, he's such a sweet boy. Don't you think so, Captain?"

"I don't think of him as 'sweet,'" Brannon said with a grin, "but I know what you mean. I think of him as a very brave young man, very skilled in his work and an asset to our crew. What you should do, Mr. and Mrs. Maybury, is to visit Paul and Constance in the States when the war is over."

"Oh, we intend to," Maybury said. "One of the privileges of being port director, y'know, is being able to travel on the liners at no cost. We intend to visit them and then go on to England. Both of us are second-generation Australians, and neither of us have seen where our people came from." Brannon excused himself as John Olsen came toward him, beckoning. He walked back across the room with Olsen to where Bob Lee was standing with his bride and Jerry Gold. The new Mrs. Lee walked up to Brannon and stopped, her eyes level with his.

"I haven't had a chance to talk to you since you were last in port and had to do that interview with me to see if I was fit to be the wife of an American Navy officer." Her eyes were glinting with laughter. "I'm so glad I passed your inspection, and I want to thank you for the lovely letter your wife wrote to me."

"She did?" Brannon said.

"She did. A lovely letter."

"Well," Brannon said awkwardly, "I did write her before we left port last trip. I felt embarrassed, having to interview you and Blake's fiancée, and I told Gloria about that. I didn't think she'd write you."

"But you knew she would if you put my name and address in your letter," Mary Ann Lee said softly. "Bob has told me that you're a very tough captain, a regular sea dog. I think you're a sentimental Irisher and I love you for that." She stepped closer and kissed him, and Brannon felt the blood rushing up his face. Mary Ann Lee chuckled and turned away.

Time passed slowly for Mike Brannon as he waited for the *Eelfish* to be dry-docked and the new sound heads fitted. For Brannon it was a critical time. Ashore a vicious political war was being waged, and Brannon wanted desperately to be able to avoid taking sides, something that was becoming more difficult by the day.

Almost two years earlier Admiral Christie, then in command of the largest group of submarines operating in the Pacific, had been summarily relieved of command at Brisbane and summoned to the United States. Christie, an expert on torpedoes, was needed to sort out and break the bottlenecks in torpedo production at Newport Torpedo Station. Admiral Christie's place at Brisbane was taken by Captain James Fife. Christie left no doubt in anyone's ears who would listen that Jimmy Fife wasn't a big enough man to fill Admiral Christie's shoes.

Christie had hardly settled in Newport when the over-all commander of Submarines Pacific, Rear Admiral Robert English, was killed in an air crash. In the resultant swirl of political maneuvering for the newly vacant job, Christie was recalled to Pearl Harbor and then sent to Fremantle to take over the submarine base there.

Meanwhile, Captain Fife, now in charge at Brisbane, had openly criticized the way Admiral Christie had handled submarines when he was in Brisbane. Fife announced that he would "tighten things up."

One of the new procedures instituted by Fife was to shift submarines about as if they were pieces on a chess board—and to require submarines to report their positions at frequent intervals. The flow of radio traffic between Brisbane and submarines on war patrol increased heavily. In the course of four weeks four submarines were lost to enemy action, and an investigation was called for. Captain Fife was exonerated of any blame.

Admiral Christie disagreed with the findings and began his own investigation. He became convinced that Fife's demand that submarines report their positions frequently by radio allowed the Japanese to use radio direction finders to locate American submarines—and send antisubmarine forces to sink them. Christie made his opinions public, and Fife, incensed, offered to resign. General Douglas MacArthur, who was fond of Jimmy Fife, intervened, and the offer to resign was dropped.

Now, two years later and across the continent of Australia at Fremantle, Admiral Christie was again being relieved of command and—again—his relief was Jimmy Fife, now a Rear Admiral.

Rumors about the reason for the change of command were thick, but neither of the principals said a word. Christie, no mean Navy politician, had a few shots left in his locker, and he meant to use them as best he could. His efforts to kill the change of command failed. Admiral Fife, it was said, had friends in high places in Washington. The change of command would go through. The submariners working out of Fremantle began to worry. Admiral Fife was known as a loner, a man who neither drank nor smoked and who disapproved highly of any indulgence in alcoholic beverages, no matter how dangerous or frightening a war patrol had been. Fife was a man dedicated to his work, and he literally lived at his desk, seven days a week from dawn until late at night. By comparison, Admiral Christie was a genial, friendly man who understood submariners and, more importantly, was tolerant of human frailties.

Admiral Fife arrived in Perth on Christmas Eve of 1944. Rather than depart immediately, Admiral Christie announced that he would be around for a while. He was due some well-earned leave before reporting for duty as the Commanding Officer of the Navy Yard at Bremerton, Washington. He made it a point not to discourage plans to hold a big reception to honor him before he left, and he pointedly did not urge anyone to invite Admiral Fife to the reception. Finally, Admiral Christie left, and the officers on Admiral Fife's staff sighed with relief and turned to the job of purging those officers who had been friendly with Admiral Christie.

Mike Brannon did his best to keep a low profile in this jungle of Navy politics, hardly daring to ask when his ship would be dry-docked, not daring at all to ask that the work be expedited. Finally it was finished, and late in February Brannon was summoned to Admiral Fife's Operations Office, where he was given a sealed envelope.

"These are your orders, sir," the Operations Officer said. "You will open them at sea and proceed to your patrol area. Good luck, sir." He did not rise, did not offer to shake hands.

Safely at sea, Mike Brannon read his patrol orders and handed them to John Olsen, who rummaged around for the proper chart among those he had brought to the Wardroom.

"Bonin Islands?" Olsen said. "Lifeguard duty?" He looked at the chart. "The Bonin Islands are directly in line between Tinian, in the Marianas—that's where the big aircraft, the B-twenty-nines fly out of—the Bonins are directly in line with Tinian and Tokyo. So now we are going to wet-nurse fliers in trouble. Hell of a way to fight a war in a submarine."

"The fliers won't think of it that way if they're sitting out in that ocean in a little rubber boat," Brannon said dryly.

Olsen read through the patrol orders without further comment until he came to the last page. "Hey, now!" he said. "We're going back to Pearl!"

"Good news for you," Brannon said. "Bad news for Bob Lee and young Blake."

"Never thought of that," Olsen said. "Are you going to tell them?"

"I don't want to, not until we're headed there," Brannon said. "I think it would hurt both of them, and there's just no need to hurt either one. So let's say nothing."

"We've got to make a pretty big detour to the west," Olsen said as he consulted the patrol orders. "I guess those people on Iwo Jima are still fighting pretty hard. I talked with some of the officers one night in the O-Club, some guys in intelligence work, and they said the Japanese resistance was way stronger than they figured it would be, that it was a hell of a lot tougher fight than they ever expected. The Marines are supposedly losing a hell of a lot of men."

"The Marines almost always get the dirty jobs," Brannon said. "That's the price you pay for being good."

"Going to be a hell of a long trip there," Brannon said, staring at the chart. "How long, in days?"

"About eighteen, twenty days," Olsen said.

"Might be a good idea to start some sort of a contest," Brannon said. "Something to relieve the boredom."

"Acey-Deucey?" Olsen asked. "Every sailor I ever knew thinks he's an expert at Acey-Deucey."

"Good idea," Brannon said. "I happen to be the best cribbage player in the whole Navy, so let's run two contests. Acey-Deucey and cribbage. First prize will be a fifth of Scotch, courtesy of the ship's recreation fund.

"Get Chief Ed Morris to draw up the pairings. He's an operator, that fellow. Figures every angle there is to be figured. He'll holler foul if someone else makes up the pairings, but if we ask him to do it he can't yell."

The two contests kept the spirits of the crew high as the *Eelfish* ran down the long sea miles to its patrol area. Chief Morris, by dint of very careful pairing and the expert use of a pair of loaded dice, took the Acey-Deucey championship from Fred Nelson.

Mike Brannon worked his way through the cribbage tournament without much trouble until he came to the semifinals. There, in a spirited battle with a young fireman, he managed to triumph, the Engine Room man admitting that the Captain was

the best cribbage player that he'd seen since his granddaddy had
taught him the game at the age of five.

In the finals, with all the off-watch crew members who could
jam into the Crew's Mess, Mike Brannon went up against Chief
Yeoman John Wilkes Booth. Brannon lost the fifth and rubber
game to Booth, who, some people said later, was the fastest man
with a cribbage peg who had ever played the game.

Eelfish arrived on station off the western side of the Bonin
Islands three weeks after leaving Fremantle. Ten days later the
radio crackled with the information that the invasion of Okinawa
had begun. The fact that thousands of men had died at Iwo Jima,
that many thousands more would die at Okinawa, made little
impression on the crew of the *Eelfish*. Invasions, battles on land,
were of a different world. Theirs was a world confined to a slim
ship that was 312 feet long and 16 feet wide at its widest point.
To the uninitiated the submariners on war patrol might seem
phlegmatic, without emotion. In truth, most were in a constant
state of anger; anger at the Japanese who depth charged them,
anger that there was a war and it had been going on for too long
a time, anger at their own senior officers, who seemed to care
little about them and the officers who served in submarines—and
not a little anger at themselves for ever volunteering to go to sea
in a submarine.

"I give us three more days on station," Doc Wharton said one
afternoon as he sat in the Crew's Mess. "I talked to Brosmer and
he said we're one hell of a long way from Fremantle, over four
thousand miles."

"Once we start back how long will it take?" Paul Blake
asked.

"About the same as it took to get here, three weeks," Doc
answered.

"You missin' that stuff you got married for, Blakey?" Scotty
Rudolph asked as he brought a platter of freshly baked doughnuts out of the galley. "Damn it, I don't see why you wanted to
get married. You know that no woman is going to cook you
chow like you get aboard this ship."

"Man could lose his appetite looking at you," Doc Wharton
said. "So it don't make no difference how good you can cook.
Blake's girl is a good-lookin' kid."

"Hell, Blakey, I didn't mean to make you blush," the ship's
cook said. "You married a nice kid. Got a smart old lady. She
asked me how I made Swiss steak at that party we had." He

jumped to his feet as the General Quarters alarm began clanging.

Mike Brannon went scrambling up the ladder to the bridge. "What have you got, Perry?"

Lieutenant Arbuckle turned, the radio telephone handset that had been installed in Fremantle in his hand.

"Mayday message from a B-twenty-nine, sir. He's got two engines still working, and one of those is overheating. He's zeroed in on us with his RDF, and he's on his way here." The handset buzzed and he held it near his ear as Brannon edged in and put his head close to Arbuckle's.

"Big Bird to Water Lily. Do you read? Over."

"Read Big Bird scale ten," Arbuckle said. "Over."

"Give us one more signal so we can get you on the radio direction finder again, Water Lily. Big Bird over and out."

Arbuckle held the transmit button on the handset down and counted to fifteen.

"Roger," the aircraft operator said. "We should be in sight in four minutes. Request Water Lily point bow into the wind. Big Bird over and out."

"Aircraft rescue party to the bridge," Brannon ordered. He and Arbuckle moved to the port side of the small bridge as Chief Flanagan led a half-dozen of the crew's strongest swimmers out of the bridge hatch and down on deck. Steve Petreshock, burdened with a one-man rubber boat, began to unknot the lashings on the boat.

"Belay that," Flanagan said. "If we need it, okay. If we don't no sense in having to lash it up again."

"Water Lily, we have you in sight. You're pretty damned small. Are you heading into wind? Big Bird over and out."

"Wind velocity is zero. Repeat zero," Arbuckle said. "Water Lily is on course three five zero. Repeat three five zero. Wind is zero. Water Lily over and out."

"Aircraft in sight dead astern, Bridge," the stern lookout yelled.

"Very well," Brannon said. Arbuckle thumbed the button on the handset.

"Water Lily has Big Bird in sight. Can you tell us your landing procedure? Water Lily over and out."

"Roger," the voice in the handset said. "We're going to come up from your back end—"

"From astern," Brannon muttered to himself.

"—and put her down in the water on your right side. Big Bird over and out. Here we come."

The B-29, trailing a long cloud of thick white smoke from its engines, was in plain sight, only a hundred or so feet above the water, flying straight up the wake of the *Eelfish*.

"My God!" Brannon half yelled. "That damned thing looks like an apartment house flying at us! What's that crazy bastard trying to do, land on my afterdeck? Arbuckle, tell that bastard to sheer off to starboard, he'll hit us!"

The big aircraft settled lower as it raced toward the submarine. Then, hundreds of feet astern, it delicately touched its massive tail to the water, lifted slightly as the abused engines stuttered and protested, and then, again delicately, touched its tail to the water. The tail raised slightly as if protesting and then settled gently, and then all of the plane was touching the water, rushing ahead, throwing up a huge wave of water that slammed into the pressure hull of the *Eelfish* as the plane's port wing eased by the starboard side of the submarine's Conning Tower only a half-dozen feet away.

"All stop!" Brannon snapped. He looked at the plane's wing, rocking and then steadying as the giant aircraft settled deeper in the water and came to a stop.

"Rig out the bow planes," Brannon ordered.

"Tell that plane commander that his port wing, that's his left wing, is over our starboard bow plane, and if he can bring his people out along his port wing we can take them aboard without using a rubber boat," Brannon said to Arbuckle.

"We can do that," the aircraft man on the radio said. Brannon leaned over the bridge rail, watching Flanagan tie the end of a coil of twenty-one-thread manila line around his waist and jump down on the bow plane.

The line of airmen inching out along the plane's wing came steadily toward the narrow end of the wing. Flanagan reached upward and held out a hand to the first man, who leaped down on to the bowplane and was assisted aboard the forward deck by Petreshock. On the deck Doc Wharton looked up at the bridge.

"Seventh man in line is hurt, sir. Might be easier to take him down the Forward Room hatch?"

Brannon, leaning over the bridge rail, nodded and gave the order. A moment later the hand wheel on the top of the Forward Torpedo Room hatch spun. The hatch opened and Jim Rice's black beard came into view.

"So that's what it looks like up here," Rice said. "What the fuck you people doin' up here, playin' games?" He braced himself in the hatch as Doc Wharton led the wounded man to the hatch.

"You just sit on my shoulders like you did with your daddy when you was a little tad," Rice said. "Papa'll carry you down into the nice submarine, and don't get any of your fuckin' blood on the inside of this hatch because I'm the guy has to clean it." Wharton and Fred Nelson eased the wounded man on to Rice's shoulders.

"Do I hang on to your beard, Sandy Claws?" the airman said in a falsetto. "Sandy Claws don't want to let the baby fall, do he?"

"Fuckin' wise guy, we got," Rice growled as he eased down the ladder rungs. "You people below, stand by to take this wounded hero off of me before he bleeds all over my dress dungaree shirt." Relieved of his burden he ran up the rungs of the ladder and dogged down the hatch.

Captain Brannon faced the plane crew on the cigaret deck and introduced himself. A slim, boyish airman stepped out of the group.

"Major John Haskins, U.S. Army Air Force, Captain. I'm the plane commander, sir. We owe you something for this, sir."

"No, you don't owe us anything." Brannon looked at the group. "I've got to destroy your plane. If you don't want to watch I don't blame you. You can go below." The young Major looked around and swallowed.

"I think I'd like to go downstairs, sir," he said in a small voice. "I've, ah, got a wounded man to see to, sir."

"I understand, sir," Brannon said. He watched as the eight men followed the young Major down the hatch.

"Forward deck gun party to the bridge," Brannon said. "Mr. Arbuckle, haul off about four hundred yards."

The plane burst into flames on the fourth shot and began to slide under the sea, nose first. The last Brannon saw of it was the huge tail slowly going under. He turned away and went down the hatch.

He found the crew of the plane in the Crew's Mess drinking coffee while Scotty Rudolph fussed in his galley making steak sandwiches.

"We'll tell your people we've got you," Brannon said to the plane commander, "if you'll tell Mr. Michaels here what command we should address the message to. We're sort of new at this. Never picked up any of you people before."

"You're not new at the business, though," the Major said.

"All those Jap flags painted on the side of your whatever it is we climbed up on, those stand for Jap ships you've sunk?"

"Yes," Brannon said. "You check on your wounded man?"

"He's okay," Major Haskins said. "Your medico fixed him up. Don't you have a doctor aboard these ships?"

"No," Brannon said. "Just a Pharmacist's Mate."

"Supposing someone gets really sick, like a heart attack?"

"I don't know about that," Brannon said. "In nineteen forty-two, on the *Seadragon*, a crewman came down with a very bad appendix. The Pharmacist's Mate made retractors out of spoons. They had some ether and a book on how to take out an appendix. So they operated on the Wardroom table. Both the patient and the Pharmacist's Mate recovered fully." The pilot shuddered.

Two hours later a message came instructing *Eelfish* to rendezvous with a destroyer detached from Iwo Jima to transfer the airmen. Four days later the *Eelfish* received orders to leave the area and head for Pearl Harbor. Brannon called Bob Lee and Paul Blake to the Wardroom and showed them the orders.

"I know it's bad news for both of you," Brannon said. "But try and look at it this way. We've invaded Okinawa. The next step is Japan itself, if they don't surrender first. It's my opinion that this war is about over. That pilot we rescued, he said he'd been carrying nothing but firebombs and blasting Tokyo. He said the city is almost burned to the ground.

"We know, in submarines we know, that Japan hasn't been able to get tankers north to Japan, that they haven't been able to get any cargo ships to Japan. They must be down to the bottom of the barrel on oil, rubber, tin, ore, everything they need. The Germans have surrendered, and I don't think this war will last past Thanksgiving."

"And then . . ." Blake's voice had a slight quiver.

"Then all you Reservists who have done so damned much to help win this war will be getting out, Paul. Your wife, Mr. Lee's wife, don't have to wait on any quota system. I went to the American Embassy in Fremantle and asked about that. Once the war is over, whether you're in the Navy or out, you just have to send them the boat fare and they can come to the States."

"It isn't so bad, Paul," Lee said. "If we went back to Fremantle we'd be there for what, three weeks? Then we'd be gone again. So we miss that one three-week leave. If the Captain is right we probably will have our wives with us before Christmas.'' Blake nodded and went to the door of the Wardroom. He turned.

"Thank you, sir," he said to Brannon. Bob Lee turned to Brannon.

"He's so damned young—what, twenty-two?"

"And you're what, how old?" Brannon grinned.

"Well, twenty-six, sir. We older types can take a little disappointment."

"Good thing we can," Brannon said. "I haven't seen my wife and daughter for two years."

CHAPTER 25

Captain Mealey and Captain Bob Rudd were standing on the pier when the *Eelfish* berthed in Pearl Harbor. The two Captains came down the gangway and shook hands with Mike Brannon. Captain Mealey looked around.

"Where's John Olsen? Captain Rudd has some very good news for him." Brannon sent John LaMark in search of the Executive Officer.

"John," Captain Rudd boomed, "never had the pleasure of knowing you before, but Captain Mealey's told me so much about you that we've decided not to send you to PCO School." He grinned, his beefy face glowing as Olsen's jaw fell.

"Any Exec who's made six successful patrol runs and can satisfy this S.O.B. here who's called Mealey doesn't need to go to PCO School anyway. Damned place is crowded with people who don't rate command half as much as you do, so we're detaching you today and sending you to take over the *Sablefish*. She's on the building ways now, and she won't go into commission until about next April. She's going to be a beautiful ship. Got everything in her that all of you people on war patrol have been screaming for." He reached out a massive hand and began to pump Olsen's hand. Mike Brannon stood by, his face beaming.

"When do I leave, sir?" Olsen asked. "I mean, I'm not anxious—yes, I am—but I'd like to take everyone to dinner if I have the time."

"Courier plane out of here at ten hundred tomorrow. You'll be on it. Captain Mealey has your orders."

The two Captains and the relief-crew officers and chiefs left, and John Olsen went down below to begin his packing. Brannon was called to the gangway by a seaman and found a serious-looking Lieutenant Commander waiting there for him.

"Lieutenant Commander Ralph Ulrich, sir," the officer said. "Captain Rudd's yeoman gave me my orders to report aboard as a replacement for Mr. Olsen, sir." He handed Mike Brannon a set of orders and waited as Brannon read through them.

"Welcome aboard, sir," Brannon said. "We're about to go to the hotel. If you wish you can report here each day and sort of oversee the refit. You're welcome, of course, to go to the hotel and meet the crew, the other officers. See me at any time you wish. I'm not being inhospitable. The crew is tired, the Wardroom is tired. It's been a very long and boring patrol."

"But a successful one," Lieutenant Commander Ulrich said. "You rescued the entire crew of a B-twenty-nine. That's ten lives saved, sir."

"The Staff calls it successful, I don't," Brannon said. "We didn't add a single flag to the Conning Tower." Ulrich looked at the side of the Conning Tower where the Rising Sun and merchant flags of the ships sunk by the *Eelfish* showed as a brilliant patch of color against the blotched gray war paint.

"I understand, sir," Ulrich said. "I'll report to you every other day if that's all right with you?" Brannon nodded and went below to pack for the two weeks of rest and relaxation that he felt he and his crew had earned.

When he returned from the rest period Brannon summoned his new Executive Officer to the Wardroom. He had the new officer's jacket opened in front of him.

"I see that you made one war patrol in the *Flying Fish*, early in the war," Brannon said. "Captain Donaho gave you good marks as an Assistant Engineering Officer. A good word from Mr. Donaho is a volume of praise from any other officer."

"I hope I earned his good word," Ulrich said solemnly.

"I'm sure you did. Now let me explain a few things to you sir. When we leave for sea this will be our seventh war patrol. With very few exceptions every man aboard this ship put her in commission and has made every war patrol. We're a very close-knit bunch of people. It won't be easy for you, coming aboard. I will do everything I can to make you welcome, because you are welcome, but submariners, as you should know, can be clannish. John Olsen was not only respected by the entire crew, he was liked." He looked at the younger officer.

"You're Academy, sir. I expect nothing but the best from you."

"I expect to give my best, sir."

"I'm sure you do," Brannon said. "I should warn you in advance that I think *Eelfish* has the best Wardroom in the whole submarine navy." He grinned wryly. "I should also warn you that the two of us are the only Academy officers in the entire Wardroom. All the rest are Reservists."

"All of them, sir?"

"All. And I couldn't ask for better men, not if I could have the pick of the top five of any year you can mention at the Academy. Half of the crew are Reservists, as well. I couldn't ask for better men. On this ship we are submariners. Nothing more, nothing less. As a crew we've gone through some pretty hellish times, one of them with Captain Mealey."

Ulrich stared at his lean hands and then looked at Mike Brannon. "I know, sir, Captain Mealey gave me a copy of all your patrol reports and action reports. I can see what you mean, the *Mako*, all that."

"The *Mako*. All that." Brannon said. He stood up. "I depend on my Executive Officer to be my right arm, Ralph. Your right arm will be the Chief of the Boat. A Chief Torpedoman named Flanagan. Called Monk by his friends because his shoulders slope downward. Depend on him. He won't let you down. No one in this crew will let you down. Now I want your estimate of the work done by the relief crew."

"It's all done except the hull check, sir. The Yard people are worried about that time you went to the bottom off Borneo."

"We went through all that in Fremantle," Brannon said sharply. "Why is it necessary to do it now?"

"Well, ah, the people in Pearl don't really trust the people in Fremantle, sir."

"Hell and damnation," Brannon growled. "The damned war will be over before we ever get back out to sea, and if it isn't there won't be any targets left to shoot at."

In the next two weeks, while *Eelfish* was waiting to get dry-dock space and during the week the ship was in dry dock, Ralph Ulrich proved his worth. No matter what Brannon wanted Ulrich seemed to know it ahead of time. Materiel needed by the *Eelfish* Chiefs for work that wasn't obtainable unless one went through endless red tape was somehow available at once if Ulrich took charge, using all the contacts he had made in almost three years as Captain Rudd's Staff Engineering Officer. Chief Morris gave his assessment of Ralph Ulrich to Mike Brannon, saying, "Good man to have around. Knows every son of a bitch in the Yard who has anything we might need. Gets it with no fuss or bother."

The day before *Eelfish* was to sail on her seventh war patrol a tall, broad-shouldered Lieutenant climbed out of a Staff car on the dock and asked for permission to come aboard.

"Captain aboard?" he asked the gangway watch.

"He's below in the Wardroom, holding a meeting with the officers," the gangway watch said. The Lieutenant dropped down the Forward Torpedo Room hatch and went to the Wardroom. Mike Brannon looked up with an expression of irritation on his face as the Lieutenant stepped through the green curtain, and then he got to his feet, his hand out, a broad smile on his face.

"By Heaven, Dusty Rhodes as ever was, as my good Irish mother used to say." He gripped the Lieutenant's hand and pumped it up and down.

"This is Dusty Rhodes, gentlemen," he said to the officers sitting around the table. "He used to be our Chief of the Boat in the *Mako*. Got bumped up to J.G. after the third run. How the hell are you, Dusty? How's John Barber, your wives, children?"

"Four-oh on all sides," Rhodes said. "Barber is in charge of all the engine room work on the boats coming in from patrol. His wife and daughter are fine. So is my wife and my sons. Your lady and daughter okay?"

"I guess they are," Brannon said. "I haven't seen them since forty-three, almost two years. This a friendly visit, or are you official?"

"Both," Dusty Rhodes said. "I'd like you to come to dinner tonight at my house, if you can. Barber and his wife will be there.

"The official part is that you're getting a few new-type torpedoes. They're called 'Cuties.' Kind of small. They'll load them this afternoon, and I've got a savvy Chief who can fill your people in the Torpedo Rooms in on how to service them. One of the officers who worked on the development of these new fish will be over after lunch to fill you and your officers in on how you use these things."

"Why that?" Bob Lee asked. "What's different about these fish?"

"Well, for one thing, they've got a sonar ear in the warhead," Rhodes said. "It picks up screws and guides the torpedo in to the screws. So to be safe you fire them from a depth of one hundred fifty feet. That way, by the time the fish has planed up to its depth set in the tube it's far enough away from you that it doesn't turn around and come back and bite you in the ass. For another thing, they're a lot slower than the Fourteens or even the electric Mark Eighteens."

"Have they been used?" Brannon said.

"Captain Bennet in *Sea Owl* had some pretty good results with the first ones we sent to sea," Rhodes said. "He said they weren't much use against a fast target but they're hell on patrol craft and picket boats, and that's about all that's out there right now."

"What will they think of next?" Jerry Gold said.

"Don't wish for anything, sir," Rhodes said with a grin. "I've got a five-inch rocket launcher up there in the shop and hundreds of rounds of rockets, and some lucky boat is going to have that monstrosity bolted to its foredeck."

"What can you use a rocket launcher for?" Gold asked.

"Shore bombardment," Rhodes said.

"Forget I spoke," Gold said hastily. "My mother wouldn't want me bombarding a seashore." Rhodes grinned and turned to Brannon. "If you can make dinner tonight I'll send a car for you about eighteen hundred."

"I'd love to come to dinner," Brannon said. "A car? Does a full Lieutenant rate a car?"

"This is the Pearl Harbor Navy, sir," Rhodes said. "Nothing but the best for the fighting men."

Eelfish slipped past the net tender at the entrance to the harbor and turned its bullnose toward the west. The destroyer that had led the submarine out of the harbor whistled in salutation and turned away to re-enter the harbor. Later, down in the Wardroom, Mike Brannon opened his patrol orders, read through them briefly, and pushed them over to Ralph Ulrich, who was sitting at the table with his charts and navigational gear.

"Doesn't sound very exciting," Brannon growled. "Lifeguard duty and sweep up any picket boats that might be around to give warning of the B-twenty-nine raids. Targets must be awfully scarce out there."

"Did you hear about the Japanese attempt to smash up the invasion fleet at Okinawa, sir?" Ulrich asked.

"No," Brannon said. "One of the things you have to learn, Ralph, is that no one tells any submarine captain anything. What happened?"

"The invasion of Okinawa took place on April first," Ulrich said in his careful voice. "On the fifth the Japanese decided to send a task force from southern Japan down to Okinawa to smash the invasion forces. The task force was the super-battleship *Yamato*, a light cruiser, and seven or eight destroyers."

"That wouldn't be a big enough force," Brannon said.

"The Japanese had been attacking the invasion ships at Okinawa with hundreds of *kamikaze* planes, sir, suicide planes that carried big bombs. The pilots crashed them into their targets. The Japanese figured that they had done a lot more damage than they did, although they did enough. They hit about forty ships with those planes. The task force was sent to mop up what was left.

"Our intelligence people say the Fleet Commanders couldn't find any oil to fuel their ships. All they had in all of southern Japan was something like twenty-five hundred barrels of oil. Not nearly enough fuel for the one-thousand-mile round trip to Okinawa. But they went anyway.

"The intelligence experts reason that the battleship ran so low on fuel it couldn't maneuver. It had no air cover, and our carrier planes sank the battleship, the cruiser, and some of the destroyers." He looked at Brannon.

"The submarines were responsible for that victory. The reason Japan hasn't got any oil or anything else it needs to fuel its war machine is the submarines."

Brannon nodded. "Set the course for Midway. We'll top off our fuel tanks there."

Eelfish reached its patrol station and began to prowl the area assigned to it, staying on the surface night and day. The lookouts and the radar watch reported constant aircraft contacts, bombers going to Japan to hit its cities and returning. From time to time there were reports of planes being ditched and the reports from submarines racing to pick up the survivors.

"The trouble is," Mike Brannon complained one evening at dinner, "we're a little bit too much to the west of the flight line from the Marianas to Tokyo. Bungo Strait, where we are now, used to be a hot spot when Japan had warships that could put to sea. Now it's dead.

"Ralph, you know a lot of people in Pearl. Draft a message asking we be reassigned to a more productive area. Send it with an information tag for anyone you think might argue our case for us."

A week later *Eelfish* was moved to the north and east. Four times in a matter of seven days *Eelfish* raced at top speed toward an area where a plane reported that it was going into the water, and four times the *Eelfish* was just a bit too far away and lost the race to a closer submarine. Jerry Gold began muttering about fuel-oil supplies and hinting that high-speed chases that were likely to be fruitless before they began were draining his fuel-oil tanks.

The emergency signal came late in the afternoon watch. It was broadcast by a "Dumbo," one of several communications aircraft that cruised along the flight route of the big bombers that were leveling Tokyo with fire raids. A B-29 with two engines shot away was coming down. Ralph Ulrich, efficient as always, had the plane's reported location on his plotting board in little more than a minute.

"We're nine thousand yards away, sir. Twenty minutes at fifteen knots. We should steer course zero four zero."

"Come left to zero four zero. Make turns for fifteen knots," Brannon ordered. He turned to climb up the ladder to the Conning Tower. "Assemble the rescue party in the Control Room. I want a constant radar search."

Five minutes later, as *Eelfish* raced toward the area where the B-29 had gone down, Rafferty reported that he had a contact on radar.

"Contact bears two six zero, repeat, two six zero. Range is one three zero zero zero yards, repeat, thirteen thousand yards, Bridge."

Lieutenant Jerry Gold turned in the bridge to inform Mike Brannon on the cigaret deck and saw Brannon beside him.

"Sound General Quarters," Brannon said. "Secure the radar for five minutes and then take another bearing." He stood to one side in the bridge, listening to the reports that came up through the bridge speaker. Five minutes later he nodded at Gold, who ordered another radar sweep.

"Contact now bears two five six. Repeat, two five six. Range is one one five zero zero yards. Repeat, eleven thousand five hundred yards," Jim Michaels's voice was calm.

"Contact course is zero nine eight, Bridge. Contact speed is fifteen knots." Ulrich's report was delivered in the emotionless tone he used in times of stress.

"Very well," Brannon said. He bent to the bridge transmitter.

"Plot, we have to assume this is an enemy ship. What does his course show in relation to our last position of the downed plane?"

"He's heading right for them, Bridge," Ulrich said. "He's a little over fifteen thousand yards from the plane. Request the Captain to take a look at the plot, Bridge."

Brannon went down the ladder to the Control Room. Ulrich pointed at the plot with a pair of dividers.

"We can come right to course three five eight, sir, and dive now. We're thirty-two hundred yards from his track as he moves toward the plane. Gives us plenty of time."

"Very well," Brannon said. He raised his voice so it would carry to the bridge.

"Dive the ship! Come left to course three five eight." He heard the thuds of the lookouts hitting the deck in the Conning Tower and the blast of the diving alarm. *Eelfish* slid downward.

"Forty feet, Jerry," Brannon said. "Raise the radar mast. I want to get one more bearing on this rascal and see if he maintains course and speed."

"He's twenty-five minutes away from the plane at his present speed," Ulrich said. "We'll have to stooge around a little, depending on how you want to attack, sir."

"Depends on what he is," Brannon said. "How did he look on the radar screen, Mr. Michaels?"

"Small, sir. Not a big pip at all."

"Probably a patrol boat," Brannon said. He looked at the plot and picked up a pair of dividers and pricked off a distance along the course *Eelfish* was on.

"I don't want to attack him when he's close to the plane, if the plane is still there. I don't want him to get close enough to machine-gun the fliers if they're in rubber boats."

"I figured that, sir," Ulrich said. "We can shoot him when he's still a little over three thousand yards from where we think the plane went down. That's well over a mile from the plane area."

"Give me two radar checks, three minutes apart," Brannon ordered. He watched as Ulrich drew in the plot as the information came to him from Michaels.

"He's on course, still making the same speed," Mike Brannon said. "We'll shoot at him with a Cutie, and if that misses we'll nail him with a regular torpedo, and if that fails, by God, I'll battle-surface!"

"We're carrying Cuties in tubes Five and Six," Flanagan said from the vent manifold. "Mark Eighteens, the electric fish, in tubes One and Two, sir."

"Very well," Brannon said. "Sixty-five feet. Sonar, start tracking as soon as you're able to get a good fix on him."

He watched the plot of the attack slowly develop, looking at his watch from time to time.

"It's time," he said to Ulrich. He turned to Jerry Gold. "One hundred and sixty feet. Talker, inform the Forward Room that we'll fire two Cuties from Five and Six at one hundred sixty feet and then come back up to sixty-five feet. I want the outer tube doors on One and Two opened as we hit periscope depth."

Blake was now the sole contact Brannon had with his target. He sat in the Conning Tower, the big mufflike earphones clamped over his ears, his whole being centered on the beat of the single propeller that he could hear coming closer and closer. As he fed his bearings to the plotting party the rate of advance of the target along the drawn-in course Ulrich had given for the enemy ship moved with mathematical precision toward the small X on the plot that marked the position of the downed aircraft. *Eelfish* slid through the sea, 160 feet below the surface.

"One minute, sir," Ulrich said. Brannon nodded. "Hell of a way to conduct a torpedo attack with no sighting of the target for, what, damned near twenty minutes. Stand by forward . . ."

"You have a solution any time, Captain," Arbuckle said from the Conning Tower.

"Now!" Ulrich whispered.

"Fire five!" Brannon said. He waited the ten seconds he had been instructed to wait between Cutie firings.

"Fire six!" Another long ten seconds crept by and then Paul Blake reported.

"First torpedo running straight away from us, sir. Second torpedo is following the first, sir."

"That's what they said would happen when they briefed me in Pearl," Brannon said. "Once the first Cutie gets clear of the ship the second one will follow the screws of the first until the first one zeroes in on the target screws. If it hits, the second fish will go right into the explosion area."

"Torpedo track is sixteen hundred yards, sir. Running time to the target should be one minute fifty seconds. We should have an indication in . . . in one minute, sir."

Brannon waited, feeling the tenseness in his legs as he stood at the gyro table staring at the plot, watching the black second hand on the stopwatch hitch its way around the dial.

"Five seconds," he whispered, half to himself, and then a distant rumbling sound shook the *Eelfish*, followed in ten seconds by another slight shock that could be felt in the hull of the *Eelfish*.

"I think that was a hit, sir!" Blake called out. "Two good big explosions in my gear, sir."

"Sixty-five feet!" Brannon ordered. "Close the outer doors on Five and Six. Stand by to open the outer doors on One and Two." He scrambled up the ladder to the Conning Tower and stood by the periscope.

"Passing seventy-five feet, sir," Gold called out.

"Open outer doors on One and Two! Stand by for a periscope observation!"

"Mark!" Brosmer read off the bearing and Arbuckle cranked the bearing into the TDC.

"He's dead in the water. Set torpedo depth two feet. Range is twelve hundred yards. There's a fire aft, on his fantail. Angle on the bow is one zero zero."

"Depth set two feet on One and Two," Flanagan said.

"You've got a solution, sir," Arbuckle said.

"Stand by forward . . .

"Fire one!" He waited, his eye glued to the periscope lens. "Son of a bitch is flying his Rising Sun flag . . . *WOW!*" A crashing explosion battered at the *Eelfish*.

"Hit! Dead center. Bring me up to forty feet. Radar search all around."

Eelfish slanted upward, and Brannon heard Michaels report there were no contacts.

"Machine gunners to the Control Room. Rescue party stand by. Ulrich, I want you with me on the bridge. Surface! Surface! Surface!" *Eelfish* shuddered as the high-pressure air slammed into her ballast tanks and she rose, bursting through the surface of the ocean with a great cloud of spray.

"Lookouts!" Brannon shouted as the three men clambered up into the periscope shears. "We've got some aviators out there on the starboard bow somewhere. All ahead full on all four main engines."

"I've got 'em!" the starboard lookout yelled. "Three small rubber boats bearing zero one zero, Bridge!"

"Come right to course zero one zero," Brannon ordered. "Make turns for two-thirds speed. Rescue party to the deck as soon as we're steady on the new course. Machine gunners to the bridge. Load and lock weapons. Mr. Ulrich, take the conn. I want to put the ship between that patrol boat and the fliers.'' He watched as Ralph Ulrich maneuvered the *Eelfish* so the bulk of the submarine was between the listing patrol boat and the three rubber boats full of fliers.

''I thought we got a good solid hit on that son of a bitch, but he's still floating,'' Brannon growled.

''He's got a wooden hull,'' Ulrich volunteered. ''They usually absorb a torpedo hit, even gunfire, better than metal ones.''

''Get those people aboard as quick as you can,'' Brannon called down to Chief Flanagan on deck. Flanagan raised an arm to indicate he understood, and with Steve Petreshock and Fred Nelson assisting he hauled the fliers out of the rubber boats and up on the deck and hustled them aft to the ladder that led up to the cigaret deck.

''Welcome aboard,'' Brannon said, smiling. ''Who's in command?''

''I am, sir, Lieutenant Colonel Roberts, Jack Roberts.'' A tall, lean man with a sweeping mustache stepped out of the group of fliers.

''I'm Captain Brannon, Mike Brannon. All your people here? Anyone hurt?''

''We all made it, no one hurt,'' the Colonel said.

''Small boat standing around the bow of the patrol boat, Bridge!'' The port lookout's voice was high, excited. ''Man in the midships section of the boat is waving at us, Bridge. About ten people in the boat. The boat is under way on its own power, Bridge.''

''Let's see what he wants, Mr. Ulrich,'' Brannon said. ''Gunners, stand by if he tries any funny business.''

''That's close enough!'' Ulrich yelled at the people in the small boat. ''Do any of you speak English, and if you do what do you want?''

The man in the center of the boat who had been waving at the submarine raised his voice. ''I speak English, sir. Can you give us a course to steer to land?''

''We'll give you a course in a minute,'' Brannon called out. ''Do you need anything else, food, water, medicine?''

''We have enough water for four days. We have no food. I have two men with burns, sir.''

''Stand clear of me,'' Brannon shouted back. ''We'll make up a couple of bags of canned food for you and give you some sulfa powder for your burned men. I'll tell you when to come alongside to get the stuff. Can you tell me the name of your ship and commanding officer?''

"I am not required to do that under the rules of war, sir.''

"Very well,'' Brannon said. He turned as Scotty Rudolph hauled the second of two clean garbage bags bulging with cans of food up through the bridge hatch. "We can make the transfer on the port side, Captain,'' Ulrich said. "Chief Flanagan has a safety line rigged, so he can put a man down on the pressure hull.''

"Very well,'' Brannon said. "What turns are we making?''

"Making turns for three knots, sir,'' Ulrich said.

"That shouldn't be too fast for him,'' Brannon said. He waved his arm at the small boat. "Come alongside. When you have the food aboard steer course two seven five. You are about eighty miles from land. Is that understood?''

"Yes, sir, and we thank you,'' the man in the boat yelled back. "We should steer course two seven five and we are eighty miles from home.''

The boat eased in toward the *Eelfish*. Chief Flanagan tied a safety line around Petreshock's waist and took a turn around the barrel of the deck gun as the torpedoman eased his way down on to the curve of the wet pressure hull, clamping the fingers of his left hand between two deck boards. Fred Nelson, crouching on the deck, handed Petreshock a bag of food. The small boat drew closer, and Petreshock could see the faces of the men in the boat, closed, without expression. He swung the bag of food back and forth, gauging the distance to the small boat.

"That's close enough,'' Flanagan shouted. The man in the boat who had done the talking to the submarine nodded and raised his right arm. Petreshock saw the sudden gout of flame, and then he collapsed on the pressure hull, legs sprawling, blood staining the sea as his body splashed into the water. Fred Nelson bellowed, grabbed the safety line, and hauled Petreshock's body out of the water as the man in the boat fired his pistol again and again.

The stuttering roar of the twin twenty-millimeter machine guns was drowned out by Booth's high-pitched Rebel yell. The cluster of men standing in the small boat went down under the hail of .20-mm shells. From the cigaret deck aft of the bridge the quad pom-pom also began to bark, its explosive shells ripping into the Japanese sailors, tearing at the hull of the small boat.

Mike Brannon leaned over the bridge rail. Flanagan and Nelson had dragged Petreshock's limp body up on the deck and were moving aft, toward the ladder to the cigaret deck. Brannon bent his head to the bridge transmitter.

"Stand by below to take a wounded man." He turned to Ulrich. "Circle that patrol boat. I want that boat sunk! We should be able to do it with the pom-pom and the twenties." Flanagan touched his Captain on the arm.

"Steve's bleedin' like hell, but he's breathing pretty good. He got it in the head, above his left ear, up in the hair. I couldn't see how bad."

"Very well, Chief. Get these fliers below as soon as you can. I'll be down as soon as we get things squared away up here." He turned as the quad pom-pom began systematically to stitch the hull of the listing patrol boat. From the gun platform below, and in front of the bridge, John Wilkes Booth was lashing at the patrol boat with the twin twenties. A sudden gush of flame erupted from the midships section of the patrol boat, followed by a dull explosion. The ship rolled over and began to sink.

"Cease fire!" Brannon yelled. "Ralph, secure the gunnery party. As soon as they're below dive the ship. I want to go to one hundred feet while we get this mess sorted out." He dropped through the hatch and went down to the Control Room. Lieutenant Jerry Gold nodded toward the Crew's Mess. "Petreshock is in the Crew's Mess, sir, with Doc. The fliers are back there also." He turned as the diving alarm sounded and a lookout slid down the ladder and manned the bow planes.

"One degree down bubble," Gold ordered. "They're probably working on Steve back there, and I don't want the poor bastard to slide off a mess table on deck."

Brannon shouldered his way through the people crowded around a mess table where Doc Wharton was working on Petreshock.

"Far as I can tell, Captain, all he's got is one hell of a deep slot cut in his skull. Bone ain't broke, though. Like every other torpedoman he's got a thick head." He looked up as Fred Nelson, his eyes glaring fiercely from either side of his great hawk nose, growled.

"I can clean the wound," Wharton said, "and give him a shot to put him to sleep for a few hours. When he wakes up maybe then we can find out how much damage was done, test his reactions, how he feels."

"Very well," Brannon said. "But if he needs more than we can give him let me know and we'll head for the nearest friendly port." He nodded to the Lieutenant Colonel. "If you and your officers will follow me, sir, we'll go up to the Wardroom and get some coffee and something to eat.''

Pete Mahaffey was waiting with a platter of sandwiches and pots of coffee. Mike Brannon sipped at a cup of coffee while the fliers ate. The Lieutenant Colonel put his cup down and wiped his mustache with a handkerchief.

"We owe you a vote of thanks, Captain," he said. "Our radioman didn't get a receipt for our Mayday call, and we figured we might have gone down with no one knowing where we were. When we saw that Jap ship coming toward us we figured it was a prison camp for all of us for sure. But then we saw an explosion. Guess that was your torpedo. It didn't make much of a noise or anything. I thought a torpedo hitting a ship would be like a bomb.''

"I think we had a low-order explosion with that warhead," Brannon said. "It happens every once in a while. Same as you get dud bombs, I guess.

"I want my Chief Pharmacist's Mate to take a look at all of you, Colonel. Then if you would give our yeoman your names, ranks or ratings, and serial numbers we can notify your home base that you're all safe." He stopped as a firm rap sounded on the bulkhead of the Wardroom. Doc Wharton stuck his head in through the curtains.

"Steve came to while I was bandaging his head, Captain. He won't take a shot. Says that all's wrong with him is a big headache. He wants to go back on watch.''

"Negative on the watch," Brannon said. "Tell him my orders are light duty only. Keep an eye on him, Doc." Wharton nodded and left.

"I can't figure out why that guy opened fire," Brannon said. He looked at the fliers sitting at the Wardroom table.

"We fight different battles, I guess, but it's been evident to us for months now that this war is over. I don't think a submarine has seen an oil tanker or any merchant ship of any size for months, now. We haven't seen a Jap warship for, oh, weeks. The information we get is that the Japs are out of oil.''

The Colonel nodded his head. "We hear the same thing. I've been flying that route from Tinian to Japan for about six weeks now. Hardly ever see a ship down there, except for those little ships like the one you just sank. Tokyo is half burned away now. Same with the other industrial areas. We drop fire bombs on 'em by the ton. But I guess they don't give up easy.''

In the Crew's Mess the off-duty crewmen surrounded John

LaMark and John Wilkes Booth, the gunners who had killed the Japanese in the small boat and then sunk the patrol craft.

"Can't figure that dude in that small boat," LaMark said. "The son of a bitch is looking right at those gun barrels, he can see that both of us, me and the Chief, are staring right at him, and he still begins loosing off rounds out of that damned pistol he was hiding. Hell! He knew that if he made a wrong move he was going to buy the farm but he did it anyway. Can't figure it."

"Man takes on odds like that dude in that boat did," Chief Booth said. "Just think what a picnic the Marines are going to have when they invade Japan itself. Jap kids will be dropping grenades on every round-eye head they can see."

Mike Brannon came in and stood at the head of the Wardroom table. "We want all of you to be as comfortable as possible," he said to the fliers, "but you have to understand that we don't have any extra bunks. Your people will have to hot-bunk it with our people. We hope you'll understand and be patient."

"You must have done this before," Colonel Roberts said.

"Only once, off the Bonin Islands. We picked up a crew from a B-twenty-nine. The plane wouldn't sink and we had to shell it. A Major was the plane captain and it upset him quite a bit when we had to sink his plane."

"Major Haskins," the Colonel said. "Kind of a short fella, always trying to grow a mustache. Never could quite make it."

"That was his name," Brannon said. "How is he?"

"Dead," the Colonel said. "Jap Zero did the suicide thing. Crashed him head on at twenty thousand feet. Both planes exploded." Brannon nodded slowly.

Two days later, cruising on the surface, the *Eelfish* was challenged by an Army B-25. Lieutenant Bob Lee, who had the OOD watch, made the correct reply by voice radio and watched as the plane swung far out ahead of him and then came back, aiming directly at the submarine. Lee yelled at the lookouts and hit the diving alarm. As the *Eelfish* passed 100 feet with a steep downward angle the B-25 dropped a string of bombs off to the port side. The explosions shook the submarine and later, in the Wardroom, Mike Brannon had pointed things to say about bomb-happy pilots.

The days wore on, and life in the *Eelfish* became difficult. The ten extra men aboard complicated the sleeping arrangements, and Scotty Rudolph swore silently as he prepared extra meals from his shrinking food supplies. Shortly after dark on a rainy night

Jim Michaels brought a message in to Mike Brannon, who was drinking coffee in the Wardroom and talking with the plane commander. Brannon decoded the message and called for Ralph Ulrich.

"We've got to get out of this area," he told Ulrich. "We're right in the way of Admiral Halsey's task force on its way to hit at Japan." He looked at the pilot of the B-29.

"If one of our own aircraft tries to bomb us I don't want to take a chance with some edgy destroyer skipper."

Eelfish raced to the northeast, and after it circled for four days Brannon asked for orders. The answer came back in 48 hours; return to Pearl Harbor. The rescued fliers groaned in unison. All their personal belongings were on Tinian Island, in the Marianas.

During the midwatch on the morning of August 8 the Chief of the Watch notified the Bridge that an Ultra radio message was coming in. Brannon left the cigaret deck and in the deserted silence of the Wardroom decoded the message. Ralph Ulrich, possessed of the intuition that every good Executive Officer must have, appeared in the doorway of the Wardroom holding two cups of coffee and stared at Brannon's ashen face.

"What's wrong?" he asked, putting the cups on the table.

"The President has announced that the most destructive weapon known to mankind has been dropped on a Japanese city called Hiroshima. This one weapon has obliterated the entire city and killed everyone in it!"

"My God!" Ulrich said. "Did he say who dropped this weapon?"

"A bomber from Tinian," Brannon replied tonelessly.

"That's the home base of our passengers," Ulrich said. "I'll get their skipper in here."

Lieutenant Colonel Roberts came into the Wardroom rubbing the sleep from his eyes. Ulrich gave him a cup of coffee and Brannon handed him the message. He read it and nodded.

"So they finally used it," he said.

"It?" Brannon said.

"We called it the 'Thing,'" Roberts said. "Two weeks or so before you picked us up they cordoned off a whole corner of the field where we flew from. Never saw so many civilians in the war zone in my life. My crew chief told me they were all big-dome scientists and they had some new weapon that could wipe out a city the size of Chicago. No one believed that, naturally. But the rumors kept flying around, and when they built up this great big bomb, funny looking thing my crew chief said, big and round and fat, and then they started building a second bomb, well, we sort of began to believe them. Some, not all."

He sipped at his coffee. "I wonder," he said in a reflective tone, "if the shock wave from something like that would affect the aircraft?"

The second bomb was dropped on Nagasaki as the *Eelfish* neared Midway en route to Pearl Harbor. Before *Eelfish* arrived at Pearl the war was over.

CHAPTER 26

The war was over, but *Eelfish* had to wait outside the harbor for the submarine net to be dragged to one side so the submarine could enter the port. The traditional welcoming party that had always greeted a submarine returning from a patrol was absent. Only a Lieutenant with a large clipboard was waiting on the dock with the line-handling party when *Eelfish* pulled in. He came aboard and introduced himself to Captain Brannon and read from his clipboard.

"We still have a curfew at sundown," he said. "There will be no R and R period at the hotel. All maintenance work necessary will be done by ship's company. Needed stores and supplies can be obtained from the Yard in the usual manner. You are to report to the Operations Office in seven days, sir. The Operations Officer will expect your ship to be ready to go to sea at that time, sir."

"Go to sea in seven days?" Brannon asked, his heart jumping wildly. "To where, Lieutenant?"

"I don't know, Captain," the Lieutenant said. "I've got seven more submarines coming in today and tomorrow, and I have to tell each one of them the same thing."

A week later Brannon went up to the Operations Office, where a weary Staff officer waved him to a chair beside his desk.

"I'm told you're ready for sea," he said.

"Yes, sir," Brannon said. "We're ready."

"One last thing," the Staff officer said. "You have to get clearance from the Materiel Office. They'll be down to inspect you day after tomorrow. You'll get your orders as soon as they give me your clearance.''

"Can you tell me where we'll be going?'' Brannon asked.

The Staff officer yawned and rubbed his face. ''I suppose so, Captain, but don't tell your crew or I'll be in hack.'' He shuffled through some papers.

"New London.''

Brannon fought to keep his face noncommittal. He stood up and left the Operations Office, trying not to skip with joy. New London was a short train ride from New York. His wife and daughter were with her parents in Brooklyn. He made a project out of walking slowly back to *Eelfish* and found Ralph Ulrich.

"We've got to get clearance from some outfit called the Materiel Office. Day after tomorrow. You did a lot of duty here. What's that involve?''

"It involves what I'd call tough luck,'' Ulrich said. ''Those are the people who go around checking up to see if you've got all your Title A gear. Your engines, periscopes, deck guns.'' He looked up and down the deck. ''The lifelines, which we don't have, and an anchor and chain, which we don't have.''

"And?''

"And if we don't have those things they won't clear us for departure from port. Where's our anchor?''

"In New London,'' Brannon said. ''They took it and the anchor chain and the lifelines and posts off before we left for the Southwest Pacific, just as they do on every submarine going into the war zone. They shouldn't want things like that.''

"They'll want things like that,'' Ulrich said in lugubrious tones. ''That's their mission in life, to want things like that.'' He paused, chewing his lower lip in an unconscious imitation of Mike Brannon.

"I know a guy who has a warehouse here, a Mustang Lieutenant, sir. Last time I was over there, before I came aboard, it was full of things like deck posts and anchor chain and bronze-wire lifelines. If I had a little bargaining power, like some whiskey, I might be able to big-deal a truck and come back here with what we need. But I know he doesn't have any anchors.''

"What's he do with that stuff, why's he got it?''

"I don't know why he's got the warehouse or what's in it, sir, but I've heard tell that every once in a while he finds a buyer for some of the stuff that belonged to submarines that didn't come back from war patrol. Ghoulish business, but some people like to make a buck.''

"Use the ship's recreation fund," Brannon said. "Get whatever you think you need to bribe the son of a bitch." He started to turn away and stopped as Ulrich cleared his throat.

"About an anchor, sir. I know he hasn't got any anchors. But I think maybe the Chief of the Boat might have an idea or two about how to get an anchor. I don't know, but you told me once that he was dependable."

Chief Flanagan knocked politely at the bulkhead of the Wardroom and went through the green curtains and sat down at Brannon's invitation. Brannon outlined the problem.

"I guess what we have to do, sir, is to steal us an anchor," Flanagan said.

"Steal?" Brannon said. "How do you steal something that must weigh a ton? If I gave permission—and I sure as hell can't do that."

"Twenty-two hundred pounds, to be exact," Flanagan said. "I didn't mean steal, sir. Borrow was the word I meant to use. Plus one hundred and five fathoms of chain."

"Mr. Ulrich said he might be able to find the anchor chain," Brannon said. "Where are you going to borrow an anchor?"

"I can't answer that, sir, because I honestly don't know. But I'll tell the Captain if I find out where I can borrow an anchor, sir."

That afternoon a small truck pulled up on the pier. Ralph Ulrich got out and summoned a working party. The seamen from the *Eelfish* unloaded a tangled mass of bronze-wire lifelines and a pile of deck posts with eyes in the tops. Mike Brannon, summoned to the deck by Lieutenant Lee, watched the unloading from the bridge and then watched Chief Flanagan drive a crew of seamen and torpedomen to install the deck posts and string the lifelines.

"Cost me a case of whiskey," Ulrich said as he climbed up the ladder from the Conning Tower. "Would have cost more, but I argued that I was showing that big-dealer a whole new field of operations, and he saw my reasoning."

"Anchor chain?" Brannon asked.

"Tomorrow afternoon," Ulrich said. "He didn't have a truck that could carry a hundred and five fathoms of chain."

The chain arrived shortly after noon. Flanagan supervised the stowage of the chain in the chain locker and led one end of the chain through the fairlead and the chain stopper, around the wildcat gears, and down the hawsepipe. He turned to Steve Petreshock.

"I want a small punt by late this afternoon. The kind the Yard uses to paint waterlines. But big enough to hold several people. I want a heavy-duty block and tackle, a marlinspike, and some rags. I want all that gear ready before dark.

"Where the hell do I get a punt?" Petreshock asked.

"You want to make Chief, Petreshock? Use your initiative. I need a punt, the heavy-duty block and tackle, a marlinspike, and some rags. Before dark." Petreshock shrugged his shoulders and went down the hatch into his torpedo room.

Two hours later he jumped out of the back end of a truck and signaled to Flanagan, who went up on the dock. A waterline-painting punt was in the back of the truck. The two men wrestled the small boat off the truck and laid it on the cement pier. Petreshock jumped up in the truck body and got a heavy block and tackle and a big marlinspike.

"I got plenty rags in my room," he said. "What do you want to do with the punt?"

"Put it in the water," Flanagan said. "Get your people and put it in the water and tie it up alongside. You get any oars?"

"You don't need oars to paint a waterline," Petreshock said. "You pull the punt along with lines."

"Don't tell me what I already know," Flanagan said. "Oars."

"Got some paddles in my bilge from those rubber boats we had," Petreshock said. "They do?" Flanagan nodded his head.

At two in the morning Flanagan, Jim Rice, Steve Petreshock, and Fred Nelson climbed down onto the pressure hull and eased into the painting punt. They wore black turtleneck sweaters and dark blue watch caps, and their faces and hands were blackened with camouflage cream. Bob Lee came along the deck as the punt disappeared in the darkness. He turned to Chief Ed Morris, who was leaning against the side of the Conning Tower, smoking his pipe.

"What the hell is going on, Chief? Who were those people? What were they doing?"

"That's the Chief of the Boat and friends," Morris said. "They're gonna go steal an anchor somewhere. Hell of an idea, stealing an anchor. If they get the damned thing in that little punt the whole rig will probably sink and with all that black stuff on their faces and hands they'll be impossible to see in the water and they'll drown."

"Steal an anchor? Have you been drinking, Chief?"

"I haven't been drinking, Lieutenant. I got the Chief's duty below decks. Sure they're gonna steal an anchor. The Chief of

the Boat is queer for stealing anchors, didn't you know that?
Does it in every port we hit."

"Wiseass," Lee said. He turned his back and started to walk
away, and then came back.

"Damn it, Chief, I'm the Officer of the Day, and I demand to
know what in the hell is going on!"

"I thought you knew, that you were kidding with me, sir,"
Morris said. "What's going on is some clown on the Base is
coming over here tomorrow, today really, it's after midnight, and
if we don't have an anchor hanging up there on the billboard we
ain't gonna get any clearance to go where they're going to send
us, which I hear is New London.

"So this afternoon I did a little scouting for the Chief of the
Boat and I found out that an LST carries the same sort of anchor
we do and there's four LSTs tied up in a nest across this arm of
the harbor. The Chief of the Boat is gonna steal one of those
anchors and bring it back."

"That's impossible!" Lee said.

"Mr. Lee," Morris said, "there is no such word as impossible
to a Chief of the United States Navy. Some things might take
longer than others, but nothing is impossible. Not to a Chief
Petty Officer. Flanagan will steal an anchor. And he'll bring it
back here. If he doesn't sink and drown."

An hour later Lee heard a gentle splashing, and the punt,
barely afloat, eased up beside the pressure hull amidships. Chief
Morris came around the Conning Tower and went down on the
pressure hull, his arm holding on to one of the newly installed
deck posts, and helped Petreshock and Fred Nelson get out of the
punt. The two men ran forward on the deck, and Petreshock
went down the hatch to the Torpedo Room. Lee heard the clank
of the anchor gear, and a fathom or so of cable rattled out of the
hawsepipe. The two men still in the punt paddled it forward. A
few minutes later Lee heard Flanagan's low order to walk the
anchor in, and there was a muted clanking noise. Jim Rice got
out of the punt, went down the hatch, and appeared a few
minutes later with a gallon can of paint and two brushes. He
dropped down into the punt, and Lee could hear the slap of the
paint brushes.

"Might be a good idea, Lieutenant," Morris's voice sounded
at Lee's shoulder, "to come with me and take a look at the moon
from the other end of the deck."

The Materiel Officer appeared the next morning with his

clipboard and a small staff. The inspection took hours, and when it was finished the officer turned to Ralph Ulrich.

"Everything is in order. I'll sign your clearance and send it to the Operations Officer. I understand you're getting underway at zero seven hundred tomorrow."

"Fuel," Ulrich said.

"Oh, yes," the Materiel Officer said. "Here it is. A destroyer coming in from Okinawa will be alongside on the other side of the pier late this afternoon. No room for her at the destroyer docks, and she's leaving tomorrow afternoon for Mare Island. The Fuel King man will be down here after the destroyer docks to unlock the lines under the pier. You'll fuel first. You're down for fifty thousand gallons. That will get you to Panama if you run at two-thirds speed on two engines. The destroyer will fuel after you do."

"That's the last thing I want to do, run to Panama on two engines at two-thirds speed!" Brannon snapped when Ulrich told him the news. He turned to Lieutenant Jerry Gold.

"That guy from Materiel said this tin can was coming in from Okinawa?" He looked at Ulrich, who nodded. "Okay, I'll bet they give liberty to two-thirds of the crew. They're over here, alongside our pier, away from their own command. I know tin-can sailors. They're a lot like us.

"The people with the watch will be bitching. Jerry, I want you to get up to the O-Club. Take some money from the recreation fund. Ulrich, you get the money, go with him. Bring back some beer and some hard liquor. Enough to get about two dozen people drunk.

"Get hold of Morris and Booth. Those two Chiefs are the biggest con artists in the submarine navy. Tell them what we want to do and have the engine room people standing by to take on fuel when the Fuel King man gets here and unlocks the valves." Ulrich looked at him and grinned.

"You're getting right into the swing of being a Navy Yard man, sir," he said. He went off with Gold, chuckling.

Chiefs Booth and Morris wandered across the pier while the *Eelfish* Engine Room people were hooking up the fuel hoses. A few minutes later Morris came walking back, and looking carefully up and down the dark pier, opened one of the Conning Tower ammunition storage lockers and took out a case of beer. An eager destroyer sailor rushed across the pier and grabbed the case, followed by another destroyer man, who grabbed the case of whiskey that Morris pulled out of the ammunition locker.

At a little after twenty-two hundred hours Jerry Gold walked into the Wardroom where Mike Brannon was playing solitaire with a worn deck of cards.

"All fuel tanks topped off, sir. One hundred and eleven thousand gallons of fuel aboard. Destroyer is fueling now, sir."

"Everything okay?" Brannon asked, putting a red jack on a black queen.

"There's two or three people in their Black Gang sober enough to shut off the valves when their tanks are full, sir."

"Good," Brannon said. "Tell the Chief of the Watch below decks that I want a zero five hundred reveille. Serve breakfast at zero five thirty. We get under way at zero seven hundred."

Jerry Gold went to his stateroom smiling gently. "Hot damn," he said to himself. "If I can steal sixty thousand gallons of diesel oil I might be able to slip an old gold crown or two into my pocket. Have to make sure my white jackets have pockets."

Eelfish reached Panama four days ahead of schedule. A three-stripe Commander came aboard, a smile creasing his red-veined cheeks.

"Been kind of a naughty fellow, haven't you, Captain?" he said genially. "You're way ahead of schedule. Can't let you through the Ditch until your scheduled time, four days from now." He looked at the bright blaze of Japanese battle flags on the Conning Tower. "There is an alternative, unless you want to fight with Pearl Harbor, and that's pretty hard to do because it takes seven days for them to acknowledge anything we send to them.

You can go through our Ditch tomorrow morning at zero six hundred. But if you do that you'll have to act as a target for a division of destroyers on the other side that hasn't had a live submarine to work with for over a year. What's your decision sir?"

"We'll be happy to act as a target for the destroyers," Brannon said solemnly.

"It's wait here four days or work with them four days, so it's all the same," the Commander said. "Zero six hundred. Tugs will be here at zero five hundred to get you into position."

The *Eelfish* cleared the Canal at dusk, pointed her bullnose north, and began running on four main engines. Down in the radio shack Ralph Ulrich stood with Jim Michaels as Rafferty listened to the signals coming over the air.

"They keep asking us where we are," Rafferty said.

"They're supposed to be submarine killers," Ralph Ulrich said. "Let them find us. We're going home!"

Ulrich went into the Wardroom and reported to Mike Brannon that the destroyer division commander was asking for *Eelfish* and what he had decided to do.

"You're getting to be a damned good Exec, Ralph." Brannon grinned. "Soon as we come within the command area of Key West, the skipper there is a guy I served under in O-boats in New London before the war, I'll throw us on his mercy, let him sweat over what to do with us."

An hour after *Eelfish* had transmitted Brannon's message to the Commanding Officer, Key West, the answer came back.

"Sorry, your transmitter must be out of order. Can't read you. Suggest you proceed original orders if your receiver will pick up this message and Godspeed."

Brannon grinned, and *Eelfish* raced toward home, past Cape Hatteras, up the long reach of the East Coast, and then, at last, the turn around the eastern end of Long Island and into the waters of Block Island Sound, through the Race, and up the Thames River, where a huge crowd was waiting on the pier. Brannon put his binoculars to his eyes as Ulrich delicately maneuvered the *Eelfish* in midstream, turning her to point in to the dock, gauging the run of the tide.

"By God, she's there! Gloria! And my daughter! I think it's little Gloria, she looks so big!" Lieutenant Lee, standing down on the main deck, smiled, thinking of his own wife in Australia.

The first two weeks in New London passed swiftly. The Reservists in the crew added up their points and were sent to Great Lakes Naval Base for discharge. When the last Reservist had left Mike Brannon walked up to the Submarine Personnel Office.

"I'm short thirty-six enlisted men and I have no officers in my Wardroom except my Exec," he said. He put a roster on the Personnel Officer's desk.

"I think we fought this war with nothing but Reserves," the Personnel Officer said.

"We'd have been in a hell of a mess if we hadn't," Brannon growled. The Personnel Officer looked at him and then down at his desk.

"You're going to be stationed here for some time, sir. You'll be used as a training ship for a while, but before that starts the people who built *Eelfish* want to put her in dry dock and go over her from stem to stern. You're the first New London boat to come back here that's suffered extensive depth charging.

"So, if I may suggest it sir, you could grant leave to your crew, what's left of it, and yourself, and your, ah, one other officer. Thirty days minimum. The engineers will be busy with your ship for at least six weeks." He looked up.

"The Command at the Submarine School has given strict orders, sir. The battle flags on your Conning Tower are not to be painted over when they paint your ship. We, everyone here, is very proud of *Eelfish,* sir, and you and your crew. You must have noticed the people here who come down to the pier and just stand and stare at the ship. They're proud, sir."

"Thank you," Brannon said. He turned and went out the door, and walked back to the *Eelfish.*

EPILOGUE

The next year passed swiftly for Mike Brannon. He was promoted to full Commander and given the extra responsibility of Assistant to the Squadron Commander. Gloria found a pleasant house to rent on the Sound that was well within their budget, and they settled into the peacetime routine of a middle-seniority career officer on his way to Flag rank. They entertained junior officers once a month and were, in turn, entertained by their senior officers.

Sitting in his office in the Submarine Base in New London early one morning Brannon saw his door open, and Chief Yeoman Booth came in carrying a tray with two full cups of coffee in one hand and a letter in the other.

"Got a letter from Chief Flanagan," he said, putting the coffee cups on the desk. "Thought you might like to hear what he's up to, sir."

"I would," Brannon said, reaching for a coffee cup.

"He retired a year ago when I was on leave," Booth said. "Went out to the Philippines. He's got a regular business letterhead with half a dozen companies listed. Everything from construction to salvage work to ships' supplies. He says he's making money at all of them."

"He's a good man," Brannon said. "Whatever he turns his hand to, he would be able to do."

"He married a girl from Tacloban," Booth continued. "Said he inherited a ready-made family. She's got twin boys about fourteen, fifteen months old." He looked at Mike Brannon, his eyes crinkling in a smile.

"Tacloban," Booth went on. "That's where he went ashore to deliver the orders to the guerrilla guy and didn't come back for a night and a day and when he came back he was passed-out drunk and Brosmer swore he smelled pussy on him."

Brannon nodded, smiling.

"Well, he's married, and he says he's happy as hell. Great woman. Good kids. You heard about Captain Mealey?"

"Made Rear Admiral," Brannon said. "Going to be our boss as head of Submarines, Atlantic. Hell of a good move."

"*Sablefish* is due in at ten hundred hours, sir. You want to meet her at the pier?"

"Hell, yes," Brannon said. "John Olsen's her skipper."

Lieutenant Commander John Olsen crossed the gangway to the pier and engulfed Mike Brannon in a bear hug. "Hah! Three full stripes. Congratulations, Mike."

"First things first," Brannon said. "How about dinner at my house at about eighteen hundred? I'm going to be tied up here, but I'll send a car to pick you up."

"Can the car pick me up at the station, the railroad station, at seventeen hundred? My fiancée's coming in on the seventeen hundred train from New York."

Brannon's eyebrows rose. "You engaged? The great woman hater? She's welcome. I have to see this wonder woman who managed to trap you.

"Now, what can I do for you before I shove off to a lot of meetings? You're part of our Squadron now and I sort of wear the number two hat in the Squadron."

"I'll give you an easy one," Olsen said. "I need a first-rate Chief of the Boat. Mine looked all right during the precommissioning, but he fell apart when we started operating out of Key West."

Brannon chewed his lower lip reflectively. "I've got Steve Petreshock in *Eelfish* as my Chief of the Boat and you can't have him. I know, Fred Nelson. He made Chief a couple of months ago and he's in excess. You know how good a man he is. That suit you?"

"Perfect," Olsen said. "If he wants to come aboard."

"He'll jump at the chance," Brannon said. "He knows he's in excess, and Chief of the Boat billets don't come along very often. I've got to run. The driver will meet you at the train station at seventeen hundred hours. See you at the house."

John Olsen walked into the Brannon's living room with a buxom, black-haired smiling woman at his side.

"These are the Brannons, dear," he said to the woman. "Mike and Gloria. Folks, meet my fiancée, Mrs. Joan Hinman." He watched as Brannon's face twisted.

"You mean?" Brannon asked softly.

"What John means, Captain Brannon, Mrs. Brannon, is that I am the widow of Captain Arthur Hinman. And I am going to be Mrs. John Olsen if this Swede doesn't chicken out on me." She looked at the Brannons, her dark blue eyes under heavy black eyebrows level and serene.

"I'm delighted!" Gloria Brannon cried. She rushed forward and swept Joan Hinman into her embrace. She released her, and Mike Brannon came forward and shyly kissed Joan's cheek.

"How did all this happen, if I may ask?" Mike Brannon said as the four sat on the shaded porch at the back of the house.

"I was stationed in Key West with *Sablefish*," Olsen began. Joan waved her hand at him.

"I went to Key West for a change," she said. "Some friends told me it was quaint and kind of funny there. I went to church one Sunday morning. A Lutheran church. Sort of an odd little place, only about twenty-five people in the congregation. The church had a little social hour after the service, coffee and doughnuts and put some money in the bowl to pay for it.

"I noticed this tall, skinny fellow dressed in a pair of old slacks and a sport shirt, and he put a dollar in the bowl and only had coffee, so I got interested. Fellow might be a big spender. Some nice lady, wife of a retired Colonel I think, came up and said wasn't it just fine that since we were the only two visitors that day that we'd already met."

"We hadn't, but Joan took care of that," Olsen said. "She said she hadn't had any breakfast and would I pop for orange juice and flapjacks? I did, and that led to lunch and to dinner and let me tell you, she's a good eater. Expensive date."

"One thing led to another," Joan continued. "He told me he was a captain of a ship and he took me to see it. I told him about Captain Hinman and he got a funny sort of a look.

"Then he told me about the *Mako* and the *Eelfish*." Her normally smiling face was solemn.

"I knew how Art had died. Quickly, the Admiral said when he wrote, and you said the same thing, sir. But I didn't know about the rest of the crew, the Psalm." She reached out and took Olsen's hand.

"John told me. It was hard for him to do that. We both cried. It sort of brought us closer together, and since then he's taught me a lot about how you people in submarines feel about each other, how close you are to each other.

"I left the Navy after the *Mako* went down. They give you that option, you know. I didn't have to work if I didn't want to. There was the pension and the insurance. So I helped in charitable things and kept myself busy, and then one day a friend told me about Key West and I went there and I went to church and there was John. The hard part was a long way back, almost three years at that time."

"She made me take her out every night," Olsen grumbled. "Can you imagine me trying to learn to dance?"

"After about three months of suffering through him being a perfect gentleman at all times I gave him a choice," Joan said. "I told him that if he had any dirty, sneaky, nasty thoughts about men and women and he didn't try to carry them out he could get out of my life." She threw her head back and rocked with laughter.

"Oh, did he have dirty thoughts!"

"She's giving up a lot to marry me," Olsen said. "She loses her pension. Shows you what a great catch I am."

"I'm a woman who looks to the future," Joan said. "If you don't make Admiral I'll divorce you and sue you for heaps of alimony."

"One other thing, Mike," Olsen said. "The wedding is next week. Will you be my best man?" He laughed as he saw the pained expression on Brannon's face.

After dinner the group moved to the porch with coffee. Olsen settled in his chair. "You ever hear from any of our old bunch on the *Eelfish*?"

"Not many of the enlisted men who were Reserves write," Brannon said. "That's understandable. They've got a living to make on the outside. Paul Blake writes every couple of months or so. He and his wife, that nice Australian girl he married in Perth, they live on a farm in Kansas. He's in partnership with his father. They've got about fifteen thousand acres of wheat. His last letter mentioned that his wife's parents came over from Perth and spent a month with them.

"Chief Flanagan is in Manila. He's apparently into a lot of different businesses and making them all go. He went there after he retired, after we got back, and he married a girl in Tacloban who had twin boys about fifteen months old." He saw Olsen doing the mental arithmetic and the two men smiled.

"Let's see, Arbuckle and Lee are both in 'Frisco. Perry is an architect and doing well. Lee is working for the state as a prosecutor. Perry said Lee's wife is there and that it's a good marriage. Perry is still single.

"Jerry Gold, remember him? He's a dentist with an office in downtown Chicago. He wrote me not long ago and said any submariner coming through Chicago should stop and get free coffee served by a beautiful nurse, and a free dental checkup goes with the coffee. He hasn't changed.

"Chief Morris, Chief Booth, they're still with me. So are most of the Regulars who brought the *Eelfish* back. The last I heard of Doc Wharton he was going to veterinarian's school somewhere in the Midwest. Charlie Two Blankets decided to make the Navy a career, and he's in intelligence work in Washington." He turned to Joan Hinman.

"You'll like it here. Good duty station. Lots of really nice wives here."

"I'm sure I will," Joan said. "I think it's time all of you were able to live normal lives again. I can't see another war, not with that atomic bomb, terrible as it is, and that other bomb they talk about, the hydrogen bomb. As long as we have those weapons and every nation knows we would never use them to conquer anyone, as long as we have those weapons I think we'll have peace."

Gloria Brannon rose. "Let me show you my garden before it gets too dark." The two women went out the screen door.

"Hell of a nice woman, John," Brannon said. "I never met her, you know. Art wrote me about her. I always wondered what kind of a woman she was. Apparently she has a mind of her own."

"Damned good mind, too," Olsen said. "After she left the Navy she started taking courses at Georgetown, economics, anthropology. She kids a lot, she's a hellion in bed, but she's got a serious side that appeals to my Swedish upbringing."

"When the women come back I want to talk to her some more

about why she thinks we won't have another war," Brannon said.

"She'll give you a good argument," Olsen said. "She hates the idea of an atomic weapon and the damage it did to Hiroshima and Nagasaki, the people it killed and injured. But she's firmly convinced that as long as we have that weapon and have control of it there won't be another war."

"I believe that, too," Mike Brannon said. "I believe it and I say 'Thank God' every night when I go to bed."

Halfway across the world in a laboratory deep in a remote area of the Soviet Union, Russian and German physicists labored at the task of putting together an atomic bomb. They would explode that bomb in less than three years.

ABOUT THE AUTHOR

HARRY HOMEWOOD was a qualified submariner before he was seventeen years old, having lied to the Navy about his age. He served in a little "S"-boat in the old Asiatic Fleet. After Pearl Harbor he reenlisted and made eleven war patrols in the Southwest Pacific. He later became Chicago Bureau Chief for *Newsweek*, chief editorial writer for the *Chicago Sun-Times*, and for eleven years had his own weekly news program syndicated to thirty-two PBS television stations. He is also the author of *Final Harbor*. Harry Homewood lives with his wife in Tucson, Arizona.

DON'T MISS
THESE CURRENT
Bantam Bestsellers

☐	24244	**GAME PLAN** Leslie Waller	$3.50
☐	23952	**DANCER WITH ONE LEG** Stephen Dobyns	$3.50
☐	24257	**WOMAN IN THE WINDOW** Dana Clarins	$3.50
☐	24363	**O GOD OF BATTLES** Harry Homewood	$3.95
☐	23823	**FINAL HARBOR** Harry Homewood	$3.50
☐	20923	**SILENT SEA** Harry Homewood	$3.50
☐	23923	**TORPEDO** Harry Homewood	$2.95
☐	23983	**CIRCLES** Doris Mortman	$3.50
☐	24184	**THE WARLORD** Malcolm Bosse	$3.95
☐	22848	**FLOWER OF THE PACIFIC** Lana McGraw Boldt	$3.95
☐	23920	**VOICE OF THE HEART** Barbara Taylor Bradford	$4.50
☐	23638	**THE OTHER SIDE** Diana Henstell	$3.50
☐	23845	**THE DELTA STAR** Joseph Wambaugh	$3.95
☐	23709	**THE OMEGA DECEPTION** Charles Robertson	$3.50
☐	24428	**DARK PLACES** Thomas Altman	$3.50
☐	23198	**BLACK CHRISTMAS** Thomas Altman	$2.95
☐	22687	**TRUE BRIDE** Thomas Altman	$2.95
☐	24010	**KISS DADDY GOODBYE** Thomas Altman	$3.50
☐	24561	**THE VALLEY OF HORSES** Jean M. Auel	$4.50
☐	23897	**CLAN OF THE CAVE BEAR** Jean M. Auel	$4.50
☐	20822	**THE GLITTER DOME** Joseph Wambaugh	$3.95

Prices and availability subject to change without notice.

Buy them at your local bookstore or use this handy coupon for ordering:

SPECIAL MONEY SAVING OFFER

Now you can have an up-to-date listing of Bantam's hundreds of titles plus take advantage of our unique and exciting bonus book offer. A special offer which gives you the opportunity to purchase a Bantam book for only 50¢. Here's how!

By ordering any five books at the regular price per order, you can also choose any other single book listed (up to a $4.95 value) for just 50¢. Some restrictions do apply, but for further details why not send for Bantam's listing of titles today!

Just send us your name and address plus 50¢ to defray the postage and handling costs.